Green Ivy Publishing

1 Lincoln Centre

18W140 Butterfield Road

Suite 1500

Oakbrook Terrace IL 60181-4843

www.greenivybooks.com

ISBN: 978-1-944680-34-3

HITLER'S BASEMENT:

MY SEARCH FOR TRUTH, LIGHT, AND THE FORGOTTEN EXECUTIONERS OF UKRAINE'S KINGDOM OF DEATH

Ron Vossler

There shall be rivers of red, a kingdom of death,

and blood washing blood to the primordial sea.

—Ancient prophecy of the long-haired Sybil

AUTHOR'S NOTE

Most people associate the Holocaust and the Final Solution with the gas chambers in Poland and with death camps like Auschwitz. In actuality, during WWII a third of the Jews were slaughtered in Nazi-occupied Soviet territories to the east in the so-called open air murders. And a tenth of those took place in a region that Hitler designated Transnistria, a region of Ukraine currently bordered by eastern Moldova, and that my Dakota German grandparents called the old country.

The reader should know that this nonfiction book is based on my own search into those responsible for such killings. To protect my sources, I've transposed localities in the US and Canada, created composites, and in accord with an archival agreement, applied pseudonyms, initials, and truncated versions for the names of people not already mentioned in the public record.

Everything in this book concerning Nazi functionaries like Leibbrandt and Eichmann and Weingartner, local police units, SS officers, testimonies, murder sites, and the former Transnistrian villages of the Volksdeutsche, a German minority living outside Germany, is as true and accurate as I could make it, except for one village given a pseudonym to protect an important confidential source.

TABLE OF CONTENTS:

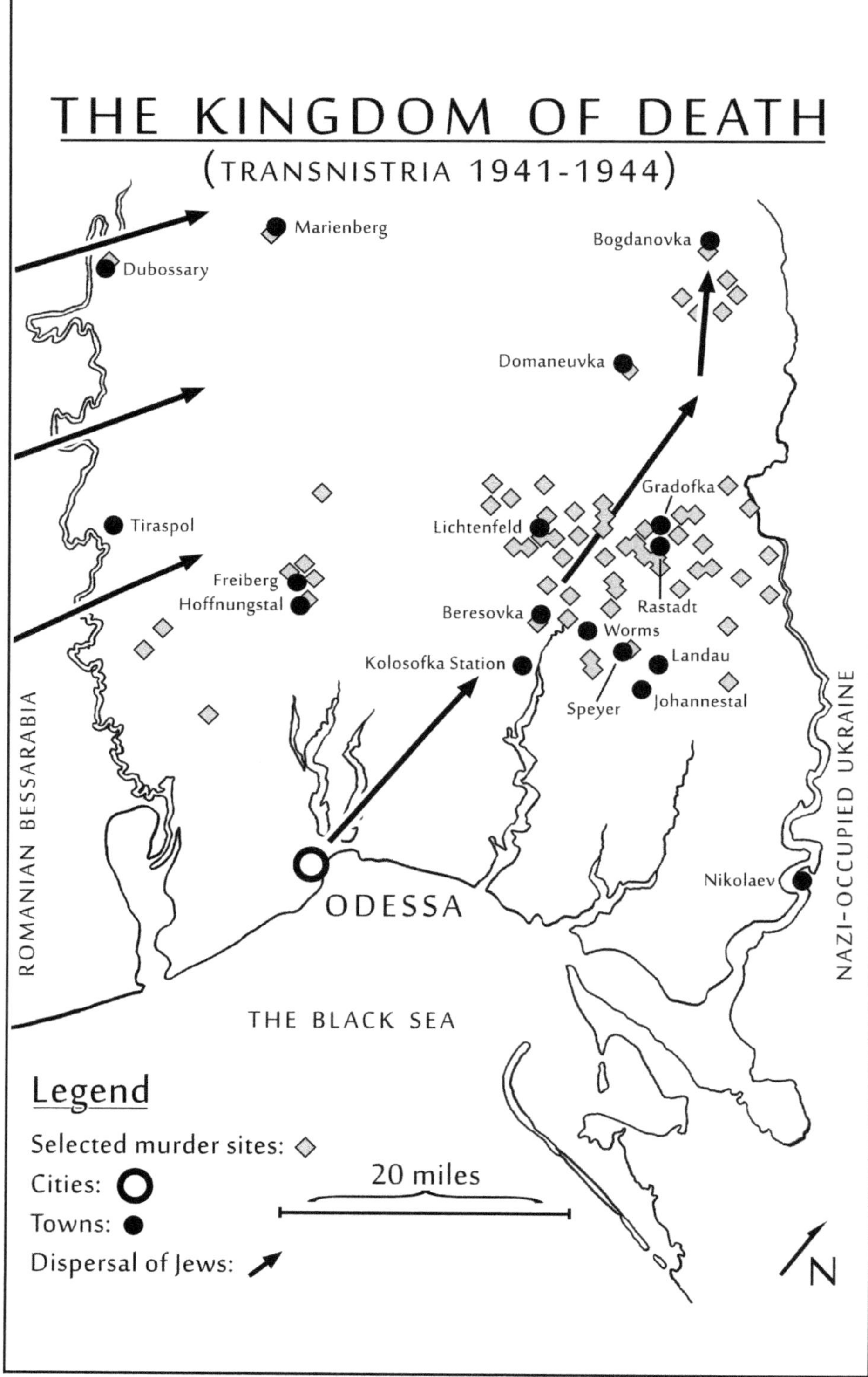

THE KINGDOM OF DEATH
(TRANSNISTRIA 1941-1944)
Marienberg
Dubossary
Bogdanovka
Domaneuvka
Gradofka
Lichtenfeld
Tiraspol
Freiberg
Hoffnungstal
Rastadt
Beresovka
Worms
Landau
Kolosofka Station
Speyer
Johannestal
ROMANIAN BESSARABIA
NAZI-OCCUPIED UKRAINE
Nikolaev
ODESSA
THE BLACK SEA
Legend
Selected murder sites:
Cities:
Towns:
Dispersal of Jews:
20 miles
N

I. INTO THE LABYRINTH

OVERTURE

This book began with a strange dream: A column of mostly old and young people and pregnant women heft packs and babies and bedrolls. They are guarded by men in white uniforms as they struggle across a prairie-like landscape I know is the steppe of Ukraine. The wind howls, and grey flakes—like the ashes of the terrible ovens I would later discover—sift down upon the grim procession.

The dream returned several times. Was I haunted by an illusion? Or was I being given an oracular vision about my grandfather's homeland? Who, exactly, were the moaning victims, and where were the white uniformed men taking them?

The dream gave no answers, and I didn't know, and wouldn't know until a decade later, in 2010: I'm in Wesseloe, an isolated village in Ukraine, just come from a bone-scattered ravine a mile away, to talk with an elderly man, an eyewitness.

We stand by his bright blue yard gate. It's his birthday actually, and though it is only midmorning, he exhales vodka fumes, as he describes what he saw as an eight-year-old in the spring of 1942—a massacre of Jews.

He is about to say, I'm certain, what I've heard at a score of murder sites. That the murderers were Nazis. Germans from Germany. But he doesn't say that. What he does say, however, sends a rippling shock wave up my spine. Just two words: "*Nimitzki colonistas.*"

"German colonists?" I say, my heart in my throat. "Are you sure?"

"*Da*. Yes. German colonists," the old man says. "The ones who did the killing."

"From where?" I ask.

"From north. From Lichtenfeld."

"From Lichtenfeld?" I'm appalled at his mention of my grandfather's birthplace.

"Da, Lichtenfeld. Police in white uniforms."

That day at the blue gate, as the old man tells me about men in white uniforms, this book begins to write itself in my thoughts, as if it's someone else, a heavenly scribe perhaps, dictating what I should say.

LOOMINGS

I can hardly believe it. I'm going to meet survivors from a place my grandparents called, in their melodious German dialect, our old homeland on the steppe; a place swept away, as my grandfather sometimes sighed, by a great rushing river of blood; which was why our family, our people, the lucky ones, now lived on the prairie, our great ethnic ark.

As the airplane heels into the Dakota sky, I press my forehead against the cool oval window and gaze down at the snow-dusted prairie that spreads beneath the wings, at dark ribbons of roads making geometric patterns, at placid lakes shining like pools of molten silver, and my thoughts fall into familiar channels:

I'm grateful for the *brairie* (my grandfather's pronunciation of *prairie*), for its wide swathes of cropland; its bushy draws, where sharp-tailed grouse and pheasants nest; even for its howling blizzards and searing droughts. I'm grateful for its heavy rocks, loosed from the devil's rucksack on his head-long plummet from heaven (as grandpa used to say) and scattered over the prairie fields for us to clear and stack along section lines, penance for having escaped the old country, where there were no rocks on the ground, just fallen fruit and death and sorrow, and the cloven-hoofed ones (as grandpa said, resorting to apocalyptic imagery), or *die verdammte bolsheviken* (as my grandpa's friends in town called them): those who gave one no rest or peace.

For the Dakotan Germans, the prairie is a great ethnic ark. As my grandfather said, *"Mir sind gluecklicha leute,"* the lucky ones, those who heeded the old prophecy. And how can I know that day, flying to California, that the river of blood, which swept all in its path meant not only enslavement of one sixth of the earth's peasantry, but also the Holocaust? Even then, part of me knows.

By the time our flight passes over the dark spine of the continent, the Rocky Mountains, anxiety is pulsing in my veins. And by the time our plane banks through swollen clouds and begins its descent to California, my heart is pounding against my ribs.

With curiosity and excitement at the prospect of meeting my elderly relatives (survivors of the doomed villages my grandfather never forgot) and with a prescient and wary fear, I'm about to enter the labyrinth of my own ethnic history, where blood and memory flow thick with secrets.

***

Helmut meets me as I emerge from my rental car in a quiet residential part of Fresno, California. He is a portly man, a retired auto worker with the distinct red hair of my mother's side of the family. He pumps my hand with blunt fingers the size of a dinner plate and guides me into his ranch-style home, talking all the way in his fragmented English about how good it is to meet a relative from the Dakotas. *"Ach yah, so gut,"* he says. (Oh yeah, so good.) Inside, Regina, his round-faced wife, gives me a hug and ushers me to their table, which groans with ethnic fare familiar to me from my own prairie childhood.

"Sit here, our place of honor," she says. "Where Leibbrandt sat when he visited us in 1974."

"George Leibbrandt was here?" I say.

Leibbrandt was a scholar whose genealogical books about the German colonists on the steppe I've avidly read. I know he was also one of fifteen Nazis at the infamous Wannsee Conference, which formalized the murder of the Jews (the first ugly tentacle of the Holocaust rising from the murky depths of Volksdeutsche history). But this is something I don't want to face. Not yet.

"Leibbrandt was our relative, like you," Helmut says. "He was from Hoffnungstal, a German colony in Ukraine. Near where your grandpa was born."

"Eat, eat," Regina says. "I hope you like strudels und sausage. That's what Leibbrandt liked so much when he was here."

Our conversation during the meal shifts to a time when there was no food, the 1930s in Soviet Ukraine, when the regime-engineered famine starved millions of Ukrainians, tens of thousands of Volksdeutsche.

"Ach, yah, *schrecklich*, those times," Helmut says, using the dialect word for "terror." "Everyone knew of the Sibyl's warning. After your grandfather and others left for America, there was no getting out."

"The Bolsheviks closed the doors," Regina says. "Und if you took all the tears we cried when they took over, that would make an ocean."

"*Gott sei dank*, that nightmare ended," Helmut says.

He explains how, after the German invasion of Soviet Ukraine in 1941, the lines of marching soldiers and trucks and motorcycles entered Hoffnungstal, loudspeakers blaring, "You are our sisters and brothers. We have come to liberate you."

"Und we cheered," Regina says.

"Und you would have cheered too, Ron," Helmut says. "*Gel?* Isn't that true?"

"Of course," I say in German dialect.

One by one, Helmut passes me five tiny yellowed photos, each an inch and a half square, that show Hoffnungstal's evacuation in 1944, the long winding line of horse-pulled wagons trundling toward the German Reich, as a hundred and twenty thousand Volksdeutsche from two hundred villages departed Transnistria ahead of the resurgent Soviet military.

"This was the last we saw of Hoffnungstal, our village," Regina says, putting the heels of her hands together, as if closing a book. "*Schluss.* That was the end. Sixty years ago."

"Und this is Weingartner," Helmut says, solemnly handing me a final photo. "Here he stands. With my father."

Something tells me to memorize the photo: the two men outlined against Hoffnungstal's neoclassical church, faint smiles on their faces, sharing a joke, but not much else. Helmut's father was a red-haired forty-year-old Soviet German in shapeless peasant clothing. Weingartner was a tall, aristocratic-looking German officer with a gaunt, El Greco–like face. He wore a military greatcoat of wool and rayon, and beneath its collar I can see something sinister: the twin lightning runes of the SS.

"Weingartner was our savior," Regina says. "He led us safely out of Ukrainia, back to Germany. Und after the war, we found our way to America—to Fresno, where we still are, as you see, fifty years later."

"To our people, who suffered more than the Jews." Helmut says. The red wine trembles in our glasses as we drink a toast.

"Helmut, *genug,* you are drinking too much," Regina says. "Enough."

"The Jews, they died fast from bullets and gas," Helmut says, his features having grown florid and coarse. "Und our people starved over many months. Let's ask Ron who had the easier death? Und who suffered more?"

"*Halt's maul,*" Regina snaps. "Quiet. No more of that Jewish business."

"Ach yah. What are they going to do, shoot me?"

He flicks his thick index finger against his temple, showing how easy it was to get shot, or even to shoot someone.

"Nobody is shooting anyone today," Regina says, soothing him. "Time for dessert. Und, Ron, maybe you will enjoy my prune kuchen-pie."

In their guest bedroom, I sleep badly. The next morning I wake with half-formed questions playing in a loop in my thoughts: What was an SS officer doing in Hoffnungstal during WWII, just thirty-five miles from Lichtenfeld, my grandfather's birthplace? And how could Helmut insist Volksdeutsche in Ukraine suffered more than the Jews?

Over breakfast that morning, whenever I try to ask Helmut questions, Regina pushes more food at me, saying, "Here, Ron, eat. Have the rest of this prune kuchen-pie. It was Leibbrandt's favorite too."

***

Back in my university office just after midterm, I write my Fresno relatives a thank-you note. I also ask a favor. Could they send me copies of those photographs they'd showed me? Although I say nothing about the photo of the SS officer, that is exactly the one I most want to see again.

"For my research. For history," I write.

At my desk that morning, I think about Helmut and Regina, all they suffered in Hoffnungstal, in Soviet Ukraine, a hellhole of murder and starvation. I think about Regina's grieving, about her refusal, as an eight-year-old, to kiss her grandfather good-bye before the Soviet secret police executed him in 1937. I think about six-year-old Helmut, robbing birds' nests of eggs for his starving mother. No wonder they greeted the invading Nazis with open arms.

When I glance up again I see—framed in my office window—several harried students skating the ice-sheathed sidewalks, obviously late for class.

"Like me," I think, grabbing my lecture notes and hurrying down the hallway on one of the few times in twenty years of teaching that I will be late.

***

OUR SAVIOR, THE SS OFFICER

Spring comes early. Students shed their parkas and stocking caps, and each day after class, I impatiently check my university mailbox. I'm waiting, I realize, for the photo of the SS officer. Perhaps if I see it again, I might better understand what he was doing in Hoffnungstal. Why on earth, I wonder, were the Nazis—the SS, even—interested in an isolated village like Hoffnungstal?

I know little of such matters. My undergraduate training in anthropology taught me human anatomy, my graduate work immersed me in abstruse literary theories, and fifteen years as an adjunct professor, discussing fiction with undergraduates, all left me ill-prepared to solve actual historical questions. Where to start? Except with the photo of the SS officer, which I eagerly await.

A month goes by before a bulky, reused envelope, addressed in Regina's angular German script, arrives in my university mailbox, and as I shuffle through Xeroxes of the photos of Hoffnungstal's evacuation in WWII, I quickly realize Regina didn't include a copy of the photo of the SS officer.

An innocent oversight? I don't know. But after I leave Regina a voice mail, thanking her for the photos and adding that she neglected to send me the photo of Weingartner, she returns my call.

Her accent seems thicker, her voice tired but emphatic: "I can't send da photo. Und I hope you can understand that."

"Of course," I say, too quickly.

"Helmut's relatives…in Germany…they are your relatives too," she says. "Und if dat photo becomes public, und harm comes…I would nefer forgif myself."

Effusive apologies ensue, from me for touching on a sensitive issue, and from Regina for not sending the photo, and in our continuing phone conversations, there is no more talk of "that Jewish business," except for Regina's aside that I need to "watch my back." I tell myself that this is paranoia from growing up in Soviet Ukraine, never certain when a few careless words in a conversation—or a letter or photo sent to or from American relatives—might result in arrest, exile, or execution.

Anyway, who am I, I ask myself in my own comfortable American perch, to question their fear? It had been "driven deep into their bones," as Helmut repeatedly told me, describing their lives under communism. The fear is still there, even if the Soviet system collapsed a decade earlier. It never occurred to me that their fear might involve something else, altogether: the murder of Jews in Hoffnungstal.

***

Our weekly phone conversations over the next few months are so Volksdeutsche, so restrained, focusing mostly on Regina's emphysema and Helmut's prostate cancer. No mention of Transnistria. Or Weingartner.

One day Regina phones to inform me of Helmut's passing. Medicated and under hospice care at his home, he'd relived the 1944 evacuation, calling out to her from where he lay bedridden: "Come. It is time to leave Hoffnungstal."

"Not this time Helmut," Regina told him. "This time you must travel alone."

We commiserate then, Regina and I, in the old Volksdeutsche way, about this whirlpool of life, our brief sojourn here, wayward pilgrims destined for heaven, our long-awaited home. I recite an old dialect proverb that came from my grandfather: "There is no herb grown on earth that cures death." Then we broach a topic I've been thinking is *streng verboten* (strictly forbidden): she starts to talk about SS officer Weingartner.

It's the strangest thing: Regina's voice suddenly changes from the craggy voice of an eighty-year-old, dredging fragments from the cellar of her memory, to the sparkling intonations of the teenage girl she'd been in Hoffnungstal, half in love with Weingartner.

She wants this story told, I tell myself, so that I (or others she'll never meet or know) will be able to follow the thread into the labyrinth and ferret out the truth, even if she can't understand or fully face that truth herself. But what is the truth?

"My family shared meals with him," Regina says. "He was a religious man. I've meant to tell you, he prayed the same prayer you prayed out loud for us before we ate when you came to Fresno."

"An SS officer, religious?" I say.

"Of course. *A Pfarrer*. A minister. Before the war. Why is that surprising?" she says. "He was one of our own people. Our people are always religious."

"Our people? You mean Weingartner was a Volksdeutsche?" I say.

"He was from Teplitz," she says, pronouncing the village the old way, *Tepleetz*, like I'd heard from my grandfather.

Teplitz is a German colony across the Dniester River from Hoffnungstal, where my own Vossler ancestors settled in 1815. I feel a shiver. For all I know, given the intense intermarriage in the German colonies, Weingartner could be a relative.

"Dat was the saddest day of our lives," Regina says. "When we learned Weingartner died near the end of the war. Und we cried."

"He died? Fighting the Soviets?" I say.

"*Nein*, not in fighting," she says wearily. "*Selbst-mord*. How do you say it?"

"Suicide," I say.

"Yah, suicide. He killed his family. His wife und his two boys," she says. "Und then himself."

* * *

One day, in a genealogical chart, I find the names of Weingartner's preteen boys, Ulrich and Hermann, the children he'd murdered before he'd taken his wife's and then his own life. Knowing their names makes them seem suddenly real, and I pour out questions about Weingartner in a letter to Alice, an elderly German friend in Munich, Germany. We've exchanged letters for years, her replies arriving *puenktlich*, exactly a month after my own missives. But this time, her return letter appears just a week later in my university mailbox.

"This is strange," I tell myself, hastily opening the envelope and reading:

10

In your last letter, you confided in me about an SS officer Weingartner, who befriended your relations. I am convinced that he seemed to be a nice and amiable man there and then. But as this man killed his family, and then himself after the war, he must have played a sinister role in the Holocaust. You find these people in Nazi history, at home they are law-abiding citizens, friendly, helpful, good family fathers—and murderers of Jews elsewhere.

You write that Weingartner was a Bessarabian Volksdeutscher. These Germans living in Eastern countries frequently joined the German army, more likely the SS when they had a chance, and since they'd experienced cruelty themselves as you know under the Soviets, many became willing tools for the Nazis. Anti-Semitism has been a terrible chapter and not only in Germany. The Holocaust, however, was unique, because it was planned and carried out systematically, and with incredible precision, with *"deutscher Grundlichkeit."*

Alice's letter angers me. Especially her linkage of Weingartner's suicide with the Holocaust. I toss the letter aside and set to work, with final grades due soon, evaluating a sheaf of student portfolios.

Usually, I read and grade quickly. This time I dither. I assign a grade, change it, change it back again. I don't want to finish grading. That much is clear.

Because then I'll have to deal with Alice's letter, which, each time I read it, makes me feel like a diver at the bottom of a murky sea, blindly groping the edges of something huge—a sunken continent or maybe a lost world.

***

LOST WORLDS

I know something about forgotten worlds. I grew up in one: an isolated triangular-shaped region of South Central North Dakota, thirty thousand square miles of rolling drift prairie, of small towns and sloughs, of pastures and glacially shaped hills and cropland, which included the northernmost tier of the counties in South Dakota. There, just before and after the turn of the twentieth century, thousands of German-speaking farmers from their ancestral villages around Odessa claimed homesteads in waves of immigration that, up to the Russian Revolution in 1917, brought one of four Volksdeutsche to America.

Saint Augustine writes of the palaces of memory, of the vastness of the past, which is how I feel about my prairie upbringing, aspects of which still shine in my memory. It was a childhood populated by relatives. There were elderly women in dark shawls and print dresses who spoke in sing-song German dialect voices, shaking handmade throw rugs from the steps of their asphalt sided homes, or washing windows with gnarled rags soaked in vinegar water. There were elderly men, retired farmers in billed slouch caps, long-sleeved shirts buttoned to the collar, as they puttered in backyards, pulling rusty nails from splintered boards, or sharpening butcher knives against pedal millstones.

The ghosts of the first prairie years haunted our lives, we'd seen those rural cemeteries, the long rows of ovals along the fence lines, children and babies dead from diphtheria or farm accidents or fevers. And outside the church cemeteries were the graves of the suicides who couldn't endure the extremes of prairie weather and died homesick for the prosperous villages they'd left behind. But at least they'd had a chance at life, far from the rivers of blood that destroyed everything on the steppe, or so went the whispers.

In high school, helping my stepfather lay linoleum in the homes of elderly pioneers retired into town, I'd sometimes seen the pinch-faced ghosts staring from old country photos—tucked into doorjambs or arrayed along shelves or on china hutches—that showed phantom families gathered around caskets so flimsy, as if assembled by mindless children. Those photos drove home the reality of my grandmother's scolding, whenever I didn't clear my plate at holiday meals: "Child, in the old country you would be happy to eat that."

Even if the land was harsh, even if the snow was so deep you couldn't find your butt with a board, as grandma said, even if there were rocks on our land, not fruit like in the old country, our lives were still better. At least here, as grandpa said, nobody ever starved, not like those on the steppe, who lost first their rights, then their sons, then their bread, finally their lives. Still, for us, for those in the later generations, those old things lay in darkness at the far edge of our grandparents' memories, in that impossibly remote past from which we had all come. As children in midcentury, we thought the whole world, if there was a world beyond our little prairie town, was rich with relatives, kneeling in rows and praying together out loud in church, or gathered around oak tables crowded with kin, because people then didn't have friends, just relatives. And if you didn't have relatives, as the old saying went, you'd be so desperate for attention you'd hug a fencepost.

"Am I related to everyone in town?" I asked my mother once, after huffing out the candles on my tenth (my only) birthday cake at a party so crowded with cousins and second cousins that it seemed more of a family reunion or church revival than a birthday party.

It was a time, in midcentury, when our people married their own distant, or not so distant relations, so I couldn't go to the local theater or get a bag of popcorn from the stand on main street Saturday night or fill a can of kerosene at the gas station without someone shouting out, "Hey, Rawney." Such calls came from the multigenerational knots of menfolk on the cracked sidewalk in front of my great uncles' bar, bald heads bathed in the glow of the front window's neon tubing that spelled out, in vaguely Germanic script, my own last name.

And it was the same when our baseball or basketball teams traveled beyond our little town (so small you could see through it from all sides to the slanting farmland around) to other towns in our county, where we were sure to find a semblance of our own genetic material, our stocky, muscled statures, our burnished, stoic faces, our hawked Roman noses in opponents, often with our own last names, cousins or second cousins or others, related by blood or marriage in the bewildering network of our families.

We knew that if our parents didn't show us enough love, God corrected the oversight on Sunday mornings by filling the pews behind us with shawled and hairnetted old ladies, usually relatives, to tenderly smooth down our cowlicks or pick lint pills from our hand-me-down sweaters, love passing to us from those knobbed and prairie-gnarled fingers. When I crossed the potholed gravel road to my grandparents' yard, a tree wasn't a tree, but a *baum*, and the potatoes you dug with a *gavel*, weren't potatoes at all, but *grundberra*. And then, when they retired from the farm, my grandparents reassembled their rural prairie life. Over a summer they brought—balanced on the huge moving beams of a relative's army surplus truck—first their two-story clapboard farmhouse, then a framed summer kitchen, a chicken coop, an outhouse, and a small garage, creating not just a replica of their Dakota farmstead, but a facsimile of their former yards in the old country, that place of ghosts.

Saturday afternoons in our small-town library, the winter sun slanting through the high windows, I'd pore over books the librarian retrieved from a high shelf, heavy volumes of Ridpath's *History of the World*, and whatever else I could find about history and the past, about archaeological expeditions and Richard Halliburton adventure stories, so by the time my grandfather lived with us so briefly, my imagination already bubbled, like a volcano, with thoughts of buried cities, forgotten empires, and lost worlds.

Evenings, I helped my grandfather limp and shuffle from my little brothers' bedroom, step by painful step, bunching up rugs along the way, to our family table, where my mother cut his food into bite-size portions just as she did for my little brothers, tied into their high chairs with dish towels. Evenings, I brought him, balanced on a tray, his cup of chamomile tea. And on one of those distant evenings, I first heard the name of his birthplace, Lichtenfeld, the Germanic syllables that meant "light in the field," tumbling from his dry lips.

Photos show me then as a dreamy ten-year-old with a heinie haircut, electric eyes focused on some inner vision, so that my grandfather could as well have said Golden Mycenae, or Persepolis, or Windy Troy, and I imagined Lichtenfeld as a shimmering aura of light on the far away steppe, a beacon of permanence, like our rural airport beacon sweeping our small town sky each night, or like the pillar of fire from sermons in our church. Someday, I promised myself then, I'd go there, to our own Canaan on the steppe: Lichtenfeld.

One evening my grandfather hinted at a darker theme in our ancestral origins. I was perched on a small homemade hassock, the kind everyone had then, fabric stretched over five metal juice cans, and Grandpa, sipping the last of his chamomile tea, sat pensively on the edge of his bed.

"Someone should know this," he said. "There is a book older than the *Bible*, written by *d' lang-haarige Sibylle*, a long-haired prophet, its origins lost in the mists of history." He'd seen the book just once, in Lichtenfeld, a tattered copy surreptitiously passed around.

"Sell hat unsera Leute oft vorher gewarnt," he said. She often warned our people. About coming hunger, about rivers of blood. Which swept away the *dorfs*, the colonies on the steppe. Which swept away Lichtenfeld, his birthplace, that far Eden his own grandfather helped found, the place from which we had all come and to which we could never return. "Not in

this lifetime," my grandfather always said. "Not while the goat people reign and devour everything."

"Now you know," grandpa said. He died not much later, after the worst blizzard in memory, snow as high as the telephone wires, with farmers shoveling down to find their barns and feed their hungry cattle.

While our little town was still digging out, we held his funeral. All of us, grandpa's children and grandchildren, all of the cousins and uncles and aunts and other relatives following the narrow, shovel-width pathway through the snowbanks to enter our clapboarded evangelical church, while the church bell clanged, once for each year of his long life.

We stood around his open coffin, singing the haunting, repetitive verses of *"Lass mich gehe"* the archaic death song of our people, wherever they were scattered, on the prairie and the steppe. And as we sang, we all knew, deep in our secret hearts, that we were remnants of a virile, bustling people, the lucky offspring of exiled survivors who'd escaped great prodigies of blood and death.

***

THE HITLER SURVEILLANCE CLUB

After my grandfather's death, a time just after two world wars against a German enemy, and during a Cold War against Russia, nobody breathed a word about our German colonist origins on the steppe. And so it was left to us, the settlers' grandchildren, to unconsciously work out in our play the unspoken contradictions of our confusing history.

During those overgrown summer days, we played war. We combed through the trunks in our basements and attics for war memorabilia that our Dakota German fathers, interpreters for the American military, brought back from the European theater: belts with "God With Us" in German, emblazoned on the silver buckles, Hitler Youth daggers, and dummy hand grenades. We added rifles and machine guns fashioned from pigweed stalks, and thus accoutered and equipped, we chased each other in the lot next to my house, through the high weeds and the sage and thistles, and around the rusting hulks of old long-necked combines and harrows once pulled by horses.

We cast my cousin, a German dialect speaking farm kid, as the rabid Nazi SS officer who wandered into our imaginations from the comic books we so avidly read. We mowed him down with our machine guns, and while he writhed in mock agony in the weeds, loosing a staccato rant of German curse words, we looked at each other, shame faced and confused. Who were we, anyway?

In early July 1961, I was twelve years old, about to enter sixth grade. My best friend Larry and I headed uptown, going along the buckled sidewalk of our neighborhood, to get some popcorn. It was Saturday night. Insects whirled in cones under the streetlights. We were just starting to like girls, and Larry was compulsively running his comb through his hair, greased back into a ducktail.

There was a small house on the corner, with asphalt siding and a built on lean-to, where an elderly stoop-shouldered man with a square moustache lived. In the middle of his neglected lawn, like an oversize mushroom, there was a crude birdbath, fashioned from leftover driveway cement.

"That's the marker," Larry said.

"For what?" I said.

"For Nazi gold."

Larry expounded on how countless stacks of gold bars were secreted in the underground chamber beneath the lawn. He didn't know all the details, but somehow Hitler escaped his bunker in Berlin, crossed the Atlantic in a Nazi submarine, and then, in a convoy of trucks laden with gold bars, found his way to our little town. There, in a borderland between fantasy and reality, we let our vivid imaginations run wild.

"Think about it," Larry said. "New Odessa is a great place to hide."

We imagined Hitler, hunched over his shortwave radio in a bunker under his house, plotting with his deputy Bormann in South America to take over the world, *noch einmal*, once again. We imagined Hitler ordering his groceries over the phone in German, just like our grandparents, and shuffling uptown on Saturday nights to my great uncles' bar, to rock and sway to live polka music. And, on Sunday nights, just a couple of blocks away from his home, sitting in a back pew in our evangelical church, where he could hear a sermon, scripture readings, and songs, all in German. Our little town, we decided, was the perfect retirement community for elderly Nazis.

Not much later, four of us formed our Hitler Surveillance Club. Somebody had to keep an eye on Hitler, Larry said. We had a secret password—Adolf. And that fall, from the trash behind my stepfather's mercantile store, we dragged an empty refrigerator shipping carton along a graveled alleyway and into the weeded lot where we played war. There, we set up our Hitler Surveillance Clubhouse. We christened it The Bunker.

We made a schedule and took turns keeping an eye on the Hitler house, just in case the washed-up dictator ever attempted a comeback. We got small notebooks in which we wrote down license plate numbers, descriptions of the large-finned cars that parked nearby, and descriptions of people who visited him.

Later that summer, our surveillance club went rogue. We convinced ourselves that we needed a secret insignia. So, using the metal tip of a math-class compass, we carved swastikas into our biceps and, pressing our torn flesh together, promised to remain blood brothers forever. When school started, we hid our wounds beneath long sleeves or under large Band-Aids, which we ripped off in unison at our after school meetings.

Once, I remember, as the sides and ceiling of our Hitler bunker sagged from a recent downpour, we'd stripped to our waists in the fetid heat, doling out code names based on the Nazi leaders whose photographs we found in *Encyclopedia Britannica*. Larry chose first, Goebbels, because it sounded like his mother's maiden name. He was a strange kid. Instead of watching the M and M boys, Mantle and Maris, in their home run chase for Babe Ruth's record, he was preoccupied with watching the televised war crime trial in Israel of Eichmann, Hitler's infamous henchman.

That day in the bunker, Larry drew his fervent, sweaty face to mine, closely examining my features. "Your lips are thin just like his," he said. "You have the same high forehead."

"Like whose?" I said.

"Like Eichmann. From now on, you are Eichmann."

Our Hitler Surveillance Club foundered soon after. It came just after we'd peeked in the old man's window and seen him kneeling in prayer and realized, finally, that maybe Hitler wasn't living in our little town after all.

Eventually the old man passed away, the swastika wounds etched into our flesh healed over, and though the other members sloughed off their code names, for reasons not my own and which I couldn't ascertain, I couldn't shed mine.

Later, at high school reunions, Larry and I and the two other former members, laughed nervously at our dark childhood imaginations run so amok. After one reunion Larry wrote me the following in an e-mail:

> We should get together more often. It was fun talking about our Hitler Surveillance Club. But don't take it so seriously. We were just acting out what many thought then, that because people in town spoke

German, then maybe Hitler, or some other Nazi mass murderer could hide there. Really, the chances of that being true are what, a million to one?

His message, up to that point, made me feel a little better, but the way he ended his e-mail disturbed me: "Hey, Eichmann, good seeing you again."

***

RIVERS OF BLOOD

That summer, Alice's letter lies on my desk in my upstairs study, an indictment that I try not to think about. I throw myself into much-neglected yard work and housework. I grow grass in several scraggly bare spots on my lawn. I prop a ladder against my house and scooped rotten leaves from rain gutters. Eventually, I run out of projects, and by the time the next semester begins, I feel relieved and happy. Until the phone call, another indication that there is an unknown hand weaving a larger pattern into the fabric of my life.

The phone call comes from an engineer and fellow prairie Volksdeutsche whose grandfather also came from Lichtenfeld. We've grown quite close, as twice a week for a year, we threaded brittle microfilm onto the sprockets of a hand-cranked film reader in the university library basement and read letters to the Dakota prairie that appeared in German language newspapers. Twice a week for a year, like in a time machine, we returned, it seemed, to the German colonies on the steppe, and we translated gut-wrenching descriptions of the Soviet famine, when people ate bark, pets, rotten flesh of horses, and sometimes each other. We also found the final letter, replete with arcane symbols and a prophecy, or fragment of one, that had the same cadence and rhythm as the prophecy my grandfather had repeated, and for a long time my friend and I puzzle over it: "From Grusia to the north, a torment of

20

hunger, fields heavy with grain, revenge on each stalk, a rain of ashes, a burning heaven of stars."

"Remember those letters we translated?" my friend says. "That stopped coming in 1936?"

"It's not like I could forget," I say. "I had a lot of bad dreams about those letters."

"I think I know why the letters stopped," he says. "Are you sitting down?"

"Executions?" I say.

"Yes," he says. "Secret police execution lists of Volksdeutsche."

"Are my relatives on that list?"

"Every Volksdeutsche has relatives on the list," he says. "Just access this website and call me back if you want to talk."

I pull up the website on the computer screen, punch the Print button, and ease back, the casters of my chair squeaking. My ancient printer churns and chugs. It reminds me of a baling machine on the prairie, pushing out rectangular hay bales. These aren't bales; these are victims—thirty pages of closely spaced Volksdeutsche names.

I scan the list. Familiar last names. Like those in small-town Central Dakota phonebooks. Like those from my childhood. Names of elderly neighbors. Of church parishioners. Of my high school basketball teammates. Twenty names, maybe more, are my stepfather's relatives, his cousins and second cousins and uncles and even an aunt: all executed—shot with a Nagan pistol in the back of the head by Soviet secret police in 1937 and 1938.

"Those are just some of the names," my friend says, when I return his call.

"There are more?" I say, incredulous.

"Tens of thousands."

"But why?" I say.

He explains Stalin's paranoia about the rising threat of the Nazis in Germany, about German colonists in Soviet Ukraine, whose supposed ties of loyalty, language and culture to Germany, might form a fifth column within the USSR.

"That's why our Dakota Germans stopped getting letters from Soviet Ukraine," he says.

After that phone call, I flip through the thick sheaf of pages, shaking my head sadly at the familiar last names, which reminded me of the photo of miles and miles of Siberian trees, flattened by a comet. Only in this case, the comet was the Soviet secret police, burning its way through the fruit and flower of an entire generation of Volksdeutsche just four years before the German invasion of the Soviet Union. No wonder my relatives cheered when Hitler's troops entered their village. No wonder my relatives befriended the SS officer.

That day, I sit in my office, the execution list heavy in my lap. My emotions churn. I feel history's bloody claw tapping me on my shoulder. Do I want to embark on another lengthy research project? That would carry me deep into the historical record, into areas beyond literature, where I have no expertise. I am, I know, a reluctant and unqualified historian, relying on instinct and prayer, hardly normal research tools. How many times, translating those terrible letters, had I prayed for strength?

In my office that day, I think about Alice's letter. About the photo of the SS officer my relatives wouldn't send. About the Soviet execution list in my lap. About the Nazi bureaucrat Leibbrandt. All of those things seem connected. Which leads to my fateful decision to pursue those connections.

***

I begin with the Nazi invasion of the Soviet Union in the summer of 1941. Operation Barbarossa was the greatest offensive of all time, with three million men, thirty-five hundred tanks, seven hundred artillery pieces, and two thousand aircraft, five hundred thousand other vehicles, and seven hundred and fifty horses. The forces were split into three groups—north, middle, and south. Each group, including one which swept into southern Ukraine, was followed by police battalions to protect the rear areas, and mobile death squads, called *Einsatzgruppen*, to kill partisans, Jews, and other enemies of the Nazis.

Cleansed of these unwanted and inferior people—so went the utopian vision—the Eastern territories, which Hitler and Himmler saw as a Nazi Garden of Eden, would be repopulated by soldier-farmers, *Wehrbauern*, ready to drop their plows and pick up their rifles to defend their spacious steppe farms against the menace of Asiatic hordes.

Hitler's *Wehrbauern* would consist not only of German military men, Eastern Front veterans awarded vast postwar acreages for service to the Reich, but also, after America's defeat, Dakota Volksdeutsche, repatriated after a half century on the prairie and bringing their vaunted agricultural skills and work ethic back to the steppe, and the region between the Bug and Dniester Rivers, crisscrossed with ravines and hills, and dotted with Schythian tumuli burial mounds, that their own ancestors had broken with the plow and tamed over a century earlier.

In Hitler's view, the repatriated Dakota Volksdeutsche and other Wehrbauern would fulfill the same role that Catherine the Great and her grandson envisioned for the original German colonists who were invited into the Black Sea region in the nineteenth century, there to act as model farmers, and to create a bulwark against eastern tribes. These Wehrbauern would become the new ruling class of the Nazi East, after thirty to forty million Slavs and Jews and other groups were killed or relocated. Those remaining, in Hitler's view, would become compliant helots, only able to count to ten and sign their names, happy with their beads and scarves.

Ukraine would become a German India, so went the totalitarian fantasy, crisscrossed by vast networks of macadamized roads to replace the churned up dirt roads of the backward steppe, creating an endless Ukrainian interstate, constructed by slave labor, over which German tourists in their Volkswagens would tour and travel, especially to Crimea, which would become the Riviera of the Eastern Empire.

That the Dakota Volksdeutsche figured into such a grandiose plan was appalling enough, but what I really wanted to learn, the history books didn't explain. What happened in the Volksdeutsche villages in the region between the Bug and Dniester Rivers during the three years of German Occupation? In fact, Transnistria—Hitler's name for that region—wasn't even listed in the indexes of major Holocaust works.

That's a good omen, I tell myself, thinking no major mass murders occurred there.

"More Hitler stuff?" the work-study librarian says, handing me the various tomes I've requested through the interlibrary loan department on campus. One book that was particularly intriguing seemed impossible to find: *Indien*, a history of British rule in India, by Ludwig Altsdorf. It was prominent on Hitler's reading list in the summer of 1942, at his eastern headquarters in Vinnitsa, Ukraine, and it came with the recommendation of Rosenberg, Reich Minister for Occupied Territories and Hitler's racial architect. It was a book the Nazi dictator meant to be required reading for the sixty thousand Germans posted to the East.

One day the university interlibrary loan office sends me a note. They've tracked down Altsdorf's book. I cross the campus quad, hurry up the steps of the library, and as I turn the first dry and friable pages of the old, battered tome, with its repaired cover, I feel a jolt of recognition: the editor of *Indien* was Dr. George Leibbrandt, propaganda minister in

Rosenberg's Ministry for the Occupied Eastern Territories. He is the same Leibbrandt who visited Helmut and Regina, my relatives in Fresno.

***

Editing a book read by Adolf Hitler didn't automatically make Leibbrandt a Nazi. But who, exactly, was he? That's what I set out to discover, and for a long while, I lose myself in the dense thickets of German and Holocaust literature, searching for him, and the prevailing ideas of his time:

The German people had long expressed interest in the East—*Drang nach Osten*, a German policy of eastern expansion. Hundreds of thousands sought new homes in a wide swath of territory from East Prussia to the Volga River, and in the early nineteenth century, thousands of German speakers, farmers and craftsmen, Leibbrandt's relatives and my own, founded villages near the Black Sea. Three thousand such Volksdeutsche colonies, islands in the great Russian landscape, eventually dotted the Czarist Empire, from Leningrad to the Sea of Azov, and from Siberia to the Black Sea.

Leibbrandt was born in 1899, his earliest years coinciding with political unrest, growing pan-Slavism, and erosion of German colonist rights. There was also anti-Germanic and anti-Jewish fervor within the Czarist Empire, culminating in a near revolution in 1905, when wealthy family farms, called *hutors*, were destroyed by revolutionary mobs, and pogroms in nearby Kishinev, Odessa, and Nikolaev—either stoked, or ignored, by the Czarist regime—further rattling nerves. German colonists felt the pogroms foretold their own destruction, for the Jews, like themselves, were an identifiable and prosperous minority, also labeled *kulaken*, a Russian word for greed. In fact, for the German colonists, especially those of a mystical bent, the social turmoil was in accord with their own beliefs in the prophecies of the long-haired Sibyl. And for the Catholics, in accord with warnings from their Jesuit

25

priests, that Ukraine would not be the final Volksdeutsche homeland.

Leibbrandt's own father, a militant minister in Hoffnungsfeld, a neighboring village to Hoffnungstal, encouraged his gifted son's prodigious reading, from several trunksful of German theological and philosophical books, carted to the Nogai steppe in 1817 by Leibbrandt's great-grandfather—books that remained in Leibbrandt's private library in Bonn, Germany, until his death. This reading certainly was instrumental in Leibbrandt's ties of culture and language to the ancestral homeland of Germany.

In 1914, as WWI broke out, Leibbrandt's father sent his fifteen-year-old son to Dorpat, Estonia, to avoid registration for the youngest round of conscripts into the Czarist military. At Dorpat's humanistic gymnasium there, he studied religion and philosophy, joining *Wingolf,* a Christian fraternity, whose motto was "All things through Jesus Christ," and whose notable members, at German universities across Europe, included influential protestant theologians and philosophers of the twentieth century like Paul Tillich.

In the spring of 1918, the nineteen-year-old Leibbrandt witnessed the German occupation army marching into Hoffnungstal during Ukraine's civil war, row on row of strong, steel-helmeted young men. This was a pivotal life event mentioned later in his Nazi party application. He volunteered as an interpreter, serving the Kaiser's military until its precipitous withdrawal a year later, which was when he joined Hoffnungstal's several hundred–man local self-protection unit, another pivotal life event.

Leibbrandt penned articles and reports about the aborted uprising and general situation in the German colonies, some of which appeared in 1920 and 1921 in *The Eureka Rundschau,* one of several German language newspapers on the prairie, which unified the scattered community of Volksdeutsche across the United States, Canada, and Europe. The *Rundschau* was published in the small farming community of Eureka, South Dakota, an hour's drive from my hometown of New Odessa, both towns within the rolling cropland and sloughs and pastures of the Central Dakotas, where hardworking immigrant Volksdeutsche farmers settled, transforming sleepy Eureka into the world's leading wheat producer, just as their ancestors, once they arrived on the steppe, had done with Odessa on the Black Sea.

The Eureka Rundschau connected new Americans, like my grandfather and his people, to the old country villages on the steppe, especially by printing personal letters in the newspapers, which made the rounds on the prairie, exchanged so often they fell apart, as the new Americans, with deepening concern read about their relatives and friends caught up in Ukraine's Civil War, as various armies—there were five of them, at least—vied for control of Russia's, and the world's, breadbasket.

In 1919, the self-protection unit in which Leibbrandt served overwhelmed the Bolshevik contingent in Hoffnungstal, an audacious move. The retreating force called to Odessa for heavy weapons, which arrived at Saddische, a railway siding twelve miles away, and after shelling both Hoffnungstal and the surrounding battlefield, they quashed the rebellion.

It was a costly uprising. In the immediate aftermath, the Bolsheviks executed many *Selbstschutz* (self-protection) members. Over the next two decades, the Soviet regime punished German colonies involved in the insurrection. In that regard, Hoffnungstal and Grossliebental suffered disproportionately, with greater numbers of their citizens exiled and executed than other national minorities during the purges of the 1930s.

Leibbrandt's eyewitness account of the German colonist uprising against the Bolsheviks, titled "Victims of Terror in Several German Colonies in Ukraine, South Russia," appeared in June 1920, in a German-language newspaper. Leibbrandt described himself as among the thousands of Volksdeutsche refugees and remnants of the White Army fleeing westward "with sack and pack." Passing through various German colonies, like Glueckstal and Kassel, the cool-headed young scholar jotted notes on the run, collecting a long list of Volksdeutsche killed by the Bolsheviks. Leibbrandt's stated goal in the account was to inform the entire Volksdeutsche community, wherever they were scattered, of what had transpired in the German colonies during the uprising.

At a border crossing on their way to Germany, the refugees were searched, and Leibbrandt, afraid he'd be arrested and executed as a spy, memorized and then destroyed the notes about the uprising. But there was another reason for Leibbrandt's anxiety about being searched, and it showed up later in his application to join the Nazi Party: secreted on his person that day was a small fortune in gemstones, sixty million dollars' worth in today's money, which he turned over to its rightful owners, Volksdeutsche in Berlin, Germany, who'd earlier fled Ukraine.

In his article, Leibbrandt lists Volksdeutsche victims murdered by the Bolsheviks, mostly innocents, and some combatants, scores of names, often first and last, along with their corresponding villages, all reproduced from memory, a prodigious feat if true, even for a young scholar. He exhorts his *Rundschau* readers to read through the names, "even if you are terrified at the death-list," because it is always better to know difficult things, instead of "hovering in uncertainty."

He ends his article with a righteous entreaty: "These names must be written in fiery alphabet letters in the pages of the history of these times, so they poke each in his eye and always give a clear reminder of what happened. May each make his own contribution to eliminate anything similar from happening in the world. As for our own Germans there on the Russian steppes, we will hope for the best and wish these times will never be repeated. May God rule."

One weekend, I take a break from teaching and researching Leibbrandt and head on a four hour journey to New Odessa, my prairie hometown. I've been invited there to tell German dialect stories and jokes for a radio program.

First, I drive south across the flatlands of the Red River Valley, then west into the rolling drift prairie, then south again on a narrow two-lane highway, which curved around glacial lakes and softly molded hills and into a broad region of wetlands, pastures, and stubbled farm fields of my old heimat. Much of the way Leibbrandt is on my mind.

He was related to me several ways, at least, according to what Helmut has told me, and his view of the Volksdeutsche as a distinct people was one I shared, from the time thirty years earlier, when returning home from college in Arizona, and toting a textbook from my favorite course, *Peoples of the World*, I had an epiphany. Standing on the one-block main street, by my great uncles' bar, it struck me just how different people in my hometown looked, the men hawk faced and bandy legged, the women hefty and shawled. They spoke differently. Theirs was an odd mix of German dialect and colloquial English, which sometimes thickened my tongue and got me teased by my suntanned fellow students. That day, home from college, I got my first inkling that the Dakota Germans were a distinct people.

A good crowd awaits me in my hometown, seated on folding chairs, row upon row under the high arching beams of my old high school gymnasium, once the best wood floor in the entire state, we used to boast, and a place dear to my heart where I played basketball, acted in high school plays, and as an eighteen-year-old at a wobbly on-stage lectern, delivered my salutatorian address.

Now, from the same lectern, I tell jokes and stories about the Volksdeutsche pioneers. Afterward, I reunite with old friends and relatives from an earlier part of my life, a few of whom venture words of German dialect: "*Yah, kennsch mich noch?*" Do you still know me?

While the high school choir sings old Dakota German dialect songs to round out the program, I ponder the fateful impulse to immigrate. Some of Leibbrandt's relatives had. If he'd come to the prairie, he might have ended up a farmer, an evangelical minister, or even a choir director, and not, as I was just beginning to learn, a Nazi involved with gas wagons, the Wannsee Conference, and the Final Solution of the Jews.

Several days later someone blogs on the Internet about my appearance at my hometown gymnasium, about my jokes and storytelling:

> What really hit home the most was Ron Vossler. His work with the heritage and history of the Germans from Russia really has made me appreciate my heritage. I didn't when I was young and I regret not getting to know my family in a deeper way before they all retired, moved off the farm and moved away…but the reality is that our family is blessed with longevity and food. Ah yes, Ron talked about sausage, what we called *Wascht*, and hearing him tell jokes, sliding in and out of English to German and back again, carried me back to earlier days around the kitchen table where English was the second language.

It is, to be sure, a kind comment. But how, I wonder, would that fan, or anyone else in my hometown audience of Volksdeutsche, react if they knew the dark and bloody direction in which I was being swept by my own research?

***

Once in Germany in 1919, George Leibbrandt, the young Christian scholar, Bolshevik fighter, and, smuggler of a vast gemstone fortune, became a peripatetic wanderer. He eventually embarked on a grand tour of sorts, traveling widely in Germany, England, Russia, and the United States, studying at six different universities, emerging with degrees in philosophy and theology and international finance. A dizzying climb, for this gifted German colonist son from the muddy streets of Hoffnungsfeld, but just the beginning.

Frequenting *émigré* circles in Germany, Leibbrandt was elected head of the Black Sea German Students' Association; by 1925 he was writing for the *Völkischer Beobachter* in Munich, which became the official Nazi propaganda organ. It was edited by Alfred Rosenberg, Hitler's racial guru and chief formulator of Nazi anti-Semitism, and an important connection in Leibbrandt's later rise in the Nazi bureaucracy, when Rosenberg becomes his boss.

In 1927 Leibbrandt made the first of three different study trips to Soviet Russia. And in 1928, the homesick young scholar visited Hoffnungsfeld, his home village, which is just several miles from Hoffnungstal. There was a brief, joyful reunion with his parents, his sister and brother-in-law and other relatives, aged in his decade away, and looking weak, having endured the searing 1922 famine caused by the Bolsheviks. It was an uncertain political situation, with Stalin in charge and about to collectivize a sixth of the earth's peasants, but one evening before Leibbrandt left, he gave a presentation to a hometown audience about his genealogical research and the origin of the region's German colonists in Germany's Swabia.

Afterward, Leibbrandt's parents and his sister and his various relatives beamed with stolid Volksdeutsche restraint. The young scholar with the limp hair nodded in appreciation as the audience gave their village's most famous son several rounds of generous applause. It was a wonderful moment, fixed forever in Leibbrandt's memory. He would never see his family again. And nearly all in attendance that evening— except for Leibbrandt and the *spitz*, the communist spy the secret police planted in their midst—would have their lives destroyed.

Within a year, Leibbrandt's closest family members, his parents, his sister and her husband, would be arrested and sent to the Gulag, likely to the island hell of Solovetski Prison in the White Sea, among the first wave of kulaks, to be exterminated as a class, a fate shared by forty thousand other Volksdeutsche from the Odessa region.

Leibbrandt's biography, overall, resembles the biographies of the ranking officers of the Einsatzgruppen murder squads, and the Order Police of Eastern Europe, especially with regard to the turbulence and dislocation of his late teens and early adulthood and the embittering personal losses. As he studied in England and the United States, he watched from afar the development of the Nazi state and its racial policy, and he already had reasons, ideological and personal, to blame his family's destruction on groups the Nazis targeted for subjugation or eradication, especially the Communists, which meant, for most Nazis, the Judeo-Bolsheviks: the Jews.

In 1931, while living in Washington DC, Leibbrandt risked losing a Rockefeller Grant, funding his study in London and the United States, by making himself available to the National Socialist Party. In 1933, after Hitler's rise to power, and after Leibbrandt was shown, by his American relatives, the shakily written hunger letters from Hoffnungstal, as a quarter of Ukraine starved to death, including tens of thousands of Volksdeutsche, he applied for membership in the Nazi party.

His application highlighted his own sea change, watching the German army march into Hoffnungstal in 1918, the lines of strong, healthy, uniformed soldiers reminding him of his German blood. He also revealed his role in smuggling the small fortune in gems out of Bolshevik Ukraine. It was Hitler's racial guru, Rosenberg, who, after Leibbrandt was accepted as a member of the Nazi Party, invited him to return to Germany.

Thus began his ambitious rise in the Nazi bureaucracy. In 1937 and 1938, through clandestine contacts with his home village, Leibbrandt learned that among the thousands of German colonists arrested during the Soviet secret police's anti-German operation were all those who attended his presentation. The Soviet secret police, obviously working from a list developed by a spy, charged each with being an agent of Hitler and with plotting outlandish crimes, such as poisoning wells, destroying railroad tracks, and otherwise wrecking Soviet infrastructure and the farm economy. Those who didn't confess were tortured in unspeakable ways. One of the accused, according to Leibbrandt, was tightly bound in a filthy Soviet prison cell while rats gnawed the flesh from his face. It was, in fact, a notorious secret police torture technique Hitler himself feared. All were eventually executed, including six Leibbrandt men, which effectively erased the ambitious young Nazi bureaucrat's family name in the Hoffnungstal area.

***

My search for Leibbrandt, however incomplete, leaves me with sympathy, and even an affinity for the former Nazi bureaucrat to whom I am distantly related. My own early life resembled his own. We'd both grown up surrounded by relatives in little villages with dirt roads and under huge skies on the prairie and the steppe. Both of us were immersed in the village church, with its rounds of revivals and celebrations. We both sang the same German songs, like the somber and ancient "All Flesh is Grass." We both pressed our faces against the pew back, lifting our voices in the communal prayers to our old God. And both of us were expected by our parents to become ministers.

Hadn't Regina and Helmut repeatedly told me how I reminded them of Leibbrandt? That we spoke German dialect the same way. That we were even fond of the same food, and ate the same way too.

"Ach you und Leibbrant both gobbled up my crispy *strudels* and kuchen-pie like it was your last meal," Regina once said.

Am I so different from Height and Giesinger, scholars from my own background who accepted the sanitized version of Leibbrandt's Nazi past? Perhaps, like me, they were still held in thrall by the old Volksdeutsche attitudes: Don't judge. Forget the past. Don't talk ill of the dead, not here to defend themselves. If you point a finger at anyone, three of your own fingers point back at you. Did those two scholars, like me, have a difficult time thinking Leibbrandt guilty because his entire family was wiped out by Soviet terror?

It seems like pure serendipity, although as my Christian friend, the writer Larry Woiwode once told me, "There is no such thing as an accident," that I stumbled onto an article in a book: *German Scholars and Ethnic Cleansing, 1919–1945*. It was penned by two young scholars of Volksdeutsche ancestry, perhaps less affected by the old ethnic strictures, since they made the claim that Leibbrandt and others collaborated "with the Nazis, using their intellectual acumen and Nazi ethnographic research to advance grandiose policies of racial imperialism in the occupied territories."

According to the article, Leibbrandt's career as the head officer in the political department of Rosenberg's Eastern Ministries put him in "an important position in the Nazi machinery of death." He made top-level policy decisions regarding the liquidations of East European Jews, and directed "the executions of tens of thousands" while overseeing the "subjugation and extermination of 'subhumans.'"

The article continued its indictment of Leibbrandt:

> In 1947 (while himself serving in prison) Leibbrandt was a key witness in the case against the Nazi Foreign Ministry. Robert M. Kempner, the lawyer who cross-examined Leibbrandt at Nuremberg, provided revealing information about Leibbrandt's complicity at Wannsee. In 1961 Kempner reflected that Leibbrandt "showed little inclination to…admit to his participation at the Heydrich-Eichmann conference [Wannsee]."

However, during his testimony, Leibbrandt did, however, refer to the "Final Solution" as *wahnsinnpolitik* (a policy of insanity). He even claimed that after the conference he protested to Rosenberg, insisting that he would not participate in such policies. Although it is true that Leibbrandt opposed some SS policies toward the Slavic peoples—whom he deemed potential allies against the Soviets—the Nuremberg documents show he was directly and actively involved in ordering the mass executions of Jews. In the course of cross-examining Leibbrandt, Kempner posed a rhetorical question: "You are a sensible man. Think about the meeting and the murder plan once more, with whom you spoke and so forth. Not one of you stood up and said, 'here I stand and cannot do otherwise.' Is that correct?" Leibbrandt remained silent. Leibbrandt's denial of complicity in the "Final Solution" already had been refuted by his immediate superior, Alfred Rosenberg.

During the Nuremberg trials, Rosenberg told Allied prosecutors that his associates—including George Leibbrandt—were fully cognizant of the program to eliminate the Jews. When the court's president asked him, "Do you agree that these five people were engaged in exterminating Jews?" Rosenberg replied, "Yes. They knew about a certain number of liquidations of Jews. That I admit, and they have told me so, or if they did not, I have heard it from other sources."

The article also martialed other salient points concerning the former high official in Hitler's Eastern Ministry:

> Some members of the ethnic German community have subsequently picked up on Leibbrandt's excuses. Many never knew the whole truth. People close to activists like Leibbrandt...naturally find this issue difficult to confront. Only a generation after their deaths and those of their closest associates can we begin putting the issues into better perspective. In 1975 one short biography claimed that Leibbrandt worked in vain

to prevent Nazi foreign policy excesses, and that, in his official capacities, he protested the "Final Solution"; it implied that Leibbrandt voluntarily resigned from his post in 1943. Nor was there any mention of Wannsee. Most biographical sketches, articles, and obituaries on Leibbrandt, never mention the Wannsee Conference, and the Nuremberg war crimes trials receive little or no mention at all. Especially as events recede further in time, the sheer ignorance concerning them increases. Today this historical "amnesia," does not necessarily stem from any ulterior motives, but the fact remains that the events are unknown to most Russian Germans—indeed to most scholars.

Despite the fact that the Allied prosecution made a clear case against Leibbrandt, and his deputy, Brautigam, they were never prosecuted, and by 1950 charges had been dropped against them and they went free. This decision, made as the Cold War ratcheted up, was based on the idea that only the highest ranking Nazis should bear the responsibility.

Another point the article made was that Leibbrandt, since he'd served as a ministerial representative at the Wannsee Conference, was one of the high ranking Nazis: "Merciless men like Leibbrandt...once again became 'respectable citizens.' After the trial Leibbrandt served as an economic adviser in Bonn and resumed his studies on the Russian Germans..."

***

The most damning evidence was a memorandum Leibbrandt penned as chief political officer of the Eastern Ministries to a Nazi official in Latvia, telling him not to worry about more transports of Jews coming to Riga because transit camps were to be "moved farther east if possible." According to some scholars, the phrase "moved farther east" was a Nazi euphemism which meant extermination, by work or other means. Leibbrandt's use of it pointed to his involvement in the Holocaust.

Equally damning, of course, was Leibbrandt's presence at the Wannsee Conference. He was among the fifteen men—mass murderers and civil servants that Eichmann called the Nazi popes—who gathered at a sumptuous villa, confiscated from its Jewish owner, outside Berlin on January 20, 1942. Those attending were inextricably involved with the murder of the Jews, or else represented territories where this had already taken place.

The conference, meant to determine how various ministerial bureaucracies would react to their projected participation in the massive operation partially underway, was chaired by Reinhard Heydrich, Hitler's fuehrer-in-waiting, with Eichmann taking notes. As for Leibbrandt, if the quasi-documentary film, *Conspiracy*, is accurate, he made barely audible but vicious anti-Semitic comments and rapped his knuckles on the conference table in approval of further genocidal procedures against European Jewry.

About that same time, January 20, 1942—while the former theological student shared cognac and lunch with Heydrich and Eichmann and other conference participants—in Leibbrandt's home region of Transnistria a thousand miles to the east, the first transport departed Odessa's Sortoriovka Station with two thousand Jews from the Slobodka ghetto.

It was the first of dozens of transports initiated by the Romanian government. Their destination—unbeknownst to Leibbrandt—was a scattering of his own beloved German colonies to the northeast, the same colonies for which he'd initiated a humanitarian effort, meant to relieve their suffering.

***

"Leibbrandt visited us in Fresno in 1974," Regina says, when I call to ask if she could add anything to what I'd learned. "He sat at our table. The place where you sat. Remember?"

"I remember," I say. "What else do you know about him?"

"He was related to Helmut," Regina says. "His aunt was Leibbrandt's *pathen*. How do you say that in English?"

"Godmother," I say.

"Yes, pathen," she says.

"Let me get this straight," I say. "Leibbrandt's godmother was my great grandmother?"

"Ach, all our people are related," Regina says. "You with us, and both of us with Leibbrandt."

"What do you remember of his visit?" I say.

"Dr. Leibbrandt gave a talk, or maybe a sermon. I don't remember."

"A sermon?" I say, aghast.

"Well, yes, like Weingartner. Leibbrandt was trained in theology."

The venue in Fresno, because of an expected crowed, shifted to the larger Reformed Church, where dozens of local Volksdeutsche-descended families with ties to Hoffnungstal, turned out to hear this respected Volksdeutsche scholar and patriarch. Did anyone know, I wonder, that this short, elderly man with the boney face and the rumpled suit rubbed elbows with Holocaust butchers like Heydrich and Eichmann? Likely not, an ignorance and political naiveté that Leibbrandt may have counted on from American Volksdeutsche.

"We had a nice time with Leibbrandt," Regina says, explaining how, after his presentation, they shared a meal, and drank sweet red California wine, much like the wine from Hoffnungstal's vineyards.

"What did you talk about?" I say.

"You know, Hoffnungstal," she says.

"Was there talk of the Jews? The afternoon Leibbrandt visited?"

"The Jewish business?" Regina says, surprised.

"Yes."

"Yes. Leibbrandt and Helmut did."

"Do you remember what they said?" To urge her to continue, I add, sneakily, "Did they talk of Weingartner?"

"Oh yes, of course. We spoke of what a wonderful young man he was. Helping the Hoffnungstalers under such ugly circumstances."

"What did Leibbrandt say about the Jews," I say. "Can you remember?"

"That I remember. Leibbrandt said the Volksdeutsche suffered more than the Jews."

"Is that where Helmut got that idea?" I say.

"That's where he first heard that, yes. And during your visit here, he repeated it to you. Remember?"

"He kept saying that for twenty-five years?"

"More than that," Regina says, in a wife's weary voice, tired of hearing her husband's repetitions.

***

"We haven't spoken in a while," Dr. Crenir says.

I'm sitting in his cluttered office on campus. He's a friend, a psychology professor roughly my own age, with a quizzical look affixed to his kind, open face. I've known him for years, but only recently stumbled onto a library database that showed scholarly articles he'd published on borderland Germans who played a substantial role in the Holocaust.

"You have a new project?" Crenir says.

I describe my Fresno visit, the photo of the SS officer that my relatives wouldn't send, my research into Leibbrandt's Nazi career, his dodging the hangman at Nuremberg.

"I wanted to ask you about something Helmut told me. His wife says he borrowed the phrase from Leibbrandt."

"What exactly did Helmut say?"

"That the Volksdeutsche suffered more than the Jews," I say.

"Did they?"

I recited the overall Volksdeutsche mortality statistics of thirty years under the Bolsheviks and Soviets—three hundred thousand deaths from shootings and hangings and a first regime-caused famine, another three hundred thousand deaths from collectivization and the terror famine of 1933, a final three hundred thousand deaths from deportations and slave labor and more executions. Nearly a million unnatural deaths.

"You didn't answer my question," Crenir says.

"No, the Volksdeutsche didn't suffer more than the Jews," I say.

"But they suffered terribly?"

"Yes, of course. What do you make of that assertion? That the Jews suffered more?"

"In Holocaust literature it's called appropriation of Jewish suffering," Crenir says.

"Why would Leibbrandt or Helmut appropriate Jewish suffering?"

"To deflect from guilt perhaps."

"I understand why Leibbrandt might feel guilt," I say.

"You mean for the Wannsee Conference?"

"Yes, for the gas wagons. For rubbing elbows with monsters like Heydrich and Eichmann at Wannsee."

"How old was Helmut when the Nazis invaded?"

"Helmut was just fourteen then," I say. "What guilt would he have?"

"It doesn't have to be his own guilt. What do you know of Helmut's father?"

"Not much. Just that he was mayor of Hoffnungstal during the war," I say.

"Appointed by the SS officer in that photo?"

"I think so."

"You know, Ron, guilt is the cockroach of emotions. Hard to root out."

"Was Helmut trying to justify something his father did?" I say.

"Perhaps. Or something the SS officer made his father do."

"What would that be?"

"Murdering Jews. The most intense killing of the Holocaust took place in Transnistria. Did you know that?"

"No," I say.

"Isn't that where Helmut's village was located?"

"Yes. Unfortunately."

"What was it called?" he says. "Where your relatives lived?"

"One place was Lichtenfeld. It meant Light in the Field. Another was Hoffnungstal."

"What does that mean, Hoffnungstal?"

"It means Valley of Hope," I say, feeling suddenly hopeless.

***

The key to understanding what happened in Hoffnungstal was, I thought, the handsome, thirty-two-year-old SS officer stationed there from 1941 to 1944.

Weingartner was from Teplitz, one of a number of Volksdeutsche villages in Bessarabia named for Napoleonic battlefields, and it lay roughly eighty miles from Hoffnungstal. Both villages were founded in 1817 by colonists whose "flame and desire"—they belonged to deeply religious, pietistic harmonies—was to settle at the supposed site of the thousand year empire of Christ at Mount Ararat.

On wide barges, they'd departed various Germanic provinces, invited by the Czars into New Russia, as southern Ukraine was then called. They floated down the Danube, singing their haunting millennial songs about the coming heavenly kingdom. They came to the mouth of that river, where they met with a devastating epidemic. The survivors sought and found new homes in Hoffnungstal and Teplitz.

By the time Weingartner was born almost a century later, in 1909 (he came from a family of Lutheran ministers and suicides, a mixture of violence and piety that characterized his later life), Teplitz had become a prosperous village of several thousand, known as far as Siberia for its sturdy wagons.

Weingartner's photo appeared in the "Famous Sons" section of a Teplitz commemorative book, assembled post-WWII by its former inhabitants, honored, so I tell myself at the time, not for his high rank or SS affiliation, but his work as a beloved minister, a Bessarabian Lutheran preacher. In that photo, he wears what appears to be a Lutheran minister's cassock, a young man, with thick hair and fine, even sensitive features. ("See, I told you he was handsome," Regina says, when I tell her about the photo I'd found.)

Dividing his formative years between Bessarabia and Germany, Weingartner studied theology for four semesters at universities in Berlin and Koenigsburg. On the strength of exceptional examinations and language skills, and without a formal university degree, he petitioned the Lutheran Council in Bessarabia to be ordained as a minister. It was a unique and exceptional move, and by the mid-1930s, he'd served in at least one parish, perhaps Teplitz, and like many young Bessarabian Volksdeutsche during this interwar period, he'd also served in Romania's military. In 1933 he demonstrated his first affinity for National Socialism, joining a crypto-fascist, and likely anti-Semitic, renewal movement in Romania called *Erneurungbewegung.*

After the Hitler/Stalin pact in 1940 swapped Weingartner's home region of Bessarabia to the Soviets in exchange for the Volksdeutsche living there, Weingartner and his wife and two children, and all of Teplitz's inhabitants, were among the ninety thousand German colonists relocated to Germany. It was a coup that these extraterritorial Germans would resettle in the Greater German Reich, bringing tens of thousands of German-speaking recruits, a rich source of manpower for Himmler's SS divisions. (Postwar Bessarabian village memory books list hundreds of young men missing in action or killed in SS units fighting for the Nazis, among these scores of my direct relatives, and Weingartner's, and in some cases, soldiers related to both of us.)

The uprooting from Bessarabia was a turning point in Weingartner's life. Shortly after that—likely on contacts made during the evacuation—he joined the *Waffen* SS, the armed branch of the Nazi Party, and served from May to September 1940. Then he filed his naturalization application to become a German citizen. His SS evaluator sang his praises as a trustworthy, valuable, and well-liked comrade—"a flawless ethnic German with unique language skills." He was then assigned first, to the staff of the highest SS police leader in Hamburg, then to the Department for the Strengthening of Germandom, the VoMi, where he worked for half a year.

In August 1941, after the Nazi invasion of Soviet Ukraine, Weingartner was called to Berlin, fitted with a uniform, awarded an SS rank as lieutenant colonel, then posted to Transnistria. He was one of the highest ranking district SS officers there, a *Bezirkmeister* as Regina called him, commandant of an entire district of sixteen villages and seven thousand people, whose capital and headquarters was located in Hoffnungstal.

About his three year tenure in that village, I know nothing, except for what Regina and Helmut have told me. Later, much later, I will catch up with Weingartner once again, following his bloody footprints, deep into the ethnic labyrinth.

***

THE MAP

One day, while congratulating myself about finding nothing incriminating about Weingartner, the gaunt SS officer in that tiny photo, I make a startling discovery. I'm going through a collection of Holocaust material, *Documents of Destruction*. There, buried deep in its pages, the following description of an event in Transnistria, which took place in the fall of 1941, leaps off the page:

> In the whole of the Berezovka district there is no Jewish woman who was not raped or beaten. Most of the women have venereal disease… After the occupation of Odessa, the Romanians evacuated a part of the Jewish population of the city to the Berezowka District where they were distributed to individual villages. In the fall of 1941, an SS detachment appeared in one of the villages and arrested all the Jews. They were arrayed in

front of a ditch by the road and told to undress. Then the leader of the SS group declared that the Jews had released the war and that the assembled people had to pay for that. After this speech the grown-ups were shot and the children slain with rifle butts. The bodies were covered with gasoline and set on fire. Children who were still alive were thrown into the flames.

It stuns me—children slain with rifle butts and thrown alive into flames, and also this seemingly benign line, which indicated that "a part of the Jewish population of Odessa was evacuated and distributed to individual villages in the Berezovka District."

That sends me to my map, which I've recently tacked up on the wall of my study—a US Army map copied from a German General Staff map used in the Nazi invasion in 1941. It shows in detail an isolated region between the Bug and Dniester Rivers, whose topography was a series of long, broad valleys, at five and ten mile intervals, crossing obliquely from northwest to southeast: sixteen thousand square miles of farmland dotted with Ukrainian and Volksdeutsche villages. I find the Berezovka district, where, as the article stated, a part of the Jewish population of Odessa had been "relocated."

What, I wonder, does that mean? The pre-WWII Jewish population of Odessa stood near two hundred thousand souls. The total makes me cringe. That means thousands upon thousands of Jews were relocated. What happened to them, the article doesn't state.

I do a quick check of the map. Hoffnungstal lay forty miles west of Berezovka. It was uncomfortably close, and so were a scatter of my other ancestral villages, Rohrbach and Worms and Josefstal and, also, my beloved Lichtenfeld, villages which supplied numerous Volksdeutsche immigrants to the prairie.

That is the origin of my pushpin map. My reasoning, more of a hunch, goes like this: if I can track down various references to massacres of Jews in Transnistria—I assume *relocated* meant *murdered*—then indicate those locations on my map with pushpins—I might determine if any murder sites were close to the Volksdeutsche villages.

Little happened on the prairie without becoming common knowledge. Smoke from fires was visible for miles, and the scent of burning carried even farther. Noises were known to echo long distances over an open landscape. Once, when a bull gored my grandfather on his rural Dakota farmstead, his relatives on their homestead three miles away heard his cries for help. The same was true of events on the prairie. Prairie people had long memories. In 2002, an elderly man described in intimate detail how my other grandfather, in 1929, stole some barley to feed to his beloved horses.

If German colonists living on the steppe in the early 1940s, in many cases direct relatives of Dakota Germans, had witnessed large numbers of Jews forced into the vicinity of their villages, or massacred near there, then the various Volksdeutsche literature and memoirs of that period should reflect that fact.

That fall, I set to work, scouring the university library, locating any volumes remotely associated with the Holocaust, with Ukraine. I lug the books up the painted stairs to my combination study/bedroom and drop them on the floor with a thud. During the typically inhospitable Dakota winter, there will be time to read and research.

Winter falls like a sledgehammer. Fierce cold early and prolonged. Over weekends and holidays, and after teaching, I become an amateur researcher, an innocuous, if grim, diversion from teaching bored university students. First, I scan and skim various library volumes, trying to find Holocaust murder sites and ghettos and labor camps in any location between the Bug and Dniester Rivers. Then, when I find them, I use red pushpins to indicate their locations on the map. Often, I awake to the Red River flatlands muffled in snow. I shovel a narrow path to the garage, and in my four-wheel-drive SUV, buck through snowbanks to teach at the university.

The snow swirls. Frost thickens on the upstairs windows. Blizzards come and go. I continue reading and marking. Sometimes I find nothing, sometimes only a single site or two in weeks of skimming and reading. This convinces me, again, that Transnistria was a historical phantom of a place, existing, as it did, for a scant three years, from the time of the German Occupation in 1941 to the evacuation of its two hundred villages and a hundred and twenty thousand Volksdeutsche in 1944.

One day, in some Holocaust literature—in a document titled "Concentration Camps and Ghettos in Transnistria"—I stumble onto a mother lode of sites with Ukrainian place names. I begin to plot those places on my map. As winter loosens its grip, I keep reading and finding sites and inserting pushpins. For months I work, face close to the map, the overall terrain a blur, squinting to read the tiny print of villages and rivers.

One evening, I clamp a lamp with a moveable neck to the desk, light flooding the map. That night, reading in bed, I glance up and see, cast across the map, the elongated shadows of all the push pins, which resemble a long column of weary figures, slogging painfully along.

"The pushpins," I tell a friend over the phone. "They look like my dream of the white uniformed soldiers."

In the spring of 2005, I stand back and survey my handiwork. The hair on my arms bristles. A cold chill runs up my spine. The pushpins on the map form a long river, a snake, or a cluster of them, winding across the map. It starts at the Dniester River, at Dubossary, near my grandmother's ancestral village, and, from there, fed by various tributaries from Odessa, it streams north and east, near exotic sounding villages whose names would later make me wince—places like Podoleanca, Berezovka, Sirotskoe, Sucha Verba, and Slepuchca. It slithers in and out of a broad, isolated, trapezoidal region of valleys and ravines and rolling cropland, dotted by Volksdeutsche villages and family estates with Dakota German names, like Wanner, Weidman, Eissinger, Trautmann, Jenner, Kraft, Lutz, Esslinger, and Schmalz. Then it butts up against, and finally ends at, a real river, the Bug, and a place called Bogdanovka. Each pushpin, I know, represents a massacre site, where Jewish blood was spilled. Is this a graphic illustration of the River of Blood my grandfather whispered about so long ago, and that the ancient prophecy foretold? Perhaps so.

But that question is overshadowed by another more pressing one. In the Volksdeutsche accounts of this period, and in my many conversations and interviews with Transnistrian Volksdeutsche, why had nobody ever said a word about the great influx of Jews forced into the region? Standing in front of my pushpin map that day, I'm already planning a trip to Ukraine.

***

II. FIRST NOTES FROM THE ROAD OF DEATH

"In the old man-killing parishes"

—Seamus Heaney

ODESSA, MY ROME

We are in Odessa, a Ukrainian city of one million, going to meet a survivor of a Transnistrian death camp. My interpreter, Laryssa, a teacher from a local business college, points the way to our driver. We turn off one of Odessa's busiest streets and into an interior courtyard ringed by crumbling balconies, where grapevines, thick as my wrist, twine around the rusting railings.

"Are you sure he lives here?" I say, feeling anxious, my voice hollow in the high ceilinged hallway as we climb several flights of well-worn steps.

"Yes, of course," Laryssa says. "One more flight."

The door to Duissmann's study is open, and we see him sitting, pigeon-breasted, amid a clutter of books and stacks of yellowed newspapers, an elderly Jew who greatly resembles the noted American writer Norman Mailer. After introductions, and after we'd seated ourselves in a couple of rickety cane chairs opposite him, I feel compelled to tell him this.

"In Ukraine it is good luck if you look like someone else," Duissmann says, smiling.

When I begin to apologize for the role of the German colonists in the Holocaust—minor as it seems at the time—

he quickly interrupts me. "Without your people, none of us would have survived."

We talk history. In the 1905 pogrom in Odessa, he says, German colonists hid Jews, and then again in 1941, when they gave Jews their identity cards. It was in this very apartment building that his own grandfather and another Jewish family, expecting to be treated fairly, like in 1918, eagerly anticipated the arrival of the German army in 1941.

"My father thought the Germans might restore private property taken by the communist regime in the 1920s and 1930s. As you can see, not all Jews were communists."

When Duissmann held up his book about his Holocaust experience, *Remember and Don't Repeat*, I snap a quick photo, which captures an eerie coincidence I note only later: he holds the book over his chest in such a way the five-pointed yellow star on its cover appears in exactly the place where the Nazis forced him, and the rest of Odessa's Jews, to wear that symbol.

"Yes, relationship between Germans, German colonists and Jews—a difficult problem," Duissmann says. "But of all the nations involved in the Holocaust, including Romanians and Ukrainians, only one has apologized. Germany."

"Mr. Duissmann would like to take you somewhere," my interpreter, Laryssa, says. "Is that okay?"

"Sure," I say.

We pile into the Nissan, with Duissmann directing our driver, Anatoli, which way to go, to Dalnik, I think, a site outside Odessa where Hitler's allies, the anti-Semitic Romanian administration, as revenge for the bombing of their headquarters in the fall of 1941, murdered twenty thousand Jews, many tied together with wire and shot in a long ditch, and the rest forced into granaries that were dynamited, burned, and machine-gunned.

We merge with the chaotic traffic—electric street cars, square Lada autos, and yellow buses that honk and spew acrid smoke. We turn once, travel past redbrick buildings with crumbling facades, and old manufacturing offices with faded signs. Then we turn again, and not much later, again, and we're back where we started.

It wasn't Dalnik that Duissmann wanted to show me, but the ghetto Slobodka, into which a large portion of the Jewish population—those who didn't flee Odessa, those not killed by the invading Romanian army—were imprisoned in 1941, during one of the coldest winters on record. Duissmann has directed us, without saying a word, around the entirety of Slobodka, to show me the ghetto's size, so that I feel part of the hugeness of the Holocaust opening in me like a chasm.

"That building, right there," Duissmann says, pointing to a low, newly remodeled structure where his physician parents treated the traumatized Jews of Odessa in a makeshift hospital at the end of 1941 and the first weeks of 1942.

While Laryssa gets out to read the inscription from the plaque on the building into my tape recorder, I ask Duissmann when he last visited this place.

"What have I lost here that I would return to look for it?" he says.

It was an odd retort, like those my grandparents made to avoid speaking of something painful. What didn't he lose here, I wonder? Except everything. His family members. His friends. The entire bustling Jewish community of his childhood that was either killed or died in Slobodka or forced from Slobodka and onto the Road of Death.

After that, Anatoli drives us into a quiet residential area, Duissmann pointing the way down a narrow, overgrown alleyway lined with a wooden-slatted fence and overhung with branches that slap at the car windows.

51

"Where are we going?" I say.

"To where Duissmann lost his brother," Laryssa says quietly, handing me what looks like a page torn from a book. "He wants you to read this before we get there."

I do. It's an account, in German, by a Volksdeutsche eyewitness to the mass murder:

> It was in 1941…I was in Odessa visiting my sister, and I came to a Romanian guard post, where I was told to return the way I had come, that I couldn't continue this direction. I went back and waited to see what would happen. After a while a long column, perhaps a kilometer in length, consisting of prisoners, Jews and their children, marched under guard into a barracks complex, which was surrounded by barbed wire. At the entrance they had to surrender all their belongings and packs on a heap. My vantage point was perhaps a kilometer distant, and I could see that various people who tried to flee were immediately shot. The stone barracks had no roofs. I could hear the screaming and the crying of these poor people who were forced into those barracks. Then there was the stench of gasoline, dark clouds of smoke rose up, and from that I realized that these poor people were being burnt alive.
>
> Deeply affected, I made my way as fast as possible to the school, where in secret I told my sister what I had witnessed, and because she had not lived through anything like that, she couldn't even imagine that what I was telling her was true. A few days later, I returned to the place to see what had happened. There were a number of workers in the enclosed area, cleaning up around twelve to fourteen stone barracks without roofs, several of which still were smoking, and at the entrance to the complex I could see, amid the various packs and possessions of the victims, a number of empty containers and benzine cookers.

We find the place where the barracks complex once stood. There is an upright granite monument, the size of a person, in a small, cultivated area, surrounded by small stuccoed houses with TV dishes. In the cramped front yards, where thousands of Jews had been immolated, I see flat-faced children, with bovine patience, busily filling plastic bottles with dirt.

Duissmann remains in the car with Anatoli, Laryssa reads the inscription into my tape recorder, and I circle the monument. In the dirt, I see a small, yellowish-white fragment. It is, as I know from an intense human biology study program in college, a human bone.

Later I will remember sites by specific bones found at each—an arthritic kneecap from Podoleanca, a sliver of shin from Suha Balca, a piece of a teenage girl's skull from Bergdorf. In future moments, I will quickly pick up each piece, but this time I hesitate. It's an inch-long piece of an arm bone, what appears to be a shattered ulna.

"What are you doing back there?" Laryssa asks.

"Taking notes," I say.

I feel a little guilty for lying. Actually, I'm tracing the outline of the bone in my field journal, and after I place the fragment back where I found it and cover it with a handful of earth, I say a brief prayer. Did the bone belong to Duissmann's brother, burned to death that day, I wonder?

"Visit me again," Duissmann says, rolling his bulk from the car once we've returned to his apartment. "Now I must go. I never miss a chance to see my grandchildren."

As we follow a modern highway—Laryssa pointing the way—I feel happy that Duissmann has grandchildren to lavish with love. We pass high-rise apartment buildings built during the Soviet era. It's obviously laundry day. Balconies are strung with clothing, a vivid pastiche of colors, like a Cezanne painting.

The road parallels the nearby Black Sea coastline, curving to the northeast, oil tankers looming in the foggy distance, following the path along which, in December and January of 1942, the Jews from the ghetto Slobodka were forced in long columns, guarded by Romanian gendarmes, toward the Sortoriovka train station on the edge of Odessa.

"Sortoriovka is the beginning of The Road of Death," Laryssa explains. "That is a place you should see. Okay?"

To get to Sortoriovka, many Jews, wading the icy water from an overflowing Black Sea inlet, froze their feet. Others expired along the road or died at the hands of Romanian gendarmes. Still others paid Volksdeutsche drivers gold and jewels to convey them in wagons, but when still other victims paid these drivers more exorbitant amounts, the prior occupants—children and pregnant women and the elderly— were forced to walk. It's a shameful episode for Odessa's German colonist population, and so is the fact that members of this group are also given, by the Romanian and Nazi authorities, seven thousand vacated Jewish apartments. But if that's the full extent of Volksdeutsche involvement, so I tell myself, then it's venality, not murderous intent.

Sortoriovka station stands amid a scatter of garbage and leaves, obviously remodeled and painted a cream-color, now ringed by frail trees and bushes. Duissmann and his family and the rest of the Odessa Jews, those who hadn't left with the Soviet army, those not wealthy enough to buy their escape, were forced onto the trains here at the rate of one to two thousand per train. Three trains departed each week, until the city was cleared of Jews.

On the stuccoed wall of the train station is a rectangular plaque, a replica of a railroad car, gaunt faces staring from barred windows, and this inscription, which Laryssa reads into my tape recorder: "From here in the years of Fascist occupation, more than a hundred thousand Jews were loaded onto freight cars and transported to different villages in the Nikolaev and Odessa regions, and there, from 1941 to 1942, exterminated."

That evening, a soft breeze rustling the curtains of my hotel room as I lay in bed, I wonder just who did the murdering? Well, at least it wasn't the Volksdeutsche, I tell myself. Or I didn't think so, since no documents I'd found mentioned the Volksdeutsche as among the SS, the Ukrainian, and the Romanian perpetrators. One document indicated that militia units organized in the Volksdeutsche villages under SS command—which would account for Weingartner's presence in Hoffnungstal—made up an overall force of eight thousand to nine thousand men, but this force "mostly participated in antipartisan actions in their own localities." That doesn't sound like Volksdeutsche militia murdered Jews. Who am I to argue with the scholars?

I wake chilled, the ballooning curtains bringing the scent of the sea into my room. I get up and stare off into the darkness, where I see a few distant lights. I close the balcony door and drift back to sleep. Then I'm floating, balloon-like, rising up, high into space, over Odessa, which from that great height seems a smoking and fiery hearth, and my gaze is drawn in the direction of Lichtenfeld, my grandfather's birthplace, and hovering over the village I vowed to go to so long ago, strange glowing pillars of light, and then I'm aiming an incandescent ray gun down at the steppe, where between Odessa and Lichtenfeld are illuminated millions and millions of white fragments, huge swirling galaxies, which as my dream tells me, are the bones of thousands and thousands of murdered Jews.

I wake with my mouth full of blood. I panic, until I realize that in my agitated sleep, I've bitten a chunk from my tongue. It's a telltale reminder that for Dakota Germans, a visit to Odessa often doesn't bode well. Some people I've known have developed strange symptoms, a lingering fatigue, or a psychic imbalance, not unlike the Volksdeutsche, leaving their villages the final time in 1944.

For many Dakota Germans, in our deepest psychic recesses, Odessa represents the old country. It's not for nothing that my own hometown is named New Odessa. Though the Dakota pioneers came from German colonies in a wide arc around the Black Sea, their mantra always was, "We came from Odessa."

Odessa existed only in the far reaches of our grandparents' memories. It was our Rome, our Jerusalem, the fount of our history, a cosmopolitan seaport where our people transacted business and marketed. And were imprisoned and murdered. The day before I gazed up at the high walls of the Odessa prison, topped by barbed wire, which once held tens of thousands of Volksdeutsche in the 1920s and 1930s. In 1937 and 1938, thousands upon thousands, the flower of German colonist youth and manhood, were murdered in KGB killing rooms. Odessa is, for me, a death-haunted place.

That night, I lie in bed, a pack of hotel ice cubes on my tongue, my thoughts a jumble. Why am I even here? Hasn't Duissmann more or less absolved the Volksdeutsche? When I wake again, my head is swimming, and Anatoli's long Slavic face hovers over me. In a fatherly gesture he lays the back of his hand against my forehead and talks to someone behind him. Laryssa?

"My wife, Sonia, she will nurse him back to health," Anatoli says. "We will take him to Nikolaev."

"Ron, is that what you want to do?" Laryssa says. "It will take a day to change your ticket to return. So we will take you to Nikolaev until you feel better. Okay?"

I sprawl in the backseat of Anatoli's Nissan for the hour-and-a-half trip to Nikolaev, Odessa's little sister, a ship-building city just up the mouth of the Bug River. Everything is a blur. Finally we bump down a rough alleyway and arrive at Anatoli's home, where his dog, Rex, comes up to me and licks my hand.

"But Rex hates strangers," Anatoli says, surprised.

Inside, his dark-haired wife, Sonia, straps an archaic looking blood pressure cuff around my arm, and in a sad, professional voice, says, "A leetle low. But you be fine." Sonia administers a cycle of homeopathic potions and folk remedies, and at midnight, a sour milk concoction. In the morning, I get up and find my hosts and Laryssa at the breakfast table, and when they see I'm feeling better and am not so pale and drawn, they solemnly cross themselves.

"Thanks be to God," Sonia says.

"Thanks to your healing powers too," I say.

"Since you feel better," Laryssa says, "we should organize ourselves."

She helps Sonia clear away the breakfast dishes, and then smooths the regional map across the table like she's petting a cat. I'm a little weak, and since I don't remember giving my approval to stay in Ukraine, I go along with her plans.

"We have been to Slobodka, here," Laryssa says. She runs her finger along the parabolic coast of the Black Sea. "And to Sortoriovka, here."

"And now?" I say. "Where do you suggest we go?"

"Berezovka. From there the Jews were distributed to the vicinity of the Volksdeutsche villages."

Anatoli bends over the map, trying to find the best road so he won't damage his Nissan. I nod in agreement. I don't know why, exactly, since I believe the Volksdeutsche weren't involved in the slaughter.

"Let it be decided then," Laryssa says, sounding like the pharaoh in *The Ten Commandments*. "Tomorrow you continue on the Road of Death."

***

57

BEREZOVKA

Berezovka was a crossroads town in the first half of the last century, a market town and rail center of twenty thousand, where Ukrainian and Volksdeutsche populations coexisted. The city sprawls in a broad valley, an ugly, medieval-looking place, known for pogroms against the Jews throughout the past 150 years and, more recently, for an ice age mastodon skeleton unearthed there, now on display in a local museum.

Anatoli pulls his Nissan in next to a battered taxi in a muddy lot in the middle of Berezovka. He asks directions to the train station. He feels camaraderie with fellow taxi drivers who ply their trade on the damaged roads of Ukraine. This cabbie, with a frayed baseball cap pulled low, launches into a long winded complaint about two broken traffic lights and incompetent city authorities. Beside him sits his girlfriend, a heavy blonde with teased hair in the shape of a helmet, chewing gum, like a scene in a David Lynch movie. Anatoli listens patiently, then asks directions again. The cabbie repeats the same litany and with such a vacuous stare that Laryssa and I joke about it well into the next day.

While we're on our way to the Berezovka train station, a trio of girls, dark-skinned gypsies, wide dresses flouncing, push a wobbly wheeled baby tram in front of our car. With ballet-like flourishes they sashay around potholes on the ravaged asphalt. It reminds me gypsies were also murdered by the Nazis in Transnistria, perhaps twenty thousand, so many that the survivors call the event the Great Devouring.

At the station, we find another plaque, riveted onto the newly stuccoed wall, another stylized railroad car, gaunt faces peering from tiny windows, another inscription, which Laryssa reads to me: "In the winter of 1941–'42 up to sixteen hundred Jews per trainload arrive from Odessa and Romania."

"See, Berezovka is another stop on the Road of Death," Laryssa says.

I know from my reading that the survivors of the journey from Odessa stumbled out of the train cars at Berezovka to a large, burning pyre of bodies, thousands of Jews, some still alive. It was so cold, the hardest winter in memory, that when a dead baby being removed from a train car was accidentally dropped, the small body shattered into pieces. An eyewitness account in my satchel indicates hundreds of Romanian Jews, after a sixteen day journey from Galatz, arrived at a train station in or near Berezovka. As they climbed out, a Romanian guard told them, "See, the Germans are waiting to kill you."

Which Germans, I wonder. SS? Or Einsatzgruppen? Or German army? Or Ukrainian helpers, as some documents call the waiting murderers?

From the platform at Berezovka, the railroad tracks curve away, under some rusted and tangled overhead wires, to the northeast, the direction that the Jews were taken by Romanian gendarmes, long columns of ragged, and doomed humanity, funneled by terrain in the direction of the Bug River.

As we leave Berezovka, I'm wondering if the term Ukrainian helpers, from the documents, might mean German colonists. A Jewish survivor later testifies he understood the language of the Germans taking control of the Jews. But would Romanian Jews have understood the High German of the Nazis? Probably not.

More likely, Romanian Jews, living in close proximity to Volksdeutsche in Bessarabia and Bukovina, understood the German colonists' tongue, a High German dialect much like Yiddish. It's a terrible thought, heavy with consequences, that I snuff from my thoughts as we head on to Podoleanca.

***

WE, THE WATER; YOU, THE FISTS

Anatoli parks his Nissan on the crumbling shoulder of a narrow asphalt road. Several elderly ladies stand there. Waiting for a bus? They turn their shawled heads toward us. That head swivel, I know from my prairie days, means we are strangers, out in the sticks.

Podoleanca is a Ukrainian hamlet of several hundred people at the far end of a long valley and the place where one of the first mass murders of Jews in the area took place.

Laryssa asks what they know about the Jews. The old ladies look at their shoes.

Finally, one of them, wearing a frayed scarf knotted under her chin like a garrote, says, "Near the beginning of the Great Patriotic War. From that way, many of them, many."

My photo catches the elderly lady in the middle of the road, pointing past brightly painted metal yard gates and shaded arbors in the direction from which the long column of Jews came. She's dressed in layers despite the warm June day and reminds me of my prairie grandfather, born not far from Podoleanca, who wore long underwear in the heat of summer. "It keeps me cool," he always said.

"What could we do?" The old lady shrugs. "The Jews came, and one young boy threw bread to them, so a Romanian soldier beat him with a rifle butt."

It is a weird hypnotic moment. We all stare in the direction she points. It's as if we can all see the haze part and, emerging from it, the long procession of Jews heading our way.

"Someone called out to the Jews," the elderly lady says, "'Why don't you fight? Or run? You are many and your guards are few.'"

"What did the Jews say?" I ask Laryssa.

A quizzical look—like a cloud—crosses her face.

"Something odd," Laryssa says. She clears her throat, she picks her words carefully. "The Jews said, 'We don't fight or run, because we are the water, and you, the Ukrainians, you are the fists.'"

Someone later explains how, in baking bread, water is added to dough, to make it easier to knead, and punch down with fists. And I finally understand it is the Jews' way of saying they know the inevitable and that after being walked in circles to weaken them, they can be more easily killed.

A few minutes later, word has obviously spread of our visit, and a placid-faced man in his forties, wearing a hat like the TV character Gilligan, steps from behind the group of ladies, and says, "I will take you there. Where they killed the Jews."

We get into the car and leave Podoleanca. Anatoli steers the Nissan from the asphalt onto a dusty path, and we go parallel to a scraggly line of shelter-belt trees. Soft grass swishes against the doors. At intervals, a dirt clod or rock rattles the undercarriage.

"Here," our guide says from the backseat. "We walk from here."

We pick our way through the sun-dappled shelter-belt trees, and emerge into a huge, open field, where faint green rows of an emerging crop stretch into the distance. Our guide points to a circular mound at the field's edge, around which the farmer who seeds this field obviously plows a wide berth. It's roughly ten feet in diameter, sunken in the middle, fringed with heavy weeds.

"This was the well where they threw the bodies," our guide says. "Some were still alive."

Our guide points down at the well, one of many such photos I snap of respectful Ukrainian villagers at massacre sites, features composed. Through Laryssa, he tells the story of the two hundred Jews, mostly women and children, brought to Podoleanca and ordered to undress near the well. The German commandant addressed the Jews in Russian, saying they must pay with their lives for unleashing the war.

After the Jews were shot, young men from Podoleanca were ordered to gather a dried plant. "A narcotic plant of some sort," Laryssa says, translating.

"Do you mean hemp?" I say.

"Yes, hemp," Laryssa says. "They threw the hemp down the well and then poured in kerosene and set fire, burning the bodies that way, and the well smoked for days."

"How does he know this?" I ask.

"From his elderly neighbor, who was a boy then, watching the murder from a haystack in an adjoining field."

"Gold teeth were knocked out with rifle butts," our guide says. "Even bread was torn open, in case jewels or gold were baked inside."

With the sun at my back, I kneel and survey the field from a lower angle. Light colored fragments litter the black earth, bits of human bones, a gnarled kneecap that looks like it came from an old man, a tiny crumbling piece, perhaps from a baby skull.

"When they saw the boy on the haystack," our guide says, "they shot at him."

"Who shot at him?" I ask.

"The killers," Laryssa says, frustrated. "Just Germans. He doesn't know."

"How long did the murders last?" I ask, and Laryssa translates a series of my questions and the answers:

"An afternoon. But at Gradofka, it was faster."

"Why faster?"

"Ovens."

"Ovens?" I say.

"Yes, ovens. Deep shafts. Like the well we just looked at."

"You mean Jews were shot and burned in ovens in Gradofka?" I say.

"Yes," our guide says, referring to the well-known slaughter of Jews near Kiev. "It is our Babi Yar."

***

OUR BABI YAR

We overnight at Yascha and Masha's nearly two hundred-year-old German house in Rastadt. A year later that will be, for a number of months, my second home. Rastadt was once a village of several thousand during the German Occupation, diminished now to maybe seven hundred souls, an idyllic place now, that some Jews during the German Occupation, called "the village of the beasts."

Yascha and Masha, a long-married Ukrainian couple roughly my own age, live off two cows, income from seven hectares of leased land, and produce from a huge garden, stored in their capacious German cellar, which Masha proudly shows me. In summers, they host American Volksdeutsche visitors who, as Yascha says, "come to find where their grandparents' cradles once rocked."

"It's a life," Masha says the next morning, one shoulder tucked under the cow's belly as she tugs at its udders. "But more difficult as we get older."

Our leisurely breakfast the next morning morphs into an obligatory tour of my hosts' backyard, and as I enter it, I'm stunned. It's so like my grandparents' yard in Dakota half a century earlier, the same gnawed wooden rabbit hutches, the same chickens scratching ovals in the dirt, the same tangles of wire and metal.

We head to Gradofka. I'm sandwiched in the backseat between Masha and Yascha, tires thumping the rough cobbles. Anatoli eases the overloaded Nissan to a smoother, dustier rural side road, edged with stubbled acreages, endless fields of dried sunflowers. Outside Gradofka, the steppe tilts into a broad pasture, and we park at a place where several dirt roads converge. I gather my tape recorder and camera and field journal and head toward a fifteen-foot-high clay wall that resembles a Dakota sandpit. There I see the ruined shafts—the ovens of Gradofka—sunk into the clay. I have an eerie feeling. These shafts, even their brown color, seem like I've seen them before. How is that even possible? It will take me ten years to answer that question.

"Okay," Laryssa says in her best tour-guide voice. "Yascha now wants to tell you how the ovens worked."

I brace myself to hear how the Jews were murdered. Instead—through Laryssa—Yascha explains how lime was rendered in the ovens. Each oven consists of a circular shaft, he says, six to eight meters in depth, plastered into the earth of a slope or overhang. Limestone blocks are added from above, catching on metal grates within the shafts, and the dried stubble, hemp, or branches are added at the base of the shaft, and at an air intake, set ablaze. The stoked oven reaches nine hundred degrees, and the lime, falling through the grate, is raked from an opening at the base of the shaft and used as fertilizer.

"Or to freshen up Masha's walls," Yascha adds, smiling.

I'm lost in a memory of my Aunt Edna telling me how the prairie pioneers brightened their sod homes each spring,

inside and out, using the same process, *weisening,* when Laryssa
jerks me back to reality

"During the war these ovens were used to dispose of the
Jews, understand?" she says.

Yascha's wife, Masha, a large, eager woman, with wispy
blond hair tucked under a scarf, matches me step for step as I
head toward the ovens. But at the slope she labors, bracing her
palms against her knees for leverage, and then, near the top,
she presents me with several fragile blue steppe flowers. It is a
conciliatory gesture, it seems. Does she think I'm Jewish?

As Masha and I approach the green ledge where Laryssa
stands, just back from the ovens, we hear her talking on her
cell phone with a local historian. "Yes, I understand. Twelve
thousand Jews were murdered at the ovens, okay." It's then
that Masha, wheezing like a tire losing air, is suddenly dizzy,
her face flushed. A stroke? I wave frantically to Yascha, and
shout what sounds odd, miles from medical care: "I think she
needs a doctor."

"It is nothing," Masha says, as Yascha and Laryssa help
her back to the car. "Just let me sit for a while."

(It's never clear why Masha grew faint. Perhaps her
high blood pressure, or perhaps, since Ukrainians rarely talk
about their bloody history, her mother on the phone —after
being told about me, an American looking for Jewish massacre
sites—confessed that seventy years earlier she'd witnessed a
mass murder.)

I stand at the lip of the rim—where the Jews waited for
the bullet. I lower myself into the upper part of the shaft, and
once my feet touch the filled in detritus below, the curving
brown oven walls seem to close around me. Yascha is yelling,
and Laryssa is leaning over the oven lip, shaking her finger at
me, saying, "Yascha says that is terribly dangerous. There is a
deep shaft under your feet."

Seeing an image of myself hurtling down a long shaft onto a suffocating bed of ashes, I clamber out onto the green ledge and survey an idyllic scene—a grazing herd of red cows, descendants of herds brought to the steppe by German colonists, and here and there, milkers perched on two-legged milking stools, drumming milk in rhythmic fashion into buckets held between their knees.

One by one or in pairs, these local peasants, in light, loose clothing, like my prairie relatives, circa 1960, approach, and through Laryssa they tell what they know: The Jews arrived in groups of several hundred at a time, overland on foot or by lorries and wagons and trucks, and in the winter, on sleighs from train stations like Berezovka, Kolosofka, or Mostove. The Romanian guards beat villagers who threw bread or otherwise tried to help. (Other documents claim some locals taunt the Jews, with chants of "To Palestine, to Palestine," while tearing at the backpacks and clothing, adding that the Jews wouldn't need their belongings, not where they were going.)

One story involves a prescient Jewish girl of five or six. She emerged from a long column of Jews struggling through Gradofka and boldly approached the Romanian commander. "I know you kill Jews. But do you also kill Russians?" she said.

"No, I don't kill Russians," the commander said.

"But I am a Russian," the girl said.

The Romanian commander ordered that the Jewish girl be allowed to leave untouched, and so she lived, while the long column struggled forward to die at the ovens.

Those stories, each an ugly door into the blood-smeared corridor of the past, overwhelm me. One milker, an older man with a paunch like a Gogol character, grabs my shoulders, maneuvering me in front of Anatoli, and then places Yascha in front of him, and himself in front of Yascha, to show how, he says, "six victims were killed with a single bullet." It's a method I will hear about later too, but there, at Gradofka, it has a cruel twist. One time, the bullet passed through five victims, killing them, but only slightly wounding the sixth, and that survivor, as if in punishment, is thrown alive into the oven flames.

Another milker, a thin faced man in a loose white shirt, tells the story of a six-month-old Jewish baby, rescued from the ovens, somehow, during the chaos of the slaughter, and raised within his own family as his sister, now a sixty-seven-year-old grandmother living in Nikolaev. His language sears me. "Yes, my mother stole the baby from the flames," he says.

When I ask him how that happened, it is too intimate a question. That the milker doesn't answer, averting his face, and wiping his tears with the tail of his loose shirt.

"Do you think German colonists were involved?" I ask Laryssa. "Rastadt is quite close."

"Just Romanians and Germans, as you have heard," Laryssa sighs. "It is just too long ago. Okay? These are just peasants. How can they tell you more?"

We leave Gradofka, Laryssa in the backseat flanked by Yascha and Masha, and as we drive in the crepuscular light, back toward Rastadt, she reads aloud idyllic passages from a book by Doroshenko, the noted author who told me once that the Holocaust is Ukraine's deepest shame Ukrainians killing Ukrainian Jews. She reads about Jewish family life in Odessa, the fathers' deep love for their wives and children. Her voice, a finely calibrated instrument, is soothing after the ugliness of the ovens.

It's a false calm, for as Doroshenko suddenly shifts the scene from domesticity to the murder pits, Laryssa's voice quivers, like fine cracks in a beautiful porcelain vase, and she is unprepared for what comes next, the description of Jews laying down in rows on those already executed, the infamous *Sardinenpackung*, having victims create more space in a mass grave by forcing them to lie down in tightly packed rows before shooting, and after struggling through this part, Laryssa hurls the book to the floor.

"Oh, this is just too horrible, horrible," she says plaintively. "My best friends in school were Jews."

***

LICHTENFELD, THE FIRST TIME

Two days later we set out from Nikolaev, the harbor bristling with the masts of yachts and huge metal cranes. With mist rising from the hazy Bug River, we cross the main bridge, the sun at our back, shadows from Anatoli's car rippling across the road ahead.

"Why go to Lichtenfeld," Laryssa asks. "I thought you wanted to learn about the Jews? Was it my outburst?"

"No, no," I say. "Lichtenfeld was my grandfather's birthplace."

I wax eloquent about my grandpa, sighing about Lichtenfeld. I talk about how my childhood imagination was set on fire, about how the village became my own lost world that I promised myself to someday visit, but getting sick in Odessa, and then discovering the ovens at Gradofka, I've gotten sidetracked.

"So here I am, keeping that promise," I say. "Going to Lichtenfeld."

The narrow asphalt highway carries us between huge, just greening fields. We pass horse-pulled carts, boxy Lada autos, and once, a rusted pickup with three pigs sticking their dirty snouts between the slatted truck box.

We travel what seems the blasted landscape of a fallen and broken world. Horse-pulled carts piled with hay, archaic WWII-era motorcycles, pedestrians with tattered tote bags,

68

solitary Ukrainian men, hefting rusted hoes and rakes, battered Argonauts tumbled from some inebriate heaven, moving in jogging, drunken sidesteps before noon. We bump through former German villages, scattering flocks of dirty peafowl, geese, and chickens in our wake. We pass rows of solid limestone houses, reinhabited after the Volksdeutsche exodus in 1944 with Ukrainians, Bulgarians, Moldovans, gypsies, and most recently, evacuees from Chernobyl.

To pass the time, Laryssa and I talk of books, of American literature, and when she talks about enjoying the jeweled precision of John Updike, I brag. "A distant relative."

I explain how Updike, the great American novelist, and another writer, Thomas Wolfe, and a third, Theodore Dreiser, all are of Pennsylvania German descent—in effect Volksdeutsche whose families left Germanic provinces for America about the same time others settled on the steppe.

That day we ride a narrow two-lane highway into a long valley, and a rutted path carries our vehicle up the side of one hill, down another and then up again, onto an isolated, windswept plateau, where we find Lichtenfeld. What remains of it. There are mostly wide, empty streets that were once lined with acacia and plantain trees, which were cut down during the Soviet-created famine of 1933 and used for fuel when the livestock died off and no longer supplied *mischt* (the dried dung villagers used in their ovens and stoves).

Lichtenfeld seems a broken, ravaged place, shattered by history. Only a few houses remain. The rest, with their limestone blocks and glazed roof tiles, have been sold off by the increasingly cash-strapped Soviet collective. And so the place is a far cry from my childhood fantasies of it.

Founded in 1867 by evangelical Lutherans from Worms and Rohrbach to the southeast, and situated on a broad windswept plateau roughly midway between the Bug and Dniester Rivers, Lichtenfeld, according to the map, seems distant from the Transnistrian killing fields. Thus, I convince myself, the villagers, and my relatives living there during WWII, weren't involved in the killing of Jews. This is a false assumption on which I will later be impaled.

For decades, prosperous Volksdeutsche farmers, like my great-grandparents, crossed the steppe from Rohrbach in their horse-pulled carriages, brought their pregnant wives—wrapped in colorful shawls I vaguely remember from church services during my Dakota childhood—to Lichtenfeld, so the would-be mothers could gaze on its pristine landscape, totter along its clean wooden sidewalks, and breath in the crystalline air, before giving birth in this place, so known for its beauty. People once traveled great distances, lining their wagons up side by side, just to gaze on the blooming fruit orchards swaddling the village, set against sweeping vistas.

That afternoon, while I drink in the beauty that remains, if not of the village itself, then at least of the landscape that scrolls and lifts into the far distance, I feel close to my grandfather, now that I've seen where he first saw the light of day so many years ago. But there is scant time to enjoy that feeling. Since Laryssa, to whose moods I am sensitive, seems snappish, exhausted from the first part of our day at Gradofka, translating the horrific descriptions from local peasants, of how pregnant women and babies and children were murdered at the ovens. Much to Laryssa's relief, I decide, though it's only midafternoon we should start back.

We turn our backs on the shelving clouds, set against the fading blue horizon, and during the quiet ride eastwards, I think about Anatoli. Except for his worry about his vehicle, he is generally a calming presence, and a nondrinker, a rarity among Ukrainian men, with two long puckered scars that crisscross his flat stomach like zippers, which he showed me once, baring his belly and explaining, "That's why I can't drink anymore. Doctors warned me. I'm lucky Sonia nursed me back to health after the operation."

That evening, back in Nikolaev, we pick burrs and hay needles from our socks and clothing, and then wash away the dust of the murder sites with tepid showers. I also restock my battery supply, for my tape recorder and camera, and catch up on my note-taking. While I greedily spoon up her thick borsch, Sonia chatters away in Ukrainian—something about where she was born. Her twenty-year-old son Pasha, home after a brief, failed marriage, translates using rudiments from his high school English class, and I finally realize Sonia is saying her parents met in prison in Soviet Ukraine during the 1940s, where she was conceived. It's the story of Ukraine, writ large in blood and suffering and prison.

Near bedtime, Anatoli disappears. The air feels thick with tension. Where is he? I wonder. Discovering new damage to his car? Pasha wonders too. We peer out the kitchen window. In the grey chill of evening, Anatoli rounds a corner, naked from the waist up, chugging a large can of malt liquor, and we see, around his porch chair, three crushed beer cans. Pasha shakes his head sadly and retreats to his bedroom.

A few minutes later, after donning a pair of worn boxing gloves and bellowing like a gored ox, Anatoli pummels the boxing bag that hangs on a metal chain from the overhead arbor under which he parks his Nissan. Even Rex, the dog, ears flattened to his head, slinks into his doghouse, whimpering. The boxing-bag chain rattles for a long time. That sound transposes itself in my dreams somehow, of strange, pig-faced men, draped in chains, hefting their rifles to the place called Bogdanovka.

***

ASHES

"Have you decided?" Laryssa asks. She calls me the next morning on my cellphone, well before breakfast.

71

"About Bogdanovka you mean?" I say.

"Perhaps you will write about Bogdanovka one day," Laryssa says.

Bogdanovka is a city of forty thousand or so, along the Bug River, where one of the first Transnistrian slaughters took place. It staggers the mind: fifty-four thousand. When I first see the total I think there are too many zeros.

"You sound tired," she says.

"I am tired," I say.

"You are also disappointed in Lichtenfeld, I think," Laryssa says.

"Yes, perhaps. But I'm glad I went there."

"We started at Slobodka and should end at Bogdanovka."

"I'll think about it."

"You sound hesitant?" she says.

"I doubt I'll learn anything new at Bogdanovka."

"Isn't that how research works?"

"What do you mean," I say.

"Not knowing what you find until you go there."

The rest of the day, I weigh my decision. Should I truncate my trip? It's expensive. A hundred dollars each day for car and interpreter. To pass the time, I play with Rex. I chat with Pasha about his future plans, maybe joining the Ukrainian army. Sonia teaches me how to cook borsch. I teach Margo, their granddaughter, a little English, and she in turn teaches me Ukrainian phrases. Since there is no evidence of Volksdeutsche involvement—although the proximity of Gradofka's ovens to Rastadt is unnerving—there seems no reason to prolong my stay.

"You have decided to go to Bogdanovka, yes?" Laryssa says when she arrives at Anatoli's the next day.

"Yes, only Bogdanovka," I say.

"Only Bogdanovka?" Laryssa says, deflated. "But Masha wants you to return to Rastadt. They want to show you something."

"No. Give my regards to Masha. I'm sure that after Bogdanovka I will have seen enough."

***

Early the next morning we drive into the rising sun, with the flat plains of the Bug River a distant haze, heading toward Bogdanovka. On the way Anatoli speaks rapidly. He glances at me guiltily, and raising his boney fist to his mouth, makes drinking motions.

"Anatoli apologizes for drinking last night," Laryssa says. "It won't happen again. He wants to tell you that. Is that okay?"

"Sure," I say. "The Road of Death makes me feel like drinking too."

Plumb line rows of trees line both sides of the road. For an instant it seems we travel an ancient Roman military road in France, and I expect to see the church spires of Alsace's idyllic villages poking the sky; but this isn't France, it's Ukraine, and soon enough, we're passing through poverty stricken villages, where behind the metal yard gates dogs bark angrily and hurl themselves against their neck chains.

Fifty-four thousand Jews were murdered at Bogdanovka in December 1941. That's nearly double the number murdered at Babi Yar, the most infamous open-air execution of the Holocaust. Yet Bogdanovka's grotesque total is unsurpassed even by the killing pace of German death factories like Auschwitz, which, at its height two years later, and using gas chambers, accounted for eight thousand victims each day.

As we approach the city, there are, stacked along the river's edge, a series of high-rise, late-Soviet-era apartments, gleaming ethereally like strange mausoleums, housing for nuclear power plant workers.

(Several days earlier, a grey-haired museum director barked a mini lecture as we stood at a marble monument in Domaneuvka, explaining that so many Jews, so close to Hitler's headquarters in Vinnitsia, sixty miles north of Bogdanovka, were considered a danger, so Hitler ordered a special operation, "A present to Stalin on his birthday." It began on December 20, the Soviet dictator's birthday, and in a dozen days, with two days off for holidays, most of the fifty-four thousand Jews in Bogdanovka were slaughtered.)

Bogdanovka's small city hall has scarred wooden doors, painted a deep Ukrainian blue, that swing on creaky hinges as Laryssa and I enter. Anatoli lopes off, just as he does whenever I need batteries or film or charcoal tablets for my bad stomach. Laryssa and I explore the empty offices, desks heaped with file folders, stacks of job applications for civil service jobs.

Anatoli returns, trailed by a spry, elderly man, wearing a clean white shirt and odd bulbous beret.

"Ron, this is Ivan," Anatoli says. "The last living witness to Bogdanovka."

Ivan and I develop a quick rapport. He tells me he'd sworn to never again speak of what he witnessed as an eight year old, because of the bad dreams and insomnia that always followed, but when I tell him that if he doesn't want to say anything that is fine, he looks at me surprised and relents.

"I will pass to you what I know." Ivan says. "And through me, you will be the last eyewitness link to what happened here."

We drive a short distance toward the river, and as we go down into a broad, low-lying area, Ivan waves his liver-spotted hand from the backseat to both sides of the road. "Here and here. Long pig sties from the collective farm. Burnt."

"Burnt?" I say.

"Burnt with all the people in them. Four thousand Jews burnt alive."

"You saw this?" I turn around in my seat to look at Ivan.

"Yes, my friends and I, from our hiding place. The smoke made us vomit."

We pass an abandoned looking building with a sagging roofline and boarded up windows, a command post of some sort.

"Here, the most beautiful Jewesses were given baths," Ivan says. "Then raped by the guards and killed."

We go up a low rise and park where two asphalt roads join. Around us there is lots of greenery, overhead, scudding clouds.

Ivan stops suddenly. He points at the dappled grass, where sunlight filtered through a profusion of leaves. "The Jews were forced to undress there. Everything was taken. If they didn't remove rings fast enough, their fingers were cut off, thrown along with the rings into a large drum."

A small man, enlivened by an astute but troubled intelligence, he often stands stock-still, as if caught in the dead center of a cyclonic universe of memory.

Ivan says that some prisoners beat on overturned buckets to drown out the gunfire and the screams as the Jews were shot, burnt to death, killed with grenades, and, according to one erroneous source, explosive bullets.

"The executioners stood there," Ivan says. He points to a line of trees parallel to the road. And at the thought of the killers, a shiver of revulsion goes up my spine. It was, I too readily assume, Romanian soldiers or Einsatzgruppen, or some combination thereof. But I don't ask, an oversight that postpones, for two years, my learning that Volksdeutsche police were involved.

"If anyone else tells you they saw what happened, they are liars," Ivan says. He speaks slowly, watching as I jot notes, and making sure, through Laryssa, that I understand him correctly. "Soldiers cordoned off the area. Only my friends and I saw. They have all died. I'm the last one alive."

We stand for an uneasy moment at the edge of the ravine where tens of thousands knelt, backs to their executioners, awaiting bullets, the land falling away to where the bodies were burnt. Between the ravine and the glistening bend of the Bug River, I see a small monument.

"Afterward, the dogs were the worst things," Ivan says.

"Why the dogs?" Laryssa looks pale and fragile as she listens and prepares to translate, like when she read Doroshenko's description. So I brace myself.

"Dogs carried human body parts, heads," Ivan says. "I swore I'd never speak of this again."

"I'm sorry I asked you to do this."

"No, it is okay," he says. "One other thing. It took a work detail of two hundred Jews two months to burn the corpses. Then they were killed too."

A pang of sympathy slices through me, for Ivan, the boy he was then, his childhood sealed away forever beneath the blood and smoke and death of the burning.

"I will show you the ashes from the burnt bodies," Ivan says. "In a nearby cemetery. A huge mound."

"No," I say. "I've seen enough."

We go to Ivan's home. Braided homemade throw rugs across wide, painted floorboards and uneven thresholds, rugs everywhere, like my Dakota grandmother's house in the 1950s. Ivan leads us room to room, talking of a TV interview and someone named George, who promised to send him a copy of a film they were making about Bogdanovka. But he has received nothing. Can I help? I promise to try.

His backyard is a chaos of wood piles and rusted metal, with a makeshift sawbuck cobbled together from spikes and twisted tree branches. And near the yard, a melon patch thick with leafy vines. "My garden," Ivan says. And beyond are thousands of plants, a proliferation of growing things, row on row of an immaculately tended garden, the largest I've seen.

"That is why I can sleep," Ivan says, gazing with love at the plants. "That and my wife."

We watch as Ivan's shawled wife transfers soft-feathered goslings, wings stirring the air, from a box to an ancient metal bucket to ferry to market and sell. She takes three at a time between her fingers, their long, nearly naked necks stretching like rubber, a vulnerable instant that reminds me of the murder ravine.

"Ivan wants to show you one more thing," Laryssa says.

"I said I didn't care to see the ashes."

"It's not the ashes," Laryssa says.

We follow Ivan through his house and into the front yard, where from close-growing bushes along the foundation he gingerly picks three red roses. He presents them, with a gentle flourish, to each of us, as good-bye gifts.

***

A day later in my Odessa hotel room, I'm packing for my return flight. I discard various items—a linen shirt torn on a piece of metal in Yascha's yard, two bottles of homemade

Bessarabian wine, gifts from a villager, and several pairs of burr-covered socks. And into the freed-up space I stuff an intricate cross-stitched runner from Sonia, books from Duissmann and Doroschenko, and also a plastic ziplock bag, whose contents, Ivan's rose, startle me, the petals oxidized into the color of congealed blood, a fitting memento of Bogdanovka.

As I leave the room, my traveler's backward glance snags on the discarded clothing on my bed, and an image comes to me of Ivan pointing to the sun-dappled grass where the Jews heaped their clothing, an image I carry with me in the taxi to the Odessa airport.

As I await my flight, the scant evidence of Volksdeutsche involvement in the Holocaust revolves in my thoughts. Yes, it's true that Volksdeutsche were beneficiaries of genocide, that Volksdeutsche families received seven thousand vacated Jewish apartments in Odessa and that some Volksdeutsche wagon drivers extorted money to ferry Jews to Sortoriovka station. But also, as I remind myself and as Duissmann told me, the Volksdeutsche helped save many Jews.

Those are my thoughts, as my flight gains altitude heading north and west from Odessa. Looking down on the hazy steppe, on the rich chernozem soil my ancestors once plowed and planted, I heave a sigh, greatly relieved that my worst fear—of Volksdeutsche killing Jews—has not been realized. That feeling, however, as it turned out, would be short-lived.

***

AFTERSHOCKS

Weaving in and out of the bustling lines of students, I'm on my way to teach a class. It's my first day back on campus, and despite the bright, clear skies and sunshine, my mind makes a grim connection. The total students on campus, I realize, is roughly the same as the number of Jews incinerated at Gradofka's ovens: Twelve thousand souls.

It's just the first in a series of connections that strike me like a club after my Ukraine trip. The next comes at harvest time in the Red River Valley, when one evening I'm pedaling on my bike, listening to my iPod, oblivious to the twelve-wheeled, multi-axle trucks, piled high with sugar beets from nearby farm fields rumbling past me, when something shriveled and black rolls the gutter beside my bike, a human head I'm certain; but it's just a mud-caked sugar beet the size of a soccer ball, jarred loose from one of the beet trucks.

That night, a dream: I'm driving one of those multi-wheeled trucks, its box mounded high, not with beets, but greyish-white ashes from Bogdanovka. The truck plows the darkness, headlights bobbing. Where I'm headed I have no idea.

My only goal is to rid myself of those ashes, but no matter how hard I jerk the steering wheel of the truck from side to side, even driving down into the ditch and up again onto the road, I can't jar them loose. Every time I check the rearview, the bone grey ashes are there, heaped in the truck box, and when I finally do jerk awake, it's with a feeling of dread.

***

FIRE AND ICE

Not much later, a cardboard box arrives in my university mailbox. Inside is a shrink-wrapped stack of documents from a major German archive, along with an apologetic note.

Somehow, as the result of new staff and high demand, the archivist wrote, this "material you requested a year ago had gotten misplaced." Perhaps these documents, he sincerely wished, might still be useful.

But they aren't, and I'm grateful they aren't. Who wants to learn your relatives might be involved in the Holocaust?

Still, out of curiosity, I spend several evenings hunkered on my couch, reading through the documents, which are responses of Volksdeutsche, resettled in postwar Germany, to questions asked by war crimes prosecutors about Transnistria. Deposed former residents of Transnistria denied the murders or located them elsewhere, confirming my opinion that the Volksdeutsche weren't involved in the killing.

Various witnesses claimed the murders were done by the Einsatzgruppen, the mobile murder squads, who swept into Ukraine, in the wake of the German army, murdering local Jews, the children of Volksdeutsche married to Jews, and those Volksdeutsche thought to be informers and collaborators with the Soviets in the 1930s. Fair enough, I thought. Nothing new in all of that.

That winter, I continue to comb over the Xeroxed material. Spring seems far off. Every evening for a week, seated in my living room, and glancing up at intervals at the television screen to keep from straining my vision, I peruse the lengthy German sentences.

On the tenth of January there has been a heavy snowfall, six inches or more, and the latest American Idol auditions play out on the television screen. Kelly Clarkson belts out a full throated number. I'm following the tangle of Germanic clauses winding like tendrils down the pages, when a series of ugly images, a description of Jews massed into wooden barracks and burnt alive, close around me. It sounds like the mass incineration Ivan told me about Bogdanovka. How, I wonder, did this description get mixed into these testimonies? I go back and reread, the light from the television flickering over the page:

> The next day, from the work camp in the village of Sucha Balka, a thousand Jews were brought to Mostove. They looked like skeletons. They were put with another

six hundred Jews from a second transport, along with others who had not perished in other murders. And all of them were murdered by the German colonists from Rastadt. They were burnt to death. They were put into wooden barracks which were set on fire. This was done at Rastadt.

Sixteen hundred souls, burnt alive in wooden buildings. But not in Bogdanovka. In Rastadt, a Volksdeutsche village. I sit stunned. A vague memory drifts back to me from the past summer in Ukraine. Yascha and I, chugging along a road just outside Rastadt in his old Lada auto, when he nodded at an overgrown, weeded field. What was it he said? Something about fire, about burning, something I'd not heeded, focused as I was on Gradofka's ovens.

I trudge through ankle deep snow in my backyard, kicking my way in bitter cold through a scatter of delicate tracks of birds and rabbits and stray cats, and a few remaining bread crusts I'd tossed out for those creatures. In my garage, in a pile of boxes, I find my field journals. I tear my gloves off with my teeth. My journal is cold as a chunk of ice. My breath rises in white puffs like smoke. After a brief search, I find the particular entry I'd made with Yascha that day, scribbled phrases angling wildly across the page, obviously written while the car was moving: "Yascha says many Jews burnt here. It's a field just outside Rastadt. On the way to Gradofka. Something about straw and kerosene and horsebarns."

Following my footprints in the snow, I return to the house. This mass burning at Rastadt sounds like the one Ivan described to me at Bogdanovka, Jews blockaded into buildings, sloshed with kerosene, then set ablaze. Were both events, the one in Rastadt and the one in Bogdanovka, done by the same perpetrators?

I check a map. Bogdanovka was just twenty-five miles from the former German village of Rastadt, where I'd stayed overnight with Yascha and Masha.

Perhaps outside of Rastadt, the SS officers from Rastadt and their Volksdeutsche police burned down the horse barns with Jews inside and then did the same thing at the ravine in Bogdanovka, or even the other way around. If my notes are accurate, it wasn't Einsatzgruppen but Volksdeutsche police who murdered Jews at Bogdanovka and Rastadt. But I can't be certain. The evidence that both mass burnings were planned and carried out by the Rastadt SS officers seems tenuous, at best. After all, how many ways are there to incinerate buildings?

I do some quick research. Two sources claim "only Romanians and Ukrainians" were involved at Bogdanova. A third source mentions that seventy Ukrainian paramilitaries, under a Ukrainian policeman named Andrusin, were the perpetrators. Could Ukrainian paramilitaries be another way of saying Volksdeutsche policemen? I don't know. I check the dates and find the mass burning near Rastadt took place months after the Einsatzgruppen departed the area.

The television flickers. I blink to clear my vision. I feel an invisible chord tugging me back into this research. Do I really want to pursue Volksdeutsche ghosts again?

That night, when sleep doesn't come easily, I make a promise to myself. Spring is three months away, and if by then more evidence surfaces about Volksdeutsche involved in the Holocaust in Transnistria, then I will proceed on this research odyssey which is destined, I fear, to shatter my illusions and break my ethnic heart.

***

The scene: my university office, the week before spring break. I am holding several Xeroxed pages from the university library's reference desk. It's a Bogdanovka survivor account that I'd been eagerly awaiting—important pages that might reveal if Volksdeutsche police killed Jews in Transnistria.

I toss the pages onto my desk in frustration. Something I haven't counted on. The document is in Romanian, a language I can't read. It seems another dead end. Finally, I place a call to the International Center on campus. Yes, I'm told, there is a Romanian student on campus. So I make arrangements, and when the student arrives in my office—an eager, bright young woman—I hand her the document.

"Yes. It is in my language. Romanian. I can translate this."

I give her a little background on the document. Romania's anti-Semitism, I explain, was as bad as, or worse than, the Nazi version. In 1941, the Romanian government ethnically cleansed its newly annexed provinces of Bukovina and Bessarabia, pushing tens of thousands of Jews into Transnistria, for supposed "economic crimes" and collaboration with the communists. The writer of the account is one of them, a survivor of Bogdanovka.

"I would like to know just what this survivor says," I say.

"In my country, we don't study such things," the Romanian student says sadly.

A week later, she returns, handing me the translation, but as I pay her and thank her, she avoids eye contact and retreats down the hallway, embarrassed, it seems, by her own country's savage role in the Holocaust.

The student has done a great job. The pages are immaculately typed. And as I read them, the names of places I visited along the Road of Death, like Berezovka and Domanevka, jump out at me. The survivor account is congruent with what Ivan says of the pig sties at Bogdanovka. "But there were no more pigs. Just empty rooms, with no doors and no windows. Awaiting us, the Jews."

Then—in a passage that alters my life—the survivor describes a Soviet war crime's trial, held in Domaneuvka in October 1976:

I recognized most of those who were the killers at Bogdanovka. Some of the accused were missing, like the Romanian gendarmes and officers, and the German officers. The one that hit my mother was there too, the one that made us go toward that smoking hole, toward death, and those who took away thousands upon thousands of lives. They were sitting in the bench of those accused. The Soviet judges were petrified. The prosecutor's indictment was harsh. There they sat, on the bench, the beasts with human faces. They were listening to the accusations against them, to the dates, numbers and statistics read by the prosecutors, and the criminals seemed interested in what they were learning, as if this was about other people, not themselves.

The survivor gives statistics: of a hundred and sixteen thousand Jews in Domanevka district alone, only six hundred survived. Just half of a single percent of the Jews from Odessa. Just one percent of the Jews from the Romanian provinces of Bessarabia and Bucovina.

On the final page of the account, the survivor gives eleven names of the former policemen sentenced to death by the Soviet court, who sat before her in court: "Iosif Gass, Vasilyimir Hipper, Alexander Fonus, Vasily Kilwein, Florian Koch, Pavel Orghianov, Vasily Pastusenko, Vasily Hendenheimer, Piotr Schtolz, Karl Ebenal, and Florian Ebenal."

Nine have Volksdeutsche last names. A shudder goes through me. I remember Ivan pointing to where the killers lined up near the Bogdanovka ravine. The killers, I thought at the time, were faceless, shadowy automatons. Now I know some are Volksdeutsche. Real people, with familiar last names. Where have I seen those names before? That's what I ask myself.

In my garage, rummaging through the boxes, I find Leibbrandt's article about the civil war in Ukraine, which contains the list of those shot down "like dogs in the street" in

Rastadt. I also find the list of Rastadt villagers executed by the Soviets in 1937. When I compare the names on those lists to the names of Rastadt policemen convicted of murdering Jews in Transnistria, I just stand there, shocked.

Two thirds of the family names from the first list reappear on the other lists. I'm not a mathematician, but it seems an obvious and statistically improbable connection. My mind churns with questions. One of which is, if the Rastadt police murdered at Bogdanovka, did they also incinerate the Jews at the horse stables near Rastadt? The answer to that, which I already know, shakes me, like a great, cascading fall of timber.

***

III. DISPATCHES FROM THE ROAD OF DEATH

AT THE HORSE STABLES

"There," Yascha says, pointing to weeded, overgrown field. "The burning took place there."

We are clattering along a cobbled road outside Rastadt, the five of us together again, Anatoli, Laryssa, Yascha, Masha, and me. Only this time I'm financed by a Fulbright Fellowship, which requires I teach at the National University in Nikolaev while researching my project, "Ukraine's Labyrinth of Memory, and the Role of the Rastadt Volksdeutsche Police in the Transnistrian Holocaust."

We turn off the road and stop. Yascha makes three parallel movements with his right hand, to indicate the orientation of the horse stables, three long buildings side by side.

"The roofs were thatched and dry," Yascha says. "The stables burnt like torches."

"Thousands, is that what your mother said?" I say.

"Yes."

"Do you think that is accurate?" My documents indicate fifteen hundred souls.

Yascha shrugs. He doesn't know. "Many," he says.

I part the weeds and enter the field. I can't see the car anymore. Masha and Laryssa have gone the opposite direction to gather medicinal herbs. Potbellied clouds scud the sky. I think of pregnant women and babies and dead souls rising up in the boiling smoke. Everything is overgrown. Holding my head high, like a dog wading a creek, I push through the tangled weeds. I think of Dante's *Inferno*, a book I'm reading because it mentions a river of blood into which murderers are thrown, and I recite aloud his famous lines about being lost, midway in his life in a dark wood.

I move in ever-widening circles, tramping through the undergrowth, searching for a place where nearly two thousand souls were incinerated, until my foot catches on a half-buried cement chunk. It takes some effort, but I finally discern what seems three long, shallow areas in the earth, each spaced five or ten yards apart. Precious little remains of the horse barns.

Perhaps typhus broke out. Perhaps the Rastadt police receive the order to kill all Jews, likely in August 1942. Perhaps the Jews barricaded themselves inside, like at Bogdanovka, not wanting to assist their executioners. Whatever the reason, the barns were torched. It took many policemen to throw a cordon around this place. Those who tried to escape were shot. It would have been a frightful inferno, of bullets and fire, like at Bogdanovka, like Dalnik near Odessa, where Jewish mothers held up babies, pleading for them to be shot and spared death by burning. Weeds scratch at me like fingernails. I drift back to the car, where I flatten one palm for balance on the warm hood, and while I pick hay needles and cockle burrs from my clothing, I notice something peculiar.

Inside Anatoli's Nissan the four sit like wax statues, Masha and Laryssa with stalks of sage in their laps. They feel it too, I think, the haunted sadness of this place from which the mind reels. I'm a great believer in monuments and plaques to inform future generations, and despite myself, I'm thinking that maybe it's good most traces of this atrocity have already been erased.

But as we depart, a strange realization jolts me. This time, unlike my previous visit to Ukraine, every murder site and every oven that I go to, I will carry the knowledge that it was likely Volksdeutsche police who did the murdering.

***

BURNING ICE

The horse stable site leaves me with a feeling of desolation. When an apartment opens up for me several weeks later, it seems a good omen.

On the day I move, Anatoli takes me aside, and tells me Rex will miss me while his health-conscious wife Sonia packs me a block of a honeycomb from her parents' village north of Nikolaev. She tells me, in a maternal tone, "Eat a little each morning. It will give you energy for your work."

My new apartment is comfortable. It's in a historic building where, as the plaque bolted on the street side indicates, Pushkin, the great Ukrainian writer once lived and wrote. For a time, I settle into a calming routine.

Programming my washing machine is beyond me, so I wash my laundry in the sink and hang it over the railing of the balcony, activities that bring back simpler times helping my grandmother hang clothing on her Dakota clothesline, and hitchhiking across Europe, washing my socks in youth hostel sinks. As the days melt away and I get my living situation in order, I plow through troves of archival material.

One day, I find a document which reveals that the murders at the Gradofka ovens were both extensive and public, the first in a series of jolts of information, which widens my understanding of the Transnistrian Holocaust:

> I was an eyewitness to columns of Jews, and their execution, from late fall of 1941, and well into the next year, 1942. During this time, I repeatedly saw columns of Jews, partly on foot, and partly driven in

89

vehicles, under guard of the SS. They came from the south and into the vicinity of Rastadt. I observed how these columns of Jews came to a halt at Gradofka, a village which lay several kilometers south of Rastadt.

During this time I saw thousands of Jews in that same situation, men and women and children of all ages, in a terrible rundown condition, all of whom had obviously suffered many difficulties and deprivation. I watched how these people were repeatedly taken to the lime-kiln ovens in Gradofka and executed in groups. I remember one particular time when 150 to two hundred Jews were shot at the ovens there. The victims were forced to undress to their underwear, and, especially, to put all their valuables at a particular place. It was winter and bitter cold; but even the women and children had to undress. The shooting proceeded in the same way as the others that took place earlier in Rastadt, the victims falling forward and into the ovens in the lime-pit. The bodies that didn't fall into the ovens were thrown into the ovens by Jews designated for that work. Such scenes played and replayed themselves, over and again, and I plainly saw many thousands of Jews killed. It was generally known that the greatest part of these people originated from the southern regions of Ukraine, as well as from Bessarabia and the Balkans. And the bodies of Jews that were shot were doused in oil, set ablaze, and in short order burnt in the ovens. The light and the smoke from the ovens were widely visible, and the air so foul anyone in the area could hardly draw a breath. I was an unwilling eyewitness to the mass extermination because I was ordered both by the mayor and the SS commander in Rastadt, to take a horse and wagon to the execution place and pick up the victims' clothing, but not the valuables, which were taken into the custody of the SS.

Soon after, I'm with Yascha and Masha again, wheeling in their old Lada through a spindrift of villages, headed to Gradofka. Nothing has changed since a year and a half earlier. Same fields of bleached stubble, same vast stands of skeletal sunflowers, same cobbled road rumbling beneath our tires. The only thing different is this time I want to follow the actual route the Jews were taken along. To that end, I'm directing Yascha along the narrow, twisting streets of Gradofka, the car's engine sounding like an overworked sewing machine. We stop at the ancient gate of the cemetery, bolted by rusty hinges to two half-crumbling brick pillars, and when Masha and I swing it open for the car, it emits an ungodly metallic shriek, as if announcing the dark underworld of the ovens, just beyond the graveyard's far edge.

Masha and I skirt several strange, medieval-looking Orthodox crosses of rough pecked sandstone, sinking into the earth, like Easter Island statues, and the mounded earth of several fresh graves, and as I feel her comforting presence at my elbow, I'm happy for her, because she's healthier than last time, her blood pressure better, drinking less. But when, at the graveyard's far edge, I slip between several strands of barbed wire fence, and hold down the wire for Masha, I realize she's returned to the car. I see her standing by it with Yascha, waving at me. So it's my first visit to the ovens alone, an emptiness opening in me, because Masha isn't with me, and because this time I'm following the Via Dolorosa along which the Jews were taken to several ruined buildings, undressed, then funneled in small groups to the ovens.

* * *

As I grow increasingly obsessed with the ovens, I overnight in Rastadt to get an early start each morning to Gradofka. Reading late into the night, I learn the village was known as Schardt, for a German colonist family originally from Pfalz, a Germanic province that supplied the first settlers to the Catholic villages of Karlsruhe and Speyer. As these German colonists spread westward, they merged at Gradofka with

91

the area's Ukrainian population. When the Nazis relocated Gradofka's Ukrainians to Bogdanovka, they renamed the "purified" village Neustadt, using the ovens for their own grim purpose.

The ovens remained generally unknown, as I learned by my late night reading at Rastadt, until two well-known Soviet writers, in *The Black Book* of *Russian Jewry*, describe the visit to Gradofka of a Soviet Lieutenant Colonel in the summer of 1944, who found the ovens choked and overflowing with charred bones—vertebrae, shoulder blades, and forearms covering the area like shells on a seashore. It was the aftermath of a mini-Holocaust. One night, after reading a Transnistrian survivor account, *Burning Ice*, I dream of young people and pregnant women, skating on a large, circular ice rink, in New York City, tracing arabesques of geometrical precision, around and around, their skate blades cutting large, circular holes in the ice, so that the skaters, like victims jumping from the World Trade Center, plummet into an uprush of flames. As I learn, the dream reflects the realities of the Transnistrian murder campaign, Jews not believing messages scratched in blood into the walls of the castle in Mostove, or with few, if any, alternatives to escape. The manner in which the Jews, dumped at railroad sidings south of Gradofka, were marched in circles for days by Romanian gendarmes, and given over to Volksdeutsche police in weakened condition, and the duration of those marches as evident in the shoes heaped up at village distribution centers across Transnistria, shoes with leather and heels so scuffed and abraded that, as a relative told me of the clothing in Neudorf, there were few takers among the German colonists.

In Rastadt each morning, in the old German bedroom I share with Anatoli, I awaken to sounds of my prairie childhood—roosters crowing, Masha's cows moaning—pastoral mornings erased by the short drive to Gradofka. There, curious locals seek me out and tell me their stories and anecdotes. Afterward, sitting cross-legged in the grass near the ovens, I dutifully record in my journal what I've been told.

One morning, I jerk awake from a bad dream and see Anatoli perched on the pull-out couch, pulling stockings onto his skinny ankles. He turns his long, sleepy face toward me, motioning that he wants to talk. We don't share a language, just a rough system of gestures and a smattering of English and German words and an occasional Ukrainian expletive. It's tiring and imprecise, this game of multilingual charades, so we conserve our energy for important issues. Like now, this morning, when it's my turn to guess.

Anatoli places his palms together, bends his head to one side, placing his cheek on his hands. Something about sleeping. Okay. He jerks his right index finger repeatedly, as if beckoning me closer. I don't understand. He snaps his finger against his temple, the same flick I've seen from Helmut. Okay, gunfire, shooting.

"Let's ask Laryssa to translate," I say.

"Da, da," Anatoli says, nodding. "Laryssa."

In the long entryway, we find Laryssa and Masha laying out breakfast on the long table, bowls of steaming kasha, black currant jelly, plum compote, scrambled eggs, blintzes, pickled cucumbers. While I spoon up kasha, Anatoli nods his long, brooding Slavic face at Laryssa, telling her something in Ukrainian.

"Anatoli says you had a nightmare," Laryssa says. "He says you were shouting."

"Da, da," Anatoli says. *"Rastrelna, rastrelna."*

"He says you have nightmares because of your terrible questions," Laryssa says.

"Asking questions is my job," I say.

"*Rastrelna*," Anatoli says, the syllables rattling off his tongue.

"Anatoli says if you keep visiting sites, you should learn that word," Laryssa says.

"Which means?" I say.

"Which means *shooting*," Laryssa says. "Okay?"

"Da," Anatoli says. "Shooting."

***

Over the next weeks, various locals describe to me what they call the conveyor belt of death that took place at Gradofka's ovens. It's a reminder that the victims didn't just line up and jump into the flames of the ovens. It took a methodical plan, stretching over 1942 and into 1943 and drawing on numerous resources and scores of Volksdeutsche police to secure the area, to move the victims on foot and in police lorries, trucks, and horse-pulled wagons to the ruined houses near the site, to guard the victims while they undressed, to escort them to the lip of the ovens and to shoot them. During the bitter winter of 1942, the kilns working in tandem, the long gullet of the first shaft choking with bodies, the second kiln, stuffed with hay and hemp and other flammables, fired up and made ready for further victims.

***

One day at Gradofka, I meet again the person whose adopted sister was stolen from the flames, and he remembers me from two years earlier. We stand there and chat.

"No visitors come here," the villager tells me. He wears the same frayed baseball cap.

"Nobody comes?" I say.

"You are the first. And the first to return."

94

At first I don't understand. On the prairie frontier, epidemics swept away babies and children, and their isolated graves, a century later, have visitors or evidence thereof, with weeds pulled from around the markers, and flowers, plastic or real, left behind. So why, I wonder, are there no visitors here at the ovens, which are, essentially graves—deep-shafted mass graves.

"Twelve thousand died here," I say. "And no visitors?"

"No, nobody comes."

"Except your sister and you."

He turns away, to hide his pain. I never get his name or the name of his sister, saved from the flames of the oven.

The rest of that day, I study the ovens. I walk the perimeter. I take photographs from various angles. Before we leave that evening, Anatoli frets about his tires. He thinks they need to be replaced. I hand him a penny, and show him how to measure, based on how much of Lincoln's head shows, the remaining tire tread.

As Anatoli duck walks from tire to tire, checking, I'm caught up in my American preconceptions, wondering about the site's lack of visitors, when I hear a whistling sound behind me. Anatoli kneels by one of his car tires, and for an instant I think he has found a nail puncture, but then I recognize the source of the sound: he's blowing into a small tube, to clear it of dirt.

"German bullet," Anatoli says, handing me the expended shell casing, from a Mauser, a German rifle. As I turn it over in my fingers and see, stamped on one end, 1938, I realize why nobody visits here to pay their respects. Not a young bride, bringing her husband, not the elderly, nobody.

Because of German thoroughness, as Alice might say. Because the bullets fired at Gradofka, like the row of victims shot with one bullet, pierced future generations. Because everyone was dead. Because there is nobody. Because the future had been killed.

***

As my obsession with the ovens grows, I often go to Gradofka by myself, in a rental car. One day, less than a mile from the ovens, I come on an elderly lady, dressed in layers despite the August warmth, patiently chopping branches with a small hand ax.

When I tell her about my research, she carefully lays the small ax across the tree stump she uses as a chopping block and turns her wizened face to me, pausing, as if accessing long forgotten memories. "It was just after the German invasion," she says. "My husband was away, at war."

"So you saw what happened at the ovens?" I ask.

"I heard the gunshots," she says, tucking a wisp of grey hair under her shawl. "I hugged my children and prayed that I would survive to care for them."

"So the Romanians brought the Jews here?" I say.

"Romanian guards with whips," Katrina says. "But they wouldn't let us help those poor people."

She tells me there was a cordon of soldiers thrown up around the ovens. The villagers were ordered to remain inside. Soon after, the murderers, wearing shiny armbands, came in lorries and horse-pulled wagons.

"Many times in the winter of 1941, and then into 1942," she says.

"That long?" I say.

"In 1942, in summer, my windows, the outside, were greasy and needed cleaning. And the vegetables in my garden were covered with soot."

After the war, she says, the communist regime recognized the suffering of Soviet citizens, not specifically Jews, so she kept quiet, not even confiding to her husband, when he returned from the war, what she'd seen.

"Everyone else is gone," Katrina says. We stood in her yard, gazing toward the ovens, toward the green ledge where the victims once stood. "I am the only one who still remembers the gunfire."

***

Whenever I visit the ovens over the next months, which is often, I'd stop and see Katrina. Sometimes I chop wood for her. Sometimes we drink chamomile tea from chipped cups, and speak German dialect, a language she has rarely used or heard since 1944, when the Volksdeutsche left this place. Sometimes she tells me about the German colonists, a good people, which helps counterbalance the gloom that pervades my thinking.

If it grows late, she motions me to stay, and there, on the worn floorboards of her tiny living room, I unroll my sleeping bag. Overseen by a faded ikon of a gaunt, byzantine-looking Jesus in one corner, I sleep, the only times I sleep well in Ukraine, under the forgiving gaze of the Savior. The next morning, before my drive back to Nikolaev, we eat an early breakfast, of crisp-fried cheese dumplings made of local cheese, washed down by tall glasses of black tea.

***

Once, at Gradofka, I position myself at the base of an oven shaft, gazing up to where, at the lip, thousands of victims once stood, outlined against the sky. Another time, I wander the periphery and find, a hundred yards or so from the ovens, where the Jews were forced to undress and where, on orders from the SS commandant, several older farmers later gathered the clothing, the scattered shoes and personal items, the rolled up packs and shawls, and ferried everything back

97

to Rastadt, where yellow stars were removed and some of the clothing was disinfected with Zyklon B, ordered through VoMi headquarters in Berlin, the same gas used later in the death camps.

On this isolated, primitive steppe, the ovens seem out of place, incongruous, and the amateur historian in me flails for meaning. The Holocaust took place in Germany and Poland and Eastern Europe, not here, not near my own ancestral villages. If the ovens, and the efficient assembly-line disposal of bodies at Gradofka weren't a model for the death camps— by the time the murders ratcheted up at Auschwitz in March of 1942, the ovens had already swallowed thousands—the ovens seem to foreshadow that development. In fact, the cross-sectional plans of furnaces to incinerate Jewish corpses in death camps, as drawn up by Nazi engineers—with metal grills spaced at intervals in long shafts—replicate, or seem to, Transnistria's ovens.

Despite these aspects of modernity, the open-air murders, as the scholar Jan Gross points out, have roots twisting deep into a Paleolithic underworld, where primitive weapons were used; where fire was used; where clubs, rifle butts, and metal rods were used; where babies and children had their skulls crushed. In that way, Gradofka is a dizzying confluence of the modern and the archaic, so no wonder my attempts to understand what happened there frequently founder. As much as I try to convince myself the killers were real people, I don't quite believe it somehow, because it contradicts everything I know about the fundamental decency and religious nature of the Volksdeutsche.

Sometimes, taking refuge in my literary background, I imagine the police murderers as avatars of death, taloned automatons, grotesque misshapen pig people, like creatures from *Lord of the Ring*, feeding living humans with industrial precision into flames. The reality is harder to accept, that it's mostly young men, from their late teens to mid-twenties, wearing swastika armbands, who after murdering the children of others, returned to their homes in nearby Rastadt and Muenchen, to their own children.

****

THE CASTLE

One Saturday, we're driving on the outskirts of Mostove, a once predominantly Jewish city also called Lachawa, on our way to the castle, which is what several documents call the large, multistoried building, which I see in the distance, its several levels of pale blue windows, floating amid a proliferate mass of bushes and trees.

As we go along the circular, pebbled driveway, I'm reminded of the life of ease and prosperity in pre-Revolution times of the wealthiest German colonists; ferried to the front door in sturdy and comfortable horse-pulled britchkas—known to sometimes force off the roads the flimsy wagons of the poor Ukrainians—met there by servants who catered their every whim. However this day it's the principal of Mostove's grade school, a heavy, earnest-faced lady who greets us.

Laryssa reads the inscription on a plaque by the front door into my digital tape recorder: "Thousands of Jews from Odessa and elsewhere were brought to this building and grounds that served as a transit camp to their deaths in nearby Rastadt and Gradofka." And I'm taken on a tour of the school.

The castle, built by a former Russian nobleman, is an exact replica of the private residence of the German colonist Esslinger, who shuttled, at the turn of the twentieth century, between his private estate several miles to the east, and his even more opulent home in Odessa. That prosperous time—as old letters says, "when the dogs slept until noon"—ended in 1919, when waves of revolutionaries swarmed such estates, forcing thousands of Volksdeutsche to leave Ukraine, which some refugees envisioned as a monstrous snake sloughing its skin, as communism showed its true face.

There are three hundred students in the first six grades, but it's a holiday, so the empty classrooms I visit that day are preternaturally quiet, and in the hallways, shafts of sunlight, flooding through the high, inset windows, illuminate the now gleaming floorboards, along which some victims were dragged to the trucks by the Rastadt police, as several documents indicate.

The castle's appearance reminds me of a short story I taught at the university, "The Blue Hotel," by Stephen Crane, a literary exploration of the role of peer pressure in violence. Were young Volksdeutsche policemen in Rastadt afraid of refusing orders from policemen they knew intimately, and to whom they were closely related? Or did they kill because their SS commanders bullied them? Or were these young, shiftless, angry men, members of a despised minority under the Soviets, quickly thrust into power, wreaking mindless vengeance on scapegoats?

In October 1942, several VoMi lorries and German army trucks dropped their endgates, disgorging a dozen hard-faced Volksdeutsche police from Rastadt. Survivors of an earlier action recognized these police, and the castle hallways echoed with their despondent wailing. "Now the end has come," they cry out. "The heartless ones are here."

There was a flurry to hide the youngest and most vulnerable. Some mothers lay their infants and toddlers on the bed of ashes inside circular room heaters recessed in the walls. Perhaps some kind soul might later discover and raise them as their own. The weak, the exhausted, the resisters were quickly shot, either inside the castle or out on the castle grounds. The rest, waiting to be loaded onto the lorries, huddled close, as if tied together with ropes. Small children trembled and cried, staring at the police, their huge eyes rolling wild in their sockets. Parents and adolescents begged: "Let us work. Let us live."

"See what beautiful things our students create," the principal gushes, as we go from classroom to classroom. She gestures at bulletin boards that display bright scenes of flying Chagall-like horses and brilliant suns floating over endless sunflower fields.

Behind the bulletin boards and artwork, in the now mortared over walls, there were bullet gouges, splatters of brain matter, and scrawled warnings in blood, in Yiddish, Russian, Polish, and Romanian: "Whoever comes here will be murdered. Flee this castle while you can."

In early 1942, during their first night in the castle, a mother and daughter heeded the warning, and creeping out into the darkness, they found refuge with a nearby Ukrainian family. From there, over the next weeks, they watched a number of actions, as a thousand or more Jews from the castle were loaded into lorries and trucks, taken away by the Rastadt police, and murdered.

One time, the mother and daughter witnessed a terrible sight in broad daylight. They had a clear view of the Mostove market, where among the shoppers they saw their fellow Jews, with whom they were taken to the castle, recognizing them from their familiar hats, scarves, and dresses. They felt a rush of joy that they'd somehow survived. Then they realized the truth, as the mother recounted: "But it was not our friends. It was the German colonists from Rastadt who came in their horse-pulled wagons to the market, wearing the clothing of our murdered acquaintances."

***

The mayor of Mostove waits on the steps of the city hall, a young man in white linen pants and expensive Italian shoes. Bruno Maglia? It rained hard the night before, and now

101

I wonder how he remains so immaculately coifed in all this mud.

"Hello, I'm Taras," he says.

"Oh, like Taras Bulba, Gogol's character," I say.

"No, like Taras Schevchenko," he snaps, then he goes silent.

I've touched a nerve, I realize, concerning Ukrainian independence from Russia and Moscow, for it is Shevchenko, the Ukrainian poet and freedom fighter, whose writing spurred and immortalized that independence.

We spend a couple of hours in Mostove's cramped city hall, as several staff members, hefty ladies, relate their childhood experiences. Yes they played near the castle. Yes they found rings and coins and bones. Later, replaying my minicassette recordings from that afternoon, I'm startled by the rushing cacophony of their voices. Was it the first time they'd dared speak of such matters?

Later, on a blanket at the stubbled edge of field, we eat our picnic lunch, and then, as the long day of unbroken light gives way to luminous darkness, we drive back toward Rastadt, going the long way around on good roads to soothe Anatoli, and as our tires hum on the pavement, I ponder Ukraine's turbulent past.

Scars of collectivization from the Soviet era of the 1930s are readily visible in the ruin-strewn former German villages, where the long collective barns, which resemble potato warehouses in the Red River Valley, were built with forced labor, using tombstones from Volksdeutsche cemeteries during collectivization, a word not enough known in the West. That was a time when churches had their steeples removed, and large wooden doors were sometimes added at the rear, so farm machinery and animals and grain could be stored inside: the Soviets, acting on the same ideological beliefs as the French during the French Revolution, turning sacrosanct places where Ukrainians and Volksdeutsche once worshipped into common stables, dance halls, and theaters.

Unlike the slaughter of the Jews which left shell casings and bone fragments littering the ravines and ovens, there is scant evidence of the starvation deaths, wrought by collectivization, grain drained from the countryside and sold on Western markets to finance Soviet industrialization. Tens of thousands of Volksdeutsche, and millions of Ukrainians were killed by the Stalinist regime, not by bullets, but lack of food. One Soviet bureaucrat described the massive starvation of 1933 as the Soviet regime turning the boney hand of famine back onto the throats of the peasantry. That year, the entire landscape through which we travel, and for that matter all of Ukraine, became a vast death camp, according to the British scholar Robert Conquest. One can visit the Nazi death camps and find watch towers and gas chambers, but in Ukraine, in every village and every house from that time, someone starved. They were horrific scenes that Volksdeutsche outlined to their Dakota relatives: "As I write this, my children pull on me, whining and crying that I should give them bread. What should I give them?"

The terror famine was so vast, that only guesses could be made about the number of victims, anywhere from four to ten million, but whatever the total, the greatest demographic decline to hit European peasantry since the Middle Ages. Entire families, entire villages died out. Even the well-fed collective officials and secret police cadres who presided over this tragedy, who went house to house in a search for grain to reach inflated quotas, were deeply affected, as a Soviet activist involved in the grain collection stated: "Those of the Communists…directly involved in the horrors of collectivization were thereafter marked men. We carried the scars. We had seen ghosts. We could be identified by our taciturnity, by the way we shrank from discussion of the 'peasant front.'"

On the last leg of our journey, the low of range of hills near Rastadt remind me I carry in my satchel a survivor account, not of the starvation, but of a massacre of Jews. The Haimovici family was among those brought from the castle at Mostove, ferried with hundreds of other Jews in lorries and trucks along this same road we're traveling, then dumped out in a field in the late summer/early fall of 1942 near Rastadt:

> We were told to line up facing the pits, where we saw something black. It was tar. We were on the slope, while the Germans crowded together on the hilltop in their black clothes with their shiny armbands…We stood there, hundreds of Jews in the open field, rich farmland all around us. Tall stalks of corn, wheat, and sunflowers…Meanwhile the beasts became drunk and began abusing all the pretty girls and women. They created a small wave of panic by shooting several small children wrenched from their mothers. Drunk, their consciences no longer functioning, under orders from their commander, they began mowing down row after row of people. The shots were accompanied by sounds of screeching and wailing that echoed throughout the German settlement…People fell, one after another, or several at a time into the prepared pits. These filled up quickly, since they were quite shallow, long rather than deep. In the hail of bullets that came our way, Father was wounded. We fell on him…

The police raped women and girls, but were too drunk to pursue the Haimovicis, who crawl into a cornfield. They watched as the corpses are doused with kerosene and set afire. They watch as bonfires were lit, and huge, unearthly shadows filled the moon-blanched valley. They watched the drunken policemen and villagers celebrate. Several hours later, under cover of darkness, the Haimovici family finally makes its escape.

When we arrive at Yascha's place, what continues to bother me is the post-slaughter revelry that the Haimovicis watched from their hiding place. How can that disturbing celebration be explained? It belongs—seems to belong—to an ugly time, void of men and creatures like them. It's a disturbing thought I quickly dismiss, because it points to the possibility that it may not just be the Nazis who hate the Jews.

***

WHEELBARROWS

That evening is chaotic. After a late supper, and homemade vodka for everyone except Anatoli and me, Yascha guides me around his solid German house. He waxes exuberant about the hundred-year-old bedroom door, showing me how, with its glazed, archaic glass panels, the door swings perfectly on oiled hinges. Growing tearful about his father's stint in the Ukrainian Guards under Zhukov, the Soviet general who captured Berlin and defeated the Nazis, he dons his father's uniform for Anatoli and me, and, like a portly model in a Soviet fashion show, walks a wobbly line across the room.

"It's bedtime," I say, anxious not for sleep, but to prepare for tomorrow. Later, while Anatoli snores in his narrow bed along the wall of our room, I'm like a child after curfew, using my mini flashlight to scan a testimony of a Volksdeutsche villager from Rastadt, describing events in 1942:

> Yes, in Rastadt, there was a self-protection unit. I was not a member, because at the time I was too young. The SS commander Hartung's office was in the priest's house next to the church. I was familiar with him because I was an apprentice woodworker at the time, helping build wooden cabinets for his office. It was well known that the murders of Jews were ordered by the SS, that they initiated the action. There were no German Wehrmacht personnel in our village or area. I don't know if the Romanians were involved in the

murders either. I didn't see the mass executions and I didn't want to see them.

Yes, several local German men, along with several Jews, were executed in Rastadt, for it was widely known that these men had collaborated with the communists before the war. I was fifteen at the time of the invasion by German and Romanian troops in 1941. There were almost three thousand inhabitants there at the time, almost all of whom were entirely German. And when we returned there in September 1941, the few Jewish families who lived there were gone.

That evening as I switch off the flashlight, the last thing I hear, besides Anatoli's snoring, is the soft patter of rain on Yascha's century old German roof tiles. When I wake several hours later, I see, or think I see, hovering in the darkness across the room, a blurry, headless figure in a white military uniform.

"Who are you?" I blurt out. "What do you want?"

I sense the answer from my dream. It's his head, lost after being hanged for war crimes, so now he wanders the earth, searching for it.

When I finally find my mini flashlight and aim its beam across the room, the figure is gone. All that remains, I can clearly see, is the military tunic, heavy with medals, just where Yascha hung it on the open wardrobe door so Anatoli and I could admire it before bed.

***

In the half-lit dawn Masha's curtains balloon into the bedroom. I lay in bed, enjoying the scent of the steppe, trying to imagine what it was like when German colonists, Catholics, arrived from Germanic provinces in 1806, wading through the long steppe grass, much like my own grandparents on the Dakota prairie, building earth and reed homes, sinking their plows in the root-ridden steppe, founding Rastadt, which they named for the city in Germany,

I decide to take a walk. Out on the asphalt road near Yascha's driveway I consult my plat map of Rastadt. It was drawn after WWII by refugees from the village. The street I'm standing on—August Eleventh Street—commemorates the exact day in 1941 when the German army entered Rastadt, ending years of purges, executions, and starvation, and long after the war the street is still called that, as if the Nazi invasion was a good thing to be remembered.

At the highest point of the village proper, I find the priest's former residence, and though a newly remodeled building, it bears no indication of its former prominence as the VoMi's Rastadt District Headquarters, established in late summer of 1941 by SS Captain Rudolf Hartung, a stocky, gap-toothed Nazi said to be an intimate of Joseph Goebbels, Hitler's propaganda minister.

In a six-week training course, Hartung shaped recruits from Rastadt and its surrounding villages and hamlets into a protean paramilitary police. If they made mistakes or disobeyed the thick-legged SS commander strode across their prone bodies, digging the heels of his polished boots into their flesh.

I want to see Hartung's former office. I go through a small hallway, pass a broken chair and a dirty mop leaning in a corner, and enter the high-ceilinged office. The heavy cabinets, which once held the Russian carbines and ammunition, are gone. A sinking feeling comes over me. This was the room where Hartung kept his wheelbarrows, heaped with brooches and watches and rings and bracelets. To gather that much loot, the police killed a huge number of Jews. That's what I think, though I have little evidence to support such a contention. Not yet.

Next door is a weeded empty lot where the Catholic church, with its double steeples, once stood. Now only a few foundation stones remain, scattered in the weeds. In Ukraine's civil war in 1919, anarchists and revolutionaries brought their wagons mounted with machine guns into Rastadt, to murder, loot, and burn. When German colonists ran for the sanctity of the church, the revolutionaries followed, riding their lathered horses into the chancel, where they forced village women to sing and dance for them. Then, according to one account at least, they raped them on the church altar.

A hundred Rastadters died, nearly as many houses were torched in that first wave of widespread destruction which included forced grain requisitions, and cleaned out colonist granaries, homes, and farms of livestock, sausage, tools, bedding, and clothing in "the greatest plunder operation in history," as scholars have called it. That was just the beginning. Starting in 1929, with collectivization, two more waves of communist violence hit, one of which is, as Volksdeutsche claim, the genocidal mass starvation in 1933, and the other, the wholesale arrests, torture, and executions of 1937.

On my way back, I scrutinize old colonist homes constructed from limestone blocks, TV dishes angling from tiled roofs, front gates painted in vivid patterns, homes in which, I know, colonists spent many a sleepless night, trying to survive those waves of destruction. Crossing his yard, in what we in Dakota call the farmers' carry, his free arm stretched parallel to the ground, to counterbalance the frothing pail of milk he carries in his other, Yascha calls out to me, "Breakfast." Then he pours the pail's contents, a blur of white, into a shiny metal container on the local cheese factory wagon stopped at his front gate behind its two mules.

In the newly painted entryway, Masha leans over my shoulder, laying out breakfast plates on the long table like she's dealing black jack. When she sees my plat map of Rastadt beside my plate, she stabs her index finger at their house, which once belonged, she tells me, to a Volksdeutsche family named L.

"Yes, L., I know that name," I say. It's a name that appears with troubling regularity on Soviet secret police documents and execution lists I've exhumed from the archives.

An epiphany strikes me. Two totalitarian world views—Stalin's and Hitler's—overlap right here in Masha's house. In 1937, several L. men were arrested, jerked from their beds in the very bedroom in which I've been sleeping, taken away in front of their women and several adolescent sons, "for nothing, and nothing again," as the colonists called the Soviet arrests to meet execution quotas. Then, four years later, during the Nazi occupation, Rastadt's SS commandants came to the house too, standing in their uniforms in what is now Masha's living room, and pressuring two L. sons, now of age, to join the police unit. Within four months, they would be turned into killers.

***

One morning, a hungover Yascha drives me to the outskirts of Rastadt, where he parks his Lada on a plateau-like rise, and from there we proceed on foot.

"This is *skolomochil*," Yascha says, meaning the place of the skulls.

"Where animal cadavers are dumped?" I ask.

"Yes, as you can see."

We pick our way through an area of bleached cow skulls, disarticulated remains, curved ribs and yellowed vertebrae. Yascha stops and points to a low area, crisscrossed by tire marks. There's a clay wall on whose surface I can see shovel marks.

"That's where I get clay to repair my outbuildings," he says.

The path curls around a knoll, suddenly we stand at the edge of the bluff, where I see the barely visible curving rim of a lime-kiln shaft embedded in the clay bank. It's an overhang like at Gradofka. But here the oven is shielded from view until the last instant. I feel a surge of anger at being tricked. Why didn't Yascha say something? Is it his way to show me, as Duissmann showed me the size of the Slobodka ghetto, how the Jews were led to the oven, killed before they could react?

It's my sixth or seventh overnight trip to Rastadt that month alone. I visit Gradofka and talk late and long with Masha and Yascha, good hosts. Patient and helpful. Why did it take Yascha so long to show me skolomochil?

"Is it because I didn't do vodka shots with him?" I ask Laryssa the next day.

"Yascha is just a peasant," Laryssa says. "He remembered, then took you there. It is nothing more. Okay?"

My research carries me down, through layer on layer of atrocities, until I reach bedrock: the first, and smallest, mass murder in Rastadt, in the vegetable garden in the heart of the village, four Volksdeutsche, alleged collaborators with the Soviets, and a dozen local Jews, shot in early fall, 1941, by the Einsatzgruppen. After that, as the Rastadt police unit is organized, drawing manpower from across the district, it takes part in the slaughter at Bogdanovka during the last week of December 1941.

From January 1942 into 1943, there are ongoing massacres, one north of the main road through Rastadt, which Masha's mother watched from afar, the naked, white bodies tumbling down a steep embankment. And there were multiple massacres directly south of that at two lime-kiln shafts on the opposite side of the same road and another at the skolomochil site. Yet another took place at the Ukrainian field two kilometers outside the village, which is the one, I think, the Haimovici family survived.

The first large massacres had roughly thirty victims per action; later, during the first months of 1942, as trainloads of one to two thousand souls per train leave Odessa, and

Romanian gendarmes bring the victims overland to the castle, or the horse-stable ghetto, the totals balloon to a hundred, then two hundred victims per massacre. When the horse-stable ghetto and its fifteen hundred souls, are incinerated, likely at the end of 1942, that marks the largest murder action by the Rastadt police since Bogdanovka.

***

On the hottest day that summer, with heat shimmers rising from the steppe, Anatoli drops me at the Odessa airport, and I cross the asphalt tarmac, spongy beneath my shoes, and board my flight, to visit a war crimes archive in Germany.

My flight floats high over the steppe, over the hazy, curving distance of what a Yale historian calls the bloodlands, which is also the title of his book. It's the site of the greatest mass killing in the twentieth century, if not history altogether: "This region experienced the worst of both Stalin's and Hitler's ideological madness. During the 1930s, 1940s, and early 1950s, the lethal armies and vicious secret policemen of two totalitarian states marched back and forth across these territories, each time bringing about profound ethnic and political changes."

Each time power changed hands—first the Soviet Union, then the Nazis, then the Soviets again—there were catastrophic results in cities across Poland and Ukraine, battles and sieges and cycles of massacres and politically motivated killing, that began not in 1939 with the invasion of Poland, but in 1933, with the terror famine in Ukraine. Between 1933 and 1945, fourteen million people died in the bloodlands, and not in combat, but because "someone made a deliberate decision to murder them."

The archives are located in a long, redbrick building, once a women's prison, just off a bustling thoroughfare in Ludwigsburg. I'm buzzed inside by a uniformed guard, who points a meaty hand at worn concrete steps, and says,

111

pronouncing my last name in a way I hadn't heard since childhood, "Go this way, Herr Fossler."

The rumpled German archivist Herr T., ceremoniously pumping my hand, leads me into in a study room with a simple institutional metal desk piled high with thick blue folders. "This iss ze material you haf requested."

These documents, which date to the early 1960s, are the result of West German investigators at the newly founded State Justice Central Office, Investigating National Socialist Crimes, located in Ludwigsburg, interviewing former German officials who served in the Odessa region during the war, as well as Volksdeutsche relocated from Transnistria to Germany in 1944 and still living in that country. By the time German investigators concluded their work in 1999, their inquiries had generated thousands upon thousands of pages related to the Transnistrian Holocaust, including the blue folders in front of me, across whose covers, in flowing German script, were three simple words—Special Command Russia. This was VoMi shorthand for the Nazi colonizing effort in Transnistria.

With the unblinking red eye of the overhead security system staring down and my grandmother's warning echoing in my thoughts ("Ach, child, forget the past"), I set to work separating out the folders that concern my ancestral villages. Somehow, I'm averse to reading these documents, anxious about what the tangled, lengthy, High German sentences, and multiple branching segments, and tortured, passive constructions, will reveal. I don't want to know, not just yet.

"Can you make copies of these?" I asked Herr T. "I need to take them with me."

After an uneasy night at a small hotel on a street named for Kepler, the famous German astronomer, and a second day at the archives, Herr T. presents me with at least ten pounds of copied testimonies that I pack in my suitcase.

On my flight across the bloodlands, I lower my tray, and wielding my knowledge of German dialect as a weapon, and consulting my German dictionary, I begin to read, to plow my way into the blood-soaked soil of Transnistria, turning up, along the way, familiar names from my own Dakota past, Kramers and Benders and Lipperts and Kienzles and Heinlies and Kreins and Dockters and Ackermans and others, which give me a shudder. Until my flight lands and I wheel my suitcase, heavy with copies, to the airport gate in Odessa, where a solemn Anatoli awaits, I hear that voice in the back of my head, telling me, over and again, "Oh, child. Just forget the past." But I know it's already too late for me, a prairie Judas about to betray his own people.

***

The new information in the testimonies signals a shift in my emphasis. I forego my usual excursions to Rastadt and Gradofka, and begin to visit sites farther south, creeping ever closer to the Lutheran villages of my own ancestral past.

My new itinerary makes Anatoli seethe. He hates these roads, more damaged than previous ones we've traveled. Despite reassurances that I would pay for damage incurred, Anatoli grows ever more obsessed, circling his Nissan like a bloodhound, sniffing out chips on the car's paint job. Driving, he stares fixedly ahead, anticipating ruts and potholes and obstructions, his long Slavic face like that of a tortured medieval saint in a painting.

One day we're searching for Krinitschki, where several hundred Odessa Jews were held in some collective buildings, when the Nissan's front tire catches the edge of a pothole, and Anatoli thumps the steering wheel with both palms, thundering, "*Yup feur mat.*"

It's one of the few Ukrainian curse words I know, brought from Ukraine by my ancestors, one my cousin and I often bandied about while working on our uncle's farm in high school. Only thing is, it's a curse word so heinous that

113

older Volksdeutsche blanched hearing it, always refusing to explain its meaning, which is, as I learn from a Russian major in college, the mother curse.

"Tell Anatoli I know that word," I say.

Anatoli's features brighten, and there ensues a discussion of the phrase and its various intricacies.

"When a person is in a bad situation," Anatoli says, "and he says, yup feur mat, that gives him extra energy to free himself."

"Like what?" Laryssa says.

"When your car gets stuck in the mud," Anatoli says. "Or you hit a pothole."

"And then?" Laryssa says, cringing.

"Then you say, yup feur mut," Anatoli says.

Wherever we go that day, we hear that phrase. From a motorcyclist, stopped at the side of the road, clubbing his broken seat into place with a fist the size of a small ham, from a leathery-skinned villager whose directions to us are punctuated with the term, even from a frustrated young mother berating her preschooler in the street: "Yup feur mat, I told you never to do that."

"Sonia doesn't want me to use that phrase," Anatoli explains solemnly as we head home that evening. "We have been arguing about that our entire married life. Thirty years."

"A thirty year argument?" I say.

"Yes, my own Thirty Years War. One I will now finally win."

"Why is that?" I say.

"Because of you," Anatoli says, his solemn face brightening. "Once you, an educated, modern American tell Sonia that you also say yup feur mut, that will tip the balance my way."

Dust billows and swirls like contrails behind the Nissan on our way back to Nikolaev. I'm tired, and amid the wafting prairie-like scents, I drift into a reverie of the summer after my senior year in high school. Anatoli becomes my cousin Rodney—they have the same long Slavic face—and the Nissan is my cousin's old push-button Buick with bucket seats. We've just finished a hot day of throwing slough bales eight layers high on a flat rack, and barreling back toward New Odessa, drinking ice-cold quarts of beer that we prop in our laps, and talk with hope about our futures.

It's a snippet of blessed memory when everyone I loved was still alive, and my young life was so thick with cousins and uncles and aunts, and by the time we reach Nikolaev, I'm rested for first time in Ukraine it seems.

But before Anatoli takes me back to my apartment, I dutifully follow him into his house and help him win his thirty-year argument with his wife Sonia.

***

One day we visit a large funnel-shaped Stuka bomb crater a mile north of Novo Pokrovka, where 120 Jews were shot down by a twenty-man Volksdeutsche police unit. The site, I see from the map, is in the vicinity of Lichtenfeld. Not good. That means police under SS commandant Liebl's command at Lichtenfeld, were involved: the first direct evidence I've found that the Holocaust may have encroached on my grandfather's birthplace.

"Let's go to Lichtenfeld," I say.

Anatoli stops the car to ask directions of a towering figure sauntering along the road. The fellow takes it as an offer of a ride, jerks the back door open, and climbs inside.

"I'm Igor the Cossack," he booms out, so loud that Laryssa scuttles across the seat to the opposite door. "Lichtenfeld, yes, I will take you there. Go that way."

While we drive a rutted path and I'm glancing around at the sweeping landscape my grandfather described to me when I was a child, Anatoli scolds Igor, "Do you have to talk so loud? You are scaring Laryssa."

The old Cossack says, "Sorry. Lost my hearing. In the mines in the far north. My friend Lang, he was with me in the mines, and he couldn't hear either."

"Lang?" I say. "I have relatives by that name."

"I will take you to Lang's grave," Igor announces.

We ride the narrow rutted path up to a plateau, down another, and into a broad valley, and after he shows us the Ukrainian cemetery and Lang's stately polished marker and grave, which he tends, the old Cossack's ideas lurch into philosophical weirdness.

Once, he booms, years ago, there were normal men in Ukraine, but now, with the advent of bottled water sold in big cities, men begin to frolic and dance around like pansy-assed fairies, unable to enjoy women or have children, seducing men away from becoming fathers, for weren't children the greatest of all joys in this wide world, even if his own children hated him? Yes he'd mistreated them, but as long as he remained strong (he balls a huge, scarred fist and shakes it like a prophet without doubt), they better watch out, or (he slams his fist against his palm), they'd get it, along with all those shit bag bottom-feeders, trying to ruin Ukraine by selling bottled water.

"Now we can go to Lichtenfeld," he says.

We need to get clear of this wild man, in whose whirling rant we are caught up, so I tell him I've changed my mind, I don't want to go to Lichtenfeld. As he climbs out of the car, I ask him what he knows of the Jews.

"There," Igor says. He points to a hummocky area in a swale between where we have stopped and a cluster of homes ahead, the hamlet Ambarova, where this grey-haired giant seems headed.

"They were killed there?" I say.

"No, where they were held."

"Where were they killed?"

He waves vaguely to the southwest, in the direction of Lichtenfeld. Then he saunters off, singing snatches of his country's national anthem, booming out the part about Ukraine not being dead yet, no not yet dead.

We find a shaded area and eat a late lunch out of the trunk, enjoying our new-found quiet and Sonia's sandwiches. Anatoli casts his worried gaze at the darkening sky. He lobbies for an early return. If it rains, this backroad will turn into a gluey gumbo, he'll ruin his car, and we'll never get unstuck, no matter how loud we shout yup feur mut.

"What about Lichtenfeld?" Laryssa says, who knows nothing of districts or police jurisdictions or my growing ambivalence about going there again, especially after what Igor has told us. "I've called ahead for you to meet people to interview."

"Lichtenfeld can wait," I say.

On the way back to Nikolaev, I remind myself that the next time I visit Lichtenfeld, I want to be prepared, emotionally. In the meantime, I want to remember Lichtenfeld as I'd imagined, amid its rainbow-like auras and blooming fruit trees, and as I found it on my first visit, a ruined paradise, atop its plateau, my own windy Troy, my own golden Mycenae.

***

It's our usual Friday afternoon of banter, drinking, and reading secret police documents. I'd been in Ukraine for nearly a year. We are seated at an outdoor cafe near my walk up apartment in Nikolaev's city center.

"There was a Ghitler here in Ukraine too," Dmitri says, and I'm struck by how my soft-spoken scholar-friend pronounces the German dictator's name, as if clearing his throat.

"Oh yes, Hitler," I say. "In the Partisan Museum I saw a photograph of Hitler's Hinkel airplane flying over Nikolaev."

"No, I don't mean that Ghitler," Dmitri says.

"What other Hitler is there?" I ask.

Everyone at the table knows the answer except me; they are members of a presidential council, whose main duty is to rehabilitate Ukrainians and Ukrainian Volksdeutsche falsely convicted during the 1930s by the Soviets, and whose grisly, but necessary work—shuffling through interrogation records deep in secret police archives—has marked each of them: Dmitri has dark smears under his eyes; Serge is a puffy-faced academic who drinks too much; and Vasily, the Marlboro Man, as we call him, nervously chain-smokes.

"The Ghitler in those documents," Dimitri says, tapping the stack of folders on the table, "was a Soviet secret police agent in the Karl Liebknecht Collective."

"That's a Volksdeutsche collective farm in the 1930s," I say. "Where my relatives were slave labor."

"Yes, this Ukrainian Ghitler shot many Volksdeutsche, hundreds," Serge adds.

"To compensate for his infamous name?" I say.

"Perhaps he shot a few of your relatives, Ron," Serge snorts, already drunk.

As the air grows tense, Vasily comes to the rescue, trying to change the topic. "You know, Ron, that grocery store that didn't give you bread that day because you didn't say bread correctly in Ukrainian?"

"I know, I should have said *khleb*," I say, making a guttural sound. "Like Ghitler."

"No, no," Vasily says. "I mean across from the store in the city square. That's where some young Volksdeutsche police were hanged after WWII. War crimes."

"Perhaps your relatives?" Serge says, slurring. "Next time I bring you names of the police hanged there."

The waiter brings more frosty mugs of beer. We divide the folders, across whose covers are written, in Cyrillic letters, KGB, one thick folder for each.

"This section seems an afterthought," Vasily says, squinting through a cloud of smoke. "How could this witness, thirty years after the fact, remember who rode with him to an execution?"

"Torture?" I say.

"Of course, torture," Vasily says, for his father, a doctor, was tortured in the 1930s, falsely charged for a concocted plot of poisoning horses in the Soviet cavalry. "The secret police pitted one prisoner against another, then filled in the rest themselves."

In the Nikolaev People's Park, an elderly woman crosses herself in front of a large statue of Saint Nicholas, the patron saint of the city, which casts its long shadow across the uneven slabs. It's getting chilly. Nearby, on concrete benches, pensioners bend their grey heads over interminable games of chess.

Visiting murder sites and delving into musty archives is a lonely, grinding affair, and I'm thankful for the camaraderie and fellowship. Who else but other Holocaust investigators could we speak to about such terrible things? This evening, as we discuss Bogdanovka, I'm surprised by their intimate knowledge of that site.

They even know of Slinenko, the radically unhinged Ukrainian policeman at Bogdanovka. In the 1920s, before collectivization, Slinenko's parents owned sixty-six hectares of land, large herds of cattle and swine. In the early 1930s the Soviets dispossessed the family of everything, naming them as kulaks, and sending them to be exterminated in a Siberian labor camp. After the German invasion in 1941, Slinenko sided with the Nazis. He was the most feared policeman at the Bogdanovka ghetto—where nearly sixty thousand Jews were held—and he associated all Jews with the Bolsheviks who destroyed his family. One day he killed three hundred Jews. Another day he murdered his own assistants for an oversight. When Slinenko's postwar mistress learned of his murderous rampages, she turned him in to Soviet authorities, and he was executed.

"Do you think some Volksdeutsche police felt like Slinenko?" I say. "Blaming the Jews for their suffering in the 1930s."

"What do you think they felt?" Serge says, turning my question back to me.

"Imagine," Dmitri mused, rescuing me from Serge's baleful stare. "There was an SS officer named Hegel from Pervomaisk, who was ordered to Bogdanovka."

"An SS officer with the same name as the famous philosopher?" I say.

"Only this Hegel killed Jews," Dmitri says.

"Wasn't it Hegel who warned about staring into the abyss?" a gloomy Serge says, referring to the detrimental effects of our research.

"No," Dmitri says. "Nietzsche said that."

"What's the quote?" I say.

"Something like, don't stare into the abyss, or the abyss will stare back," Dmitri says.

"Which means?"

"Which means," Vasily says, lighting another cigarette, "that all this research affects us. Look at Serge."

"Dmitri looks worse than I do," Serge says, bristling.

Our talk shifts to Dmitri's theory that Stalin, a former Soviet nationalities commissioner, diabolically pitted Jews against other minorities, using Jews in Ukraine's secret police to do the regime's dirty work.

"Which fueled grass roots anti-Semitism in Ukraine," Serge says.

Vasily, who is Jewish, even though to me he usually denies the fact, suddenly flails with both palms, wildly, knocking his lit cigarette from his lap, before it burns a spot in his linen pants.

After that, he seems unfocused and lost, and so we call it an evening, Dmitri and Serge head one way, and Vasily the other, and as his angular frame slides into the shadows, his voice floats back to me: "Ron, if you are unhappy with your apartment, call me and I will find you another."

To tire myself, I take the long way home, nervously clutching my satchel of secret police documents to my chest. I realize I've walked a huge circle back to where I started, Lenin Prospect, two chaotic arteries buzzing with traffic, separated by a wide grassy berm with trees and metal park benches. Along this way, if I remember correctly, ten thousand Jews were led to the city cemetery to be executed by the Nazis, but on the way, some young Jews created a disturbance, which allowed scores to escape.

On one corner looms a large statue of a Cheka agent. He wears a tight-fitting balaclava-like cap, like those worn by the apes in *The Planet of the Apes*, which gives the supposedly heroic figure a sinister appearance, more in keeping with the reality of the Cheka.

(During several months of 1918, in what was known as the Red Terror, Lenin's Bolshevik regime and its Cheka agents executed roughly the same number of its political enemies—6,185—as the Czarist regimes of the entire previous century. Cheka agents were also involved in the murder of sixty thousand Volksdeutsche, in the context of forced grain requisitions. They were also involved in the public hangings of hundreds of Ukrainians and Volksdeutsche on Lenin's orders, to promote terror in Ukraine. The civil war period gave Stalin and the Cheka their taste for obscene violence and homicidal solutions, which escalated in subsequent decades, during which Ukraine, one of the world's leading grain exporters in 1913, became a place where, in both 1922 and 1933, food was used as a weapon, cannibals ate human flesh, and millions starved.)

Familiar street names tell me I'm near my apartment. Finally, I cross an open, bustling square where Vasily says the young Volksdeutsche policemen were publicly hanged at the end of WWII. While prosecutors and officials in postwar Germany often applied leniency for Volksdeutsche perpetrators used by the Nazis and emerging from two decades of mass death and Soviet oppression, postwar Soviet courts commute few, if any, death sentences, even for those who were seventeen or eighteen at the time of their crimes. At least in my view, those youngest ones are more like the child soldiers of Africa than hardened, culpable killers.

Finally, I reach my apartment building. The heavy metal gate clanks open, and I hurry up the steps. It's my favorite time of the day just ahead. Wrapped in my only sweater against the evening chill, I usually sit on my balcony sipping chamomile tea, whose taste gives me Proustian memories of my grandfather. Sometimes, from a curbside accordionist plaintive Ukrainian melodies rise up to the balcony. And always, before bed, I kneel and pray for a peaceful heart and mind to continue my research.

On the second flight of steps, it occurs to me that from my beloved balcony I can see the square where the war criminals were hanged, and I know that every time I go onto my balcony, I'll think of those young war criminals, jerking at the ends of ropes.

Before I turn the key in the lock of my door, I'm on my cell phone, calling Vasily, asking if he could quickly help me find another apartment.

***

From various sources, I assemble a rough understanding of Nazi rule in Transnistria. After the Nazi invasion of the Soviet Union, Hitler granted two conquered provinces, Bukovina and Bessarabia, to Romania for its help, especially in securing Odessa. He also ceded them limited control of Transnistria, an isolated agricultural region east of Dniester River. He does, however, demand extraterritorial authority over the region's hundred and thirty thousand Volksdeutsche in two hundred farming villages founded nearly a century and a half earlier.

These once prosperous villages, which lost a quarter of their population in immigration to the American prairies under the Soviets, fell into ruin and despair, their population so decimated by deportations, mass starvation, and wholesale executions, that half of all households are without a male head. In addition, retreating Soviet security forces, suspecting the Volksdeutsche of being a fifth column, destroyed crops, and removed agricultural equipment, horses, cattle, and all men of military age beyond the Bug River. When the Wehrmacht units swept through the region, they found the Volksdeutsche villages in woeful condition, with few resources. Numerous elderly, women, and orphans were without proper clothing, medicine, or nutrition. In short, it was a humanitarian disaster.

Enter, Leibbrandt. He called a meeting. It took place in a smoke-filled Berlin cafe. The walls were painted with aryanized scenes of German life, mothers in colorful aprons, and blonde youth frolicking on a village green. There were nine men, most of Volksdeutsche background, half in military uniforms. Leibbrandt was in his element, drawing on his intimate knowledge of his home region and on his position in the Eastern Ministries. The relief operation they were organizing for the beleaguered Black Sea Germans, he determined, should start in Hoffnungstal and go from there.

In July of 1941, that relief operation, spearheaded by the German Red Cross, sent a number of nurses, physicians, and others to seek out—by train, by car, and horse-pulled wagons—the beleaguered German colonists of Transnistria. At the same time, the VoMi, Himmler's Ethnic German Welfare Office, was organizing its own relief operation. Until that can be set into motion, however, Himmler orders Einsatzgruppen D, one of four mobile killing squads still in the area, along with an elite unit of Volksdeutsche soldiers, the Brandenbergers on the mend from previous battles, to care for the German colonists, valuable Aryans, according to Himmler, Hitler's SS police commander.

The Einsatzgruppen D, in their string of blue buses and lorries and motorcycles, already bore the dubious distinction of being among the first units to kill not only male Jews, but entire families, after forcing Bessarabian Jews across the Dniester River. In that sense, they were the tip of the spear of the ramped-up policy of death.

It was a strange task, indeed, for Einsatzgruppen D, with its roll call of about five hundred, mostly hardened killers if not psychopaths, to conduct welfare activities. While they rendered medical and humanitarian aid to the Volksdeutsche, the units continued their genocide, combing the region for Jews. Sometimes, the two disparate activities, the murdering and the helping, overlapped, as beds and furniture and clothing taken from Jewish victims were distributed to the German colonists.

Meanwhile, the VoMi bureaucrats, under orders from Himmler, organized a relief operation that morphed into a colonization effort, *Sonderkommando R.* (Special Command Russia). Its personnel gathered at Stahnsdorf, the Wehrmacht headquarters south of Berlin, in the first weeks of August 1941. In mid-August, outfitted with the same equipment given the four Einsatzgruppen death squads which preceded them—everything except shovels and a bulldozer to bury the victims—they embarked for the East.

It was a long convoy of two hundred sedans and personal vehicles, Volkswagens, motorcycles (some with sidecars), staff cars, specialized radio and vans, and dozens of two- and three-ton Opel Blitz trucks, their doors inscribed with VoMi in large German letters. Riding in the vehicles was a small percentage of the sixty thousand Germans eventually posted in the East—SS officers, National Socialist drivers, pharmacists, Eastern Ministry bureaucrats (known as Golden Pheasants for their distinctive uniforms), and German Red Cross nurses and educators and social workers, the vanguard of Nazi culture meant to transform the Volksdeutsche into a people loyal to Hitler and to create a Nazi Garden of Eden in the East. At the forefront of the educational effort were the nurses, educators, and social workers, many of them women, whose job was to establish schools, kindergartens, nursing stations, and birthing centers.

They were also to teach local Volksdeutsche about Nazi racial hygienics, teaching and reinforcing anti-Semitic notions about the necessary destruction of the Jews and ensuring understanding that the Jews were the cause of Bolshevik terror during the 1930s. ("Yes, a Jewish baby is beautiful," a

German midwife once counseled a teenage Regina. "But it too will grow into a bloodsucking parasite.")

The VoMi convoy traveled for nearly two weeks through Nazi-occupied territory. It went by way of Lodz, Poland. At Zhytomyr the convoy divided, sending half of the vehicles and personnel to Nazi-occupied Ukraine and the other half to Transnistria.

There the VoMi—after releasing the Einsatzgruppen units of their caretaking responsibilities so that these units continue their killing in the direction of Crimea—established its headquarters in Landau, hijacked Leibbrandt's relief operation, and because no civilian authority was yet established by the Eastern Ministries, assumed control of the two hundred Volksdeutsche villages of Transnistria.

It's interagency squabbling of the sort Hitler encouraged, but for Leibbrandt, even if the VoMi was led by SS bureaucrats with whom he'd agreed to work in the best interests of the Volksdeutsche, Special Command Russia—with its heady mix of totalitarian despotism and Utopian planning—would bring disastrous consequences onto the very people he'd so long sought to protect.

***

"WHO WILL TAKE THIS GIRL?"

While our vehicle pitches in the ruts of a bad road, I'm explaining to Laryssa what I know about Landau, the village we are fast approaching. I tell her its wartime population, in excess of three thousand German Catholic Volksdeutsche, is now only a third of that, and there is little to indicate its former importance as the VoMi capital of Transnistria. Except its headquarters, which I want to find, whose buildings once contained three hundred bureaucrats, administrators, and SS officers under General Horst Hoffmeyer, a Leibbrandt acquaintance, chosen to rule over that portion of the Nazi colonial empire.

I explain how Hoffmeyer and his boss in Berlin, Werner Lorenz, were the architects of VoMi resettlement of a million Volksdeutsche from Bessarabia, Poland, Western Volhynia, and the Baltic States, an ingathering of Germanic blood before the Nazi invasion of the Soviet Union in 1941; Volksdeutsche, whose young men were drafted into SS units, and whose educated class, with their multilingual abilities and knowledge of regions beyond Germany, were useful in Nazi colonization, especially of Transnistria.

"Like Weingartner, the SS officer your relatives admired?" she says.

"Yes, he was Bezirkmeister," I say, my voice sounding oddly proud, like Regina's when she spoke of him. "He commanded an entire district. Seven thousand people. Sixteen villages."

"And killed Jews?" Laryssa says.

"There were no Jews forced into Weingartner's district," I say, hoping I'm right. "Not like in the Rastadt area."

"What about other police units," Laryssa says. "Like in Lichtenfeld?"

"I'm still working on that," I say, knowing Lichtenfeld was twenty kilometers from Rastadt.

Our vehicle surmounts a rise, and there it is, spreading from one side of the valley to the other—Landau. We stop a middle-aged man with the saggy countenance of an overworked opera singer and ask the way to the former VoMi headquarters. He gives an indeterminate jerk of his head, as if the location were self-evident. When I snap a photo of a nearby ruined building that looks official, he gets frustrated.

"No, no, the building down the road. With bars on the lower level," he says. "When the Nazis came, the Gestapo was housed in that building and used the torture equipment left behind by the Soviet secret police."

"So Ukrainians were tortured first by the Soviets, then by the Nazis," I say.

"Of course. Every system needs a prison," he says, sounding like a character from an Ambrose Bierce short story. "But if you are to be killed, you want to be killed by someone who speaks your own language."

We leave this home-spun philosopher and drive on. Anatoli steers the Nissan between two pillars, and a cobbled road funnels us into a central plaza, ringed by solid buildings. It's the belly of the beast, the former VoMi headquarters, now an orphanage, where children with shaved heads are planting flowers in fresh, overturned earth. Anatoli pulls in his neck, and shudders; later he tells me his mother nearly abandoned him at such an institution.

The orphanage director, an attractive woman with the heavy hipped grace of my Dakota aunts, meets us and embraces her old friend Laryssa. Then she shakes my hand. "My name is Tatiana F. My husband is of German ancestry."

"Yes, I know that name," I say.

At least four victims from the Soviet execution list of 1937 and 1938 had her last name. There was also a Volksdeutsche family by that name, who in 1942, was discovered to be hiding a half-Jewish baby. An SS officer showed up, and with the mother watching, swung the baby by its legs against a wagon wheel, just one of many murders of mixed Jewish/Volksdeutsche children across Transnistria.

Mrs. F. ushers us into one of the main orphanage buildings. I stand there, stunned. After the dung-ridden streets of poverty stricken villages and the squabbling flocks of geese and ducks, this building's floor-to-ceiling windows and the gleaming floors make me feel I've been transported from rural Ukraine to modern Europe.

It's likely what Hartung and other SS commandants felt, motoring from their cramped offices in the muddy villages, for quarterly meetings here, where they decried the impossible logistics of the steppe, complained about the pig-headed Volksdeutsche, and discussed evolving mass murder methods.

While the director and Laryssa get reacquainted, I walk past the former VoMi offices, which extend off the long hallway. These are offices in which VoMi bureaucrats made decisions, from the mundane to the murderous. Now, they are dorm rooms for orphans, with delicate window curtains and narrow bunk beds covered by bright, multicolored, familiar-looking quilts. On one of them I find a series of small red hearts and this message, stitched in red thread: "Made with love and donated by the Church Ladies of Tuttle, North Dakota."

One of these VoMi offices also belonged to an assistant paymaster and Volkish/Nazi writer, an SS officer named Karl Goetz, who knew Leibbrandt and was also a confidante of Reichsfuehrer Heinrich Himmler. In 1937 Goetz toured North Dakota, contacting German-language newspapers and giving talks and slide shows, an unsuccessful Nazi project to draw Dakota Germans back to the Reich.

On the opposite end of the hallway, the director is speaking Ukrainian on her cell phone. Laryssa beckons to me and says, "She's contacted a person about a massacre near here. I will translate for you, okay?"

So I jot down notes: During the Fascist Occupation in a German colony near Landau, a German officer ordered the villagers to assemble at a nearby ravine. There the colonists found sixteen Jewish families, nearly fifty people huddled together and guarded by an armed unit of men, whose officer, leading a small Jewish girl of five or six by the hand, walked in front of the colonists.

"Who will save this child?" the German officer said.

Nobody offered. The colonists cowered. They feared they were next. The girl ran back to her parents. The officer ordered his men to fire. The force of the discharge knocked the Jews into the ravine.

"Bury them," the officer barked to the colonists, pointing to a couple of shovels. "Or you are next."

The director folds her cell phone. We stand there together, the sun slanting in through the high windows. When I ask Laryssa, who in turn asks the director, just who the killers were, I'm told, as always, "Germans. Just Germans."

We say good-bye to the kindly director and go on our way, northward, to seek out the massacre site, Landau sinking out of sight behind us. If it was August/September 1941, then the killers were Einsatzgruppen D, whose grisly convoy swung through this area on their line of march toward the Caucasus. If it was later, spring or summer of 1942, then the killers were a Volksdeutsche police unit under SS command. It troubles me not knowing.

"Did the orders for massacre come from the offices we just visited?" Laryssa says.

"Maybe," I say.

"But how were they relayed to the SS officer who oversaw the murder?"

"By a Nazi courier on a fast horse." Later I'll learn one of the couriers, perhaps even this courier, was someone my own mother knew.

I try to explain to Laryssa that the result of the orders we've just heard described has been relayed by a modern cell phone, seventy years after the fact, back to where the orders originated.

Laryssa says nothing. Knowing I've failed to convey the ugly irony to her, I hear myself talking, trying to expunge an idea that sticks like shrapnel in my brain.

It has something to do with the pulsing light of a long dead star returning to its point of origin, something with how the colonists felt watching the murder, something with not wanting to think about the little girl.

***

There are, at first, a dozen VoMi districts in Transnistria—these are later subdivided—each with its own SS commandant, usually an *obersturmbannfuhrer* (the equivalent of a lieutenant colonel), one or two lower rank SS officers, as well as police trainers and drivers, along with various VoMi personnel brought by the convoy, with secretaries, receptionists, mechanics, stenographers, cooks, and maids recruited from local Volksdeutsche and paid monthly salaries in the range of two hundred German Marks.

The VoMi SS headquarters in each district were in centrally located buildings, like schools, former parsonages, and Soviet governmental or secret police offices. Their identifying placards indicated the district's number and VoMi affiliation and were prominently placed in front of the headquarters. SS commandants provided security in their districts and decided upon agricultural matters—what crops to plant and when to commence harvest—and in some cases whether young recruits could marry. This was a projection of Hitler and Himmler's vision of an Eastern Germanic Kingdom, which considered the Volksdeutsche as Nazi darlings, even if many SS commandants saw them as only slightly better than Slavic *untermenschen*, or "Russian pigs who must be reeducated with the German spirit," as one SS commander put it as he railed at his Volksdeutsche police recruits.

The procedure for establishing a local police force, or Selbstschutz, as the self-protection units were called, was the same across Transnistria. At a mandatory meeting, all district men fit enough for military training, and of proper age—from sixteen to fifty in some locales and from eighteen to forty in others—were drafted into the local police.

Recruits were given a four- or six-week training period, at either Nikolaev, across the Bug River, or in nearby Sadowka, in the Beresan District. In the string of Catholic villages northwest of Odessa the Romanians shaped Volksdeutsche recruits into a protean self-protection force, before the VoMi assumed authority over them.

Active policemen were often billeted in the headquarters, where they ate hot meals in the SS canteen. Reserve police were called from their homes, when needed, by a predetermined signal, usually a gunshot. With old Russian carbines, local police guarded important buildings, patrolled the village streets, enforced the 8:00 p.m. Nazi curfew, and guarded against widespread thievery by Romanian soldiers. They also patrolled against mostly nonexistent partisans and bandits, and guarded VoMi lorries, the commandant's personal auto (if he had one), and other vehicles, captured from the Soviets and kept in repair by local mechanics, since the policemen were "always coming and going in a flurry of activity."

Police units were variously clothed. Some in cast-off Wehrmacht uniforms, with identifying designations removed. And if survivor reports are accurate, some police units wore black uniforms, or perhaps just dark clothing. Others donned white uniforms for winter operations, and a few local Volksdeutsche commanders donned field caps with a death's-head insignia. Most policemen wore armbands with a black swastika imposed on a red background, a visible indication of Nazi power, that made some elderly Volksdeutsche uneasy, not because they feared these young men they'd known their entire lives, but because they remembered the precipitous withdrawal of the German army in 1918, and the two-decade-long communist punishment for welcoming that army.

What if the Nazis left or were defeated and the Soviets returned? The repercussions would be huge. Even these wary oldsters couldn't imagine what was about to occur; even these wary oldsters couldn't know or foresee that four short months after the invasion in 1941, under SS orders, they'd be heaping their own farm wagons with the clothing of Jews murdered by these same young men they knew from local police units.

***

One day I accept Vasily's invitation to spend a Sunday afternoon on the deck of a yacht moored on the Bug River with a bevy of former Soviet KGB agents.

"You are always KGB," the oldest announces. "Even if you quit."

They are hard drinkers and sloppy eaters—more like portly businessmen without manners than hardened KGB agents. One of the younger men—in his mid-forties—asks me to hold his vodka bottle, then leaps overboard, dog paddles around in the waters of the bay, boards again, towels off, and continues our conversation about Stalin, repeating nearly verbatim what the history department chairman at my American university told me:

"Stalin got things done. He pointed to a map and said 'I want a canal here,' and that canal got built. Sure, he killed people. Every leader does. You can't help but admire such a man."

The yacht sways, the agents drink, Vasily along with them. At one point the Stalin-loving agent mimes his interrogation techniques. He shows me how he used to sneak into suspects' homes, jamming his high-powered flashlight into sleeping faces, startling his suspect to confess. "It's effective," he says, gloating.

He asks me to hold out my hands, which I do without thinking. Before I know it, he slaps a real pair of handcuffs onto my wrists.

"Now we take you to prison," he jokes, leading me around the yacht.

It's not a joke—not to me anyway. That day, as the yacht thumps against the dock like the fitful beating of a troubled heart and as a tiny sliver of fear goes up my back, I know what the Volksdeutsche, my many relatives among them, felt during Stalin's 1937 German Operation, before they were tortured and killed by Soviet Ukraine's secret police.

***

TO THE SEA

My rental car's tires thump a tattoo over the cobbled road into Josefstal, a once bustling former Volksdeutsche village in the Beresan, now fallen into ruin.

I drive up and down Delke Street. It's named for my stepfather's people. Just a few gables peek out above thick foliage, for the majority of homes, built with limestone blocks from the local quarry, were sold in the cash-strapped final years of communism, entire neighborhoods moved away.

Helga's house, the same blue color as my own in Dakota, is easy to find. I'm looking forward to meeting her—she's related to my stepfather in a tangled way I can't comprehend—and also to a good Volksdeutsche meal and an afternoon not thinking about ovens and ravines, since Josefstal, as far as I can tell from the documents of death, was not involved in the Holocaust.

As I knock, I admire the *dachsiegels* (glazed roof tiles), which form an overlapping array of greens and blues, falling away from the sinuous roofline, so that Helga's house, perched on its sloping yard, looks like a prehistoric iguana sunning itself.

She meets me at the door, a sad looking elderly woman whose swarthy features—she's of mixed gypsy and Volksdeutsche parentage—are framed in a bright shawl.

"I saw you admiring my dachsiegels," she says.

"Of course," I say. "How could I not. They're exquisite."

We chat about relatives, about how, if the economy doesn't improve, she will sell more of her beloved, century-old glazed tiles, to grace the roof of some wealthy person's dacha outside Odessa, ninety miles to the southwest.

"What a shame," I say. "*Shade.*"

The table we eat at has a wobbly bench set against an uneven wall, which is entirely covered by a backdrop of an idyllic copse—it's obviously a hugely enlarged photo—where a narrow brook flows over a bed of polished stones that look like dinosaur eggs.

Helga moves between the table and the nearby kitchen, bringing me a bowl of soup, whose finely sliced homemade noodles I spoon up greedily. The crocheted rugs spread over the wide floorboards and the family photos arrayed across the freshly calcined walls remind me of my grandmother's home on the prairie. Except for the flinty-eyed faces, gaunt with suffering, staring out of the photos.

"Arrested," Helga says, pointing at the photos. "This one died in a labor camp. These two executed. These starved. *Verstehe?*" (Understand?)

I understand only too well that underworld of suffering and death, so unknown in the West, when millions of starving people tottered around, features so blackened and grotesque that their own children ran from them. I shudder, and it seems criminal to be eating so heartily in a place, even perhaps in this very house, where people starved, so I put my spoon down, and trying to steer our conversation to a less horrific topic, I ask Helga about when Josefstal was a quiet backwater during the German Occupation.

"Finish your soup first," Helga says. "Then I answer."

I try to joke. *"Ein Befehl?"* (An order?)

"Yes," she says sternly. "Ein Befehl."

When I finish spooning up those thick, wonderful noodles, old Helga heaves a sigh and places a hand on her brow, as if locating a lost memory. "This happened when the Jews of Odessa were forced from their homes, and among those poor people was Eva, the most beautiful woman in Odessa, *gerade wie e' Engel aus Himmel g'falla.*" (Like an angel fallen from heaven.)

"When the Jews got out of the train car at Berezovka, the night sky was lit from great fires, German and Romanian soldiers burning the bodies of the Jews. What can I say? It was a dark time. Jewish women were raped. Eva smeared her face with soot, and wore a large shawl, so she looked old and awful, like me now. So she escaped that fate for a worse one.

"From there, the surviving Jews were forced over the steppe, and that's how Eva, this angel from Odessa, stood naked at a kalk-oven, waiting to die.

"When the SS commandant gave the order, the police, young men from the village went down the line and shot, and the bodies fell into the flames of the oven. One of the police was just a boy, from a good family destroyed by the Soviets, and when he saw Eva, and was struck by her naked beauty, he lowered his rifle. She held out her arms, like she wanted to hug him, and when he took a step in her direction, she threw her arms around him, and jerked them both backward, into the flames of the oven."

Helga gets up quickly and goes into the kitchen. I'm left at the table, wondering about the story, which sounds familiar. I know I've read it before, in a document about Gradofka and its ovens. I'd assumed it took place there. Now I'm less certain. Could it have happened in Josefstal? I feel like I've been carried into the heart of a terrible mystery.

When Helga returns with a bowl of mottled, Oreo-like cookies, which she sets on the table in front of me, I look at her carefully. She looks pale and drained now, but in her time she must have been a great beauty. It gets me to wondering. If Helga was fifteen in 1941, could that have been her?

"What happened to Eva? You didn't say."

"What do you think happened?" she says.

"How do you know so many details?"

"Eat, eat," she says, pushing the bowl of mottled cookies toward me. "That young man carried the scars from the oven the rest of his life." She pulls up the collar on her blouse.

"And Eva?" I say.

Silence.

"I will show you a place where Jews died. When you finish eating."

***

On the outskirts of the village, we get out of the rental car, and look over a low-lying area, which was once the village pasture where herds of German colonist red cows once grazed.

"It happened here," Helga says, standing on a rise and pointing down.

"Eva's murder?"

137

"No," she says. "The murder of a Jewish family from Josefstal."

She describes the murder, first, of a local teacher who begged in German dialect to be spared, then her husband. Then a week later, after VoMi racial experts found insufficient Aryan features, the couple's two children were killed—a ten-year old girl, shot while bending down to tie her shoe, and her younger brother, zigzagging to avoid the bullets fired at him. The last of five or six bullets struck him, and with his bloody scalp hanging down, he ran several more steps before collapsing.

(The photo I snap that day shows Helga pointing to a sloping area where the bodies were buried. But years later, as I look more closely at the photo, I realize that there is the telltale circle of a partially buried oven shaft that I didn't see at the time because I didn't want to see an oven in my stepfather's ancestral village.)

"But who fired the shots?" I say that day.

"Yakov Leidel knows of such things," Helga says. She shrugs fatalistically, mentioning the name of the man whose blood dark footprints I will only later follow back to my prairie hometown. "After the war he went to South Dakota. Isn't that where you live?"

"I live in North Dakota," I say. "But it's near."

While we drink a final cup of tea before I go, she tells me one more thing, in an oracular tone. It seems to echo the prophecy of the long-haired Sybil, and what she says stays with me now, years later, writing this, a hint I chose to overlook of many murders in Josefstal.

"In the years the Fascists were here," Helga says, "The *balkas* (ravines) ran red with blood, and if all the blood spilled in all the villages flowed together, it would make a terrible river, sweeping everything from its path, before it emptied into the Black Sea."

***

After Josefstal, I redouble my efforts, visiting so many sites in such a short time, that Laryssa's bangs hang into her eyes, and Anatoli's eyes jump around in his head like the jackrabbits we flush from the weeds of the steppe.

One day, I ask them both, "Are all these murder sites depressing you?"

"It's our job," both say without conviction, which stokes my fear they'll both abruptly quit.

So to cover myself, I hire backups, Mikhail, a leathery-skinned retired engineer, and Pavel, a tall, blond Nordic-looking university student, both of whom, on Laryssa's and Anatoli's days off, I ease into my schedule.

This new duo and I fuel early at the same gas station on the outskirts of Nikolaev. From a silver-toothed lady with a scruffy cat curling around her low stool, we buy chunks of grey halvah in Plasticine wraps, meat-stuffed buns, and cinnamon-spiced *bladgina*, pastries that taste like my Dakota grandmother's.

Gingerly sipping steaming coffee from soft plastic cups, we head westward to the least accessible sites, and it is with Mikhail and Pavel that I travel the greatest distances, and have my wildest adventures.

Mikhail, the driver, is fearless, with sharp reflexes he likes to test, just as he likes to test his old Volga with its high clearance. He continually tells me he can take me anywhere I ask and even places I don't, skirting the precarious edges of ravines, or plunging headlong into rain-sodden fields.

Sometimes we get stuck. Once, during *rasputitsa* (the muddy period), we search the edge of a field at Nova

Kantakovoska, where sixteen Volksdeutsche police from New Kandel killed 120 Jews. The Volga, mired to its axles in mud, lists like a sinking ship. Mikhail and I swear a blue streak, and unload our yup fuer muts. Pavel and I put our backs against the rear fender and heave, and the spinning wheels spatter our clothing with clots of mud. I have an idea to place burlap sacks from Mikhail's trunk under the wheels, and so we rock the tormented Volga back and forth. When that doesn't help, Pavel, a war buff like Mikhail, blames me, saying, "You Germans never did fare well in mud." It's a snide reference to the Nazi advance mired down west of Kiev during WWII. Finally, several locals, stumbling home drunk after a funeral, come along and push us out, so we continue on our way.

Mikhail and Pavel tell stories of Nazi occupation, of young people rounded up as forced laborers and taken to the Reich, of flat cars of trains heaped with rich chernozem soil for fascist gardens in Germany, and of current Ukrainian villagers so backward they only know of borsch, not soup. Sometimes, in isolated villages, rocking on weathered wooden benches, we see these troglodytes, jaws moving in a bovine manner, empty gazes drawn beyond us, toward the blue horizon line.

"See," Pavel says. "I told you."

Once, the old Volga slaloms down a slippery hillside, in a spine-jarring ride, the vehicle sliding sideways, its windows lashed wildly by sunflower stalks along the field's edge, its engine stalling and dying: until Mikhail—using a farmer's trick—lets the vehicle roll under its own weight, pops the clutch, so that the cylinders cough and sputter into action.

"Like a tank," Mikhail says, repeating his mantra.

We cover a lot of ground, the countryside flashing by in dreamlike images, Mikhail gunning the engine, flocks of geese and ducks scattering in our wake. We pass various military monuments, Soviet tanks on pedestals, or howitzer-like artillery pieces, barrels angled to the sky, like prairie grain augers. We bump and rattle through half-deserted villages with euphonic Ukrainian names, like Bonderevka, Jeremejewvka, and Tschemerlejewka, and places with medieval-sounding Germanic names like Windhaag and Hahnhafen.

Sometimes, visiting hamlets and hutors with Volksdeutsche family names like Lutz, Jenner, Oschner, Ehly, Zimmerman, Anton, Wanner, and, near the Black Sea, Hornbacher and Meuchel, we seem to travel the Dakota prairie. Sometimes, seeing the huge, abandoned Volksdeutsche churches, like at Karlsruhe and Selz, I feel I'm in Mexico and Central America, viewing from afar the great temples and ruined cities of Chichen Itza and Tikal and Palenque I read about as a child. Sometimes we come on forests of cement pillars, row on row of pillars, from huge, collapsed collective barns as if fashioned by a vanished race of giants. Once, near the end of a long day, in the distance I see pillars of light, like those I'd imagined as a child, hovering over Lichtenfeld, lights reminding me how everyone on the steppe must have seen, must have smelled the great fires from the lime-kiln ovens.

Ukrainians are anxious to help, unless they see my mini-recorder with its blinking red light, and think I'm a secret police agent, gathering information to incriminate them. Wherever we find them, in city halls, or tending gardens, they tell us what they know. And they point the way to the mass graves, which we find in ravines, open fields, abandoned wells, bomb craters, silo holes, hastily scooped out pits, plowed-over antitank ditches, hummocky areas, clay pits, limestone quarries, drop-offs, and, of course, the twenty foot oven shafts, sunken and reclaimed by the earth, with scant evidence of those incinerated. But once, looking closely, I find a tiny fragment that crumbles in my fingers. It is, I think, an unborn baby's clavicle—that small.

If time sweeps away the names and ranks and affiliations of the murderers—"Germans, just Germans," as villagers told me, regardless if it was Romanian gendarmes, Einsatzgruppen, Volksdeutsche police, VoMi SS officers, Kalmuck SS, or once, Luftwaffe pilots who flying overhead saw a massacre underway, and landed to take part—the techniques of those murders remain, embedded like grenade fragments in local memory. It's older Ukrainian men, usually, who describe these cruel techniques so specifically I wonder if their fathers and grandfather weren't eyewitnesses, or even participants.

One technique: the killer shoots a mother holding a baby, so both die from the same bullet. Another: the killer lifts a child or baby by the hair, shooting it with a pistol. At times, it seems I recognize the handiwork of specific killers, like SS officer T. or local Volksdeutsche commander R., or Max Drexel, the infamous Einsatzgruppen officer, whose own daughter, on learning postwar what he had done, disowned him.

Wherever we go, Ukraine's bloody past seems on display. One day, a Soviet veteran, an elderly man in a heavy wool suit coat laden with war medals, sits in the shade of a wilted tree telling me about the Jews of Gorivo.

"Sixty souls. Killed up in those hills," he says. "By the Fascists."

There is a hot wind. The old man takes off his old slouch cap. Beads of sweat in his matted grey hair. On my map I search unsuccessfully for Gorivo, an agricultural settlement of Jews in the middle of Transnistria.

Mikhail asks the old veteran about his war medals. The Great Patriotic War, the old man says, where he met his wife, at Stalingrad. Rest her soul. He trained dogs for that battle, and also for Kursk, the greatest tank battle the world has ever known.

He explains the process. First the dogs were starved, then fed with food placed under a military tank, so they associate the tanks with food. On the battlefield, fitted with metal antennae detonators, they run under the Nazi Panzers, and satchels of dynamite strapped around their bodies explode.

"My dogs were the world's first suicide bombers," he says proudly.

Sometimes I feel like Chichikov, the main character in Gogol's novel *Dead Souls*, who travels Czarist Ukraine, buying up rights to deceased serfs. His is an idiosyncratic journey, with humor giving comic relief to an earnest task. In that way—except for an occasional strange person we come on, like the wizened Yoda-like woman with her multicolored cloak and gnarled staff who scares Pavel and points us in the wrong direction—Chichikov's journey is mostly unlike my own. Even the musical and multisyllabic names of the sites we visit, that roll off of Mikhail's tongue, like Novopavlivka, Babinka Balka, Staraja Balka, and Akmachetka, don't quite ease the sadness of what happened at them. But at times, it's true, there I feel a sense of peace and hope, like the day I hear, bursting from the reconstructed church tower of my grandmother's ancestral village, the clear, liquid sounds of bells, and I ask Mikhail, "What's the Ukrainian word for bell?"

"*Kolokola, kolokola,*" he says, repeating the word whose sound mimicked that of the liquid bells.

Like Chichikov, I keep a record, filling page after page of my field journal with my deteriorating scrawl, and as the sites blur into a ragged pastiche of sunflower fields, of villagers with metallic teeth, of ugly ravines that slash the countryside, I scribble this nearly illegible sentence: "To visit all the massacre sites in Transnistria would take a small lifetime."

***

RAIN

My second apartment in Nikolaev encompasses nearly an entire single floor of a late Soviet-era apartment building, different balconies offering views of neighboring high-rises and weeded fields filled with slabs of buckled cement.

143

My new apartment's security is tenuous at best. Unlit hallways and a security man absent from the front door make me nervous about break-ins, and I fear arrest, or even blackmail, for possessing documents Dmitri regularly brings me from secret police archives.

My first weeks in the new apartment, I carry those documents in my latched satchel through that wasteland of fatigued cement and weeds on my way to teach at National University. On the way, I'm harried by a pack of skinny, predatory looking dogs that grows larger each day, and seems to sense something in my satchel, the interrogation records, I tell myself, some of which, I'm sure, are spattered with blood and human matter.

One morning I forget to pack my lunchtime sandwiches, and for the first time in two weeks, on my usual walk to the National University, there are no dogs anywhere. Strange, I think—until I realize it's because I'm not carrying food in my satchel. That brief drama of the hungry dogs, now in hindsight, is just one of a series of early indications about my distressed state of mind, all of which I ignore.

About this time, I make a shattering discovery, or more accurately, Alexa, my student from National University, does. She's a dark-haired intelligent beauty with an expressed interest in Ukraine's dark history, which worries me. I fear that her vibrant personality may be affected, especially if she translates some of the horrific documents I handle daily.

"Just allow me to try," Alexa importunes me again one day after class. "I do good work from you."

"Okay," I finally relent, handing her what I think is innocuous material from the archives concerning a large, rural collective farm called New Amerika.

"Let's see how you do with this first batch," I say.

Which is why we arrange to meet that Saturday at a cafeteria near the National University. With rain cascading in glossy sheets against the windows, she'd shown up in the entrance, shaking her umbrella, sending raindrops in a luminous scatter, and after she slides into the booth across from me, we sip hot tea and talk about her education and prospects. Given a chronically high unemployment rate in the wobbly democracy of Ukraine, not to mention rampant corruption, and Putin's invasion threats (as I write this, the threat has become an invasion), how will she ever secure a stable future? I'm more worried than she is, it appears.

"Dr. Vossler, I have brought the translations."

The sheaf of papers she hands across the table are immaculate, stapled, double-spaced and errorless, and as I glance over the material I feel my stomach constrict.

"These are the keelers," Alexa says, pointing a polished fingernail at a list of Volksdeutsche policemen. "A dozen of them."

That's the shattering discovery. That the translated documents reveal, in addition to the main Rastadt police, another group of prolific killers, also under Hartung's overall jurisdiction, from a nearby hamlet, New Amerika. The Soviets executed several of them in the 1970s.

"Here are the places where they did the mordering, and how many they mordered," she says, handing me a list of villages, hamlets, and collective farms in Eastern Transnistria, and the estimated Jewish victims at each:

Novay Uman—a hundred people were shot.

Suha Balka—350 people were shot.

Mostove—three hundred people were shot.

New Amerika—three hundred people were shot.

Shevchenko—a hundred people were shot.

Podoleanca—three hundred people were shot.

Stepanovka—360 people were shot.

Yastrabino—six hundred people were shot.

Novay Ilinka—189 people were shot.

Babina Balka—six hundred people were shot.

The local Volksdeutsche police commander, Alexa tells me, who wore a field cap with a death's-head insignia, starved hundreds of Jews in a makeshift ghetto in New Amerika. He also raped and murdered twelve- and thirteen-year-old girls in his custody, crimes for which he was convicted.

"I didn't sleep after translating that document," she says. "Some of these men were real monsters."

I give her background on the decade before the Nazi invasion, which unraveled the character of Ukrainians and Volksdeutsche alike. It was, I tell Alexa, such profound starvation that government food stores—where grave robbers traded gold and silver for bread—posted large public service announcements on their walls: "It's a crime to kill and eat your children."

Once people are dehumanized, I say, primed by witnessing cruelty, they seek scapegoats, and are even more cruel, in turn, to their own victims. I get lost in my arguments, and don't know if I'm talking about Bolsheviks or Nazis or Volksdeutsche police or all of the above. It sounds like I'm excusing what the Volksdeutsche policemen did—like I'm saying the two immense blood lettings, the Holodomor and the Holocaust, are related, one birthing the next. Truth is, I have no real answers, and after months clambering in ravines and ovens, all I can offer are several reductionistic points. Meanwhile, Alexa's eyes glaze over. She is obviously thinking about something else.

"Vhat you think, Dr. Vossler?" Alexa says, finally.

"About what?" I say.

"Is possible you take me to New Amerika, to the massacre pits there?" She mispronounces the word massacre, putting the accent on the middle syllable— masSAKer.

"We'll see," I say. "We'll see."

As she strides away, umbrella angled against the cold rain, I feel suddenly protective of her, wishing I'd told her what was so often told me, "Oh child, forget the past." I already know that when I do go to New Amerika, to its murder ravines, I won't take Alexa.

***

I've long been intrigued by New Amerika. I've often seen the name of the hamlet on my map of Transnistria, assuming it'd been named in honor of turn-of-the-century Volksdeutsche who went to the Dakota prairie. I never do go there, even after someone at National University urges me to visit the broad, fertile valley, to see its immense sunflower fields of astonishing brightness, because it has nothing to do with my research, or so I think.

During Soviet 1930s, the hamlet was part of the Lunacharskiy State Grain Farm, named after the first Soviet commissar of education—a Marxist critic and playwright and Trotsky supporter. Its vast, rolling fields produced huge quantities of grain, which, dumped on Western markets, helped finance Soviet industrialization and erased the already scant Depression-era profit margins of the Dakota farmers, close relatives of the Soviet Volksdeutsche in the collective. Only after the German invasion, and after its Ukrainian population was moved, was it renamed New Amerika.

Two different times I draw close to New Amerika, once at Suha Balka, and once at Novaya Uman. Both times, a nervous Anatoli, fearful of damaging his car, argues me out of going

147

either place, just a valley or two away, claiming, "Not good. Too many bad roads." Four months after I learn from Alexa's translations concerning the New Amerika police unit, I finally go there, by myself.

It's near the end of a long, hot Ukrainian summer, with fields of dry corn and sunflowers crackling in the parched heat, and dust clouds billowing like horizontal cyclones behind my rental car.

New Amerika's mayor, metal teeth flashing, explains how the Jews were ferried in lorries, twenty at a time, from collective buildings for chickens where they were held, to the edge of a sloping farm field, a mile away. During an afternoon, several hundred Jews were executed—just one of a dozen such actions by the New Amerika police.

Visiting New Amerika reminds me I've not seen Alexa in a while. Perhaps she has dropped out of the university. Still, I feel I've done the right thing, not involving her. Look at what it has done to Laryssa and Anatoli and other adults, with better coping mechanisms. Or to me, I tell myself that day, stumbling along this winding, labyrinthine ravine at New Amerika, knocking loose clots of damp earth, crazed and claustrophobic. How could this be good for any young person?

When I check the New Amerika killers against the list of Volksdeutsche executed in 1937 and 1938, I find that, just as with the Rastadt and Vorwerk policemen, nearly all lost fathers, grandfathers, uncles, and brothers, executed or exiled on trumped up charges as kulaks and wreckers of the Soviet farm economy. Small wonder, then, that the Nazis could use their smoldering resentment and that so few protested when they were ordered to join the local police.

Others in New Amerika, however, just as in Hoffnungstal, Neudorf, and other Volksdeutsche villages, made an initial and intense outcry against the murder of the local Jews in the fall of 1941:

At first, a gathering of the inhabitants of New Amerika was called, and once Hartung, the SS commander from Rastadt, arrived, the question was asked by a villager as to why the Jews were to be shot. Hartung repeated that since the time of WWI, the Jews had acted as traitors to the German army and state, giving victory to the Germany's enemies. He says many other things about how bad the Jews were. That was the only time that Hartung ever spoke to us, simple policemen, about the crimes of the Jews against the German nation.

In fall of 1942, many local Volksdeutsche remained *aufgeregt* (distressed) by the murder of the Jews, which was why the New Amerika police were ordered to mask the noise of continuing gunfire, and as one eyewitness pointed out:

In New Amerika, they held the Jews in ruined houses. I don't remember if these Jews helped with the harvest. The number of Jews I also don't know. I do know there were Stalin tractors set up near those houses, and their motors were allowed to run.

My house lay perhaps five hundred to eight hundred meters from the ruined houses, so that I clearly saw what was happening. At that point it was clear that the Jews would be shot. Before that, nothing was known about if they would be murdered. From my house I watched the Jews climb out of the lorries, guarded by the policemen from the village, who carried out the murders.

The commander of the police unit I didn't see, since I wasn't allowed to leave my house. I heard later from some policemen, but from whom I can no longer say, that the SS officers Hartung, T., and R. were all there. We never talked about the number of Jews murdered. It was, as others have testified in the neighborhood of 350. And yes, I also heard that the commanders of the police unit actively took part in the murders. I did hear that at this execution R. was said to have shot a small child. How did I learn this? I will tell you. I was arrested by R. one Sunday for refusing to work, and held in a room in the school in New Amerika, I overheard a conversation in the main room where the police unit gathered. R. had coaxed a mother to give her small child to him, to care for it, he said, but when the mother handed it to him, R. held the baby high with his left arm, and with a pistol in his right hand shot the infant.

The final mass murder at New Amerika, I think, took place in the fall of 1942, just after Himmler's order to eliminate even those Jews engaged in agricultural labor. With the sunflower crop only partially harvested, the local Volksdeutsche commander told his five-man New Amerika police unit to gather the Jews from the local ghetto: "Just let them think they are going to work today. But we don't take them to work. Instead, we will shoot them."

***

WESSELOE

We pull over and stop on the weedy shoulder at the top of a long hill out of Mostove, where two gravel roads angle off the main road. Our map shows both roads lead to villages named Wesseloe. We wait to ask directions of a local man in a filthy coat churning slowly up the hill on an ancient bicycle, a large bag of walnuts strapped to the back.

Pavel and Mikhail take a smoke break, and I flip through an eleven-page confession describing a murder action at Wesseloe. It's from a former policeman arrested post-WWII in Akjubinsk in the Ural Mountains, by the name of Andrew E., a direct relative of a retired Dakota German farm couple I used to work for. After reading of my Fulbright Fellowship in

150

the local newspaper, they'd sent me a card, saying that they'd pray for me in Ukraine, that I should seek the truth. "Let God guide you," they wrote.

When the bicyclist arrives at the top of the hill, and we ask directions to the massacre site, he jerks his grimy thumb to the right, toward the larger Wesseloe, still just a hamlet, at the end of several miles of washboard-like road.

A local man with a piebald complexion and threadbare suit coat agrees to guide us. He rides with us outside of the village, to a long collective building of white limestone blocks. It's a former sheep barn inside which several hundred Jews were held, and around which, if E's confession is accurate, the police unit bedded down for the night, while the rest of the Jews were held in chicken barns in the village. Details that indicate to me the massacre was sizeable, at least four hundred.

Next to the sheep barn is a roofless, ruined house where the victims were taken in small groups, and forced to undress. I go inside—there is no door—and stand within the swagged mud walls, the layers of sloughed plaster and detritus shifting under my feet. Then we drive to the ravines, half a mile or so, the distance the naked Jews were taken in small groups, circled by armed policemen.

"They were once deeper," our guide tells us, as we stand there, and survey a series of ravines that slant off the higher roadbed where we stand.

Clutching at weed stalks, I slip and slide down the side of a ravine, my camera held high, weeds slapping and scratching at my clothing like invisible hands, and when I hit the bottom, I am bobbling my camera like a wide receiver, an instant which gets inexplicably winked into permanence. Two years later, an indistinct photo turns up in my files, one I don't remember, snapped from a lower angle, and showing several blurry figures, Volksdeutsche police on a raised road-bed, awaiting more victims? After some checking, I learn from my field journal that the photo's date coincides with my skid into that Wesseloe ravine, so that it really shows my driver, interpreter, and guide, sharing a smoke there. Still, it's an abiding mystery, or seems so, that an accidental photo would reveal what dying Jews might have seen.

"There is an eyewitness in the village," the piebald man says as I climb from the ravine onto the roadbed. "I will take you to him."

We follow the path the killers took, lorries stuffed with Jewish clothing, into Wesseloe. On the way I read E.'s description of the end of the massacre:

> Shortly before the end of the shooting, Liebl, S., and Z., the mayor, drove away in their personal autos toward Lichtenfeld, and the operation continued under J., the local Volksdeutsche commander. As happened at other times, the unit no longer shot as a group, but randomly, and during this time there was much crying and screaming and begging from the victims. Many asked to live, and said they were not guilty of anything. But we shot them anyway. The shooting ended about five o'clock in the afternoon…and afterward, we gathered in a woman's home on the edge of Wesseloe, washed our hands, ate a midday meal and drank homemade schnapps. Because there were so many policemen, we ate in two or three groups at the table.

This post-massacre mealtime at the far edge of the Nazi empire follows Himmler's instructions of 21 December, 1941 to his SS murderers in the eastern territories that there should be served a meal "at which alcohol should not be abused… and at which the men should sit and eat at table in the best German domestic style…It is the holy duty of senior leaders and commanders personally to ensure that none of our men who fulfill this burdensome duty should ever be brutalized or suffer damage to their spirit and character in doing so."

Mikhail stops at a house with a blue gate, and a few minutes later our guide returns, helping along an older fellow, wobbly on his feet, exhaling a cloud of vodka and sweat.

"Here he is," the guide says. "The eyewitness."

"It's my seventy-sixth birthday," the old man says, giving me a bleary stare. "Will you join me?"

"I appreciate the offer, but no," I say.

We make small talk. Finally I ask him, "What do you know about the massacre near here in 1942? The one out at the ravines."

The old man speaks rapidly. As an eight-year-old, he watched a massacre and, much like Ivan at Bogdanovka, has lived a lifetime with the aftermath.

"I wanted to see what they were doing out there," he says. "So I went there."

"How close were you?"

"From here to your machine."

He points to our car. My eyes snag on the rutted earth. The car is just ten feet away. That close. The old man shudders. He rocks back and forth. Through Pavel he tells me that his wife, whenever she butchers a chicken or rabbit, does it out of his sight, cooking all meat thoroughly until it is crisp.

"Blood brings nightmares," he blurts out in epigrammatic fashion. His hands chop the air. It happened in the spring, he says, the muddy time. I think I hear the words *Niemtzi colonistas* (German colonists). But I can't be sure.

"Who were the killers?" I ask.

The old man's speech slurs. Jagged fragments of trauma in the deepest layers of memory.

"What is he saying?" I ask.

"Just a minute," Pavel snaps, annoyed.

The old man wrings his stubbled face in his hands, a strange, ritualistic cleansing gesture.

"He is saying," Pavel says, "that some Jews ran away."

The old man's mind leaps around. There were rapes. He gives the name of a local Ukrainian who used his own horse to hunt down those who run away, dragging them back to be shot. Other villagers threw bodies into the ravine and shoveled dirt over them. The earth heaved afterward. Not all the victims were dead.

"If I wasn't so drunk," the old man says, "I could tell you more."

"Who were the killers?" I ask again. "Can you describe them?"

"Nimetzki colonista," he says.

A shock goes up my spine. It's the first time I've heard an eyewitness, or anyone, say Volksdeutsche police were involved. Averting his face from me, Pavel scuffles his white tennis shoes in the dirt. He wants the old man to stop. He doesn't want to repeat the grisly details.

"What is he saying?" I say, irritated.

"He is saying…he is saying," Pavel blurts out, "that they shot the Jews up the ass. And other things."

"Where did they come from, the murderers?"

"From over there," the old man says, pointing vaguely to the north, in the general direction of Lichtenfeld.

"That's enough," Pavel says. "Let's go."

"Uniforms?" I say, though I know, or think, that except the Rastadters, most Volksdeutsche police wore civilian clothing. "Ask him about their uniforms?"

"He is old and drunk," Pavel says, exasperated.

The old man totters like a bowling pin. He thrusts out his arms to balance himself. He speaks of Wova, his best childhood friend, and Wova's mother, a beloved teacher named Christina, both murdered at the ravine.

"Wova's jacket was just like this," the old man says, pinching the piebald man's shirt. "Just like this."

"Ask about the uniforms," I insist to Pavel. "I think he misunderstood. Ask him what Wova's killers wore?"

The old man is like a sleepwalker, exploring an archaic catastrophe. He rocks back and forth.

"White uniforms," the old man says. "The ones who killed Wova wore white uniforms."

"White uniforms?" I say. "From Lichtenfeld?"

"Da, Lichtenfeld," the old man says, and when he does, I feel the direct connection between my dream of the white-uniformed soldiers that first spurred my research, and this book, which began to write itself in my thoughts.

***

SMOKE

I'm sitting on the front steps of my apartment building in Nikolaev, waiting for Mikhail. We are going to Jastrabino, one of many sites associated with SS Untersturmfuehrer Johann T., and in the ambient morning light, I'm glancing through T.'s folder, the thickest folder I've compiled thus far. He was Rastadt's second-in-command, in his mid-forties from the

Heidelberg area in Germany, a former street fighter and Nazi party hack, whose main responsibility, a number of people said his only responsibility, was organizing massacres.

T.'s folder is so replete with descriptions of his killing activities, that at intervals I glance up to get relief from the disgusting details, my gaze drawn across an interior courtyard to what seems a tableau of peasant patience from Ukrainian history. There, seated on a stool draped with a tattered sheepskin, in front of a small, tin-roofed shack, is an elderly watch-lady, her mouth moving, praying I think at first, until I realize under her ragged scarf she is talking on the mouthpiece of a cell phone headset.

T. was one of the most active killers in Transnistria. Overall, he orchestrated and participated in at least thirty thousand murders, not including fifty-four thousand victims at Bogdanovka, where he was also reportedly seen, pacing the perimeter of the killing grounds. Testimonies placed him at Podoleanca, Stepanovka, Babina Balka, Guthof Schewtschenko, Woltschoi Balka, Gradofka, Sucha Balka, and Rastadt, all of which I've visited, except for Jastrabino.

Volksdeutsche villagers described most of the SS commandants and their assistants in the two dozen Transnistrian districts in a satiric vein as bald, bad tempered, paunchy, and snaggletoothed. It's a far cry from the blond Nazi superman stereotype. That is how T. appeared, with his grandfatherly grey hair, like a retired clerk, more in accord with Hannah Arendt's phrase, "the banality of evil," but up close, as testimonies indicate, T.'s beaked nose and cadaverous face, gave him a vulture-like appearance, terrifying victims and the police under his command alike.

While Hartung often concluded massacres, using a machine pistol to mow down rows of Jews, like he did at Podoleanca and Woltschoi Balka, in a stuttering and terrifying Gotterdammerung of death, T. gravitated to killing the most helpless at point blank range, babies and children, and afterward their sick and weak mothers.

Waiting for Mikhail that morning, I find two incidents that document Volksdeutsche police under T.'s command refusing to murder Jews, one at Jastrabino, and the other at the ovens of Gradofka, which unfolded in the following manner:

Before being chauffeured away early in his personal auto by his driver, Hartung ordered T., and G., the trusted local Volksdeutsche commander, to complete the massacre, which had reached its midway point, typically a time when policemen rotated duties, and those overseeing the undressing, replacing the executioners near the lip of the oven. But not this time. There was a problem with this well-oiled conveyer belt of death, when two Volksdeutsche policemen, twenty-five-year-old friends Johannes W. and Florian E., sat down amid some heaps of clothing, rifles across their laps, and said:

"We are not going to shoot anyone."

This, one of the first rebellions, takes the assistant SS commandant aback. After conferring with the local commander, someone who had known these men for years, T. grabbed Johannes W. by the collar, leading him to the oven, where he "pushed [him] into the position from which [he] was to shoot." Still, the policeman refused, tossing his rifle aside, while T. cursed and fumed, and then, finally, with an angry wave of his pistol, ordered his driver to transport the two shirkers back to Rastatt.

Later that day, the two young policemen stood in Hartung's small, high-ceilinged office, crowded with several wheelbarrows heaped with watches and jewelry and gold from thousands of Jewish victims. The beefy-faced, gap toothed SS commandant behind his desk leveled an ugly stare at them and said: "You will be sent to a military tribunal in Landau for disobeying a direct order. Now get out of here." After that, the young policemen, no longer detailed to police activities, and never officially dismissed, remained fearful of reprisals, until the evacuation of Rastadt and Transnistria in early spring, 1944, when they no longer saw their SS commandants.

Waiting for Mikhail, I feel relieved to learn about the two Volksdeutsche policemen's refusal to murder at Gradofka, and for a while, at least, my spirits buoyed, for which I'm grateful, because on my visit to Jastrabino I'll need, I know, all the optimism I can muster.

***

Two hours later, after steering around potholes, and listening to Mikhail's out-of-tune renditions of an old WWII Soviet army tune, "We drive our machines through the bombs and the bullets," we arrive at Jastrabino, pick up the village mayor, a heavy blonde woman in a red sweater. Then head toward the murder site.

The homes we pass, set back from the street, have swirls and arabesques in their plastered exteriors, and curlicue decorative elements under the roof gables, none very Ukrainian-looking.

"Romanians," the mayor says, answering my question. "It was Romanians who built those."

When I ask, the mayor tells me about the yellow uniformed Romanian gendarmes and Volksdeutsche police in plain clothes and swastika armbands, who brought a long column of Odessa Jews, most carrying small bundles, to Jastrabino, housing them in chicken coops. There, the mayor tells me, they were held for a month, fed by the local population.

Mikhail steers his old Volga off the main road, and we chug up a muddy path onto a low rise, the same path along which the Jews, escorted by Germans with machine pistols, some riding motorbikes, were taken on the execution day.

158

"There," the mayor says, pointing to some underbrush, so I almost jump out of my skin. "Right there, some Jews escaped."

We surmount the hill, engine churning, the Volga tilting precariously, the narrow green tunnel of overarching trees and roadside bushes closing around us, so I feel a surge of claustrophobia. I hate small, narrow places.

"See," Mikhail says. "High clearance. We can go anywhere."

"Through bombs and bullets," I say.

Jastrabino is the least accessible of all the sites I've visited, and its rough terrain, buttes and dense undergrowth test Mikhail's driving ability and my patience. We go up a rise, down another, and after a series of spine-jarring jolts, we finally come to a halt.

The mayor leads the way on foot. We sidle along, taking small steps to negotiate the downward slope; on the way I grasp several bushes, and as their stalks slide through my fingers, I see the bushes have red berries, the color of blood, and strangely elongated, the shape of bullets, a disconcerting image, like the burrs and cockles on our clothing, that sticks with me as we slip and slide down to the low-lying area.

"Some Jews climbed onto the top of this well," the mayor says, pointing to a small brick structure which caps the well. "They held up their gold and shouted 'Long live Stalin,' then leapt into the well, so the Fascists wouldn't benefit."

The ideological overtones of the mayor's story, and the logistics of a human being leaping down this narrow shaft, make me uneasy. Would someone even fit in there? There are various accounts. One says the Jews were shot in open pits, another says in tunnels, a third, an archival document, shows cross sections of five wells dug, and indicates a postwar Soviet excavation found one well shaft completely stuffed with clothing. A fourth account claims the Jews were machine-gunned, bodies falling into pits, children jumping in afterward—a nightmare scenario that makes my heart fling seizures, because after the pits were covered, the earth moved, which means the children were buried alive.

Two things are quite certain: onlookers gathered behind an embankment watched, and policemen from Rastadt and New Amerika used yard-long wooden cudgels to force the Jews from where they undressed, under a railway arch, to where they were shot. These accounts contradict one another, or seem to. If the bodies were burnt, how was it possible the children were buried alive? And perhaps the bodies were thrown into tunnels or pits or wells or some combination thereof, which indicates, I think, multiple massacres.

"People grew ill from the stench of the smoke," the mayor says.

"But the village is two miles away," I say, feeling queasy. "Was there that much smoke from the bodies?"

"Yes, that much smoke," the mayor says, shrugging her heavy shoulders. "It smelled of hair and bone."

The mayor and Mikhail and Pavel talk quietly off to one side. About me, I imagine, this strange American, intent on unearthing ghosts. It's a recurring paranoia I usually ignore, or stave off, by combing the ground for bone fragments and shell casings, pacing distances for the rough maps I sketch in my field journal, or taking photos.

The Jastrabino site, a low-lying area, where billowing smoke choked victims and perpetrators alike, seems a worse hell than even Gradofka, whose ovens are located on a higher, windswept area. Burying children alive here is what one source says contributed to a revolt, just a handful of Volksdeutsche police, to be sure, but a possibility to which, as I pace the killing site, half expecting to see T.'s long, lanky figure, striding through the scrub brush, I find myself clinging.

Single file, we go up the slope, ahead of me, the mayor, who when she reaches the bushes with the bullet-shaped berries, presses her hands against her heavy hips, like Masha on my first visit to Gradofka. When was that, three years ago? How many sunflower fields, spine-jolting rides, and ravines and ovens between then and now?

Crowded again into our vehicle we retrace our path. We grind up the incline, go back into the green tunnel, past where some Jews escaped, and, finally, spill out onto the street of Jastrabino. We thank the mayor, and drop her at her home, and when she gets out, I see her red sweater, and think, she'll be busy picking off all those burrs and hay needles.

We start back to Nikolaev. Dusk falls over the steppe. On the way, we stop at a shabby roadside stand. Small, dried river fish, laid out in rows on a makeshift table, plastic bottles of smoky-colored honey, which the elderly proprietor, another shawled woman with a cell phone, offers at a cut rate price, but I decline, even though I love honey, knowing that each time I'll see or use that honey, I'll think about smoke.

***

DIRT

"You need to see these," Dimitri says, waving a sheaf of papers when we meet again at the outdoor cafe.

He hands me a list of Lichtenfeld policemen detailed to the murder pits. I scan down the column of names.

"You look like you just saw a ghost," Dimitri says.

"I did," I say.

"A name on the list?"

"Wilhelm Y."

Y. is my mother's maiden name and Wilhelm is my brother's first name and also the middle name of an uncle.

"It's a shock to see our family naming tradition reflected in a secret police document in Ukraine," I say.

"You mean you are shocked to learn a relative killed Jews," Dimitri says.

"Something like that."

I chatter about everything but the name on that list. Compulsively. About my mother's clan, hardworking Dakota farmers. About their congenital sweet tooth, eating cookies from ice cream containers that doubled as field lunch boxes. About their quiet fun, checkers and board games, but not the dancing or gayety of their prairie Catholic neighbors. About their height, six feet, tall for Volksdeutsche, and their blue-eyes, which reflects their Silesian German origins.

"They sound like good SS police material," Dimitri says.

"You mean physically," I say quickly.

"Is it hard to imagine this Wilhelm murdering Jews?"

"Of course," I say, in no mood to discuss my killer relative, and since Dimitri leaves for Crimea the next morning, we leave the cafe, parting ways early.

In my apartment, I scroll through several old letters on my computer screen, letters from the Y. clan in Rohrbach and Lichtenfeld, my ancestral villages, to my Dakota relatives. As the new collective system was forced onto the Volksdeutsche in the early 1930s, the Y.'s, avoiding even the indirect mention of the imposed starvation and the arrests, instead solicited advice by mail from their American kin, more advanced in terms of technology, asking how long a tractor lasts, and if it was worthwhile for their local Soviet collective to buy one, and if one of the uncles there in America, could inquire about the costs of shipping a tractor to Ukraine.

Then I find the Wilhelm Y. letter, written in the early 1930s, a decade before being detailed to the murder pits, in which he asks a favor. "Could one of you send a Bible with flaps, to carry to the fields and read during breaks, but small," he said, so it could be secreted, I'm sure, from his communist overseer. If this fellow's father immigrated to the prairie, he'd have been born in a crude *semeljanka* (sod home) on the Y. farmstead southwest of my prairie hometown, and like the rest of my inveterate church-going clan, like my uncle on the family homestead, raising wheat and barley and ushering in our evangelical church for half a century, ending up, like other relatives, at our house in New Odessa during Easter or Christmas or other holidays, just another white-foreheaded farmer perched on our doily-covered couch and armchairs, quaffing my mother's coffee and complaining in German dialect about the vagaries of Dakota weather. Instead, he ended up at the murder pits.

Dmitri's other documents indict an entire murderous cast of characters from the Lichtenfeld headquarters: the fanatical but weak-stomached SS commandant Franz Liebl; his SS assistant S., known to demonstrate on living victims, the correct manner of murdering ("Like this," he screamed. "This is how you must shoot a person"); Z., the reluctant mayor bullied into participating in massacres; J., the brutal local Volksdeutsche commander; and his diminutive squad leader D., an assiduous killer in his own right, to whom Liebl presented an award at a special ceremony, an alarm-equipped pocket watch, "for all your good work."

It's troubling to learn, through a policeman's confession, that when Liebl departed massacres early, leaving J., and D. in charge, the massacres spun into an orgy of torture, rape, and sadism, with bodies scattered all over and local villagers searching the corpses and dumping then into the ovens. It's even more troubling to learn that both times the policeman confessed a list of his fellow perpetrators, the name of my relative, Wilhelm Y., appears in direct proximity to D.'s.

Wondering if I'm seeing connections that don't exist, I think of calling Dmitri, always so level-headed, but it's after midnight, so I call Don in the United States, where it's eight hours earlier. He's my closest American friend, a retired teacher with a curious mind, someone with whom I grew up and share relatives on both the prairie and in Transnistria.

We've not spoken since I moved to Ukraine, so I give him a rambling update of my visits to ovens and ravines, to which he listens intently, asking pointed questions. But when I describe my descent into the Wesseloe ravine, the list of Lichtenfeld police, and then mention that Y. is also implicated in the murders, the usually affable Don falls quiet.

"Read me that list again," he says.

I recite the policemen's last names. It's a mantra from our childhood. Names of classmates, friends, Main Street business owners, family members. It occurs to me, suddenly, that he may not want to know this, but I'm like Laryssa, caught up in that LaBrea tar pit of Doroschenko's awful descriptions.

"It sounds like the New Odessa phonebook," Don says, finally.

"I know."

"You better have your ducks in a row. If you go public with this…"

"I'll never publish the real names," I say.

"If you go back home to New Odessa, people there will grind you up into *Schwatamaga*." (Headcheese.)

"Do you really think so? For what?"

"For digging up all this dirt."

That phrase—digging up dirt—haunts me for days. It's a reference to a Dakota German attitude—that the past should be forgotten, that silence was better than speaking about the dead, who are not here to defend themselves. That silence spared those of us in later generations from the traumatic events, the systematic starvation and execution of our relatives in Soviet Ukraine, which our grandparents knew from letters and their German language newspapers. That silence also kept us from thinking about ourselves as victims. But it left most American Volksdeutsche—I included myself in that category—mostly ignorant about our ethnic history, which was, for us growing up, so riddled with lacunae and empty places that were filled with what seemed embellishments, like the oft-mentioned great grandfather serving as a personal bodyguard to the Czar, or how none of our ancestors remained behind in Ukraine, or how some Volksdeutsche were actually of Jewish ancestry. Who wouldn't prefer such romantic ideas, to the succession of tragedies that befell the Volksdeutsche people, and required a broad knowledge of geography and history and politics to understand?

My friend Don knows enough of our complicated and tragic history to be troubled by what I've uncovered, that much I know, and it contributes to my own sense of guilt and shame—a feeling that I'm betraying my own background. Those feelings are, I tell myself, vestigial emotions, remnants of old ethnic attitudes, like the ghost pain in an amputated limb. Anyway, I tell myself, in uncovering Holocaust killers with Dakota Volksdeutsche last names, the worst has already surfaced. But I'm wrong about that.

***

GHOSTS OF TRANSNISTRIA

I'm wondering why I didn't stay in bed. It's my day off from teaching, and though a Ukrainian winter is benign compared to subzero Dakota, I'm in the Nikolaev archives, blowing into my closed fists to warm my fingers. Around me, in the long, narrow, badly lit room, is a chaos of combustible material, sagging file cabinets, and stacks of yellowed folders

165

that any self-respecting fire marshal would automatically declare a fire hazard.

It's a slog, shuffling through documents that another human might never again set eyes on. But I proceed carefully, trying not to miss even the tiniest clue, which might be the Ariadne's thread into the labyrinth of the past. It's labor intensive work, like that done by young boys I'd seen once in Pakistan, cracking fist-size rocks with small hammers, rock by rock by rock, doing their part to build a roadbed.

Whenever I despair, which is often, I remind myself it's markedly easier doing detective work on Transnistria seventy years ago, as opposed to what my archaeological training prepared me for, using slash marks on animal bones and wear patterns on human dentition to reconstruct events from centuries or even millennia earlier.

My layman's grasp of events in Transnistria is elusive at best, despite all the documents and testimonies I have pored over, despite all of my site visits. In my worst moments, the three years of German Occupation seem a terrible hurricane of death, the two hundred Volksdeutsche villages situated at the exact dead center of that storm.

Each day, before I climb down into the murder pit that is Ukraine's past, I pray for guidance. I turn my worries to a Higher Power, remind myself to do the best I can, and if I uncover or don't uncover anything, *so isch's halt* (that's how it will be). It's God will. In that way, I see myself as working within the larger pattern woven by His hand. Researchers rarely, if ever, talk about the role of faith in their work, though they may know it by its other, more superficial delineations, like serendipity, or luck, or intuition, and that morning in the chilly archives, at least one of those terms applies to me.

At first glance, it's just another document—out of hundreds of High German documents from the early 1960s stacked around me on the tables. Just another document of mostly innocuous information shuffled by West German bureaucrats to their Soviet counterparts during a new wave of investigations and trials. It doesn't seem to be anything that concerns Transnistria. Until the hook of history reaches out and grabs me, and I recognize the mailing address for Nazi Transnistria: *Feld Post* (field post) Number 10 520.

Below it is this explanation: "Under this unremarkable field post number the 'Sonderkommando R' of the VoMi camouflaged its annihilation of fifty thousand Jews from Odessa."

It's an extortion document, I realize, aimed at SS officers who built successful postwar civilian careers, including SS General Hoffmeyer, the former VoMi head who by the early 1960s was manager of a powerful bank, Bundes Deutscher Osten, whose chairman at the time was the powerful prime minister of West Germany: Oberlander.

The extortionist, Walter V., is a forty-year-old businessman and former SS officer, in charge of wartime wireless communications between the main VoMi office on Unter den Linden in Berlin and its Transnistrian headquarters in Landau. As a former businessmen, he also supervised a canteen/lounge on the VoMi grounds. Both of these positions provided him access to a range of information, from formal communiques, written documents, and personal conversations with those engaged in the Holocaust in Transnistria.

During quarterly meetings in Landau, at what was more or less a convocation of genocidaires, the SS district commandants and their SS aides gathered, giving reports, trading information, learning what Himmler and VoMi headquarters required of them, and, afterward, drinking in the canteen. That was where Walter V. plied them with alcohol, listened to their drunken confessions, and for their return journey provided the SS commandants with crates of wine and vodka and beer and other spirits, to drink themselves, or dispense to their policemen, to lessen the burden of killing Jews. It was not, however, from any of the SS commandants that the extortionist gathered personal information about the slaughter of the Jews, but from a young, blonde National Socialist driver with a Norwegian surname, R., whose name appears numerous times in testimonies and documents often in conjunction with the Rastadt commandant Hartung and several times in conjunction with the killing of babies. R. was at the Bogdanovka ravine, at the Gradofka ovens and was likely at the burning of several thousand Jews at the horse-stables in Rastadt. Later, transferred to the Selz district, he became a driver for Obersturmfuehrer Paschowell, an overall "swine-*hund*" as one villager later described him, who was deeply implicated in the murder of Jews and said to have burned down houses in which Jews hid, but he was never convicted of war crimes.

One day in the latter part of 1942, the young driver, R., confessed to the extortionist over drinks what he knew about the Jews, whether men, women, or children, taken by the hundreds and thousands onto the steppe and led to old chalk-ovens. There, after they undressed, they were shot through the neck, their corpses thrown into the ovens and burnt, their clothing divided up among the Volksdeutsche villages. At one point, the young driver spilled the contents of a rucksack onto the table, gold rubles, rings, watches, and jewels—a small fortune, just part of the plunder in Hartung's wheelbarrows. The young man's intent, however, was not clear. Did he want to demonstrate to the older SS officer, Walter V., that Hartung was stealing Jewish property that belonged, as per regulation, to the Nazi state? Was it to even a personal score with the aggressive SS commandant he chauffeured around? Or did he want the man plying him with drinks to fence the material?

After the war, Walter V. assembled the brief but damning chronology of the VoMi's activities, basing his accusations on those private conversations with the young driver and the radio and shortwave communications that came across his desk, into the extortion document I hold in my hands that chilly morning in the archives.

It's what I've long sought and long feared to find, these cogent paragraphs which summarize the brief but bloody history of Transnistria. And as I read over the stages, which, in effect, transform the Volksdeutsche police into murderers, a terrible sinking feeling comes over me:

—Summer, 1941, when German troops marched into Russia, SS Obergruppenfuehrer Lorenz, the VoMi head in Berlin, was tasked with setting up, as soon as possible, a commando unit to secure the welfare of a hundred and twenty thousand Volksdeutsche villagers in the Black Sea region.

—In August 1941, Sonderkommando unit R, led by SS *Standartenfuehrer* Hoffmeyer departed Germany. Their goal: Odessa, on the Black Sea.

—After looting museums, in which they found, among other things, a precious golden saddle which they sent to the VoMi head Lorenz in Berlin, they set to work in the Romanian controlled region of Transnistria.

—They divided the various German colonies they found, which carried familiar German names, like Landau, Speyer, Rastadt, and Johannesfeld, into a dozen districts.

—When long columns of Odessa Jews were forced into the vicinity of several German villages, SS General Hoffmeyer flew to VoMi headquarters in Berlin, returning with direct orders that the local police units in the German districts be used to annihilate the Jews.

—How many Jews were annihilated? After communications by this correspondent with the commanders involved, it was determined that in Hartung's Rastadt district thirty-six thousand Jews, and in Liebl's Lichtenfeld district, sixteen thousand Jews, were liquidated.

The extortion document I read in the archives that day troubles me because it includes only the number of Odessa Jews who were murdered. There is no reference to the two hundred thousand Romanian Jews later pushed across the Dniester River and, in part, also murdered by Volksdeutsche police. What also troubles me, from a personal point of view, is that the police of Lichtenfeld, my grandfather's birthplace, murdered sixteen thousand Jews. It's a staggering total for a small police unit from such an isolated hamlet. In 1926 it had only 420 people. But like so many other German villages across Transnistria, Lichtenfeld's male population had been repeatedly decimated, first by the deportations of the collectivization era, then by the starvation of the government created terror-famine of 1933, and finally by the wholesale executions in 1937 of Stalin's Great Terror.

That day, in the archives, a tremor of anxiety goes through me at this thought that Lichtenfeld's police unit would have been drawn from a limited manpower pool, from males too young to be shot in 1937, who by the time of the Nazi occupation, having lost fathers and brothers and uncles to Soviet repression, and in their late teens, were old enough, as police recruits, to do the Nazis' bidding. It's nothing I want to think about, because Lichtenfeld's small population increases the chance that my grandfather's relatives, still living there in the German Occupation, were detailed to the murder pits.

That day in the archives, with the extortion document shaking in my fingers, as the Lichtenfeld slaughter of sixteen thousand is borne in upon me—I feel the Holocaust draw near and tell myself: "I will go to Lichtenfeld later. I will visit its ravines and ovens later. When I feel stronger. When my nerves are healed."

***

Not a few people enriched themselves personally in the Transnistrian Holocaust. Those with the opportunity to most benefit were the SS commandants in districts where

170

the greatest numbers of Jews were murdered, like Hartung at Rastadt, known to spread out and admire the newly acquired gold and jewelry on his desk, and like another SS district commandant who mailed to his home in wartime Germany a certified package of three and a half kilos of gold and other valuables taken from murdered Jews.

Local squad commanders and Volksdeutsche mayors could also benefit, if they were present often at the ravines and ovens to access Jewish clothing and belongings. Sometimes arguments broke out. In New Amerika some policemen jockeyed to guard the victims just before execution, so they could be the first to search discarded clothing for valuables sewn into the seams, hidden in hollowed-out heels, or even secreted on the Jews themselves.

What happened to the rest of the Jewish gold? There is ample evidence that a lively trade in Jewish valuables developed in Odessa. One former Volksdeutsche mayor— the same person who fired a salvo of shots at the retreating Soviets in 1941, at the start of the German invasion— assumed a position two years later in an SS affiliated concern in Odessa. There he sold various Jewish items, miniature gold Torahs, gold brooches, and other valuables acquired from the numerous massacres in the district where he was once mayor. Later, in postwar Germany, he used his illicit gains to finance his own business concern of buying and selling milk.

Some gold was used, as per orders of Sonderkommando R leader Hoffmeyer, to fix the teeth of his SS men. In January 1944, after the Soviet breakthrough on the Bug River, and knowing Transnistria would be evacuated, Hoffmeyer had a chestful of gold, of rings and chains and watches packed up and sent via personal currier to Berlin, to the home of his superior, Obergruppenfuehrer Lorenz. There, the stolen Jewish gold, marking the VoMi's murderous presence in Transnistria, joined the priceless golden saddle looted from the Odessa museum at the onset of the VoMi's purported welfare mission for the Volksdeutsche three years earlier.

***

Several days after my archive visit, I go to a Chinese restaurant in Nikolaev, where I meet my new friend Jeremy, a talkative Missourian in his early twenties. I'm relieved that he asks no questions about my research. Over supper, we talk about his matchmaking business, pairing Ukrainian ladies and American men. "Ukrainian women are like kittens," he says, speaking from experience, he added, having married a Ukrainian woman himself.

"You marry their whole family," Jeremy says. "I call her father Dad, like he is my own father. Which, in addition to my American father, he actually is."

With Jeremy, I avoid politics. He thinks Bill Clinton is a cocaine fiend, and his view of American presidents, while at times accurate, is a tad extreme: "There hasn't been an honest one since Lincoln," he told me once.

We are joined by Jeremy's friend, Gilad, a shaven-headed Jew from New York in his mid-forties, and sporting expensive snakeskin cowboy boots. At one point, Gilad pulls from his wallet a plastic-enclosed photo an elderly man with a bristling head of wild hair who looks more like the psychologist Fritz Perls than the new Messiah, which is how Gilad's sect views him.

"This is Schneerson," he says.

"I've never heard of Schneerson," I say.

"How can you not know about the Messiah?" Gilad says.

"Hey, I'm a prairie person," I say, defensive about my abysmal ignorance of Jewish history. "Do you know who Weivoka is, or Sitting Bull?"

An awkward silence settles over us, until Jeremy, a natural born peacemaker, tells Gilad I'm researching the Holocaust, and then things proceed more smoothly.

"I will introduce you to the rabbi at our synagogue," Gilad says. "He will help you."

The next day Gilad takes me to see the rabbi, and on the way I keep thinking, who could know more of the murder of Jews than a rabbi in Nikolaev? We stop at a solid, building, not far from the market where I shop. Its windows are reinforced by ornate metal bars meant to look like decorative elements, just like the side door through which we are buzzed, is reinforced with rivets and wide bands of metal, like the portcullis door of a medieval castle. Gilad and I go down a hallway with numerous turns, that leads us into the depths of the synagogue basement, and along the way we pass a large, cheap-framed photo of Schneerson, hanging askew on the wall.

"He was born in Nikolaev," Gilad says, nodding at the photo. "And then he became a famous mathematician."

Handing me a yarmulke, Gilad leads me in a large meeting room, where the rabbi, a short, dark haired man, seated at a table, is having an intense conversation, obviously about marital problems, with a young woman.

"You are on your own now," Gilad says.

While I wait to see the rabbi, I study a large wooden wall display of Ukraine. It shows the various provinces outlined in black, and each province has a large Jewish star, and within each star, the estimates, in tens of thousands, of Jews murdered in WWII.

When the rabbi finally approaches, and I realize he speaks little or no English, I try to explain in my stuttering pidgin of German dialect and Yiddish the research in which I'm engaged. He nods, I'm not sure he understands.

I talk about Gradofka, and holding my arms wide, as if hugging a thick tree, I demonstrate the circumference of the ovens in Gradofka. I tell him at least ten thousand Jews died in them. I've not spoken about my research for weeks, not since my call to my friend Don, and my voice sounds hoarse and disembodied, even angry, as I lead the rabbi to the wall display and stab my index finger in a triangular section of Transnistria whose corners are Lichtenfeld, Rastadt, and Worms.

"There were fifty thousand Jews from Odessa murdered here, maybe more," I say. "Not to mention the Jews from Bukovina and Bessarabia, yet this display shows nothing."

The rabbi gazes at me in surprise. How strange this American is, he seems to be thinking, yammering in barely decipherable German dialect about incorrect murder totals.

"I can see how difficult this research is for you," the rabbi says. "I can help you I think."

"I would appreciate that," I say.

"This weekend there will be a gathering here at the synagogue. Please come. To meet several elderly survivors."

The rabbi leads me through the dim hallway, back to the reinforced door, where I hand him my yarmulke, and we solemnly shake hands, his eyes searching my flushed features, which resemble, I'm sure, those of a tortured Dostoevsky character.

"Keep your spirit strong," he says. "This is important work. Remember that. And please come here this weekend, on Shabbat."

"Thank you," I say.

Before I go out the door, I already know I won't come. Because I couldn't bear to look the survivors in the face, for fear that they might recoil from or recognize, in my distinctly

Germanic features, in my distinctly Y. features, the face of one of their Volksdeutsche police tormentors.

***

Meanwhile, I spend countless hours reading verbatim transcripts of interviews with Volksdeutsche settled into new lives in Germany, interviews which take place in the early 1960s, as war crimes prosecutors, using local authorities, and questions derived from Jewish survivor accounts, troll for information about Transnistria.

Some refused to be interviewed, saying things like, "I am sick and want to be left alone." Others claimed too much time had passed to accurately remember anything. German investigators noted the broken mentality of some they interviewed, and Volksdeutsche witnesses cited ill-health, tumultuous lives, and the desire to forget starvation, exile, war, and executions. "Let us alone. We have suffered enough."

Some Volksdeutsche misunderstood some questions, either on purpose or by accident, issuing responses that sound like denials, evasions, and dodges. Some focus replies on local Jews murdered by Einsatzgruppen squads, not knowing about, or avoiding the fact that, Jews from Odessa and Romania were murdered in the vicinity of some villages. If pressed about discrepancies, some quickly backpedaled: "In my first testimony I thought you meant our Jews…not the ones brought into the area."

Other Volksdeutsche pleaded the complicated, much-intermarried state of German colonist life: "You have the wrong person. There were several people by that name in our village." And they were accurate in that assertion, for Volksdeutsche on the prairie and steppe were predictable, often repeating the same names from generation to generation, a difficult genealogical puzzle that at times defied attempts by investigators to locate witnesses and perpetrators. The Volksdeutsche *only* complicated things with vigorous denials: "These accusations are false." "No, I never saw…" "I only heard…" "It was common knowledge that in other places…" "You have the wrong person and wrong family."

For some Volksdeutsche, like the French after WWII, the testimonies were less about truth than evening old scores dating back to the Soviet 1930s, when, in a hothouse atmosphere of arrests and executions, the social fabric of the Volksdeutsche villages unraveled as "brother accused brother and neighbor, neighbor," to save themselves by collaborating with the Soviet secret police. When questioned postwar, many Volksdeutsche reflexively protected loved ones, in particular young policemen.

Some former policemen maintained that their main responsibility was to fight partisans. One interviewee says no policeman in his village ever murdered a Jew, and that he hadn't even seen any Jews, this despite the fact that his own home stood, as my village plat showed, on a main road along which—a scant few yards from his own windows—thousands of Jews passed to a temporary ghetto. Some Volksdeutsche admitted seeing columns of Jews brought to their villages, but couldn't or wouldn't identify the killers, not wanting to indict their own relatives, or because, as some claimed, in the terrible cold of 1942, the killers were unrecognizable, bundled in heavy clothing, scarves wound around their faces. Others blamed Romanian gendarmes, which was sometimes, but not always, accurate.

One witness testified that the February 1942, massacre at Novo Petrovka, north of Lichtenfeld, was done by the Romanians. It was true that the Romanians took a hundred Odessa Jews to the village of Krinitschki. It was, however, Volksdeutsche police who took the victims from the chicken barns where they were held to a large bomb crater near Novo Petrovka, and in gunfire that lasted until evening, murdered them then burnt the bodies. Evidenced, in part, by the fact that in postwar Germany, two Nova Petrovka Volksdeutsche police were convicted of those murders, serving several year sentences.

Several older Volksdeutsche women who'd worked as housemaids for wealthy Jews in Odessa offered the most detailed admissions. One lady offered a long list of perpetrators from her village, their full names, their fathers' full names, locations of policemen's homes, and descriptions of murder operations. Another admitted that after an execution near her village, she surreptitiously went there the next day, turning over bodies to see if policemen murdered Jews she might have known in Odessa.

Despite being Himmler's supposed darlings, Volksdeutsche suffering in Transnistria was very real. A number of SS commandants were active, ruthless Fascists, not afraid to use extreme measures, and German colonists were routinely beaten or bludgeoned to death. SS officers often demanded total obedience. Even for minor infractions, like not giving a Hitler salute, keeping a German officer waiting, or not mounting a horse quickly enough, German colonists often were ear boxed, cursed, even beat with shovels and hammers and clubs. Even police recruits were regularly abused. One police recruit was jailed, because his SS commander saw him attending the reopened village church; another was jailed for refusing to work in his fields on Sundays, a Volksdeutsche religious tradition.

Most Volksdeutsche felt helpless under the Nazis. What could they do? "Nobody asked us what we wanted," one village mayor said. All they wanted was to rebuild their lives and sleep again without fear of arbitrary arrest, the norm under the Soviets. "We were glad to be left alone after the fear of that time."

Most Volksdeutsche interviewees claimed ignorance of the VoMi or Sonderkommando R, the overall designation of the district command centers in Transnistria, even if the VoMi logo was conspicuously displayed on the numerous lorries that plied the roads of Transnistria, and on the identification placards outside of each of the two dozen district headquarters. "We had nothing to do with all that," they said. What they do remember, however, are the SS officers' names, where they came from in Germany, and, along a wide spectrum from beloved to hated, how they ruled.

The greed of their Nazi overlords was not lost on the Volksdeutsche. They saw these supposed members of the master race, squatting over corpses, using rifle butts to knock gold teeth from victims' mouths, or rifling through heaps of Jewish clothing at murder sites, even ripping apart bread the victims carried in backpacks, in a relentless search for gold and secreted valuables. The Volksdeutsche ridiculed the SS officers, behind their backs of course, and as part of a long-standing tradition of mockery, doled out nicknames to fit their idiosyncrasies. One SS officer was called Commander Lens, because of his photography hobby. Another officer, who rode a white stallion to executions, was known as the Horse Minister. And others were called the Berserker, the Jew Slaughterer, the Blood Licker. One SS officer, initially stationed in Landau at the VoMi headquarters, later assigned to a district post, was dubbed the Screamer, because of his outbursts. Once he stopped an execution, pushed a Jewish man to an oven, shot him in the head, and shouted: "That is how you kill a person."

The Transnistria that emerged from the Volksdeutsche testimonies, often seemed a cruelly imagined place, like the ghoulish island in Kafka's *In the Penal Colony*, and some SS commandants seemed as bad or worse than imaginary characters, like Kafka's island commander, or the Judge in McCarthy's *Blood Meridian*. Hartung at Rastadt, with his penchant to mow down Jews with his machine pistol, and his second-in-command T. with his affinity to kill the weak, both certainly fit the bill, and so did Dr. Eckhart, the shadowy SS commandant of the Speyer district.

Known to have several advanced degrees, and rumored to speak nine languages, Eckart was liaison officer with the Romanian authorities in Eastern Transnistria. While being chauffeured around his district, much like the death camp commandant in *Schindler's List*, he regularly and randomly shot German colonists, Ukrainians, and Russian prisoners of war. He was poisoned, so went the rumor, by a jealous SS colleague, and because of his early death, his name was omitted from the roster of VoMi SS men sought for postwar questioning, and so his crimes, as far as I could determine, also went uninvestigated.

For some reason Dr. Eckart's name remains with me. It's a matter of intuition. If I'd learned anything, it was to trust my intuition. To trust that an unknown hand just might be weaving a larger pattern in the fabric of my research, just as with Weingartner. As it turned out, Eckart's name did resurface later, in conjunction with my tracing a former policeman's bloody footprints back to my own Dakota hometown, back to my very own neighborhood, back to my very own family.

***

SQUARE FOOTAGE

Long after Ukraine, Suha Balka haunts me. It's a ruined, Soviet collective farm situated in a broad, flat valley, and whenever I see its name on maps or in documents, I feel myself back there again, on the morning of my visit, the strangling mists rising from its cratered acres.

"It looks like this place has been carpet-bombed," I say.

"No. Those are not from bombs," my guide Michael says, misunderstanding.

"I know. Murder pits," I say. "Carpet-bombed is a figure of speech."

Michael, my guide, is a tight-muscled Ukrainian with short grey hair, and as we pass mounds of rubble of collapsed Soviet collective buildings, we talk, however imperfectly, in our only common language, German.

He's a fan of all things German, even if earlier he'd confronted my interpreter for speaking Russian, not Ukrainian, and then, turning to me, had asked, "What language should be spoken in a nation?"

"A nation, to be a nation, should have a common tongue."

His face lights up, and I realize he's in favor of the Ukrainian language, as his country, a fledgling democracy, establishes its identity apart from Russia.

His father, it turns out, was in the Galician SS Division, Ukrainians fighting for the Nazis, a division known to slaughter Jews.

"My father said the Jews went passively to their deaths," Michael says.

And I wonder if his father's unit was at Suha Balka. Is that why he seems to know so much about the Jews killed here?

"Yes, I have heard that," I say. "But the Volksdeutsche were also passive."

The issue bears further exploration. Both groups—Jews and Volksdeutsche—were battered by Soviet totalitarianism into compliance by starvation and hopelessness. What could either group do but accept their role as victims? That applied to Volksdeutsche police too, handed a rifle by the Nazis.

"The Jews are not like us," Michael says. We stood near a long line of still-standing, preformed concrete pillars, hundreds of them, bleached white, like the ribs of a monstrous whale beached on the shores of history. "They didn't value their own lives."

It's a slur, a justification his father might have used, victim blaming to explain the eerie dignity with which some Jews went to their deaths, which unnerved the perpetrators, as

Biberstein, an Einsatzgruppen commander, mentioned at his Nuremberg trial.

We come to one pit—sunken in the middle—which stretches for some thirty feet. I stride the perimeter, where Jews knelt or stood, count my paces, and enter them in my notebook. Later I'll try to calculate the full square footage of earth moved, and man-hours needed to complete the grisly job. The previous summer, using a tiling spade, I'd dug a small grave in my tulip bed for my beloved cat, Torpedo. After just ten minutes of digging in the stubborn, root-clogged Red River Valley chernozem—the same rich soil as in Ukraine—I come away winded and dripping sweat. That's how I know the pits at Suha Balka required a huge expenditure of labor, likely by a commando of Jews, who were then, in turn, killed and buried in graves they'd dug themselves.

I'm confused by the overall numbers. The extortion document claimed thirty thousand were murdered in Rastadt's jurisdiction. Another document claimed twenty thousand in Rastadt and Suha Balca. It's not clear if those totals overlap, but my own rough figures—from multiple actions around Rastadt, the horse barns, skolomochil, Gradofka, and New Amerika, already total thirty thousand victims, and this vast acreage surely holds thousands more. So I know the overall total for Rastadt and Suha Balka totals well over thirty thousand.

Suha Balka is mentioned frequently in the testimonies. Not a good sign. That means lots of murders. There was a ghetto in Suha Balka to hold Jews brought from Kolosofka station, ten miles to the southwest, or from the ghetto and castle at Mostove, eight miles due west, or from Rastadt, close-by. That accounts, I think, for some of the hummocky areas, remnants of temporary structures grubbed into the earth. The ghetto dated earlier stages of the Holocaust, when agricultural Jews worked on collective farms, bringing in the harvest, and it also held gypsies, who fashion combs, which they sold for a meagre income. My grandmother's cousin, a twenty-year-old farmer, lived at Suha Balka during this period. After the war, his name was given to investigators as someone to be questioned. He'd be ninety now. His role at Suha Balka is unclear. A policeman guarding the ghetto? A farmer trying to stay alive?

We head back. Our shortcut takes us between narrow rows of just emerging crops. I glance over my shoulder. In the dew-laden grass, I see the dark marks of our passage, like hieroglyphics from this forgotten empire of suffering. At the car, Michael tells me of his uncle, who fled the Bolsheviks in 1919, perhaps alongside Leibbrandt, ending up in the United States.

"Can you check on him, on his family?" Michael says.

"Yes," I say, jotting the name in my notebook. "I will check."

His uncle's last name is the same as a conservative TV commentator with whom I share a strain of American political belief. It's an anti-Marxism, prevalent in Ukrainian, German colonist, and Eastern European diasporic communities inoculated by the wrenching suffering, and hundred million corpses generated in the twentieth century by such central-planning systems.

At one point, I kneel and gaze across the broad field. There—between the rows of just greening crops—I see a scatter of glinting bone fragments. I'm glad that, at the time, I couldn't yet put names and descriptions to the Suha Balka killers, to the trio of malefic baby killers from Rastadt, the cadaverous SS officer T., the young, blond National Socialist driver R., and the local Volksdeutsche commander G., rarely without his death's head cap; as it is, the place is haunting enough: witness my vague memory of finding a reference in a document of a sizeable revolt of Volksdeutsche police at Suha Balka. That revolt—the third one I've learned about—remains long in my thoughts, even gives me a semblance of peace. Yet when I try to track down the archival material, I find nothing. It's a dream, I realize, that I've somehow generated to cast a ray of light into the prevailing darkness of Suha Balka.

Late in the morning, we head to the nearby Esslinger hutor, the ruined family estate of a wealthy Volksdeutsche landlord whose family fled Bolshevik terror just after the Russian Revolution. On the way, in my field journal, I'm trying to compute the square footage of the largest pit, because numbers, if they aren't numbers of the dead, and just quantities of earth, are a good place to hide from blood and suffering.

So I compute and multiply, and find various possible totals of earth, until our vehicle hits a rut, and pitches so violently, which sends the tip of my pen skating wildly across the page—into an indecipherable and mutilated line.

***

MASTERS OF DEATH

Dimitri showed up at my apartment one day, waving a thick folder with large, black Cyrillic letters of the Soviet secret police—KGB—spelled out across its cover.

"I finally found them," he says.

"The confessions of Volksdeutsche police at Bogdanovka?" I say.

"Yes," Dmitri says. "After the war the Soviets interrogated the policemen in the Nikolaev prison."

"The redbrick one high on the bluffs above the Bug River?" I say. "No wonder I get the willies each time I see it."

"Prison Number One, it's called," Dimitri says. "Nobody ever escaped from there. It is like your prison…what is that place?"

"Alcatraz," I say.

"Yes, like Alcatraz."

"Men from Rastadt no doubt," I say, flipping through the confessions, and seeing the names of policemen.

"Not exactly. From villages near a collective farm called Vorwerk Bogdanovski."

"I've seen that place on a map. It's eight miles from Bogdanovka and thirty miles from Rastadt."

"Hartung and his second-in-command drove there to recruit these local men into the police," Dmitri says.

"Forced them to join the police, more like."

"That's true for most police," Dmitri says. "But the Vorwerker police unit might be different."

"Based on what?" I say.

"On the numbers."

"What numbers?"

"The numbers of murders. Which makes the Vorwerker police some of the bloodiest genocidaires of the Holocaust."

"That's a new word, genocidaire," I say, feeling depressed.

"You will get used to that word," Dimitri says.

"That's what Laryssa told me about the other word."

"What word was that?"

"Rastrelna," I say, the syllables rattling off my tongue. "Shooting."

***

Two days later, I'm crossing the flood plain of the Bug River south of Bogdanovka, retracing the bloody footsteps of the Vorwerk genocidaires.

Not that my newly hired duo—my driver, Valentine, a swarthy veteran of the Soviet invasion of Afghanistan and my new interpreter, Mitya, a university professor with a sense of humor and a penchant for open-weave leather sandals—know or care. Which is how I like it.

With Valentine and Mitya there's no carping about bad weather or bumper damage, like with Anatoli, no out-of-tune choruses of Soviet military songs like with Mikhail, no questioning the Holocaust like with Pavel.

We even tell jokes, as we wheel past long barns of several Soviet collective farms, and huge fields of drying sunflowers with drooping heads, which might seem like sacrilege, but which provides at least some relief. The joke I'm telling, if it can be called that, is based on the ten million deaths from Soviet collectivization policy in the 1930s.

Question: "What's the best way to get rid of lice?"

Answer: "Collectivize them. That way half will die, and the other half will run away."

Valentine chortles and Mitya nods. It's his turn now, so he unloads another worm joke, of which he has an entire repertoire.

Once upon a time, Mitya says, there was a worm family living in a pile of dung. One day the young son, sticking his head out of the dung, noticed a bright, shiny apple nearby, inhabited by another worm family.

"Why do we live in a pile of dung?" the son asked his father.

"Son," the father-worm replied, "nobody gets to choose his own homeland."

Valentine guffaws bitterly at the not-so-veiled reference to Ukraine. It's as if he is asking what sane person would choose Ukraine as a homeland. It's a cynical attitude I've encountered before, in soft, brainwashed American academics, and third world countries where the past a horror pit, and national pride is in short supply. In fact, Laryssa once told me that the 2005 Orange Revolution that brought democracy to Ukraine was obviously orchestrated by America, because no Ukrainian was capable of such organization.

"Where are we going again?" Mitya says.

"No place in particular," I say. "Out on the steppe to calm my nerves."

I feel terrible lying, but the truth, if I told it, would make me feel worse. Dealing with my own emotions, especially the feeling I'm betraying my own people by tracing the path of the Vorwerk genocidaires, is hard enough. Taking others to the murder sites, as my jaunts with Laryssa and Anatoli have taught me, unnerves me somehow, and only complicates my job.

"My brother-in-law has a resort in the Carpathian Mountains," Mitya insists. "You can relax there. And do whatever you Americans do to calm yourself."

"What do you do to calm your nerves?" I say.

"We drink," Mitya says. He snaps his forefinger under his jawline, the Ukrainian gesture for drunkenness. "Valentine and I go to my dacha outside of Nikolaev and get blind drunk."

"You think I should do the same?" I say.

"Of course," he says.

I can muster no response to such strange logic, an outgrowth of Ukraine's alcoholic culture. As we fast approach Vorwerk, a poor farming hamlet of older, mostly ruined German colonist homes, I motion to Valentine to slow down.

"Why are we slowing down?" Mitya says. "This is the middle of nowhere. There is nothing here."

"It's like Afghanistan," Valentine says. "Where we chased *dhuki.*"

"*Dhuki?*" I say.

"Ghosts," Valentine says. "Mujahideen fighters. That's what we called them when I was a Soviet soldier in Helmand Province."

"Why ghosts?" I say.

"Because they attacked without warning. Then disappeared."

"I'm chasing dhuki too," I say.

The village we are entering was once home to roughly half of the twenty man Vorwerk police unit, one of the greatest concentration of mass murderers in Holocaust history: a unit organized in early fall of 1941. SS officers Hartung and his second-in-command, T., motored in their staff car from Rastadt police headquarters, and went house to house in Welikova, Vorwerk, Anetovka, and Markarova, four hamlets south of Bogdanovka settled with Volksdeutsche families from Rastadt during Soviet collectivization.

"It is your duty to the German Reich to join the local police unit," the SS officers said, pressuring the recruits. Three months later, ordered to Bogdanovka, the Vorwerkers are among those who murder fifty thousand Jews in less than ten days. That's nearly the total victims of the Nagasaki atom bomb blast; nevertheless, just the beginning of their killing.

Valentine stops near a ruined house, obviously German in construction. I want to stretch my legs, I say. I get out, and nonchalantly wander through the blighted, weed-smothered yard, then duck into this house, and in a low-ceilinged back room, find, I think, the bedroom where the bloodiest Vorwerk policeman, as the old Volksdeutsche documents say, "first saw the light of the world." It was a normal birth, with a *Hebamme* (a midwife/faith healer) in attendance, and baptism two weeks later in pre-Bolshevik times, when churches were resonant with Sunday prayers and music.

By the boy's fourteenth year, the typical time for religious training, the Soviet regime had lopped off all the steeples, converting the churches into cinemas, banning religious ceremonies, and murdering and exiling thousands of priests and religious leaders. Soviet oppression of that sort—so goes my own reductionist theory—opened a spiritual chasm in the inherently religious Volksdeutsche—a chasm which filled with demonic forces, which the Nazis harnessed for their own purposes.

At his postwar trial this policeman admitted to killing four hundred Jews. That was not his real total. At Bogdanovka alone, he likely murdered double, even triple, that number. Of course he didn't offer the real totals. Why would anyone admit the full total, even if they knew? In March 1942, the Vorwerker police and their families were transferred to Gradofka. There, within walking distance of the ovens, the men murdered thousands more, along with the fifteen hundred, or more, incinerated in the horse stables. It is likely that this single Vorwerker genocidaire destroyed two thousand human beings, four or five times his admitted total.

It's true that the SS officers regularly threatened the Vorwerkers at the Bogdanovka ravine: "If you don't follow orders to kill, you will end up in the same pit as the Jews." That the policemen would murder under such circumstances makes sense. What choices did they have? What the Vorwerkers did, however, on their way to and from the Bogdanovka ravine in their horse-pulled wagons over several weeks at the end of 1941 and the beginning of 1942 does not make any sense.

Without being coerced or ordered, and out of sight of the SS officers, the Vorwerkers were caught up in a dizzying spiral of murder. These smaller-scale killings took place in the roughly one hundred square miles of their home region, bounded by Bogdanovka to the north, Domaneuvka to the southwest and the Bug River to the east. This became their own killing field—a microcosm of slaughter within the Kingdom of Death.

The Vorwerkers searched out those Jews who escaped ghettos and massacre pits, those who'd fled the long columns winding over the steppe, and those who found refuge somewhere in the vast countryside.

On those mornings, they rode like a plague of merciless death across the steppeland, toward the rising sun, and then after a day of killing at the Bogdanovka ravine, rode back home, the setting sun in their eyes, squinting and searching the countryside for movement, any hiding place, which likely meant more victims. Despite the rough, isolated terrain and the distances traveled in horse-pulled wagons, the Vorwerkers killed—ten Jews hidden here, eight there, groups of three and four women with children elsewhere, all hunted down and murdered. They killed a young Jewess in a horse stall in Anetowka. They discovered a number of Jews hidden in nearby straw stacks, took them to the Bakshala River, shot them in a ravine, and left behind the smoldering corpses. One policeman shot thirty-five Jews by himself in the same vicinity. Several members of the unit shot fifty-five Jews on the outskirts of Makarova, then another thirty Jews in the nearby collective farm of *Komintern*.

The Vorwerkers went to hutors and family estates and collective barns, killing wounded women who'd survived other massacres, sick and starving Jews flushed like wounded quail from cattle stalls or chicken houses or blacksmith shops, victims too weak to flee. They slaked their blood lust on those hiding in haystacks, on Jews rounded up by local villagers and locked up in collective buildings. They raped women and young girls. They lifted children by the hair and shot them. They tore unweaned babies from the arms of their mothers, bludgeoning them with rifle butts or swung the tiny bodies against the wheels of their wagons, and tossed them aside, blood spewing from the fontanels. Then they shot the mothers. They took the apparel, especially if the Jews were wealthy, and wore silk blouses and embroidered dresses and well-stitched leather boots, whatever would fit their loved ones, or themselves, replacing their own brain-spattered and blood-stiffened clothing.

They murdered of their own free will, or appeared to, which seems to support Goldhagen's thesis that the distinction between criminal Nazis and ordinary Germans is a false one, although I'd argue that the Vorwerkers were in no sense ordinary, having endured forced starvation, waves of arrests and executions, and the general oppression of collectivization. So I'm not ready to endorse Goldhagen's theory. What I know is that the Vorwerker unit, like other Volksdeutsche police units, consisted of closely related, and much intermarried, villagers. So perhaps a single charismatic Volksdeutsche policeman—perhaps an older, local leader, imbued with the murderous anti-Semitism of his SS commanders, influenced the Vorwerkers to cleanse their home area of Jews.

By midafternoon, a sharp pain radiates down my left arm. It's a heart attack, I feel sure, from pondering such ghastly matters, but my driver, Valentine, nodding at the concrete-like ruts over which we bounce, tells me "Just a pinched nerve, I'm sure. Lucky for you I'm a part-time massage therapist."

While I lay across the hood of the car like a gutted deer, and Valentine, with his elbow and fingers, loosens the knots and cords of my neck and back, Mitya wanders off. When I'm feeling better, I scan the horizon. He's nowhere I can see. We wait. I sit on the car hood. The countryside is flat, like the Red River Valley in Dakota. Finally we see a dark speck on the horizon, Mitya, wading through a field of knee-high grain. Ever the dandy, he is sniffing a blood red flower, a *mukh* (poppy), which reminds me of the German dialect word *mukha* (fly) White death squads used during Ukraine's civil war. A Volksdeutsche translator has told me Nazi death squads used it too, twenty years later. If a person couldn't correctly pronounce that word, that meant they were Jewish, and they had to die.

As we drive on, Mitya launches into a joke, set during the collectivization period, when a peasant, granted an audience with Stalin, stood in front of the Great Leader, chewing a mouthful of hay to show just how miserable life in the Soviet Union had become.

"Comrade farmer," Stalin said, addressing the peasant. "For ten years we have been trying to teach you how to farm in a Socialist manner."

"What does that mean?" the peasant said.

"In summer you are supposed to graze," Stalin said. "Save that hay for winter."

Valentine chortles, Mitya falls into a self-satisfied silence.

I'm left to ponder the Vorwerkers. There is a growing body of literature on war criminals, monsters and killers, and how they are created. One book, *Evil Men*, explores the mentality of killers, not only the Nazis, but also American soldiers at My Lai and Japanese soldiers during WWII. The paramilitary Vorwerkers, however, for reasons I don't understand, fall outside all those categories and explanations.

I think back to what Regina and Helmut told me about the prolonged Soviet brutality of the 1930s. Especially after the wholesale arrests during the Great Terror of 1937 when Volksdeutsche arrested in large numbers, tortured in ways too ugly to describe that tore at the victim's personhood. Each secret police unit in the main Soviet cities in the 1930s had its own expertise. In Hoffnungstal, the victims' relatives, allowed a final visit, no longer recognized their loved ones. "We lost our feelings toward other people, and human life meant little," Regina once told me. If that was true for Regina, just a year younger than the young policemen, was that also true for the Vorwerkers? Likely.

Several Vorwerkers, while admitting in postwar Soviet trials to murdering scores and hundreds of victims, also insisted that while standing guard at Bogdanovka, they allowed Jews, even entire families, to escape. Other Vorwerkers in the docket, charged with horrendous crimes, claimed they didn't take the victims' clothing or belongings. Was that to bolster the argument that they didn't murder from venality but because they were threatened?

A couple of Vorwerkers disputed the official number of deaths attributed to them. "No, I did not kill one hundred and eighty as the transcript shows," one defendant stated. "I killed no more than one hundred forty." That correction seems strange. What difference did forty fewer victims make to ghastly totals? For a time I wonder how the Vorwerkers could return to their own homes and families, to play with their children and sleep in their own beds, then continue killing the next day. Eventually, I realize this return to normalcy, celebrating holidays with their families, was actually what allowed the Vorwerkers to engage in such prolonged destruction of human beings. In my worst moments I read from a small book of meditations by the medieval mystic Jacob Boehme that I keep in my satchel. One passage in particular explains, I think, the Vorwerkers' mentality: "It is not to be thought that the life of darkness is sunk in misery and lost as if in sorrowing. There is no sorrowing. For sorrow is a thing that is swallowed up in death, and death and dying are the very life of the darkness."

Heading back to Nikolaev, I feel an unfocused fear, my nerves stretched tight like barbed wire. Panics and other psychosomatic symptoms, as Dmitri frequently reminds me, are normal for any Holocaust scholar, even an amateur like me.

"Just catch the panics early," Dmitri says. "Calm yourself. Let them happen. Don't fight against them."

Mitya is saying something about vacations, about taking things too seriously, about drinking, but the tendrils of my anxiety have morphed into a full-fledged attack, which carries me beyond myself, to a far country where not everything buried is dead, where in the gathering dusk behind our car, I sense the Vorwerkers, in their wagons, chasing me.

***

THE WAVES SWALLOW

Several times a week I enter the bowels of an imposing totalitarian structure that is Nikolaev National University, a huge slab of cheap, poured cement and open stairwells, designed for tropical Africa, but because of the cash-starved later Soviet era, constructed near the Bug River in Nikolaev.

Each day I get there by crossing a movable bridge over the river, and one morning, stepping over a gap between the rusting metal partitions, I see human bodies bobbing in the water, but thankfully they're just logs. But this is indicative of my bloody state of mind. In my classes that day, I find it necessary to impress upon my students that I have discovered, on the list of murderers, one of my own relative's name. My students receive this news with baleful stares. To them, I'm sure, I look as the old man at the blue gate did to me, stuttering half-baked ideas.

That night, a bad dream clots in my subconscious. I'm in a ravine, kicking through tangled weeds, when I come upon an SS officer, furiously digging with a spade, the blade grating against the pebbled earth. It's Weingartner.

"This is your grave," he says, turning his gaunt, sweaty face toward me.

What does that mean? Digging my own grave by pursuing this research? Losing Volksdeutsche friends with uncomfortable truths? Perhaps. On a practical level, the dream reminds me of one thing: though I've explored several

193

districts, I know precious little about Hoffnungstal, and SS officer Weingartner's wartime tenure there.

***

The early-morning sun, a split melon, pours blood into the cloudless sky as we head to Hoffnungstal. Anatoli drives, Dimitri rides shotgun, and I'm in the backseat, studying a tattered old photograph.

"The photo. Relatives?" Dimitri says.

"Yes, the C. family," I say. "My mother found it in a photo album recently and sent it to me."

The photo, I explain, shows Christian C., a flinty-eyed, beetle-browed redhead, his thin-faced, sickly looking wife, and—wobbling between them—a chubby toddler, Helmut, his tiny hand enveloped by his father's blunt, spade-like fingers. Christian sent this photo to his sister, my great aunt, Margarete, in New Odessa, North Dakota.

"Now, three quarters of a century later," I say. "It's come full circle."

"Helmut's father looks like somebody you didn't want to mess with," Dimitri says, peering at the photo, and I bristle as usual, although I know he's likely right, as always.

To my left, a line of low hills, and, atop them—set against the pale blue sky—the saw-toothed outline of vineyards once owned by Helmut's family. As the narrow asphalt road unwinds like a dirty ribbon, I explain to Dmitri the history of this broad valley we are entering, the Valley of Hope, named in 1817 by The Children of God, survivors of a large group of millennialist pilgrims.

The pilgrims departed from German principalities, floating down the Danube River on wide rafts, singing haunting millennial songs. Their final destination was Mount Ararat, where Jesus would return and usher in the Thousand

194

Year Reign of the Just. After an epidemic swept through the pilgrims at the mouth of the Danube River, the survivors—my own ancestors, along with Leibbrandt's and Helmut's and Regina's—barred by the Russian Czar from proceeding further, helped to found the German colonies of Hoffnungstal and, just across the Dniester River, the birthplace of Weingartner—Teplitz.

"Hmm, that Thousand Year Kingdom sounds familiar," Dimitri says.

"I know, I know. Hitler's Thousand Year German Reich," I say.

"It was the Einsatzgruppen who did the murdering in Hoffnungstal?" Dmitri says. "Jews from a nearby village, Freiburg, wasn't it?"

"Yes. The people in Hoffnungstal, when they learned about those murders wept and were outraged."

"Your relatives told you that?"

"Yes," I snap. "Both Helmut and Regina said that."

"You act like the murders taint you. You know, collective thinking, collective guilt," Dmitri says. "What happened to your American individualism?"

"It took me a long time to accept how widespread the murders were in the Volksdeutsche villages."

"Are you afraid of what you might find in Hoffnungstal?"

"Well, yes."

"You said there were clues?" Dmitri says. "Like what?"

I explain how, at a time when I knew little of Weingartner, less of Helmut's father, and nothing of the Jews, I'd done a google search, and discovered Freiburg, a hamlet of Jews just two kilometers from Hoffnungstal.

"So I called Helmut and asked him about it," I say.

"You asked him about the Jews of Freiburg?" Dimitri says. "What did he say?"

"He told me those Jews fled in August of 1941 to Kazakhstan. To get away from the invading Germans."

"And you believed him," Dimitri says.

"At the time, yes. I had no reason not to."

"Something changed your mind?"

"This," I say, handing Dimitri a single Xeroxed page that a friend discovered in a back issue of a Volksdeutsche journal and sent to me in Ukraine.

Dmitri scans the eyewitness account of a mass murder of forty-nine Jews outside the village on a foggy Sunday morning in early September of 1941. Uniformed men ordered the victims to undress and kneel at the edge of a washout, then they shot them in the back of the head with Lugers. Afterward, the murderers smoked, told "filthy stories," and when the earth moved, shoveled more dirt over the mass grave and then drove off in their trucks.

"Likely an Einsatzgruppen action," Dmitri says.

"You mean use of the Lugers?"

"Yes. But the question is, were there murders of Jews after the Einsatzgruppen left the area? If so, then the Hoffnungstal police were involved."

"No. Weingartner wouldn't have allowed that," I say. "He was a decent man."

"Your relatives told you that? Let me guess, you found evidence Weingartner denied killing Jews."

"Yes, a Hoffnungstaler asked Weingartner directly."

"And?"

"And he *verneint* it."

"*Verneint?*"

"Strongly denied it," I say. "Weingartner strongly denied killing Jews."

"That's not surprising. But he knew. I'm sure."

"Why do you think that?"

"Because he was…what did your relative call him?"

"Bezirkmeister," I say. "Master of the entire district."

"So your beloved Hauptsturmfuehrer was involved. Even if your relatives told you otherwise."

"You're sure?" I say, downcast.

"Just my opinion," he says.

"So you are sure."

"What if you learn your relatives and Weingartner were involved? What then?"

"You're telling me my relatives were involved? That they are not any different?"

"Why would they be different? Lots of Volksdeutsche were involved, whether they wanted to be or not."

"You mean in killing centers and labor camps across Europe, not just in Transnistria?"

"Not only Volksdeutsche," Dimitri says. "But also my people, too, Ukrainians. You know, the Demyanyuk case."

"So you think some Hoffnungstalers were also murderers?" I say.

"Again, why would they be different?"

"They were decent people," I say, but now I had my doubts.

***

The rest of the way to Hoffnungstal—tires humming quietly on a new patch of narrow two-lane—Dimitri and I pass documents between us. We are reconstructing, as best we can, the life of Hoffnungstal's former mayor, and Helmut's father, Christian C.:

Helmut's father was a contemporary of Leibbrandt, and like the Propaganda Minister, born into one of the founding families of Hoffnungstal, and like most Volksdeutsche of his era, he'd fought, as a Czarist conscript on the Bulgarian front in WWI, returning with a growing hatred of Russians and a pair of knee-high leather military boots, that he was still wearing a decade later in a family photo sent to my Dakota relatives.

In 1919, he fought alongside Leibbrandt in the failed uprising against the Bolsheviks, and while the latter fled the country, C. remained in Hoffnungstal, where, as records show, he worked as a vineyardist, marrying and fathering several children, and keeping his young family alive during the famine of 1922, which killed millions. C.'s wife, Christine, maintained correspondence with a number of Dakota Germans, especially her husband's sister, my great aunt, describing a period scholars call The Dark Valley: an unprecedented decade, the 1930s, whose mass deaths from starvation, disease, and execution brought on the greatest demographic shift in European peasantry since the Middle Ages.

Christine's letters sometimes contained invisible messages, scrawled in urine or milk between the lines, such as "Even a stone has more feeling than a brutal bolshevik," or "Send this letter to your newspaper so the world can learn what is being done to us": dangerous, anti-Soviet comments that revealed themselves once the reader held the letter near an open flame. These letters arrived in the rural mailbox of a large, two story farm home my great uncle and his wife called "the Ranch," just outside New Odessa, North Dakota. Letters that described the confiscations of private property, and the imposition of inflated grain quotas, to starve the small landholders, who survived on a grisly diet of mice, earthworms, family pets, even horse manure, for the grain seeds it contained.

In 1933, Christine wrote her Dakota relatives about her husband:

> I would like to let you know, dear brother-in-law George Y., that Christian has been arrested again and is now held in Odessa. I am at home with five children and nothing to feed them or myself. Everything has been taken from us, and no one knows what will happen next…I should tell you why Christian is being held. On January 2 they held him in custody, nobody knows why. At the same time they also arrested sixty other men from the village for not filling out the correct bread forms, or so they say. Several men were charged, several talked themselves free, and Christian, after being held for two months, became free again, not charged. He was home for a month when they brought tractors to work the corn, and put him in charge of overseeing the working of the land. There were five tractors and twenty two workers, and almost all of the workers stole corn at night. And so Christian was charged with that… and we have so little food that two of our children are already swelling. It tears my heart apart that we must live this way, but to whom should I complain?

Helmut's father was sentenced first to internal exile, at a vineyard south of Odessa, and later as a slave laborer on the White Sea Canal, one of Stalin's pet projects, which claimed tens of thousands of victims. He'd survived, somehow, returning to Hoffnungstal, in 1937, where he narrowly missed being rounded up by the Soviet secret police, a mass arrest of several hundred men shot by year's end in the Odessa prison, to fulfill the execution quotas of Stalin's "German Operation."

Four short years later, in the second week of August 1941, my great uncle Christian C., and his wife and sons, including fifteen-year-old Helmut, were among those villagers cheering as the German army marched into Hoffnungstal, liberating the Volksdeutsche from the scourge of Soviet totalitarianism.

***

We follow the main highway that brought the German army into the valley in August, 1941, and entering Hoffnungstal, pass limestone homes that lined the road, including one with green shutters and a large yard, that belonged to a prosperous farmer whose entire family, as Helmut once told me, was sent to Siberia in 1929, so the centrally located property could be used for secret police headquarters, and its long barns as a jail and torture center.

Anatoli parks in Hoffnungstal's village square, near the steepleless church, in which, for over a century or more, my own relatives worshipped. We get out and stretch our legs. I point out, near the church, where the photo was snapped, the one I saw in Fresno of Helmut's father and the SS officer Weingartner.

"Why do you think they wouldn't send you the photo?" Dmitri says.

"They say they were afraid of what it showed," I say.

"What did it show again? Enlighten me."

"It showed Helmut's father and Weingartner smiling. Like they were sharing a joke."

"So they had a relationship? What did they have in common?"

"Both were Volksdeutsche. Raised in villages ninety miles apart."

"You forgot one thing," Dmitri says. "Both were *Randvoelker.*" (Borderland Germans.)

200

"So you think both were anti-Semites?"

"They likely had an understanding."

"An agreement about destroying the Jews of Freiburg?" I say.

"Yes. But that is just my opinion."

I hate hearing that, because whenever Dmitri says something is just his opinion, he's usually right.

***

"Why do you want to know these things?" Rosa says.

"Because my relatives lived here in Hoffnungstal until 1944," I say.

I was sitting at a wobbly table in Rosa's front yard. She's the last of the Jews of Freiburg, a diminutive woman with frizzy hair pulled into a bun; when she doesn't respond to my reply, I'm not sure she heard.

"These peels must dry in the sun," Rosa says. "So they don't give off smoke when I use them for fuel."

She is flipping curled potato peelings, the color of a dark bruise, which gives me a bad feeling. How, I wonder, did Rosa escape the slaughter of the Freiburg Jews?

"Before we talk of other things, let me tell you something," Rosa says, flipping over the last peelings. "The German colonists who lived in this valley were good people."

She tells me she attended school in Hoffnungstal, the same one as Leibbrandt, albeit two decades earlier. She was, I realize, the same age as Regina, eighty-two now, a little younger than Helmut, and I am fairly certain she might have known Rosa, who seems to read my thoughts.

"Your relatives, if they are still alive, might remember me," she says. "My sister and I wore brightly embroidered Ukrainian blouses. We had long braids down our back."

201

Then she recites the string of Lutheran ministers in Hoffnungstal, like the starting lineup of a baseball team, all the way back to WWI, and it's clear she has rich memories of when Volksdeutsche and Jew were neighbors, children attending school together, dancing together at the village festivals. Each time she says "Hoffnungstal," each time the Germanic syllables roll off her tongue, I'm struck again that she pronounces the village exactly like Regina.

"Do you know, the Hoffnungstalers didn't drink water if they were thirsty?" she mused. "Only wine. Wonderful wine."

We discover our mutual love of Heine's poetry—he was a German Jew who predicted the Holocaust—and recite, together, "Die Lorelei." As we do, Rosa claps her hands with joy, and when we come to the part where the waves swallow the sailors, I have a foreboding, which I quickly suppress, that my Hoffnungstal relatives helped destroy the Jews of Freiburg.

After the German army invaded, Rosa says, Jewish families suspicious of the Nazis, and those with the means, with horses and wagons, like Rosa's parents, flee Freiburg, spending the rest of the war in Central Asia. The rest hid, or were hidden by friends in Hoffnungstal.

"The mayor of Hoffnungstal protected the Jews at great risk," Rosa says, and I'm wondering if that was my relative, Christian C. When that mayor was replaced, the edict was quickly posted that all Jews must register for a census, and those who queued at the registration office in Hoffnungstal were arrested.

"The most beautiful Jewesses were used for fun by the soldiers," Rosa says. "Then executed with the others outside of Hoffnungstal."

After the war, her family returned. With the same wagon and same faithful horse, all the way back from Kazakhstan. Her father dug up the mass grave and identified the remains of his sister and Rosa's eight-year-old cousin by their clothing, by how their skeletal fingers were still entwined from the moment of execution.

Telling me that last part, Rosa weeps, and I feel a wave of despair that I've made her recount her painful past. So I end the interview, and after giving her a hug, I fold her fingers over a wad of 100-grievna bills. "For the upcoming Jewish holidays," I say.

"Oh, this is just so very much," she says.

As I leave, I'm thinking, "No, it is nowhere enough." Or do I say it aloud? This is well before I know the truth of what a relative did.

***

Wherever I go that day, down the once-wide, now tree-lined streets fringed by thick weeds, along once-broad sidewalks now pebbled pathways, and especially, up the cupped wooden church stairs to the church balcony, where young women like Regina once gazed down in admiration at the handsome SS officer preaching at the pulpit: wherever I go, I feel, hovering over me, the uneasy spirit of Theophil Weingartner.

In the final week of August, 1941, Weingartner's driver, an Austrian of Bessarabian derivation, eased the staff car over the churned up ruts into Hoffnungstal, and the first thing that the Hauptsturmfuehrer, a former Lutheran minister, standing on the running board, notices is the missing steeple and bells of the hundred year old neoclassical church, not to mention the deteriorated condition of what had been the most prosperous, and most unique architecturally, of the German colonies within the region.

Weingartner was only too well aware of Soviet religious persecution in the 1930s, a time during which Lutheran ministers, and Catholic priests alike were heavily taxed, exiled to labor camps, and murdered outright. That might have been his fate too, he knew, if he'd been born on this, the

Hoffnungstal side of the Dniester River, not in Teplitz, on the Bessarabian side. Growing up, Weingartner was cognizant that the dividing line between Romania and Soviet Ukraine was the Dniester River, the line between those Volksdeutsche who had food, and those starving during Stalin's collectivization scheme.

When the Bessarabian Germans tried to send truckloads of grain and foodstuffs to their friends and relatives across the Dniester River—they were, after all, the same people— the paranoid communists turned them back. That was all Weingartner needed to know, he said later about the Soviet regime. He entered Hoffnungstal in his staff car at the head of a string of vehicles, including a couple of motorcycles (one with a sidecar), several heavy trucks, and five or six lorries with the VoMi logo emblazoned across their doors, ferrying Weingarner's people, as villagers called them, two SS aides, his National Socialist driver, his two Red Cross nurses, his police trainer, and others, to their new posting in the East. By that time he was already anticommunist, if not anti-Semitic, which, in Nazi parlance, meant blaming the Jews for communism and capitalism.

Of the dozen district SS commandants in Transnistria, Weingartner was the only Volksdeutscher, and as Regina insisted, much loved, as one of their very own, and his assignment was a homecoming, of sorts, to a village he considered his second home. Hoffnungstal bore many similarities to his native Teplitz. It was on the same huge steppe, with the same curvilinear roofing tiles on homes and cellars, with the same round of religious festivals, like *Ernte-Dankfest*, the autumn harvest celebration, when the church, its balcony and chancel, just as he remembered in his native Teplitz, was decorated with pumpkins and watermelons and sheaves of wheat, in praise of God's bounty. Most importantly, Hoffnungstal was populated, like Teplitz, with descendants of German-dialect speaking millenialists, who sang the same songs in their church, and prayed aloud, in communal prayers, to the same Old God.

His first act, fraught with symbolism I will only understand later, was to build a jail—Weingartner's jail, as locals called it. It was in the basement of the hastily constructed barracks, whose puddled concrete-like walls also house the Selbstschutz police training area and canteen, and very near the Lutheran church, where he also begins to meet the religious needs of the spiritually starved Hoffnungstalers. One Sunday in September of 1941—Regina remembered it as a warm, Indian summer day—Weingartner presided over a day-long religious service. Sacraments, outlawed for a decade under the communists, were performed en masse for parishioners who crowded the refurbished church. It was a joyful day for the Hoffnungstalers, legitimizing in the eyes of God the backlog of marriages and especially baptisms, which by tradition took place in the first weeks of an infant's life. On this Sunday, the long row of teenagers who came forward to the baptismal font amply illustrated the duration of Soviet oppression, outlawing all religious ceremonies. And when, at first, Weingartner, in his SS uniform, disallowed confirmation, villagers were angered. Then he explained why. He wanted to personally instruct the hundreds of confirmands, and then, in a mixture of religion and politics, have them pass confirmation and become church members in a special ceremony on the birthday of the Fuehrer.

Weingartner delivered regular sermons, in his full-dress SS uniform, from the pulpit of the Hoffnungstal church, impassioned orations that, in the perfect acoustics of the high ceilinged church, brought tears to the eyes of the Hoffnungstalers. He also entertained a regular stream of visitors to his headquarters. They invited him to share meals with them, so they could show their deep appreciation for the Nazis rescuing them from the nightmare of communism.

The Hauptsturmfuehrer's name showed up regularly in the Nazi newspapers of the time—mastheads displayed a large swastika clutched in the claws of an eagle, and linotyped columns included propaganda articles blaming the Jews for various crimes—and his Volksdeutsche background, aristocratic appearance, and folksy manner made him much in demand, and he crisscrossed his own district and Transnistria, giving speeches, making presentations, and giving out awards at Nazi celebrations to Hitler Youth groups, male and female. It was a demanding schedule for any healthy thirty-two-year-old, and more so for Weingartner, diagnosed with malaria, a catchall term for an unknown malady that sapped his energy and gave him the gaunt appearance I've seen in the photo in Fresno. Like the bulk of SS district commandants in Transnistria, Weingartner was disqualified from active, frontline duty. Still, he was one of the best and brightest of the VoMi's colonization effort, and long after the war, in Volksdeutsche memoirs, he remained admired as the least repressive of the VoMi's district commandants.

As the German front line collapsed in spring of 1944, Weingartner and his driver and confidant, L., were point men for the evacuation of the Hoffnungstal district, going ahead in his staff car, and using his rare language skills to negotiate safe passage across Eastern Europe for the long lines of horse-pulled wagons, and the hundred and twenty thousand Volksdeutsche, trundling in his wake. He kept discipline and anticipated problems. At one point he confiscated money the Volksdeutsche received for some butchered cattle, knowing that many, leaving their home villages for the first time and experiencing a severe sense of displacement, would use the money to buy alcohol and drink themselves into insensibility.

Once the Volksdeutsche refugees resettled in the Greater German Reich, Weingartner discarded his uniform and retired to his modest estate in Schleswig-Holstein, which, despite his exemplary Nazi record, he had difficulty receiving, primarily because he was Volksdeutsche. There, he lived quietly with his wife and two boys until the approach of the Soviet army in 1945. Then using his Luger, which he rarely carried in Hoffnungstal, he shot his two boys, his wife, and then himself. But why? Because of his fear of what the Soviets would do to him and his family? Perhaps. Or because he helped murder Jews? That's the question that has remained from the beginning of my research, and it nags me that day in Hoffnungstal.

***

Dmitri and I find the mayor's office, or *Amt*. It's a stuccoed building with a high false front. Once an orthodox church, it's now empty, its front door bolted with a large, rusted, medieval-looking lock. For a time I stand where, as Rosa says, the Jews of Freiburg lined up for the census. Nearby, a mirror image of the mayor's Amt, is Weingartner's former SS headquarters, the *Kommendatura* as it was called, with the same high false front and stuccoed exterior, and set back from the street. We go inside. It's now Hoffnungstal's pharmacy, and the pharmacist, a broad Slavic-faced woman in a white smock, glances up from filling orders.

When we tell her our business, she says, "Yes, it was a Fascist headquarters. Please, look around all you want."

Weingartner's office has a low door (the tall SS officer had to duck while entering), and inside we find walls painted the same eggshell blue as the interiors of Volksdeutsche sod homes on the prairie, and, set deep in the south wall, and with interior shutters, a single tall window, offering a view the former Lutheran minister would have liked, of the nearby church. Near the window, where Weingartner's desk once stood, and where he made his *entscheidungen* (decisions), is a cheap desk of fabricated wood and a tall book case, filled with billing records and small pharmaceuticals boxes.

"Rosa told me the mayor here protected the Jews," I say. "Hiding them."

207

"That mayor would have been replaced, quickly," Dmitri says. "To get someone amenable to murdering the Jews. You say Helmut's father was a mayor here?"

"Yes," I say. "So you think he was the mayor who protected the Jews?"

"No, I don't," Dmitri says. "I think he was the mayor who posted the census that got the Jews killed."

We walk down a dark, narrow hallway off the office, and returned, and as I blink against the light, a pall falls over me.

"You think Weingartner and the mayor agreed to kill the Jews?" I say.

"Yes, likely in here," Dmitri says. "In this office."

"So then the decree was posted?"

"Yes, the ruse to get the Jews into the village. So the Einsatzgruppen could kill them before that unit moved out of that area."

"And you think the mayor signed off on it?" I say.

"Of course," Dmitri says. "Tell me, Ron. What happened to Helmut's father, the mayor?"

"The usual Volksdeutsche story."

"Let me guess," Dimitri says, reciting a staccato list of points. "Caught in a Soviet dragnet in Germany at war's end. Returned to the Soviet Union in a cattle car with thousands of others. Placed on trial. Right so far?"

"Yes," I say. "The trial took place in Odessa in the early 1960s, a political trial."

"That's what Helmut told you—a political trial? He was acquitted, right? For lack of evidence?"

"Of course," I say. "What evidence could there be?"

"That photo your relative refused to send you. It connected Helmut's father with Weingartner and, thus, with the murder of the Jews."

"So no photo, no case?" I say.

"Exactly."

Outside, we stand near the church, eating sandwiches out of the trunk of Anatoli's car and talking quietly about Helmut's father.

"I get tired just thinking about his life," I say.

I tick off various aspects thereof—fighting in WWI, fighting in an armed rebellion against the Bolsheviks, surviving several mass starvations, a stint as a slave laborer on the White Sea Canal, several arrests, an acquittal in a Soviet court for the murder of the Jews of Freiburg, a conviction on a lesser charge, exile to Siberia.

"The man was a survivor," Dmitri says.

"Is that why he caved to the demands of Weingartner, the SS officer? To survive?"

"I don't think he caved," Dmitri says. "If anything, it was the other way around."

"Just your opinion?"

Dmitri doesn't say anything.

"Maybe both Weingartner and the mayor were caught in the Nazi machine," I say. "And had no choice."

"I doubt it," Dmitri says. "Hoffnungstal was on the far edge of the Nazi's colonial empire. The VoMi authorities didn't oversee what was done in these districts."

"They didn't have to kill Jews?" I say. "Is that what you are saying?"

"Maybe. What happened to Helmut's father after Siberia?"

"In the late 1980s, after communism fell, he returned to Germany," I say, my voice trailing off as I realize where Dmitri is going with his questions.

"And Helmut flew to Germany for a final reunion?"

"Yes."

"You asked Helmut about that reunion?"

"Yes," I say. "But he didn't have much to say."

"About meeting his father for the last time?"

***

Midafternoon, we retrace the journey of the doomed Jews of Freiburg. We start from the village square where we parked. We go past the ruined barracks structure that once held Weingartner's jail.

"I'm not sure Weingartner's new jail was built yet," Dmitri says. "And I'm not sure where they held the Jews. In the old jail most likely, and maybe the remainder in the church, like in other villages."

"No, the remainder of the Jews were held in the school gymnasium," I say. "That's what Rosa told me."

"The Einsatzgruppen loaded the Jews into trucks," Dmitri says.

"Do you think Weingartner and the mayor were there for the loading?"

"My opinion? Yes."

We drive on to the school gymnasium, where the Jews were held and where Leibbrandt, as a student, exercised, an intersection of his early life with later Nazi policies that also included his penning guidelines for the indoctrination of "indigenous security units" (i.e. Volksdeutsche police units) "emphasizing the Jewish face of Bolshevikism."

"Now where?" Anatoli says.

"This way," I say.

We leave the village and go onto the steppe, along a meandering dirt path. We get out and gaze over the steppe, over the rough, tilting pastureland.

"Where was the murder?" Dimitri says.

"I don't know."

"You don't know? I was sure you knew. You know every murder site in Transnistria, but not this one?"

"Just east of the village, but I could be wrong," I say. "At a place called the *Klinge*."

"*Klinge?*"

"Yes," I say. "It means a cadaver dump, I think. Like skolomochil in Rastadt."

"No, klinge means blade," Dimitri says, sounding like an entry in a German dictionary. "It can be used with a German phrase, *'einem uber die Klinge springen lassen.'* To be put to death, put to the sword."

"I don't see anything like that here," I say, cursing myself for not asking Rosa the klinge's exact location.

"Let's go to Freiburg," Dimitri says. "Where the Jews once lived."

We leave Hoffnungstal and drive two kilometers north, Anatoli turning off the asphalt, and slipping the Nissan into its lowest gear, as we idle along a rutted path, passing a motley series of low structures, along only one side of the path, long-abandoned homes, yards smothered in weeds, walls shedding mortar. The road, if it can be called that, peters out near the base of sculpted, wind-scoured hills, like those just east of my Dakota hometown.

"There were two other mass murders of Jews, up there in those hills," Dmitri says.

"You know an awful lot about Hoffnungstal," I say. "More than you admit."

"I'm just giving you a sip of truth once in a while."

"Einsatzgruppen?" I say, about the murders in the hills.

"Einsatzgruppen, or else…" Dmitri says.

"Or else what?"

"A patrol of Weingartner's police."

"I doubt Weingartner used his police to kill Jews."

"Surely you aren't saying the murders around Hoffnungstal, at the klinge, and those up in the hills were all done only by Einsatzgruppen?"

"Weingartner might have used his SS men from his headquarters. But not his police. Not anyone from Hoffnungstal who knew the Jews."

"How do you know that?"

"My opinion," I say. "Just my opinion."

***

MAYORS

Two weeks later Dmitri and I sit at an outside table at the cafe in the city center park, tearing apart smoked salted fish. We pop chunks into our mouths, and chase them with

212

frosty mugs of beer. It's Indian summer, or feels like it, soggy mulberry leaves underfoot. We are reading documents from the secret police archives.

"Bad?" I say, looking up.

"Do these documents ever have good news?" Dimitri says.

Dimitri divides his document stack between us. I read a secret police report about a Volksdeutsche policeman with a familiar Dakota German name. His interrogations began in Novosibirsk in 1954 when he was just thirty years old, which makes him seventeen or eighteen when he takes part in four different mass murders.

"Do you want to start shots already?" Dimitri says, looking up, his brow furrowed. "Or save them for later?"

"Later. A beer will work now."

Drafted into the Waffen SS in 1943, the young policeman fought in the Balkans and elsewhere on the Eastern Front. He survived brutal street fighting in rubble strewn Berlin only because—so he told his interrogators—a pocket watch stopped a piece of shrapnel from piercing his heart. What he didn't tell his interrogators was, as I know from other documents, that he received the watch from his police commandant for slaughtering Jews.

At war's end, tens of thousands of Volksdeutsche, this former policeman among them, were forcibly repatriated to the Soviet Union. Several years later, Soviet war crimes prosecutors tracked him down in South-Central Siberia. He was charged with murdering innocent Soviet citizens.

"Can you imagine," I say to Dimitri. "That's just his life from seventeen to thirty."

"I have more on his early life," Dimitri says, waving for the bartender. "You need a shot to read this."

"No, I don't need a shot," I say.

"I'll order you a shot."

We trade testimony pages. I scan the former policeman's biographical details, the same howling litany of Volksdeutsche life in the Soviet Ukraine in the 1920s and 1930s. Parents and grandparents starved and executed and worked to death in labor camps. Raised by others. Moved from place to place. Impaled on two horrific famines, in 1921 and 1933. He came of age absent food, love, education, and religious training, everything pre-Soviet Volksdeutsche prided themselves upon.

"Small wonder this guy murdered people," I mutter.

"His life sounds like Simplicimuss during the Thirty Years War," Dimitri says.

"That was a novel, the first novel, actually. This is real."

"Scholars do call this period in Ukraine another Thirty Years War," Dimitri says.

"From 1918 to just after WWII?"

"Yes, of course."

We pause to drink shots.

"Imagine Ukraine is a woman," Dmitri says.

After several intense months of studying documents with Dmitri, I know he poses metaphors and uses them to answer complex questions. So I let him talk.

"A woman repeatedly starved and raped. That is what happened to Ukraine. Over hundreds of years. Multiple times by Moscow. Then by the Nazis. What can one expect from such a woman, from such a country?"

"Yes, of course."

"What would you have done?" Dimitri says, tapping the confessions on the table. "If you were one of these men."

"The youngest were hardly men," I say. "The equivalent of the child soldiers of Africa. Seventeen years old. Eighteen years old."

"That's no answer."

"You mean if someone gave me a rifle when I was a teen and told me to kill?"

"No, if you were older, with that same background. And someone gave you a rifle and told you to kill."

"If I was in my thirties or forties, like some of the local police leaders?"

"Yes, with the same past," Dmitri says.

We conjecture about the older local Volksdeutsche police leaders—like G. at Rastadt, F. at New Amerika, and B. and R. at Worms—all with fathers, grandfathers, uncles, brothers, executed by the Soviets in 1937 and '38.

"The mayors and the police leaders survived more brutalization and suffering than younger policemen," Dmitri says.

"So you think the older men chose to murder. While the younger police just followed orders?"

"Yes. After twenty years of oppression, would you kill?"

"What do you think I would have done?" I say.

"Now you sound like a Ukrainian. Turning back the question."

"It's different for everybody."

"Well, that's my point." Dimitri says. "Some Volksdeutsche mayors went along with the murders, even abetted them."

"Like my relative in Hoffnungstal?" I say.

"While other mayors refused to kill Jews."

"Do you know this for certain?"

"Just my opinion," he says. "But next time I will bring documents to support my opinion."

***

The next time we meet, there is a crisp, early winter chill in the air so we install ourselves at the long counter inside the cafe.

"I have interesting news," Dimitri says.

"Only interesting?" I say. "Not horrific?"

"Interesting first. Then horrific."

Over beers, we talk about what he'd found in the archives.

"In some villages there were two or three different mayors during the first months of the German Occupation."

"Which means?" I say.

"Which means some mayors refused to get involved."

"And were replaced?"

"Not always. A Volksdeutsche, Hirsch, from Tschernova, sixty kilometers from Rastadt."

Hirsch's background—as I see from the document Dmitri hands me—fits the parameters of mayors appointed by the SS—someone who hated the Soviets. Arrested multiple times for unstipulated political crimes. Jailed for two years with thirteen thousand others in Odessa's overcrowded prison during Stalin's Great Terror in 1937, when up to fifty Volksdeutsche were executed each night. It's a typical story, except Hirsch, as he said, was released "because nothing was found against me."

Hirsch, it seems, retained enough moral clarity to distinguish between "the worst of the Jews," meaning, in some cases, Soviet officials who were Jewish and responsible for hundreds of deaths in each village, and innocent local Jews he protects, as he clearly spells out in his postwar testimony:

> After a few days the Wehrmacht troops abruptly pulled out of Tschernova, leaving only an SS commando group of sixteen to twenty men temporarily stationed in the hospital in our village, and the leader of this group was Lieutenant Gruenwald, who as I recall spoke German with a Saxon accent. In our village there were seventy to eighty Jews, who were known to all. I even worked with these people for several years, and always was treated well.
>
> One day, two sergeants major came to me and said, "Herr Hirsch, we will stay here only two more days. You must give us the Jews. We must shoot them."
>
> I asked why, and he said, "The Jews are our enemies and therefore need to be liquidated. That way nothing will happen once my men are no longer here." I told him I didn't fear them, and anyway, I added, "The worst had of the Jews already left this area before the war even began."
>
> I didn't give him the list of Jews, and he didn't order me to comply. Instead he said, "If something happens later, don't blame me." Two days after that, Lieutenant Gruenwald and his SS men departed, and I never saw them again.

"What do you think?" Dmitri says when I finish the document.

"I think some mayors were brave," I say. "Like Hirsch."

"While others, like Hoffnungstal's mayor encouraged the murders of the Jews?"

"We don't know if that's true."

"Maybe your relative believed Nazi propaganda that Jews were all communists?"

"I have a hard time accepting that."

"Well, I'll do more digging in the archives"

"To find something to poke in my eye?" I say.

"There is an old proverb about eyes."

"Not another Ukrainian proverb."

"Dwell on the past, lose an eye."

"Let me guess the rest," I say. "Forget the past and go blind."

***

One chilly morning, wrapped in the sweater Sonia made for me, I sit on the front steps of my apartment building, waiting for Anatoli, when Dmitri, on his way to teach for the day, shows up. He hands me a sheaf of documents.

"Maybe these will cure you," he says.

"Of what?" I say.

"Of blindness," Dmitri says ominously.

He strolls away, toward the grey hulking edifice of National University that loomed over the Bug River. By the time I think to warn him about the packs of dogs, his dark figure has disappeared in the distance. When Anatoli pulls up in his Nissan, and as we depart Nikolaev, I stuff the documents from Dmitri into my satchel for later reading.

Completing my survey of murder sites seems an impossible job, especially since I keep discovering more of

218

them, including one in Helenental, which is where we're headed now.

Helenental, a former Volksdeutsche colony of evangelical Lutherans that lies fifty miles due west, isn't hard to find. Nor is the place where forty kneeling Jews were shot in an antitank ditch near a razed cemetery. Locals, however, aren't sure if the killing took place at the end of 1941 or the beginning of 1942. They also didn't know whether the murderers were Volksdeutsche police or Einsatzgruppen or Romanian soldiers.

After going along in my usual half crouch, searching for empty cartridges in the trench, which might indicate the weapons used, and, thus the perpetrators, I come up empty-handed, so we headed toward Johannesfeld, where I want to locate the VoMi's lager or prison for Volksdeutsche. After that, I want to swing north to Berezovka, to find the former Jewish quarter, where I've heard there is a road completely paved, during the Nazi Occupation, with Jewish tombstones. I want to photograph those tombstones, some of which, as I have been told, bear recent anti-Semitic slogans. My plan? To show Crenir that if guilt is the cockroach of emotions, then its long-lasting and indestructible twin, in the realm of prejudices, surely has to be anti-Semitism.

We head toward Johannesfeld, our car breasting the swells of the landscape, my curiosity growing about the documents Dmitri handed me that morning, documents which indict, I'm quite sure, Hauptsturmfuehrer Weingartner. I scan several pages, but the lengthy German sentences slithering and sliding across the page are unreadable.

"Let's take a break," I say. "For one hour. Right here."

Anatoli pulls the Nissan to the edge of the road. While he circles the vehicle, running his hands along its fenders like he's stroking the fetlocks of a thoroughbred, I read through the testimonies, my legs swung out of the car, a soft wind riffling the pages.

The testimonies, conducted after the war by war crimes officials, deposed Weingartner's three assistants, his two SS officers and personal chauffeur, L., an Austrian with Bessarabian Volksdeutsche roots, who had much in common with his commandant. He was bilingual, and Weingartner appointed him to read out the death decrees that he'd written out in Russian, so the eight or ten partisans caught with weapons in their homes, could hear, before their execution, the charges against them in their own language.

Weingartner was already in Hoffnungstal, L. maintained, when the Einsatzgruppen murdered the Jews and the Volksdeutsche collaborators with the Soviets; but after that twenty-man unit withdrew, he asserted, no more Jews or Volksdeutsche were murdered. He did remember finding weapons in a house search and arresting two young Russians and a young Russian woman. After the men escaped from the barracks jail, the woman, on Weingartner's command, was shot near Hoffnungstal by the Selbstschutz police. Two other Weingartner assistants, SS Obersturmfuehrer H., in his thirties, and SS junior officer H.J., in his mid-twenties, agreed with L., admitting only the execution of partisans, which under general rules of warfare was allowed, maintaining that after the Einsatzgruppen murder of the Jews at the klinge, there were no more executions of Jews in Hoffnungstal. All of which, if true, means that they and Weingartner were innocent of war crimes.

I sit there awhile and think about what I've read. I rest my eyes by watching several large, dark birds, hawks or raptors of some sort, wings spread, outlined against the bleached sky, riding air currents. I'm inclined to believe these testimonies, which seem to show that Weingartner and his people just did their military duty—nothing more, and they also support everything Regina told me of Weingartner's SS officers and driver. (Hadn't they helped the Hauptsturmfuehrer with his pastoral duties, carrying babies to the baptismal font, handing out communion wafers on the day of the en masse sacraments? Hadn't HJ, the young SS man adopted Hoffnungstal as his new home, marrying a local Volksdeutsche woman in a mid-war, jubilant celebration, and so concerned about Hoffnungstal's church records that at the time of the evacuation trek that he'd taken personal charge of the thick ledgers, with more than a century of Volksdeutsche genealogy, of births and deaths and marriages, and toted them across Eastern Europe and back to the Greater German Reich?)

But it's a trap. Set by Dmitri. He's arranged the documents, so I read, first, those in favor of Weingartner's innocence. Which I've done. He also wants me to read the remaining documents, which, if I know Dmitri, support an opposite conclusion, the Hauptsturmfuehrer's guilt. That is what I do, somewhere between Helenental and Johannesfeld, hawks circling high over the steppe, and I continue by reading this brief paragraph which concerns something that happened in Hoffnungstal in 1942:

> As my sister has already told you, our brother Richard was required to attend the training sessions in the barracks in Hoffnungstal where the policemen stayed. At the time he was still a child, just sixteen years old, and he confided to me, in the greatest secrecy, "An execution took place at the local sandpit, not far from the barracks, in which prisoners were forced to shoot other prisoners." That's what he told me. But who gave the order for this shooting, I can't say.

If this new information is accurate, and if prisoners were used to shoot other prisoners—which is akin to my learning the Rastadt police used cudgels—that points to numerous massacres in Hoffnungstal. It also means that whoever orchestrated these prisoner-on-prisoner murders did so either as sadistic entertainment—as per Doestoevky's view that if a human being controls another, atrocities will follow—or else to limit the spiritual burden on the killers. The latter was, strangely enough, a major concern of Reichsfuehrer Himmler for his eastern executioners. Was it also, perhaps, a major concern of Weingartner, the ex-minister with his own fastidiousness about not overburdening those who carried out his orders?

I read on. One Hoffnungstaler claimed that Weingartner himself shot five Jews with his pistol. Another testimony leveled a similar charge. Still another told of a Hoffnungstaler, Mrs. Metzger, who after stating in the Hauptsturmfuehrer's presence that Germany would lose the war, disappeared.

Other damning testimony came from two German women posted in Hoffnungstal: one, a German Red Cross sister, claimed that Weingartner's main assistant, Obersturmfuehrer H., drunkenly confessed to her in Odessa in 1942 that he'd been a member of a headquarters-sanctioned execution unit of Jews in the village, and the other, a former kindergarten teacher, who said she'd learned from locals that Jews had been murdered after Weingartner and his people established district headquarters there, adding that L. admitted to her he'd also participated in the executions of Jews in Hoffnungstal.

The most telling testimony came from Helmut's close friend, GM, a Volksdeutsche policeman in his early twenties, in charge of the main desk in the Selbstschutz barracks in Hoffnungstal. He signed visitors in and out to the jail in the basement and guarded and transported prisoners. GM claimed he'd never been detailed to executions, because Weingartner's order expressly forbid local Selbstschutz police from taking part, a task that belonged, he says, to the trio of SS men from Weingartner's headquarters. GM described an incident, in which Weingartner ordered him to transport two Russian partisans to the klinge, which he did, leaving them with H., HJ, and L. He claimed that Weingartner's driver, L., shot the two victims as they knelt. In this instance, GM revealed the identity of the executioner because, as he likely knew, the execution of partisans under the rules of war was a legal act.

GM admitted that from time to time Jews were caught by the Selbstschutz police patrols, and that small numbers of Jews, on various other occasions were brought from Schoenfeld, a Volksdeutsche village twenty miles to the north. These executions took place, as usual, he said, at twilight at the klinge. He didn't know the identity of those executioners, he insisted, and his memory failed him again, about the executioners in October 1942.

That was when several prisoners, Volksdeutsche from nearby Hoffnungsfeld, Leibbrandt's home village, were arrested and brought to the jail. GM has a front row seat as to how Hauptsturmfuehrer Weingartner agonized over this decision. He paced. He took long walks. Various testimonies indicated his decisions took a week or more. In this case, on the tenth day, Hauptsturmfuehrer Weingartner sat down at his desk and wrote out in longhand an order, which his secretary typed, for the execution of the Hoffnungsfelders. GM was ordered to convey the Volksdeutsche from Hoffnungsfeld to the klinge outside Hoffnungstal, which he did at twilight. Just as in the previous incident, the young policeman told war crimes investigators he couldn't identify the executioners. That was likely because he knew if he named them, and if they were still alive, they could be prosecuted for the extrajudicial murder of civilians.

I swing my legs back into the car, and as an impatient Anatoli drives us on toward Johannesfeld, and Berezovka, I lay my head back, thoughts churning. I feel like I did at Wesseloe, large blocks of information seeming to fall into place. I understand with forceful clarity why the Volksdeutsche from Hoffnungsfeld were executed: these were the spies thought responsible for giving to the Soviet secret police in 1937, the names of all the audience members in attendance at Leibbrandt's harmless genealogical presentation in Hoffnungsfeld in 1928, and, thus, spies responsible for those deaths. Only one question remains unanswered. Who gave Weingartner the names of the spies, the Hoffnungsfelders collaborating with the Soviet secret police? Was it Leibbrandt from the Eastern Ministries in Berlin? Likely, even very likely, and if not him directly, then it was Volksdeutsche from Hoffnungsfeld, sympathetic to Leibbrandt.

Regardless, it is just one of many cycles of violence and revenge that played out in three short years in Transnistria, and I will uncover several others too, some of which, concerning my own relatives, will bring those cycles of revenge and death much closer to home.

***

The next day, when I come upon Dimitri in the dim hallway of National University, I tell him, "You were right."

He puts down his book bag and looks at me. We stand there in the hallway.

"It's true," I say. "I was overly invested in Weingartner not being a killer and in Hoffnungstal being different."

"You aren't the first person to live in denial," Dimitri says.

"But the war crimes prosecutors in Germany in the 1960s did dismiss the case," I say.

"Yes, of course. Too much conflicting testimony. Too many dimming memories."

"And Weingartner's suicide," I say. "It helped close off prosecution of his SS aides and Hoffnungstal police."

"Well, he gave the orders. So he was the most culpable."

"In an odd way, Regina was right. Weingartner was their savior."

"How very Christian of him," Dmitri says, an edge in his voice.

"You don't agree? That with his suicide he took full blame onto himself?"

"I might agree," Dmitri says. "But don't forget. He did shoot his wife and kids."

***

What else can there be to Hoffnungstal's story? Nothing I can imagine. Another ugly twist, however, like the whiplash ending of a Flannery O'Connor short story, provides another glimpse, not the last, into the Aeschylus-like tragedy of Hoffnungstal.

224

It happens this way. As I'm completing the previous section of this book, I receive a phone call. Bad news. Regina had passed away. It seems an omen. I deliver the sad news to others in the Volksdeutsche network, and I end up in a long phone conversation with Timotheus, a retired American military man with a wisp of a Volksdeutsche accent, Helmut's best friend.

They came to the United States at the same time, in the early 1950s, and over the years, they drove hundreds on hundreds of miles cross-country, so their growing families could celebrate holidays together. Both of their fathers, Timotheus told me, were mayors under the German Occupation.

"Helmut's father was the Hoffnungstal district mayor," Timotheus says. "And my father, who was mayor of our little village nearby, was responsible to him."

"And both answered to Hauptsturmfuehrer Weingartner?" I say.

"Yes," Timotheus says. "And Helmut was a teenager then, a little older than I was, and he often helped his father."

"In the mayor's Amt?"

"Yes," he says. "His father had him run errands with the horse and wagon."

"Did Helmut know what was happening in Hoffnungstal?"

"He knew too much, I think. At times during our visits here in America, he got real upset whenever we talked about his father."

"By upset, you mean…?"

"Ach, his face twisted around. An ugly sight. Some kind of trauma," Timotheus says, pronouncing the word, *trowama,* lingering on it.

"Because his father posted the edict?" I say. "And helped Weingartner kill Jews?"

"Possible."

"What was Helmut's father like?"

"A gung ho Nazi," he says. "A gung ho Nazi for sure."

I take a deep breath. "Did he wear a pistol?"

"Well, yes, my father wore one too," he says. "After all, they were civilian officials, serving at the pleasure of the Nazis."

"Did they use the pistols?"

"Helmut's father may have."

"I'm not sure I follow," I say.

"Well, I can't say more," he says. "Just that it's possible."

***

WITH THE TOURISTS

I'm in the Tourist Hotel in Nikolaev, seated in a high-ceilinged private dining area; there's a long mirror covering an entire wall, and I'm making remarks to an American Volksdeutsche tour group, which includes two of my relatives from Nebraska.

The small audience titters as I tell a few German dialect jokes, keeping the mood light, until the retired American minister who organized the tour group raises a toast: "Let's give thanks to God that today we could visit the village where my grandfather's cradle rocked."

It's a pleasant time. Curious, I turn to the tour member sitting next to me, the minister's wife, and ask, "Where was it you visited?"

"A Catholic village across the Bug River," the minister's wife says.

"Rastadt?"

"Yes, Rastadt. How did you know?"

226

"Just a guess. What was his grandfather's last name?"

"G.," the minister's wife says. "My husband's grandfather had a much younger brother who didn't immigrate."

I toss back a vodka shot, and I hardly notice that it burns my throat: G. was the name of the local Volksdeutsche police leader in Rastadt, a cold, methodical killer.

"What's wrong? You look pale," my Nebraska relative says.

"It's the vodka," I lie. "It went to my head."

As we eat borsch and *gurka salat*, our conversation shifts, to our own ethnic creation story: of our Volksdeutsche forefathers departing prosperous villages on the steppe a decade before the communists took over, of an uncertain ocean crossing, huge waves hammering the steamship like great fists.

It's good to hear stories of our shared rural past, of sod and clapboard churches where our hardy ancestors pray aloud in German dialect to their old God, and it reminds me of the essential goodness of the Volksdeutsche, and counterbalances the dark tape running in a loop in my thoughts, of G., the ruthless local Volksdeutsche police commander in Rastadt, especially one incident:

When a transport of Jews was brought to the horse barns outside Rastadt, in spring of 1942, the ever-thorough G., to identify potential problems in the genocidal assembly line, went there and noted a muscular Jew, a former boxer, who appeared healthy and strong. The next day, before the action, he warned his policemen, "Watch him. He could cause trouble."

Wielding meter-long cudgels, thick as a man's wrist, and their rifles, G.'s policemen forced and kicked several hundred Jews from the horse barn to a steep drop-off outside the village, likely north of the mill. As the Jews undressed in small groups, G. struck the boxer from behind, two vicious blows with his cudgel, breaking the man's arms, making him easier to kill.

Afterward, cries emanated from the murder pit, an unnerving, insistent noise of a baby. G., a father of young children himself, ordered a policeman into the pit, and after treading over the bloody bodies, he found the source—a crying baby pinned under the mother's corpse.

"Of course it was difficult," the policeman who killed the baby admitted later. "We had to do that, or we would have been killed ourselves."

That evening, in the mirror along one wall of the dining area, I catch a reflection of a strange pale person, swaying slightly from the vodka, amid the well-fed tourists. It's me. With my unkempt hair, and my best pair of pants hanging loose on my hips and grass smeared from clambering into ovens and ravines, I look like a gaunt-faced zombie from American television. Why am I so thin? When was the last time I shaved?

My Nebraska relative invites me to accompany them to a Volksdeutsche village the next day—an offer I gladly accept. It's been months since I've conversed with a native English speaker. At midnight, I step outside and hail a taxi. We speed along the busy thoroughfare, long rows of trees looming on the berm between the separated lanes.

"This is Nevsky Prospect," the taxi driver says over the noise of raucous American hip-hop from his radio, and I realize it's the route along which a convoy of thirty German army trucks went in 1942, heaped with naked Jewish corpses, headed to a mass grave, one of many within Nikolaev itself.

Small wonder I sleep badly that night. I jerk awake, arms flailing, from a nightmare of being buried alive by strange, pig-like men wielding cudgels. My chest heaves. I try to calm my ragged breathing. But the talons of the panic are buried deep.

In anticipation of such an emergency, I pop a tranquilizer, and then another, which knit together my frayed thoughts, and for a few hours I sleep.

***

The next morning, the minibus echoes with American voices. We are heading to Katherinental, a former German village named for Catherine the Great, whose Manifesto and grandson were instrumental in inviting German colonists onto the steppe.

I feel like a tourist again, except for my paranoia about my satchel, bulging with secret police documents. Which I'm afraid to leave in my apartment, lest there be a break-in, and lest I end up like a Ukrainian scholar interrogated for twelve hours by Ukraine's current secret police.

"He was doing research like my own," I tell Dmitri. "I saw him one day in the archives."

"Oh, you worry too much about those documents," Dimitri tells me. "They won't pull your fingernails out. You're an American. Ukrainians, well that is another story." Vasily takes a different view of such matters. Once, after receiving an e-mail in which I used the initials KGB, Vasily confronts me, shaking his finger.

"Don't ever do that again," he says. "The secret police scan e-mails for those initials. I don't want to end up in prison like my father."

On the way to Katherinental, my Nebraska relative and I share a seat, poring over a plat map of that village, marveling at how the streets and houses form a huge cross, symbolic of how religion permeated the German colonists' everyday lives.

"Like the Nazca effigies in South America," my relative says. "So huge they can only be seen from above."

"Dakota Germans did the same with their mischt piles," I say with a laugh, explaining how dried bricks of cow dung and straw were stacked on prairie farms so viewed from above they formed a cross, a mix of sacred and the profane.

Our minibus plunges between great fields of sunflowers whose brilliant yellow heads follow the sun, on a vast steppe which appears uninhabited. But I know better. Ukrainian villages lay concealed in long, low folds in the earth, then rise up seemingly out of nowhere, and that is what happens as our minivan surmounts a rise, and there, a couple of miles ahead, is Katherinental, a village of several hundred souls.

Our destination is a museum, remodeled in German colonist style, with fabrics and furniture artifacts on display, and the curator, an attractive, middle-aged woman, and recipient of an award from the Ukrainian government for historical preservation work, meets us at the door, and leads us from room to room in her museum which showcases, she says, German colonist daily life, which ended here in 1944.

On the living room wall, above a German colonist *wigge* (cradle), hangs a framed, smaller version of the village plat map my relative carries. The museum's plat shows sections of long streets and houses, outlined in black, areas burnt by Bolsheviks who destroyed a good part of the village in 1919, shooting down Volksdeutsche citizens in the street. None of which the curator mentions. Does she know, I wonder, that her plat map marks the historical moment that German colonist hatred of the Bolsheviks began?

I take the museum curator aside, and ask if she knows of the massacre of Jews outside Katherinental. She shrinks back, and lowers her voice, so the tourists, milling from room to room, won't hear.

"It was Romanians who did this terrible thing," she says.

A year earlier, I might have believed her. What she says might even be true in some cases. In general, however, the

Romanian gendarmes guarding the Jews turned them over to the Volksdeutsche police units for disposal, not wanting to "dirty their own hands," as documents indicate.

I decide to take a walk, and on my way out, toss several twenty-dollar bills into a wicker-woven donation basket near the door, heaped with loose dollars—"green candy," as Ukrainians call American currency.

Even if the director knew the particulars of the two mass murders near her village, it's unlikely she'd relay that to her visitors. Why undermine her own cottage industry, hosting American Volksdeutsche on their ethnic pilgrimages to their ancestral villages? What visitor wants to learn his relatives may have helped murder Jews?

I cross the street, and go into a grassy area, enclosed by a chain link fence lined with trees, and stand in the exact center where the church once stood. On a cool marble bench next to a plaque to the Soviet war dead, I get out a document that Dmitri had scanned and sent by e-mail that morning, along with this appended note: "Ron, read this when you get to Katherinental."

It's the testimony of an official of the German Catholic Church of Romania, describing his visit to Katherinental on a warm September day in 1942, a day much like this one. As his vehicle approached the village, going along the same road by which we've entered, he was stopped: "I found myself suddenly surrounded by a group of young men who thought I was a Jew, and who told me they carry old Russian carbines to liquidate the Jews who during the Soviet times, from their high positions in the collectives, were guilty for the deportation of numerous German farmers." He had a hard time proving he was not a Jew or a communist or a partisan, and only after the official showed his identity card was he allowed to go free.

The official described meeting priests placed in German colonies like Munchen, Rastadt, Sulz, and Katherinental, who told him of the wrenching, guilt-ridden confessions from parishioners, of the great number of Jews they helped to murder, Jews forced to dig their own graves or burned, some still alive, in local lime-kiln ovens. So many murders, the official says, that "throughout the entire night the sound of gunfire echoed, and the fires in the ovens never went out, smoking day and night from the burning of the Jews."

On my way back to the museum, I follow a rut, churned deep in the roadway. My glimpse into the paranoid mentality of the young policemen makes me wonder, should I show this document to the curator? To the tourists? The Americans spill from the museum, blinking and smiling in the bright sun, as I approach. I decide against it, and for the rest of the day, wherever we go, I let their banter and optimism wash over me like a healing balm.

Soon enough, I know, my research focus will shift, though I'll put that shift off as long as possible, from the Catholic villages like Rastadt and Katherinental, where the murders seem distant from me, to a cluster of villages to the south, to the villages of my own protestant ancestors, where it will be a different story.

***

KARTAKEI

> *"For so much suffering, I tell you, someone plots revenge."*
>
> —Aeschylus

Several days later, in the slanting grey light of dawn, we depart from Nikolaev. Two hours after that we enter Kartakei, the former German village of Kunersdorf, and there, in a labyrinth of freshly painted school hallways, I meet the local historian.

He's just leaving his classroom, a fastidious-looking man in owl-rimmed eyeglasses, a grey vest, and pepper-grey hair in a buzz cut. On our way outside I explain myself.

"I'm here on a Fulbright fellowship," I say. "Investigating sites where Jews were murdered during WWII.

"There is one such a site here," he says. "We can walk there."

It is a dirty village, with an Asiatic squalor I've seen in rural Pakistan, smoking piles of leaves, skinny dogs milling around, and under some trees shawled rag ladies, short, heavy women, bending over and retrieving something.

"Are they sorting rubbish?" I say.

"No, picking up walnuts," my interpreter, Pavel, says. "Very healthy. All the poor collect them."

With an absent-minded air the historian leads the way. We go along the road to a potholed alleyway that stinks of urine. To avoid the puddles, we press ourselves against a rough brick wall, sidling from shadow to light.

"There," the historian says.

He points toward the naked folds of hills in the distance. Kartakei is situated at the end of a long valley, near other massacre sites, like Michaelovka and Zavadofka, and not far from Lichtenfeld, my grandfather's birthplace, where, as testimonies indicated, the sounds of rifle volleys carried, ten, twenty miles, over the steppe. In 1942 everyone in this vicinity knew of the slaughter. Even children.

"In the hills?" I ask.

"No. Near the stream there. At the base of the hills," he says. "Bones wash out after heavy rains."

"Were the bodies burnt?" I ask, wondering if I should look for charred remnants, and remembering the Berezovka train station, just several miles away, fifty-five hundred bodies burnt on a pyre, that left the soil, which I pinched between my fingers, oily to the touch.

I don't get an answer, because the historian has launched into a story of his aunt, an eyewitness at Bogdanovka. From her garden directly across the river—using a pair of Wehrmacht binoculars from a German officer billeted in her home—she watched the huge pile of victims, writhing in the fire like worms.

"Who were the murderers here?" I say, frustrated. I've already had enough ugly images about Bogdanovka crowding my thoughts. I don't need more.

The historian ignores my question. My interpreter shrugs. We cross the field, littered with garbage, and on the way, the historian tells me that there were two hundred victims, among them sixty communist officials, the rest women and children.

"The documents say seventeen German colonist policemen from Kartakei murdered 650 Jews brought from Hulievka," I say.

"Impossible," the historian says. "Soviet people would never do such a thing. Not to their own countrymen."

"This man is a patriot," Pavel interjects, proudly, obviously enlivened by this new twist, this denial.

The pasture near the rivulet is strewn with animal bones and plastic bottles and scattered garbage, an ugly and desolate site, like so many places where Jews were killed.

"The children and the babies…they were not shot," I say.

"Impossible," the historian says.

My interpreter didn't use the Ukrainian word, rastrelna, I know, because I didn't hear those rattling syllables which always remind me of gunfire, so I realize he says "not killed" to the historian, instead of "not shot."

"No, I mean the children were killed in other ways," I say. "Have you heard that?"

"No," The historian says.

"There was a Volksdeutsche woman here," I say. "She volunteered."

"Volunteered?" the historian says, quizzically. "For what?"

"To murder the babies and children of Jewish officials from the Kartakei collective."

"Impossible."

The historian doesn't believe me. He doesn't want to. If he did, it would mean that instead of creating a new Soviet person, the communist regime spawned vengeful baby killers, capable of murdering their fellow citizens with alacrity.

"I am not saying I believe it, or it is right," I say. "I am saying this woman blamed the Jews for administering regime policies that starved her children in the 1930s."

"No. Impossible."

"It was a common delusion then," I say.

We start back. Crossing the fouled pasture—just over my shoulder—I sense the raging, stringy-haired peasant Medea, wielding her rifle as a club. The ugly image of children being killed remains with me as we pass through the pungent ally and reach our car on Kartakei's main street.

"I will walk home from here," the historian says, walking away in short, measured steps.

Under the scraggly trees, a rag lady mutters to herself, pockets bulging with walnuts.

"What's she saying?" I say.

"Something bad about her family," my interpreter says. "Something that happened long ago. Only God knows."

***

The next day, on my wall map of Transnistria. I can't find Kartakei. I was busy reading documents while Mikhail drove me there, so I have no idea where it is. I place my index finger on the map, on Rohrbach, and from there, search in widening arcs. Nothing. It's not strange I can't find it, I tell myself. Some places have four, even five different names, Ukrainian, Volksdeutsche, pre-Bolshevik, and then, in the 1930s, a collective farm named for an obscure Soviet official. Finally, I give up. That's when I see it was under my finger the entire time. Uncomfortably close. Less than ten miles from Rohrbach. Where my grandfather once lived, where other relatives of mine lived during the German Occupation.

Kartakei appalls and confuses me. Is the rifle wielding Volksdeutsche woman an aberration, an isolated occurrence, occasioned by a viciously cruel collective leader in the 1930s who happened to be Jewish? Or is she indicative of a broader pattern of virulent anti-Semitic revenge taking during the German Occupation? The Nazis tried unsuccessfully, to orchestrate "spontaneous" pogroms among indigenous Ukrainians, and local Volksdeutsche.

What happened in Kartakei is an indication—and the document that I read in Katherinental is another—that I don't understand the extent of anti-Semitism in the Volksdeutsche villages. I propose to remedy this during my next holiday, cloistering myself in my apartment—I've learned that from Dimitri—and for a full week, I live a curious inner life, as I plow through the various books and documents, the issue swaying like a hooded cobra in front of me.

For most of the nineteenth century, initially amicable relationships existed between the two groups, with Jews

236

buying grain from the colonists and funneling that grain into the ports on the Black Sea. That relationship shifted—as noted by the foremost Volksdeutsche scholar Height—when young Jews from Odessa, embittered by bad conditions in the ghetto, eagerly joined the Revolution, and non-Jewish Jews, as the historian Paul Johnson calls those who relinquished their Judaism, including women, who enlisted in the secret police and Red Army began to assume leadership positions.

Bolshevik grain requisitioning squads, anarchists, and revolutionaries raided Volksdeutsche villages like Katherinental, Worms, and Rastadt in 1918 and 1919, and as Height claims, some of these squads that murdered and pillaged and raped were under leadership of Jews who spoke the German dialect and were familiar with the economic status of the villages. Other sources cited incidents of Bolsheviks torturing German colonists to learn the location of hidden grain stocks.

The role of Bolshevist Jews in the Ukraine, Height claims, was formidable, with four hundred Jews among the leading Soviet functionaries in Russia itself, so in some Volksdeutsche colonies, the Jews were perceived as the public face of the regime, even if, in reality, they were far from wielding the power attributed to them. In 1918, a Jewish regiment from Odessa went to Landau, arrested the German colonists active in the Citizen's Home Guard, and executed them. In the early 1920s, in Selz, the Bolshevist commissar, a Jewish woman, was notorious for "treating the people like dirt." In the Beresan district, an Austrian Jew set up a Bolshevist regime, ordering numerous Volksdeutsche executions.

The tens of thousands of Volksdeutsche refugees who fled Ukraine during the civil war period, carried their anti-Semitism—which blurred distinctions between the Jewish people and the homicidal methods of the Bolsheviks—across Europe, and their letters, in German language newspapers in America, point to an anti-Semitic environment in some Volksdeutsche villages in the early 1920s.

One letter, penned from Kirtum, Latvia, by the daughter of a Volksdeutsche pastor who once ministered in Grossliebental, a village south of Odessa, painted an ugly picture:

> Grossliebental has become a large hospital with only sick people and no remedies. Each day they must go to the cemetery and watch as the corpses are buried...In one grave four to six corpses are placed without caskets. Papa himself prayed at many of these burials, as entire families are buried, with husband and wife buried together and their children on either side. Weak, hungry people stumble around on the streets like drunks...All of the death is because the final provisions were taken from the storehouses belonging to the farmers. If they had been helped to protect their provisions, there would have been enough to nourish everyone, but the Jews took the food and the rest starved...

The pastor's daughter accuses a Jewish communist, an orphanage house-father at Grossliebental, of murdering Volksdeutsche orphans under his care, "to see if there won't be fewer of them, by first exposing them to the elements and then allowing them to starve..." Her letter ends with a bone-chilling threat that sounds more like Nazi Germany than Ukraine in 1922: "This situation will give rise to such a slaughter of Jews such as history has never known before. Even the babies in their cribs will not be spared, for the Jews have earned this terrible reward."

Some scholars, like Lumanns in *Himmler's Auxiliaries*, maintain the Volksdeutsche were more anti-Semitic than the average Reich German, that their view of the equivalency of Jews and communists was, if not as virulent as, then roughly congruent with, the crude anti-Semitism of the Nazi occupiers. An Einsatzgruppen commander Biberstein, under Allied questioning at Nuremberg, in perhaps self-serving statements, described the rage the ethnic Germans harbored against the communists. He said he was, in particular, "terrified by the bloodlust exhibited by students from nearby Volksdeutsche villages, those who had lost their elders to executions by the communists during the 1930s." These students, along with Russian prisoners of war, willingly lined up to help slaughter Jews.

One Transnistrian memoirist admitted that with the arrival of German troops in 1941, the people were "happy to have been delivered from the Jewish yoke." However much that statement was "colored with ideology," he says, it was not inaccurate and quite close to his "own experience of actual views held at the time." Most disturbing were the statements of Sister Fanny, a German Red Cross Sister, placed in the Rastadt hospital in June 1942. She was told in the strictest confidence that some local Volksdeutsche had "a hatred against the Jews," and that prior to her arrival, masses of Jews had been murdered and their bodies burnt. Sister Fanny was also told that, among the Rastadters, there was a general understanding to remain silent because their own young men in the local police were involved, and those who felt the murders were a terrible crime dared not speak out.

***

KOLOSOFKA

"This is the road to hell," I say.

We are somewhere on the steppe, bumping toward the Kolosofka train station, Mikhail downshifting to soften the spine-jarring jolts, Pavel busy correcting my American misconceptions.

"No, not to hell," Pavel says. "Road to heaven."

"Road to heaven?"

That morning, before leaving Nikolaev, Mikhail ran his dirty fingernail along the road, marked yellow on the map to indicate its good condition. But the road we travel isn't good, isn't even a road. Construction funds have been funneled off by corrupt bureaucrats, and this is more a washboard-like prairie path. Even Mikhail's old Volga, with its high clearance, has difficulty negotiating it.

"Yes, road to heaven. Narrow and difficult," Pavel says. "And filled with aster plants."

"Aster plants?"

"Yes, aster plants have thorns," Pavel says.

"Like the thorns in the crown of Jesus?" I say.

"Yes. So this path is very difficult."

"Like the road to heaven. Okay, I understand."

We are tracing the route of trainloads of Jews, originating from Odessa. Kinder transports I call them, because, as one document claimed, at least a third of the victims dumped out at the Kolosofka station were children and babies.

In the rust and ruin of rural Ukraine, the Kolosofka station is a startling anomaly, a large, modern building, with a glistening bank of slanting windows, which Mikhail has stopped to admire, while doubting Pavel clutches his coat around himself, mumbling: "I don't think Jewses were brought here to kill."

This spurs me to circle the spectral, honey-colored old station next door, snapping photos, and to bleed out my anger. I imagine an outburst, aimed at Pavel: "Every Jew brought here was murdered, so this whole station is, as far as I'm concerned, the portal to hell."

On the Kolosofka platform, my mind does jogging sidesteps at the hugeness of the Holocaust, which stretches from Struthof, a Nazi concentration camp with gas chambers I once visited in the Vosges Mountains in France, all the way across Eastern Europe, to Ukraine, and its seven hundred murder sites, including sites west and north of the Kolosofka station, and others farther eastward, and still others, across the Bug River, which dot the former Nazi-occupied Ukraine.

Mikhail and Pavel join me on the Kolosofka platform. Snow laces the ground. It's a familiar Dakota-like cold. My life on the prairie flickers—a distant light on a far horizon. How long have I been chasing these ghosts, an entire summer and autumn and part of a winter? Or is it a year, plus the better part of a second year? I don't quite remember. It hardly matters.

Thousands of Jews brought to Kolosofka station went directly from the freight and cattle cars, and depending on the season, into the hands of the Volksdeutsche police, into their sleds and lorries and wagons, or were forced into long columns which stretch out over the steppe. There are children, many children. Which troubles the balding Nazi fanatic, Untersturmfuehrer Liebl, stationed in Lichtenafeld, heard complaining one day in his office to his adjutant: "Today I must struggle through another difficult day, removing the young."

Removing the young. A tortured euphemism for annihilating innocents. It's reflective of Liebl's attitude, a mix of self-indulgence and perverse Nazi morality, of toughness and brutality as inversions of Judeo-Christian tenets. Even Volksdeutsche youth groups in Transnistria, both male and female, were taught such patent nonsense.

The wind whistles in the whorl of my ear. I'm chilled and depressed. Mikhail and Pavel stand close, like cattle in a storm, faces turned from the bitter wind. I need to make a decision. I'd made plans to visit Worms, also known as Vinogradnoye, especially its Evangelical Lutheran Church where some of my relatives and my childhood neighbor, Mrs.

Sayler, were baptized and confirmed before immigration to Dakota. It would be a sentimental journey, unrelated to my research, because as far as I know, the Worms police weren't involved in the Holocaust. The only murders there were done by an Einsatzgruppen unit, who came in a blue bus and several motorcycles, in the fall of 1941, and took a group of Jews, locked overnight in that same church, to a nearby sandpit, where they were executed.

"Vinogradnoye?" Mikhail says. "Is that where you want to go?"

"No," I say.

He jabs his forefinger at the map, at Sirotskoye, through which Jewish columns passed on their way to Domaneuvka and Akmachetka, and then at Michaelovka, the site of another massacre.

"Mikhail says we have enough daylight to visit both and be back by evening at Nikolaev," Pavel says.

That day, shivering on the Kolosofka platform, I direct Mikhail to drive us back to Nikolaev, not knowing I've drawn close to the dark heart of the Transnistrian Holocaust, to where it first began: my ancestral village of Worms.

***

In January 1942, when the first column of Jews passed through the Zerigol Valley and came into the vicinity of Worms, alarm bells were raised, and twenty-eight-year-old Obersturmfuehrer Berhard Streit, the SS commandant of that district, was notified.

Four months earlier, Streit established his district headquarters in the most substantial building in Worms, the former Institute for the Deaf-Mute, and drawing manpower from nearby Volksdeutsche villages, like Rohrbach, he established what was likely the largest overall police unit in Transnistria.

When Streit learned of the columns, all of the dead and diseased bodies left scattered along the road from Beresovka, and anticipating further columns of Jews passing through his district, he appeared at VoMi headquarters in Landau, asking for guidance. His superior, Dr. W.—the fanatical Nazi who later used plundered Jewish gold to "put into order" his and his own wife's dentition—orders Streit to stop the Jews from encroaching on the Volksdeutsche villages and, if necessary, to use force.

At the same time, SS General Hoffmeyer, the VoMi head, sought advice in Berlin. What should he do about the columns of Jews struggling over the steppe of Transnistria? He returned with two recommendations, neither of which appeal to him. The first, that SS officers from the VoMi do the killing, the second, that Ollendorf, the Einsatzgruppen D leader, headquartered in Nikolaev—later hanged at Nuremberg—use his mobile death squads.

When Ollendorf refused, General Hoffmeyer traveled to Odessa to get the Romanians to stop the transports of Jews from that city, but without success. He raged against both the Romanians and the bureaucrats in Berlin for getting him involved in this dirty business, but Hoffmeyer reluctantly decided that the Volksdeutsche policemen in Transnistria should liquidate the Jews.

***

The initial murder of Jews by Volksdeutsche police was haphazard. It took place on January 20, 1942, several kilometers outside Worms, at a cultivated acreage called the Beresofka Field. That's according to a canteen cook at the SS headquarters in Worms. On her way to get water from an outside well, she heard the excited voices of local policemen standing outside the headquarters. Curious, she went closer:

> I heard them talk of being ordered to go and kill some Soviet citizens who were Jews. When I asked one of the policemen what is going on, he tells me, "There

243

is a transport of Jews out of Odessa being brought to the Beresovka Field, and we are going to give them a hot reception." At that point, the SS commandant Streit appeared, and the police formed in their ranks, and Streit, riding high in the saddle, led them to the Beresovka Field.

A policeman said:

> It was on a Saturday that I was in the police canteen in Worms, when S., the local Volksdeutsche police leader entered, ordering all of us to get our weapons and necessary ammunition and fall into formation, ready to march. We were led behind the village and out to the Beresovka Field. Once there, S. told us that a large column of Jews was approaching. Our orders were to not allow the Jews to enter Worms; instead, we were to turn them in the direction of a hamlet named Vinogradofka. There were approximately fifty policemen from the barracks, and an hour later twenty or thirty more policemen joined us, and all of us met the approaching column of about five hundred Jews.

The policemen could discern, in the reflected light from the snow-covered field, dark forms moving their way. Obersturmfuehrer Streit orders the police to encircle the column and block its forward progress. When an elderly Jew comes forward, insisting the exhausted, bedraggled column be allowed passage into Worms, one of Streit's SS officers draws his pistol, shoots the old man in the head, announcing to the shocked policemen: "That is how you deal with such people."

Streit gives the order to shoot. Some policemen discharge their rifles so their bullets go wide or high, others fire directly into the massed Jews. The shooting lasts two hours. Many are killed, and the survivors struggle in the direction of the Kolosofka station, eight kilometers away. Streit dispatches several policeman to turn over the bodies and administer the coup-de-grace to the wounded.

Several days later, the canteen worker goes to the Beresofka Field. She finds:

A terrible scene…bodies lay scattered for several kilometers in the direction of the Kolosofka station… many young children, from two to six years, and their mothers, grown and half-grown males and females, and older people, all of whom had been shot and killed, except for several babies that, trapped under some corpses, froze to death. Overall, there were about three hundred bodies.

Over the following weeks, other columns, large and small, arrived at the Beresofka Field, with similar results. As bodies accumulated, Streit ordered a work detail of elderly men from Worms and Rohrbach—a number of them were close relatives of the Dakota pioneers—to gather the corpses. There were three thousand, according to one report, and they burned them on a huge wooden pyre in the Beresovka Field.

***

By February 1942—on Hoffmeyer's orders—Streit's police continued to meet the Jews struggling toward Worms. Now, however, several rings of police were thrown up around the columns, and not just the weak, sick, and exhausted were murdered. All were annihilated.

Several Worms policemen, under Soviet interrogation, testified to a dozen or more actions of indeterminate size. Enough actions so that one policeman's chest, an eyewitness claimed, was covered with black and blue bruises from his rifle's recoil. After the war, a Soviet newspaper claimed twenty thousand Jews were murdered by the Worms police, a number likely inflated for propaganda purposes. My own estimate, based on eyewitness statements, not coerced confessions, is that there were at least four different actions, and roughly, at least forty-three hundred victims.

One former policeman angrily testified there weren't murders in Worms in January of 1942 and that the number of Jews murdered was based on forced confessions. He said that S., the accused local Volksdeutsche commander, had been transferred to Wesselinovo, a village twenty miles from Worms, so how could he have led murder actions? Wesselinovo, however, was also an active murder locale. At least three thousand Jews were killed there, along with two groups of gypsies killed and buried in mass graves several kilometers outside that village, an additional number of gypsies shot and thrown down a local well, and an unknown number of Jews and gypsies killed and buried in a mass grave halfway between Rohrbach and Wesselinovo. If S., the local Volksdeutsche commander, was transferred to Wesselinovo, then it was to a place to where as many, and perhaps more, Jews were killed than in Worms.

***

About that time I find a roster of the Volksdeutsche policemen detailed to the Beresofka Field slaughters. The list reads like the phonebook from my hometown of New Odessa, and other Dakota towns in my home county, common Volksdeutsche names of people I'd known intimately—Mindt, Schmierer, Ackerman, Trautmann, Frank, Schmidt, Ebel, Remmich, Adam, Bohlender, Hochhalter, and Wolf.

My body breaks out in a rash, a scatter of red dots on my chest, weird stigmata that to my jaundiced eye resembles the sites that mark my pushpin map. I wake shuddering. At night, a red stain, like blood, seems to seep under my eyelids. I grow sluggish and dispirited. A visit to a Ukrainian doctor reveals nothing.

"Everybody has at least one thing wrong with them," the doctor says.

"It's a spiritual malady," Dmitri says, crossing himself solemnly when he comes. "From the Holocaust. Remember we spoke of Nietzsche's abyss? This is what happens. It is staring back at you. You better take a long break."

I take his advice. I pray. I lay in bed for days. My thoughts drift back to a time long before my Transnistrian research, when I first met my grandmother's ninety-three-year-old cousin. After sponsorship by the Baptist Church, he'd become a naturalized American citizen, and his apartment door in Tucson, Arizona, emblazoned with patriotic stickers, showed how glad he was to live in America. While he'd told me about his past, I kept glancing sideways at a framed photograph on the living room wall, three men, two brothers and himself, in SS uniforms.

He told me how, drafted into the Waffen SS from his home village in 1943, he'd calmed his young wife's fears that he'd never return by doing a Bible reading, an old Volksdeutsche faith healing practice. He'd let his Bible fall open, and his finger landed randomly on Psalms 91:5, which gave him, he says, divine evidence he'd return unscathed: "Do not be afraid of the terrors of the night, nor fear the dangers of the day…though a thousand fall at your side and ten thousand are dying around you, these evils will not touch you."

"That's the prophecy I carried in *mein* heart," he told me that hot day in Tucson, tapping his sunken chest with long elegant fingers, and it was that "letter from heaven"—the Bible verse—copied out and carried in his breast pocket, that allowed him to survive, not just two years of military action in the SS, as bullets and shrapnel left him untouched, but also Magadan, a postwar Soviet gulag death camp, where he'd been imprisoned because of his SS affiliation, and where hundreds upon hundreds of frozen Volksdeutsche corpses lay stacked like cordwood outside the drafty barracks: the thousand and the ten thousand that would fall by his side, as predicted by the verse. And then, after his release from Soviet captivity in 1955, and thanks to the Baptist Church, which sponsored him, he and his wife came to America.

Lying in bed in Nikolaev, I also remember an incident he told me about in Tucson that day, an incident that still haunted him, he said, that took place in 1942. As a teacher in a Nazi-run school in Pervomaisk, he made a holiday trip to Odessa, traversing Transnistria from north to south, and on the way, the wheels of his auto thumped with regularity over body parts strewn across the highway, the remains of Jews forced over the steppe. That was, I realized, my first glimpse into the Holocaust in Transnistria.

The next morning, I decide to do a random Bible reading. I prop myself up on my elbow, squeeze my eyes shut, and after allowing my Bible to fall open, let my finger to fall randomly onto the page, onto this verse: "Yet a little while the light is with you. Walk while you have the light, lest darkness come upon you, for he that walks in darkness knows not where he goes."

In this modern age few believe, and many might mock what they'd call my archaic fantasy about divine guidance, but to me the verse is the only meaningful thing I can muster against the forces of darkness and blood that threaten to overwhelm me, and the verse means my maladies will cease, that from some inexhaustible source my energy will be renewed, so I can continue my research. Which is what I continue to do, going from murder site to murder site after that, making notes, knowing that despite my weakness I am doing God's work.

***

Mid-fellowship I fly to Germany for a brief vacation, my first in a long time. I soak in a tiled tub the first night in Berlin's refurbished Hotel Adlon. I'm cognizant of the great abyss between amenities of modernity and the isolated, muddy villages on the steppe. I'm unaware, thankfully, that my Berlin jaunt will drive a final stake through the heart of my mythical view of Lichtenfeld.

The next morning, I'm whisked across the city by the whisper-quiet subway to meet my friend at the Pergamon Museum, a political science professor with JFK University. I arrive early, passing time in the nearby Neues Museum, where classical frescoes still are pockmarked from WWII bullets, which remind me that there were hundreds of Volksdeutsche fighting in SS units in the bombed-out city as Hitler's forces made their last stand in 1945.

Once my friend arrives, we pose for photos by the great lion at the entrance to the Pergamon Museum. Afterward we visit the section of Berlin where Hitler's Chancellery once stood. From a park bench, she motions me forward, but she herself refuses to draw near that place, which symbolized the destruction visited on her own family, uprooted from a German colony in Ukraine. Her grandfather went missing in the *Volksturm*, Hitler's civilian army, and her grandmother's brothers were killed in the Budapest encirclement.

"What did you see there?" my friend asks later.

I tell her about the rusted, mangled rebar, poking up like fire-scorched filaments of an alien plant. I tell her about how I stood on the place where, beneath yards and yards of thick concrete, Hitler's bunker was located.

"Did you think of your own Hitler bunker?" she says.

"Yes. I did."

My Volksdeutsche friend from Berlin is the only person I've ever told about the Hitler club, or my grotesque nickname, Eichmann, or the bloody swastika I'd carved into my arm. That came about one day while we're sunning ourselves on her balcony, when she traced, with a quizzical look on her face, the faint, scarred outline.

"You don't want to talk about it?" she says now.

"Not exactly," I say.

Later, strolling the *Kufurstendamm*, a string of cafes, shops, and hotels along Berlin's Broadway, my friend says, "Eichmann's office is nearby. Do you want to go there?"

We find 116 Kurfurstendammstrasse, circling the surprisingly modern-looking high-rise office building in which *Referat IVB4*, Eichmann's office, was once located, and coming around to the front, I catch a full length reflection of myself, the first since the tourist hotel in Nikolaev, and though I don't look unkempt, I jerk back.

"You act like you've just seen a ghost," my friend says.

"Well, maybe I have," I say. In my emotional exhaustion, I think I see, etched into my aging features, guilt for betraying my Volksdeutsche background with this research, and it shocks me just how much I resemble Eichmann at the time of his trial in Israel.

"Don't do that American emotional striptease with me," she says. "Next thing you'll tell me is that you look like Eichmann."

"Don't I?" I say.

"Ach. Oh, misery," my friend says, shaking her beautiful head. "Why don't you get a pair of black glasses and make your transformation complete?"

"You are saying I need this vacation?"

"I've made my point. Let's find your office Eichmann."

On the main floor of the building, we find a bank, and in a tableau of Germanic efficiency, employees bustle from office to office, a blur of white shirts against dark wood paneling.

"Here, in these same offices, Nazi policy toward the Jews evolved," she says.

Three different stages, she explains, all headed by Eichmann, a territorial solution, emigration, and finally, between July and October of 1941, after emigration is replaced by extermination, and ministerial squabbles ensue.

"So that's when the Wannsee Conference was organized?" I say.

"Yes, at the behest of Heydrich, the Fuehrer-in-waiting," she says.

The Wannsee Conference was, as Eichmann called it during his trial, a gathering of "the Popes," the various senior officers and representatives of Nazi ministries considered suitable to carry out the Final Solution. They meet at a confiscated Jewish villa outside of Berlin on January 1942.

"Do you think Leibbrandt knew, by the time of Wannsee, that they were killing Jews in Transnistria?" she says.

"I don't know how he didn't know," I say. "There was an uproar in Hoffnungstal about the murder of the Freiburg Jews. And Wannsee was four months later. So he knew. From his many contacts in Hoffnungstal."

We headed back the way we had come, leaving the former Referat IVB4, our conversation centered on how Eichmann was connected with Transnistria.

"I will tell you this," she says. "And then, enough of such talk for this evening?"

"Okay," I say.

"It's a decision Eichmann made in early 1942," she says. "From Referat IVB4."

His decision disallowed, she explained, the passage of two hundred thousand Jews, ethnically cleansed by the anti-Semitic Romanians, from crossing the Bug River into the Nazi-occupied Ukraine; Eichmann also disallows their return across the Dniester River back to Romania. That traps the Jews—those arriving on foot or by railcar from Romania and

Odessa, those already forced overland in long columns—within Transnistria.

At a street-side vendor, my friend buys a small basket of crisp French fries, dipping them in a tangy sauce. She starts to eat.

"So it was Eichmann's decision that..." I say.

"I will say it for you. So you don't have to say it. Yes, Eichmann's decision turned the Volksdeutsche police in Transnistria into killers."

A pained look clouds her features, a reminder that it wasn't only my relatives, but also her own, forced into the police units, used to kill Jews.

"But eat your French fries," she says. "No more talk about Eichmann. You are on vacation."

My last day in Berlin my friend and I, go to our favorite cafe, high-atop the Wertheim building. We drink strong German coffee, read, and chat. At one point she looks up from the paperback she is reading, *Tracks*, by Louise Erdrich, a Native American writer, whose novels are set on the prairie, a place that my friend, in metropolitan Berlin, can't quite imagine.

"It's like this view," I say, nodding at the wide plate glass windows that offer a long view over Berlin's rooftops. "On the prairie those open spaces affect people."

"Hitler said something like that about Volksdeutsche," she says. "In a transcript of his table talk conversations."

"Yes, it was something about how the Volksdeutsche seemed stunned by the steppe," I say.

"Speaking of transcripts, I want to read you this. From Eichmann's trial."

"So my vacation is officially over?"

"Yes," she says, pulling several pages out of her purse, and clearing her throat. "Just don't tell me that my accent sounds like an old Nazi, agreed?"

"Agreed."

What she read me that day, high atop the Wertheim building in Berlin, from a verbatim transcript of Eichmann's trial in Israel, 1961, gave me a psychic jolt.

> State Attorney Bach: I now submit to the Court several Romanian reports relating to the district of Transnistria.

> Presiding Judge: Do we know under whose command these camps in Transnistria were?

> State Attorney Bach: Your Honors, later on we shall produce another witness who will describe conditions in Transnistria for us. As I demonstrated by that Tighina Agreement, it was actually a joint German-Romanian administration…

> The next document is number four seventy-six, which reports that twelve hundred Jews were transferred to the area of the constabulary post in Huliacovka, and from there to a certain collective farm, a *kolkhoz*, and that afterward SS men from the German settlement of Lichtenfeld took these Jews and shot them. The information is reliable.

"Well, what do you think?" my friend says. "Lichtenfeld mentioned at Eichmann's trial."

"It's depressing," I say.

"Didn't you already know that?"

"Of course, I just don't like being reminded."

"Have you visited Lichtenfeld yet? You've had a year, or more, to go there."

"I've visited Lichtenfeld."

"I know," she says, in her prescient way. "But that was before you knew of the sixteen thousand Jews killed, wasn't it?"

"Let's pretend I'm still on vacation, okay?" I say.

After that, until my flight leaves Berlin's Tegel Airport that evening, we avoid talk of Hitler and Eichmann, but it is there, even in our silence, the past that will not pass away.

***

RETURN TO LICHTENFELD; RETURN HOME

On the days I don't teach, and over weekends and holidays, I'm on the road with Mikhail and Pavel, and in the evenings, on my wall map of Transnistria, when I mark with a red x the murder sites I've visited, my heart contracts at the foreboding and essential truth: since my trip to Germany, I've been moving in an ever-narrowing circle whose center is Lichtenfeld.

"Later. I will go to Lichtenfeld later," I tell myself each time, though later would come more quickly than I expected.

Early one morning we cross Nikolaev's main bridge, thick fog rising from Bug River, headed to find Krasna-Vladimirovka—a murder site in a long valley west and north of Berezovka. There are gusts of traffic, a couple of boxy Lada and other older autos, then just us and the steppe.

The road narrows, and we pass into what seems a tunnel of overarching walnut trees and white poplars, which then opens to an immense sunflower field of withered stalks, curling leaves, and heavy heads hanging down, like an endless procession of mourners. We bump through former Volksdeutsche villages, homes of limestone block with corrugated metal roofs bristling

254

with TV dishes, and overgrown yards where I see steep-roofed outdoor cellars like those built by Dakota Germans on the prairie.

We get lost. Where was Krasna-Vladimirovka? A strange woman, with a Medusa-like tangle of hair, points one way, and an unshaven workman repairing a new John Deere combine roadside waves his greasy wrench the other.

"Just when you think you are lost," Mikhail says, repeating an old Ukrainian proverb. "Then you are there."

We find a hamlet, turn at its cemetery, where, amid a couple of weathered, rickety tables, laden with empty bottles and rotting scraps of food for the dead, several medieval-looking pecked-limestone crosses stand like sentinels.

Our potholed road finally peters out into muddy ruts of a long incline, edged by sunflower fields, and engine whining, our auto skidding sideways down the wet slope of the other side, a wild slalom ride that brings us into a wide valley of swales, alluvial folds, and ravines.

"Lots of places to kill and hide Jews here," Mikhail says.

At a house on a sloping hill outside a village we stop. A tall, ruggedly handsome man lifts his pepper-grey head from under the hood of his semi-truck.

"Yes, this is Krasna-Vladimirovka," the man replies. "My mother knows about the Jews."

He gestures with oily hands at heavy clumps of Muscat grapes, hanging from an overhead arbor under which we stand. "Eat if you are hungry," he says. "I will wash up and take you to see my mother."

We eat the dark grapes, they're small and ripe, the sweetest grapes I've ever eaten, and just a handful quells my hunger.

"He is a Volksdeutsche," my interpreter, Pavel, says. "Or his father is."

"How do you know?" I say.

"I just know," Pavel says.

The big trucker guides us to his mother's house, and in a back room inside, we find a seventy-five year old woman, with an open Slavic-looking face, framed by a worn headscarf. She is busy pouring honey into plastic bottles.

"*Kumm herein*," she says. (Come in.)

In her *stupe* (living room), and brushing stray strands of grey hair from her face with the back of her hand, she tells me about her background, mixed Volksdeutsche and Ukrainian; some of her father's people—U.'s—immigrated to the prairie.

"Yes, I know the U. name," I say, but I didn't say I knew it from the Worms police roster. "My great aunt in Washington married a red-haired U."

"That is his grandfather's brother, I think," our host says, nodding at her son.

"Most U.'s have red hair," the son says. "Except mine is now grey."

"They brought the Jews here. When I was a little girl," our host says. "You can see the barns where the Jews were held. They still store grain there."

That evening, she adds, the village women, her own mother among them, secretly passed loaves of bread to the Jews in the barns.

"Who were the executioners? "I ask.

"People from here," she says. "And Volksdeutsche police. In white."

The massacre we speak about likely took place in fall of 1942, when four hundred Romanian Jews, mostly children and babies and pregnant women, were brought overland from the direction of Berezovka to this village, also known as Wasserthal. It is one of a dozen or more villages and hamlets under Liebl's Lichtenfeld command. That likely means D., the diminutive squad commander, and also my relative Y., were among the killers.

"When my mother and other villagers brought food again the next night, the barns were empty," our host says. "The killings were done secretly."

Secretly? That seems impossible. Shoot several hundred Jews in the middle of the night? The gunfire would have alerted everybody. Not to mention the flames and the stench. Some accounts say locals, just like at Wesseloe, helped with the murders.

"I will tell your driver to take you there," the woman says.

We pile into the Volga, and while we cross the bottom of the valley, I dig in my satchel for the Wasserthal folder, and read an eyewitness testimony:

> From a distance of two hundred to three hundred meters, I watched the second action at Wasserthal. It was evening, at twilight. Because of the flames coming from the lime-kiln, and the sounds of gunfire, I grew curious, and crept as close as I dared to the place. I saw that there were small groups of Jews in front of the burning lime-kiln, and that it smelled of bone and hair.
>
> Members of the police unit used carbines to shoot the victims in the head or the neck from behind. The victims then tumbled forward into the oven, and local Ukrainians threw the bodies into the flames. I did not see babies thrown into the flames alive, but there was talk of that later in Lichtenfeld. Here I must add

that these events were not openly spoken about, and if
so, only to one's closest kin and friends…

From my observation point, I watched three
different groups being shot, with each consisting
of about ten persons, I returned to my house. With
certainty I can say that among those police unit
members who did the shooting there were people
from Wasserthal; I knew them personally. The clothed
victims were searched for valuables beforehand. One
police unit member told me later that they looked
carefully between the toes, because sometimes the
Jews hid their rings there. I also know that one Sunday
clothing of executed Jews was given to the locals by
the police.

Mikhail parks our vehicle near the local village
cemetery, which tilts on a hillside, and across the road there is
a long low bluff. Pavel and I get out.

"There is nothing here," Pavel says.

He goes off to join Mikhail and the big trucker for a
smoke-break, while I skid down the slope of the bluff to a
low-lying area much like the one at Gradofka. I scan the edge
of the rise, set against grey clouds, and see, at thirty or forty
foot intervals, like a monster has taken huge bites from the
bluff, oval indentations: the ovens.

In the nearest oven—what's left of it—I kneel and part
the weeds and grass. It's what I do at every oven. What am I
looking for? Some certainty, I suppose, that hundreds, even
thousands, were murdered there.

Letters I'd translated from Wasserthal, to my
grandmother's family in Dakota, describe how, during the
starvation of 1933, squads of men go house to house, removing
grain and other foodstuffs, payment in kind for inflated regime
quotas. Mostly they find dead bodies. Locals called these men
the Undertakers. One letter harangued my relative on whose

land near New Odessa I used to hunt, for forgetting about "me, your only living aunt in all of Ukraine, who now must starve."

The Volksdeutsche and Ukrainian villages bury ten, twenty victims per day in mass graves. People break into the churches, closed by the Soviets, and in the darkness pray for death. "If the Lord does not help we are lost. My husband and sons are swollen like barrels. People are turning black again. By autumn, if we are not allowed grain, we will eat one another." People find bits of human fingers in sausage from the market. It's a horrific time out of which my surviving relatives stagger, forever seared. My own theory is that it is these people— those most psychologically and spiritually and physically damaged—whose thinking has most profoundly deteriorated, who conflate the Jews with the Soviet regime who starved them: the people who help the police murder Jews.

Pavel returns from his smoke and stands over me as I grub in the dirt of an oven. "There is nothing here. No evidence. Only God knows if anything even happened here."

Can't he see the outlines of the ovens? Why is his English clear only when he complains? Why can't he say Jews, not Jewses? For a long time I've been like a nervous dog, twining its leash around the post to which it's tethered, and now, at Krasna-Vladimirovka, I feel I've reached my limit.

"My God, babies and children were burnt alive here," I say, a flare of anger shooting through me. "Their screams carried for miles. I'll find you evidence."

Bent over, like a half-mad hunchback, I scuttle along the shoulder of the road, and then—as if willed by God—in a churned up tire-track I find a sliver of charred bone.

"See this," I say, wheeling around in a shameful display of self-righteousness. "This is a piece of bone. Human. Expelled from an oven seventy years ago."

Pouting, Pavel heads back to the car, and I follow. In the backseat, after calming myself, I apologize, and he accepts. Good for him, I think. At least he doesn't carry his ancestors' graveyards on his back. Which means I do.

Back at our host's home, the trucker fills a tray of shot glasses to their quivering brims with a clear liquid from a green plastic bottle, and we toss shots against the back of our throats. I'm disturbed at how animated everyone is.

While the ovens smoldered, our host says, some Volksdeutsche raked ashes into the clearing. Then, like an academic making air quotes, she shows how the villagers combed the still warm ashes, for whatever the Jews took with them to the ovens, for bracelets, gold, jewels. So that helps show the villagers knew the Jews had valuables, because earlier, at the barns, the Jews had bartered those valuables for food.

When the Soviets regain control of Ukraine near the end of WWII, my host says, a Volksdeutsche policeman from Lichtenfeld, one of the most brutal participants in the Wasserthal massacre, is captured and brought back to the village.

"We should do another round of shots," I announce.

The trucker, in one long pour, fills all of the shot glasses on the tray, and as I have another, and warmth spreads through me, I know the captured policeman is likely D., the murderous little squad leader, or even, perhaps, my grandfather's cousin, Y. On a hastily erected gallows in the center of Wasserthal, the former policeman is publicly hanged. By order of the Soviet government, as a warning to the other villagers, his corpse dangles for weeks, eyes plucked out, flesh torn away by sharp beaked hawks. I have another shot of the clear liquid, but that ugly image stays with me.

"Finally the body was cut down," our host says.

Everything seems unearthly sad, moves in slow motion. Our host returns from the back room with a jumble of plastic bottles of honey, of Muscat grape wine, of the clear liquid, and a round slab of brinza cheese, pressed against her breast. Thus laden we say our good-byes and stagger out to the car. On the northern edge of the village we stop at several long, low barns.

"Is this the place," I say, thick tongued but insistent. "Is this where she said the Jews were held?"

"It's here," Pavel says. "The Jewses were held here overnight."

His mispronunciation, Jewses, doesn't bother me this time. Strange, I think. I push open a large door and enter. It is cool inside. Mote-ridden beams of light strain through barred windows. There is a single pile of grain.

Using the bars of the windows, I hoist myself up, like doing a chin-up. It's doubtful the starving Jews were strong enough to do that, so it seems logical that if food was passed inside, perhaps bartered for something of value, it came from unseen faces. If the bars were wider, then maybe a small child or baby might have been saved. I curse myself for not asking our host about survivors. Likely not.

Back at the car, Mikhail and Pavel, grinding their cigarette butts into the dirt, look like they are doing a weird dance.

"Lichtenfeld?" Mikhail says.

"Are we that close?" I say, startled.

"Very close," Pavel says, glancing up from the map, spread across the hood in accordion-like folds. "Seven kilometers. That way."

The crumbled asphalt road meanders into a rutted pathway, which disappears onto the steppe.

"You'll damage your car getting there," I say.

"Volga is tank," Mikhail says. "It can go anywhere the police lorries went."

It's a weird reversal. After months of cajoling Anatoli, who balked at even good roads, I find myself trying to dissuade Mikhail from driving what looks like nothing but bad road ahead. My thoughts whirl, my legs feel like rubber, I feel stupid and lost.

"What was in those shots? I say.

"It's *samahonka*," Pavel says.

"I know that word *samahonka*," I say, feeling a jolt of terror.

"Yes, home-made vodka," Pavel says. "*Samahonka*."

It's what the policemen at Wesseloe and Rastadt and other sites drank to dull their senses, before and after murders. It's what Volksdeutsche policemen were forced to drink at Pervomaisk, before shooting tens of thousands of kneeling Jews at an antitank ditch.

"There is an old saying," Pavel says. "If you drink samahonka, you need three legs to walk."

"What do you think," Mikhail says, smiling broadly, enjoying seeing me, his American boss, stupefied. He traces his dirty index finger along the path to Lichtenfeld.

The map spins, I see the village, perched atop a high broad plateau, centrally located, situated in a long valley, ringed by a cluster of former state and collective farms, hamlets and family farms, like Christophero, Grigorjewka, Serotskoe, Wolkovo, Slepucha, and Guter Mauch. The nearest market town, Mostove with its castle, is ten miles away, and railheads like Berezovka and Kolosofka station, double that distance.

"Remember the Road to Hell?" Pavel says. "This path will be easier."

"To Lichtenfeld?" Mikhail says in German, because he knows I like to hear the language.

"Nach Lichtenfeld," I agree.

When we leave the collective barns, I'm fumbling in the back seat for the plastic bottles our host gave us, and soon enough, as our vehicle bumps and jostles slowly up the long gut of the valley, we are passing, back and forth, the bottle of Muscat wine, the bottle of samahonka.

***

Once, I'd prayed to understand more clearly what happened in Transnistria. Now, after months of research, and those prayers answered, I feel haunted by the knowledge. The isolated valley we travel toward Lichtenfeld actually runs parallel to another long valley to the east, where in the endless snowfalls of early 1942, just as Leibbrandt sipped his cognac at the Wannsee Conference, three thousand Jews from Odessa were struggling for their very existence.

Forced by their "Romano-German butchers" from the ghetto Slobodka in Odessa, by way of the Sortoriovka railway station, the Jews were shipped in cattle cars into the heart of Volksdeutsche villages and settlements. Their first stop, the Berezovka train-station, where they see the Romanian gendarmes and Germans, their set-in-stone faces illuminated by the immense flames of a bonfire, are busy "burning children alive, burning people alive."

On foot, the Jews who survive find their way to Sorotskoe and Mostove, ill-clothed, hungry, harried by not only the elements, but also drunk Romanians, policemen, and local bandits, who steal, rape, and kill them. At Lidievka, a Volksdeutsche village, just 6 percent of the three thousand Jews remain alive, and go from there on their final, overland journey to the death camps of Domaneuka, Gorka, and Bogdanovka.

That grim scenario, much on my mind as we head to Lichtenfeld, brings my thoughts back again, to Bogdanovka, to where the first Volksdeutsche police were forced to murder, so it feels like, by coming full circle, I've waded into the river of blood as deep and as far as possible without drowning, a realization that there just isn't enough samahonka to fully expunge.

***

Chattering in a pidgin of English and Ukrainian and German, we're ragged argonauts, buzzed from the samahonka, and the bottles of Muscat wine drained along the way, and when we reach the outskirts of Lichtenfeld, empties rolling on the floorboards, we have lapsed into near imbecility. Until our front tire snags the edge of a large pothole, and the auto shudders, and Pavel, chipping his tooth from his final drink of our only glass bottle, turns to Mikhail and snaps, angrily: "You're a goddamn *sosonia*."

"What's a *sosonia?*" I say.

"Someone who leads," Pavel says, picking a chip of enamel off his tongue. "But leads badly."

"Volga is Abrams tank," Mikhail says, oblivious to Pavel, sounding like the Groot character in the movie *Guardians of the Galaxy*.

Lichtenfeld looks smaller than I remember, either because we are enter from the opposite direction, or because of the scrambling effects of the wine and samahonka. Lichtenfeld is the smallest, population wise of the two dozen VoMi capitals across Transnistria, its central location explains the SS headquarters located there, and its police manpower totaling from two hundred to five hundred, depending on which source I consult, drawn only partially from Lichtenfeld, whose manpower has been severely depleted by the Soviet arrests and executions of 1937, with the rest of the men coming from the surrounding hutors and German villages and hamlets.

264

We drive the streets. My grandfather, and his siblings, I'm quite certain, were born in one of the still-intact old German homes, set back from the road. Which one, I don't know. In part because there is no available plat map for Lichtenfeld, an evangelical daughter colony of Worms and Rohrbach founded late, in 1867, in part because I don't want to know. In fact, the baldheaded Untersturmfuehrer Franz Liebl—he of the bad stomach, the maudlin self-pity about murdering children, and the same last name as Eichmann's wife Vera, and one of her relatives—was quartered in one of these substantial homes, even perhaps, and I shudder at the thought, the house where my own grandfather "first saw the light of this world."

Liebl's SS police headquarters is an innocuous looking building at the highest point of the village, and it offers a view of, clinging to both sides of the valley, a series of collective buildings, mostly open pole-barns for livestock, and in the distance the far horizon line of the boundless steppe.

I get out and teeter around the former headquarters. I cup my hands around my face, to peer through a dirty window, but jerk back when I see that a boney face, my own reflection, looks back. The building resembles a rural school or cafe on the prairie, circa the 1950s, and at different times, it served both purposes; in between, from late 1941 to 1944, it was the nerve-center of Nazi murder operations in the district. At one end, Liebl's office—in the middle an armory with Russian carbines, chests of ammunition, and heaped Jewish clothing and belongings—and at the opposite end the police canteen. On the steps of Liebl's former headquarters, I sit down, and read a testimony I've carried in my satchel for months, but have put off reading because it concerns my beloved Lichtenfeld. It's by a Volksdeutsche woman, who was a cook in the canteen:

> One day in 1943, one of the police lorries left Lichtenfeld in a hurry and I asked several guards in the building who was in the vehicle, and they said it was SS officer S., and two German Red Cross sisters, Christine

and Anne. A few hours later the lorry returned, bringing a Volksdeutsche policemen, accompanied by the two Red Cross sisters, who entered the canteen in the command center where I was then working as a cook.

As the policeman washed up I saw how terrible he looked, like he had seen a ghost, so I asked what was wrong. That was when he sat on a sofa in the canteen and told me that he had just come from the execution site. There, he says, a little girl who resembled his own daughter begged him, "Uncle, please let me live. I am German like you, for my father was Jewish, but my mother is a German."

He told me that the face of the girl and her words struck his soul so deeply that he passed out. That was when the German Red Cross sisters administered a medication to return him to his senses, so he could continue with the killings. The two nurses standing there in the canteen agreed with everything the policeman told me. A little later I witnessed an exchange between SS officer Ra., one of Liebl's lieutenants, and the policeman, who now that he'd returned to his senses, was ordered to return to the execution site.

"Untersturmfuehrer Ra.," the policeman said. 'Please. I just can't do that anymore."

"But you must," Ra. repeated. "You have no choice."

The rest of this exchange I could no longer overhear. But everything that I have said is true. As for how many Jews were killed on that particular day, I can't say, but in any case the police were always coming and going.

***

Since my first visit to Lichtenfeld, I've learned the first mayor during the German Occupation was Gottlieb L., my grandmother's cousin, who quickly agreed to take the post. In postwar testimony, L. says: "Everyone knew the Jews were being murdered, but about actual murders I know nothing. I never saw or heard anything and am not aware of any incidents." Why then did he resign just weeks into his term as mayor?

He was quickly replaced by Jacob Z., a local locksmith, mayor for the rest of the three year Nazi occupation. When questioned postwar, Z. denied knowledge of the murder of Jews in Lichtenfeld, and recited the mantra of German colonists helpless against Nazi power: "We were just a small dumb people. We did as we were told, or we would be stood up against the wall."

Z.'s twelve page testimony focused primarily on his fear of Liebl, and how their relationship was rife with threats: "You must understand the atmosphere of the times." Liebl bludgeoned to death several Volksdeutsche, used threats and physical intimidation on others, not just Z., and one day, when Liebl handed Z. the mayor's official stamp, he warned him: "if you lose this stamp, you will also lose your head."

These examples are consistent with reports of widespread brutality and killings of Volksdeutsche and other draconian actions by SS personnel across Transnistria. In fact, the brutalization of German colonists by VoMi personnel was so ongoing and significant that in 1943, General Hoffmeyer, the VoMi head, established a lager/jail in Johannesfeld, where offending Volksdeutsche, wearing the same striped uniforms as Jews in concentration camps, served out judicially determined sentences, instead of enduring arbitrary punishment by the VoMi's SS men.

Z.'s testimony raises some questions. Once, Z. says, Liebl cuffed the ears of the mayor of Ambarova, a neighboring village, for not properly responding to an SS officer. That is, oddly enough, the exact German word, *Ohrfeig* (ear cuffing), Z. used to describe what a nameless *SD*, or security police, officer did to Zimmer, a local Volksdeutsche communist, before having him murdered in the summer of 1941. Z. claimed the same SD officer assembled the entire Lichtenfeld community, those working in the fields, and the widows of fifty four Lichtenfeld men Zimmer purportedly sent to their deaths in labor camps in the Soviet 1930s, to watch the extrajudicial punishment.

"This piece of dung sent fifty four men to their deaths"—Z. quoted the SD officer as saying, while he beat Zimmer viciously about the head. "And for that he is going to be shot." It is curious testimony, because other Lichtenfelders claim it was Liebl, the SS commandant, who beat and shot Zimmer. Why would Z. blame an unnamed SD officer unless he was worried, through his mayoral association with Liebl, that he might be prosecuted?

Despite Z.'s denials, various Volksdeutsche policemen placed him at the center of the mass murders; he stood, they say, on the train siding at Kolosofka while Jews were unloaded directly into the custody of the Lichtenfeld police; he murdered Jews multiple times; he was seen personally delivering "chests full of bullets" to a massacre at Gut Mauch, a hamlet near Lichtenfeld, and it was Z., seen riding in a police lorry with Liebl, and his adjutant to Wesseloe to complete massacres there. Z. claimed that he learned second-hand about mass murders of Jews in Lichtenfeld, sometime in January 1942, and never saw the long columns of Jews that others said passed through Lichtenfeld, destined for the murder pits and ovens. He claimed he only heard the echo of gunfire from afar, and as for a swearing in ceremony just outside Lichtenfeld, at which others claimed hundreds of policeman attended, to watch the execution of a gypsy woman, he couldn't remember anything like that happening.

Z.'s own testimony is peppered with details only someone present at the murders might remember. He'd heard, he said, the murders at Krasna-Vladimirovka lasted two full days; he'd heard, he said, that locals there and at Wesseloe helped with the murders. His purported presence at the Kolosofka train-station was not, he insisted, to meet a trainload of Jews, but to arrest a German deserter sent from Odessa. That is precisely what Liebl claimed in a deposition in the early 1970s, which suggests the former mayor and Liebl may have coordinated statements to escape prosecution.

In the early 1960s, the seventy-three-year-old former SS commandant Liebl, living openly as an architect under his own name in Germany, sketched out for war crimes investigators his career with the Nazis. He was an official with the VoMi in the winter of 1939 and 1940, helping resettle Bessarabian and Lithuanian Volksdeutsche in Poland and Germany; at the time of the invasion of the Soviet Union in 1941, congruent with Weingartner's experience, he was called to Berlin, granted SS Untersturmfuehrer rank, then posted to Transnistria as Lichtenfeld's district SS commandant.

Leibl denied the assertion that he and his SS adjutant followed the columns in a police lorry, shooting stragglers. It was true, Liebl testified, that some Jews did pass through his district in the winter of 1941 and 1942, coming from the direction of Berezovka and, headed toward Worms, leaving behind corpses. It was General Hoffmeyer, his superior at VoMi headquarters in Landau, who ordered him, Liebl says, to meet with the Romanian prefect, Popp in Berezovka, and tell him to bury the corpses.

Liebl also says that the execution of the communist Zimmer, in direct opposition to Z.'s claim, was the result of a written order from General Hoffmeyer at VoMi headquarters in Landau. The actual execution, Liebl stated, was done by J., the local Volksdeutsche police commander, who assumed full responsibility for the murder, and even told Liebl as much. Other accusations, Liebl says, whether from former policemen or Lichtenfeld villagers, were bald-faced lies to settle personal vendettas.

Liebl's testimony stretched the bounds of believability, rivaling Z.'s patent falsehoods. Several Lichtenfelders painted an alternate picture. Liebl was, they testified, an ardent Nazi, a berserker with an unwavering will to murder Jews. Lichtenfelders testified that volleys of gunfire could be heard in their village for hours on end, once for two days, punctuated by the terrified screams of still living victims, doused with kerosene and set ablaze. A former policeman described the multiple times he'd seen long columns, of one to two thousand Jews straggling through his home village of Bergquelle, just seven kilometers from Lichtenfeld. The same policeman also described his swearing in as a policeman in either 1942 or 1943:

> It happened at the end of January or the beginning of February, in the time of the snowmelt, when five hundred police recruits gathered from the various villages in the district...Before the swearing-in oath, we were told to go to a muddy pit just west of Lichtenfeld, where we waited, not in formation. A number of policemen I didn't know personally, but all from Lichtenfeld, finally arrived under the command of the SS officer H., and J., the local Volksdeutsche commander. They brought with them a young woman... whose father was a tailor...and who was known to be a Jew...As she was forced to undress, J. asked her if she had a last wish, and she replied, "Yes, that my parents should be able to live."

> Immediately after that, the local Volksdeutsche commander, J., gave the command to fire. The policemen, using their carbines, shot from a distance of about three meters, and the young woman fell backward into the pit. I watched everything from ten meters away...At that point, J. had us line up, and placing firmly in each of our hands a list of our responsibilities, led us back to the place where Leibl led us in the swearing-in oath of loyalty to the Fuehrer and the Reich, which we repeated in unison.

***

While Mikhail drives us along the empty, rutted streets of Lichtenfeld, the various voices from the testimonies, of Liebl, of Z., rattle around in my thoughts. There are, I know, in the testimonies concerning events in other villages in Transnistria in the same three years, as murderers blame their crimes on others, similar contradictions, counter-narratives, and opposing viewpoints, and that most perpetrators went unprosecuted, and the lack of justice, even in my half-drunk state, is depressing.

The weeded Lichtenfeld cemetery has been razed of all its tombstones, like all, or most, colonist cemeteries across Transnistria, punishment for purported Volksdeutsche collaboration with the Nazis, and as we drive past, I see the mounded earth beside Zimmer's empty grave. His body was exhumed in the 1960s and accompanied back to Germany by his son, an unusual favor granted by the Soviet regime, because Zimmer is a local communist hero, despite the number of deaths he directly caused, and he even has a street in Lichtenfeld named after him.

Zimmer was just one of thousands of Soviet desk murderers during Stalin's collectivization scheme, which enslaved and oppressed nearly one sixth of the globe, and as I'm mulling that, I realize that the street we drive along is, in fact, Zimmer Street, so it's not only American university professors who admire and celebrate Marxist killers.

At the far end of Zimmer Street, we find three women in brilliant head-scarves knotted under their chins, peering blankly, like inmates of an asylum, I get out and snap a photo. It's the last photo I will snap in Ukraine.

"So Americans can see what stylish scarves you wear," I tell them.

What do they know of mass murders around Lichtenfeld? Nothing. They shake their heads. I'm relieved. But they know someone who does. A neighbor.

"We can summon him," they say.

The shortest woman waddles back to the house. I wax eloquent about my childhood, about the pastoral vision of Lichtenfeld's aura, shimmering over the steppe. Maybe the ladies will invite us in for vodka. It seems forever since Laryssa phoned ahead, warning prospective hosts not to push alcohol onto me, this American who didn't drink; forever ago Yascha and Masha teased me, saying, "The mourners at your funeral will gaze into your coffin and ask, 'But what did Ron die from? He had no bad habits.'"

"Here he comes," one lady says, as a leather-skinned guy in a battered slouch cap rounds the corner, his stubbled face squirms around a cigarette butt, and like Dmitri he has sleepless dark smears under his eyes. Every place on the steppe has someone like him: a local Memory Artist, a Secretary of Death. This guy is Lichtenfeld's. But I can't convince myself to care, and feel caught in a panic, like I'm running along an endless ravine, just ahead of a great tide of blood.

"He knows where the Jewses were killed," Pavel says. "Many, many Jewses. Some burned alive. In several places. He will show us."

I make a snap decision then, born of exhaustion and claustrophobia, and like the first tree in a cascade of falling timber, out of that decision come other bad decisions, some that haunt me now, years later, writing this.

"*Nach hause?*" Mikhail says. "Go home now?"

He studies my face closely. Like he can see in my eyes, the thousand spine-jarring paths we've traveled, the potholed roads, mud humped with ridges, shining with rain water in summer, and furred with frost on shivery autumn dawns.

"Nach hause," I say. "Let's go back."

It's the first step on the long journey home. Before we start back, I press a wad of twenty dollar bills into hand of the unshaven man, his face lapsing into stricken surprise, that I'd rejected his offer to see Lichtenfeld's murder sites.

We pass through half-ruined former Volksdeutsche villages, yards smothered with weeds, rusted hulks of farm machinery around long collective barns. I wish I could show all the college professors, wannabe Marxists and faculty lounge communists, this stillborn Utopian project, to cure them of their delusions; I'm deluded too, caught up in my own Lichtenfeld fantasy, which I don't want besmirched.

Mikhail and Pavel chatter. We bump into a once prosperous German-Catholic village, its reconstructed church, where Volksdeutsche in Germany, in memory to all those murdered by communists, have erected a large statue of Mary, and outside that village, and as a herd of cattle, minded by several leathery-faced herdsmen with thick cudgels, crosses the road, we stop and watch.

My thoughts boil with numbers. Sixteen thousand Jews murdered at Lichtenfeld seems too low. A couple of eyewitnesses claim the slaughter there was worse than Rastatt. Seventy six thousand Jews murdered by the Volksdeutsche police in Transnistria also seems low. Does that number include the Romanian Jews? Or twenty thousand gypsies dumped there? What am I, but an accidental and amateur historian who has gone too far, lost himself in the Kingdom of Death.

Mikhail pops the clutch after the final cow passes, and the car jerks forward. It is then I see the kitten. It lays mid-road, obviously struck by a passing vehicle, its tiny ribcage heaving, head seeping blood. It is the first time in Ukraine, during months and months of crawling along the ravines and climbing into ovens, that I've seen anything dying.

My head swims as archaic rural scenes unfold around us, half abandoned villages with old German churches, steeples replaced by orthodox domes, rows of solid limestone houses, and melon gardens where vines thick as snakes crawl the earth, and shriveled yellow melons and pumpkins piled against small haystacks, and rows of blue cabbages, that to my unravelling state of mind look like severed heads that Marlowe, the main character in Conrad's *Heart of Darkness*, found at the end of his journey upriver.

Back in Nikolaev, I pace my apartment. In my fraught state I feel like I'm wading in blood, and the rooms fill with occult forces, with small, black coffins. I arrange an Internet flight to Istanbul for the next morning. For rest, for relaxation, I tell myself. I'll visit Hagia Sophia, the ancient Church of Holy Wisdom, the greatest church of ancient Byzantium.

I'll kneel in its dimly lit interior, one of the largest enclosed spaces in human history, and on the cool floor I'll pray, and light candles in remembrance of the murdered Jews. Where will I find enough candles? Even if one candle represents ten thousand, I'll still need two hundred candles. Maybe, after that, I'll return to Nikolaev. Resume my teaching. But I will cease all of my visits to ovens and ravines.

Part of me knows it's a fiction I'm telling myself. If I go back, I know, I'll seek out more murder sites. I don't want that. So I jettison all my maps and village plats, handfuls of shell casings, bottles of honey from Krasna-Vladimirovka, everything connected to my research. I don't want reminders. I sit on the front steps of my high-rise apartment building, and wait for Anatoli, a relief to be outside, since I'm under the impression there will be an earthquake, floors pancaking like those of the World Trade Center Towers.

A few mangy dogs—from the pack that harried me earlier—mill around piled-up garbage beside the apartment building. When I shout at them, they lift their ears and growl, refusing to leave. My own private Greek furies.

A somber Anatoli drives me to Odessa. On the way to the airport he casts anxious gazes at me. We get caught in a downpour, the streets flood in seasonal rain. Vehicles seems to move backward. He crosses himself again. His Nissan plunges through foot deep water, a ritual of cleansing I hope. For the first time since I've known him, Anatoli seems less worried about his car, which is up to its bumper in water, than about me.

At the Odessa airport we hug. His troubled face mirrors my own. On the way to the airport gate, I turn to wave, and he pumps his clenched fist at me, as if to say, "Stay strong."

Several hours later, as my plane banks over the dark waters of the Bosporus, I glimpse Istanbul, and inside its ancient city walls, see Hagia Sofia, the ancient church, squatting amid its elegant minarets like a huge frog.

I pass in a flash through Istanbul's sleek airport, the most modern I've seen, board my flight, and in less than twenty hours, pass from the seething quiet of the ravines and ovens to take my place amid the bustling humanity in a series of airports, New York, Chicago, and Minneapolis. Each time my fellow travelers line up, like cattle in a chute, it seems to me, and passively remove their shoes, and deposit their wallets, computers and purses in plastic trays on the conveyer belt, Hartung's injunction to his victims, an auditory hallucination echoes in my inner ear: "Give me your valuables and then you will live."

***

My abrupt departure from Ukraine disappoints many people, myself included. For several weeks I avoid calls, e-mails, and texts from everyone except Dimitri: "I don't know how you lasted as long as you did. Now you understand why I avoid eyewitnesses and prefer documents. A pity we didn't write our book on Bogdanovka. Remember, most Holocaust researchers end up feeling as you feel. I've been there. This too shall pass. Try to be happy, slowly."

A younger brother dies unexpectedly; then a younger sister I'd been supporting, emotionally and financially. It suddenly occurred to me that I'd also been doling out money, tens of thousands of dollars for plane tickets, rental cars, drivers, interpreters, eyewitnesses, and archivists. Next to nothing remains of my retirement funds, and I feel I've just awakened from a spendthrift dream.

The Dakota winter, with its raging blizzards, and fierce cold, mirrors my mental state. On one thirty degree below zero day, it is so cold spit freezes before it hits the ground, and smoke from chimneys rises straight up, like pillars supporting a leaden grey sky. I'm caught inside for days at a time. Claustrophobic, I wade through the heavy snow to the garage, grateful for my four-wheel drive vehicle. Only movement calms me, and as I slide over the icy streets, gunning the car engine, I caterwaul country-western lyrics that reflect the disorder of my life, or seem to: "Looking for a place to fall apart." And, "Are we rolling downhill like a snowball heading for hell?"

I limp toward spring, plagued by strange dreams, gorged with complex literary and religious and ethno-political symbology, none of which I understand. In one dream, the staccato sounds of gunfire draws me out of a cave. Peering around a concrete slab, I watch an execution: row on row of people blasted into an open trench. Jews? Moving among the executioners, cloaked figures, raising high Eastern Orthodox crosses, seeming to bless the murders. Some are Cheka agents, the early Soviet equivalent of the Nazi SS; others wear the arched headgear of Jewish high priests; one figure, a red-cloaked Grand Inquisitor-like character, swinging a fuming censer, as if he'd just wandered from the pages of Dostoevsky's *Brothers Karamazov.* Another dream: I'm clinging to the steering wheel of a five-ton beet truck, which I drive at a headlong pace across the pitch-black steppe. My destination—a pillar of light in the distance, a heavenly manifestation and sign, which means Lichtenfeld, but once I arrive there, the pillar of light I've been following is, I realize, the deathly glow of body burnings in the ovens which surround that village.

Are these dreams meant to guide me? I don't know. I pray, and try to turn my troubles and confusion over to God. But that long first winter back from Ukraine, He seems singularly absent from my life. Be patient, I tell myself. Prayer and reading do help calm me. *The Confessions of Saint Augustine* occupies me for weeks, and some passages seem aimed at me:

> What nature am I? A life various and manifold, and exceeding immense. Behold in the plains and caves and caverns of my memory, innumerable and innumerably full of innumerable kinds of things…So great is the force of memory, so great the force of life, even in the mortal life of man. What shall I do then, oh Thou my true life, my God? I will pass beyond even this power of mine which is called memory; yea, I will pass beyond it, that I may approach unto Thee, oh sweet light.

I also read and study the Bible, the verses in Habakkuk about the strangeness of God's ways, in Psalms about how silent and inactive God seems in my life. So I wait, in hopes my new path will be revealed to me. All I know for certain— so I think—is that the next stage of my life won't involve the killing fields of Transnistria. But I will be wrong about that.

***

A DISTURBING CONVERSATION

"Are you sure Old Peter says that about the Jews?" I say.

I was on the phone with my mother, and we were talking about my stepfather's cousin, Old Peter.

"Yes," my mother replies. "And more too."

My eighty-five-year-old mother, like most of her prairie generation, is phobic about the phone. She uses it only to report disturbing news, or a death, in our widespread Dakota clan.

"Did you believe him?" I say.

"It's not up to me to believe or not believe," my mother says.

I imagined her, white-haired and pensive, gazing out her condominium's picture window at the snow-covered prairie distance.

"What exactly did Old Peter say?" I ask.

"What do you mean?" she says. "I already told you."

"The actual words he used. Do you remember them?"

"'That the Jews murdered our relatives."

"He actually said it that way? That the Jews murdered his relatives?"

"Murdered *our* relatives," she corrects. "They are your relatives too."

"When was this?" I say.

"The other day when we drove to visit him. And on our way inside, your stepfather stepped into a cake pan cooling on the porch. *Ach Gott!*" (Oh God!) "Did we laugh. Even his wife laughed."

"Why did you say even his wife laughed?" I ask, probing her subtle, and sometimes veiled, manner of communication.

"Because she has Alzheimer's," my mother says.

"People with Alzheimer's say wild things."

"*Hanna yo*," my mother says, using the old words. "Of course."

"What kind of wild things did she say?" I ask.

"She said they were Nazis. Can you imagine?"

"Nazis? Weren't they both born on the prairie?"

"No, no," she says. "In the old country, both of them."

"Old Peter and his wife were born in Ukraine?"

"They came to the prairie after WWII," she says. "DPs, your stepfather calls them. Displaced persons."

"I didn't know that," I say.

"There is lots you don't know."

"Like exactly what Old Peter says?"

"Oh, he's said worse," my mother says.

"What's worse than blaming Jews for killing his relatives?"

"*Our* relatives," she says. "You mean *our* relatives."

"What's worse than Old Peter saying Jews killed our relatives," I say.

"*Das brauchst du nit vissa*," she says. (That's something you don't need to know.)

"What am I not supposed to know?" I say.

"Whatever Old Peter told me," she says, with a pained laugh.

"What did he tell you?"

"I won't say what he told me," she says. "But I'll tell you what your stepdad said."

"What did he say?"

"Your stepfather says if Old Peter says it happened, it happened," she says.

"Do you have Old Peter's phone number?"

"That I can give you," she says.

***

I was shaking after my mother's phone call. For years I'd chased the ghosts of Transnistria, searching everywhere but in my own Dakota family, and though I didn't know Old Peter, he'd joined our family in 1987 after my mother's remarriage—his name had popped up with regularity in my phone calls and visits. I needed to know how Old Peter became part of my stepfather's family, so I called my ninety-year-old stepfather who told me the following story:

It happened in the early 1950s. My stepfather's parents, elderly Volksdeutsche immigrant farmers retired into a midsize Dakota prairie town were hoeing weeds in their garden one afternoon, when they saw a disheveled fellow, an unemployed carpenter, trudging along the sidewalk in front of their home.

He looked like he didn't have a friend in the world, so out of simple Christian charity, they invited him inside; while he quaffed cups of chicory-flavored coffee, and wolfed down several slices of kuchen—"Just like my mother's," he said in a familiar sounding German dialect—he told them of his tragic past in Selz, Ukraine, how in 1937, his own father was executed in front of him. When the Germans occupied Ukraine in 1941, Peter joined them as a translator, and then, after the war, he found his way to the American prairie.

"So here I am now," he said.

At one point, while peering at an old country photo of his elderly host's family on the living room china hutch, Peter froze. He pointed at the photo and said. "That man is my father."

"And my brother," my stepfather's mother said. "Which makes you our nephew."

After that, Old Peter became a fixture in my stepfather's extended family, joining them for holidays and other celebrations, mostly staying in the background.

"When I married your mother in 1987," my stepfather tells me on the phone that day, "Old Peter was the first to offer us congratulations."

***

Not much later, my mother reluctantly gives me Old Peter's phone number, and so I call him, and just as I was going to hang up, an accented voice answers and says, "Yah, vhat?" It was Old Peter.

"I'm Alma's son," I say. "I wonder if we can talk sometime. About the old country."

"Ach Gott, Ukrainia? Well, shur," he says. "Not on d' phone."

"On my next visit to see my folks then?" I say.

"Call first," he says. "I take care of my wife. She has the Alzheimer's."

"Okay," I say. "Once spring gets here."

"Yah, dann ve can make *Maistub*. Do you know Cherman?"

"Yes," I say.

"*Gut*, then we visit *auf Deutsche*," he says. "Next time you come und see your parents."

***

In early spring, on the four hour drive to see my mother and stepfather, and following the narrow two-lane, where snowbanks melted into themselves, and making my way into the Volksdeutsche triangle of the Central Dakotas, I rehearsed the questions that I wanted to ask Old Peter, about mass murders in Selz, about the torching of a home hiding Jews, about Paschowell, the district SS commandant.

By the time I arrived at my mother's condominium in South Dakota, I felt a mixture of dread and curiosity. My elderly mother met me at the door, and after we'd hugged, and I'd blurted my plans to visit Old Peter, she gave me a strange look.

"He went fast," my mother says.

My heart sunk. At the kitchen counter she searched through a small pile of clippings from the local newspaper, then handed me Old Peter's obituary.

"Your stepfather hasn't been well," she says. "So we missed both funerals."

"Both?" I say.

"His wife passed away just after. You know, like most couples married a long time."

I plopped on the couch and read Old Peter's obituary. Nothing of his birthplace in Ukraine; nothing of Transnistria, just the usual focus on his American life, his trade, the names of his grown children, and his beloved grandchildren.

"I'm sorry you didn't get to meet him," my mother says.

We sat there like Faulkner characters, my mother and I, there among family photographs on the wall and arrayed across an oak sideboard, our images reflecting from the curved glass of her beloved china hutch: she, the youngest of an old Dakota German farm family, trying to forget the past, and me, the youngest child from her first marriage, made prodigal by my research.

"Why do you dig up this stuff about the old country anyway?" my mother says.

"This dirt you mean?"

"Well, that's one way to put it," she says.

I explained how our ancestral villages lay at the heart of the Holocaust killing zone in Transnistria, how our relatives who didn't immigrate, and lived the first part of their lives in the old ancestral villages, like Old Peter, knew of the killing of Jews, and a few were even involved.

If Volksdeutsche admitted what they knew, what had been done, then the world might accept their own suffering under the Soviets, a million dead over three decades, not to mention their brutalization under the Nazis.

"Ach, let it go, child," my mother says, sighing, worried about me, about what I was trying to find. "Can't you just forget about it?"

***

That evening, I called Old Peter's son, David, a German professor, at a university in Montana, to express my condolences about his parents.

"Who are you again?" he says in clipped, academic tones.

"Your father and my stepfather were cousins," I say. "They were often together at family gatherings and holidays."

After some small talk, we spoke of Old Peter, his father.

"He was a *dolmetscher* for the German military," he says. "That's what he always told me,"

"An interpreter?" I say.

"I have a photograph of him. In uniform."

"Wehrmacht?" I say, hoping.

"No, SD."

"SD?" I say, my stomach falling. "Are you sure SD?"

"Yes, SD," he says. "Security police."

"I'm not judging your father," I say. "It is a terrible problem, what was done to the Volksdeutsche in the 1930s, and how the Nazis used them."

"I can tell you when he began hating," he says.

"He told you that?"

"Yes," he says. "It was in 1933."

"During the terror famine?"

"Yes, he was twelve years old, and they were starving. And he watched his father, my grandfather, trade his wedding ring at a government store."

"Yes, Soviets used the government-run stores to extort gold and silver for foreign exchange from the starving populace," I say.

"The Jew who worked there gave him several loaves of bread. So he could feed his family. That's when my father says he first started to hate."

I explained how educated Jews were a visible presence in the collective hierarchy and secret police, enforcing Soviet policies and creating the impression, the illusion, which was far from the truth, that Jews were Stalin's favorites.

"One Fourth of July," Old Peter's son says. "I was still in high school, in the 1960s, and we had a picnic in a park on the edge of town. My father wandered away."

He'd followed his father out onto the prairie, and found him dazed and shouting at the top of his lungs in German. It was a flashback, his father told him later, a traumatic memory, of being knocked out in a battle, and coming back to his senses, buried alive in a heap of bodies. Somehow he snaked his arm between the blood-slick corpses, waving frantically until one of his own men finally saw him and shouted, "Our Lieutenant is still alive."

There was a slight tremor as he related this story, so I decided not to tell him that when Einsatzgruppen D, the mobile death squads, swept into Transnistria, it took on young bilingual Volksdeutsche as translators, and some of them, perhaps his own father, ended up at the ravines and ovens, helping decide who should be murdered, or, even, helping with the murders. But he could sense my indecision.

"Whatever it is," Old Peter's son says, "tell me. I want to know."

"I've told you everything I know," I lie. "But one favor. Send me the photo of your father in his SD uniform?"

"Yes, of course," he says, also lying. "I have your e-mail."

Before our conversation ended, I knew I'd never see Old Peter's photograph in his SD uniform, because, like the photo of Weingartner, it too was held tightly by another son, troubled by what his father might have done in Transnistria.

***

SHOOTING GRAVES

"He couldn't have killed Jews," Freda wailed. We were in her walk-up apartment in U., north of Frankfurt, Germany, talking of Old Peter, her cousin.

Perched uneasily on her couch, I waited for her to quiet. She was crumpled in the armchair nearby, her gaping mouth a tangle of yellow teeth.

She'd known Old Peter her entire early life, she says. They'd sat next to one another for four years in their German village school in Selz, a row of cousins, all with the same last name.

285

"So how can you, an American relative, accuse him of such horrible things?" she says, using the old dialect word, *verwandt* (relative), so that a pang of guilt slid through me.

I'd learned of Freda, cousin to both my stepfather and Old Peter, through a Canadian friend, and in one of the letters we exchange, she described how, as a twelve year old near the Volksdeutsche village of Selz during WWII, she'd been forced to dig *schuetzengraben*. That word electrifies me. It means, I'm certain, massacre pits. What else could it mean? Too impatient to write Freda and await her snail mail reply, and on a trip I could ill afford, I fly to Germany.

On the way to Freda's, the autobahn clogged with miles of perfectly maintained cars and small trucks, I congratulate myself. Even Israeli war crimes prosecutors haven't uncovered evidence of a mass murder of Jews in Selz. It looks as though I've solved that mystery. My reasoning goes like this: If Freda dug schuetzengraben, she must know about, or must have witnessed, a massacre. It may even be, as occurred in some areas of Ukraine, that the Nazis ordered her to trample on the corpses, to force more bodies into a massacre pit.

Yes, I tell myself, going up the three flights of her apartment building several steps at a time, Freda will tell me about schuetzengraben in Selz. Yes, I tell myself, I've finally come to the center of the labyrinth.

The woman who meets me at the door, Freda, is a clone of my mother's ninety-five-year-old cousin in Dakota, with the same shy, hospitable smile, and after we embrace, she ushers me inside to her couch. We make small talk about relatives, about her cousin, my stepfather, until finally I ask about schuetzengraben. With palsied fingers she painstakingly sketches out, in my notebook the shaky dimensions of the long trench she and other teenage girls were forced to dig in 1941, soldiers waving rifles and barking at them, "*Davai, davai.*" (Hurry, hurry.)

"Davai?" I say. "That's a Russian word. Wasn't it Nazi soldiers making you dig murder pits?"

"No, Soviet soldiers, Soviets," she says. "Making us dig antitank trenches."

"Schuetzengraben were antitank trenches?" I say, incredulous. "To ward off Nazi panzers?"

"What did you think?" Freda says. "Jews were killed there?"

"Yes. Were there Jews murdered in Selz?"

"That I don't know," Freda says. "If it happened, then at night, in secret, and maybe the bodies were buried in schuetzengraben."

The trip to Germany, I realized, was not necessary, not if I'd looked up the word schuetzengraben in my German dictionary; but since I was already there, ensconced on her couch, I listened, not to the usual Volksdeutsche mantra of suffering I'd expected, about the starvation, but to how her husband was forced into the Soviet *trudarmia*, the ruthless slave labor army that during WWII and just after built roads and railroads, where each railroad tie laid—here she held up a thick, disfigured finger—cost one Volksdeutsche his life.

Her husband survived, among the lucky ten-percent, and reuniting with Freda in the Ural Mountains long enough to father a child, and then, health broken from exposure, dying young. After the fall of communism, German legislation rectifying the wrongs of the war brought her and her disabled son back to Germany, where she'd lived only briefly during the war.

"Yah, so jetzt sind wir hier," she says. (Now we are here.)

Freda wobbled on arthritic hips into the adjoining kitchen, returning with a lunch tray of rattling dishes that she set on an end table between us, and after we bent our heads and prayed together the Come Lord Jesus from our childhoods so far apart, and the food we shared, chunks of sausage and cheese and pickles, spurred Freda to talk of a time when there wasn't any, her childhood. Okay, here it comes, I told myself, steeling myself, and I wasn't wrong. During the famine of 1933, pillows and tables and chairs were pawned or traded for bread, and her father, denied pay by the collective, stumbled home, weak from hunger.

"His empty hands meant no food," she says. "And no food meant we would swell again and turn black."

Suddenly, Freda's eyes roll wild in their sockets, and she is wringing her hands and wailing, *"Des han die Juden gemacht."* (That is what the Jews did to our people.)

That's how, on Freda's couch, it grows clear that what happened to her seventy years ago was still not buried, and would never be, not in this world, not even in the deepest schuetzengraben.

***

BACK TO MY OLD LIFE, ALMOST

As my return flight from Germany speeds high above the icy, barren ridges of Greenland, images of Freda's tortured face hover in my thoughts. Like her cousin Old Peter, she grew up in what some scholars called an anti-Semitic environment. Two decades of suffering under the Soviets, and then Nazi propaganda in Transnistria—namely Hitler's crude equivalence of Jews with communists and partisans—only cemented that prejudice.

It is, I know, futile to argue with Freda that the Jews, as a group, shouldn't be blamed for the actions of some of its members, just as the Volksdeutsche, as a group, shouldn't be blamed for what some of their police did. No, wielding reason like a scalpel to excise Freda's anti-Semitic tumor was an educated American's illusion. But as a Holocaust Museum scholar once told me, in confidence: "It was an easy mistake for the Volksdeutsche to make, thinking Jews controlled the Soviet regime in the 1930s." Especially, he'd added, since the German colonists had only a limited view of the situation. In ways, it may have been a moot point. Even if the German colonists, and their policemen, weren't anti-Semitic, they were in no position to disobey the Nazis. "It was either shoot the Jews or end up yourself in the same pit," as one policeman put it.

At Minneapolis, I begin the last leg of my journey home, and boarding with me are my former university colleagues, historians and sociologists and theoreticians of literature, returning from academic conferences. I avoid them. After the collapse of the Soviet Union, some of these same academics— Rococo Marxists, as the author Tom Wolfe called them once— pejoratively called me a "triumphalist," because I thought that collapse a good thing.

My own experience at the university—which has included one professor telling me how much he admired Stalin, another posting Lenin's image on her door, and a third telling me he was in sympathy with Stalin's deportation of the kulaks, which resulted in twelve million deaths—has only confirmed Wolfe's view that Marxist historians would never render an honest reckoning of communism's destructive effects, not to mention the pervasive suffering of the Volksdeutsche under the Soviets.

Our flight whistles through the clean, crisp air. Rural Minnesota spreads below the airplane wing, with frozen lakes that look blue in the evening light and fertile squares of Red River Valley farmland, lightly dusted with snow. Half an hour later we land, and while driving the icy streets homeward, I think, for an instant, I hear Freda wailing and keening, and perhaps across the ocean she still is. But the sounds are, I know, from my car's engine, its squealing fan belt fighting the cold.

***

One aspect of the Transnistrian Holocaust I don't fully understand is this relationship between forced labor and genocide, though I do know that when it was time to kill the Jews, a common ruse was to tell them they were going to work. The New Amerika police unit used it, and so did the Worms police unit, enough so that, in the macabre shorthand of the times, mid-1942, the response to anyone inquiring about the Jews was, "We're taking them around the corner," or "We're taking them to work." Instead, they were being taken to be murdered.

Some Volksdeutsche police units, as I learn from a book by Schachan, in addition to patrolling their own locales, ventured far afield, to Tulchin, Balta, and Mogilev in northernmost Transnistria, securing "Jews for labor purposes," some of whom were executed roadside or in antitank ditches.

A second Schachan passage stuns me.

> In the southern Transnistrian regions, local Germans would go out in groups of thirty and forty people to the labor camps or to other concentrations of Jews and would demand that Romanian gendarmes hand over Jews for labor. Everybody knew what type of "labor" was in store for the Jews, and thus the Jews' lives were in the hands of the Romanian commanders. In most cases Jews from the camps closest to the slaughter were summoned to bury the dead, and sometimes the German farmers would bury the dead in lime to obscure their deed. After the war, numerous mass grave sites, covered with lime, were found in the area between the Odessa district and the Berezovka district.

This passage blames local German colonist farmers, and so does a less credible Internet source, The Nizkor Project, which asserts groups of Volksdeutsche, armed to the teeth, traveled in horse-drawn wagons to the Jewish ghettos in Transnistria,

290

to retrieve Jews, killing them immediately or after using them for forced labor. I doubt these armed Volksdeutsche were civilians. Certainly, police units wearing swastika armbands in lieu of uniforms could be mistaken for civilians, and if groups of colonists toted weapons, those weapons came from police headquarters where they were kept in an arsenal, under lock and key. It seems unlikely that the SS commandants would indiscriminately arm civilians.

Most likely the armed Volksdeutsche were police units ordered by the SS commandants—many of whom controlled agricultural aspects of districts—to procure Jews for seeding and harvest and other projects. Nevertheless, many of these Jews were murdered, and it is these widening circles of involvement, and the use of Jews as slave labor, which placed them alongside Volksdeutsche laboring in the fields, that is profoundly dispiriting. It means knowledge of the murder of the Jews must have been widespread. An insight I want to avoid thinking about, and in that way, I am not unlike some postwar Volksdeutsche.

****

IV. FINDING HITLER'S STEPPE-CHILDREN

I VISIT A FORMER POLICEMAN

From an upper level of a huge convention complex outside Stuttgart, Germany, I'm looking over a vast sea of people, gathered for a Volksdeutsche reunion called a Bundestreffen. Despite the celebratory strains of live music that float from a lower level, I'm thinking dark thoughts. Somewhere among the fifty thousand souls gathered here, which is roughly the same number of Odessa Jews murdered in Transnistria, are some of the genocidaires who killed them. The question is, can I find one to interview?

Outside the convention center that day, I'd joined clots of Volksdeutsche emerging from Binder tour buses parked along both sides of the highway, and lining up to pay an entrance fee. I'd noted hefty, broad-faced women, mothers and daughters, in pantsuits and nondescript dresses, and uncomfortable looking younger men, wide shoulders stuffed into tight suit coats, like construction workers on their days off.

But there were few elderly men. I did some quick calculations. If a young man of twenty was drafted into a police unit at the end of 1941, and wasn't among the tens of thousands of Volksdeutsche and the several million German soldiers dead on WWII's Eastern Front, he would now be in his mid- to late-eighties.

Now I follow a long hallway, hung with artwork, hundreds of framed pieces, in pencil and oils and tempera and watercolors, of bloody images, of hammers and sickles, of graveyards and jackboots trampling prostrated victims: symbols of Volksdeutsche suffering under the Soviets.

On the lower level, around long tables with placards displaying village names familiar from my research—Worms, Rohrbach, Selz—I come upon elderly Volksdeutsche, whose distinctive Germanic features and physical appearance, seem so like the beloved relatives of my prairie childhood. I remind myself these people never lived in the United States: the oldest, I know, born in the German colonies in southern Ukraine, evacuated back to the German Reich in 1944, where they were settled on farms in the Polish Warthegau; drafted into the German military, often the SS, and, at war's end, the unlucky survivors repatriated to the far reaches of the Soviet Union, remaining there until the fall of communism in the early 1990s. Now, they'd come full circle, back to the land their ancestors, and my own left two hundred years earlier.

Some *aussiedlers*, as the newly returning Germans were called, line up at the nearby North Dakota State University Library outreach-sponsored American Booth to get help contacting American kin, with whom they lost contact during the Stalinist purges of the 1930s. They carry small items tattered by war and exile, photographs creased and folded, relatives posing by new American autos, or homes, envelopes scrawled with addresses of places their relatives settled in Kansas, Idaho, South Dakota, North Dakota. One hefty Siberian aussiedler leans forward on the information table, and says in German dialect: "I search for American relatives. My name is Pius Gross."

"Pius Gross?" the well-fed American at the information table says. "That's my name too, Pius Gross."

There is a shock of recognition—like in a Borghese short story of parallel universes—the two Pius Grosses, who shared a great grandfather, and shaking hands, reuniting after a century two branches of that family, those who remained in Ukraine, and those who immigrated to America.

I meet an elderly fellow named Valder who has an amazing shock of white hair, and when he tells me he is from a village near Selz, Ukraine, I ask if he knew my stepfather's relatives, E.'s.

He snaps, eyes flashing with old anger. "E's? Of course. My neighbors. Peter and Franz. Shot by the Soviets. 1937."

He seemed the right age to have been a policeman, and when I asked him about the German Occupation, he quickly skips to 1943, to his SS Maria Theresa Division, fighting in Budapest, Hungary. Slicing the air with his hands, he describes how he and his SS comrades, fighting from the sewers under the streets, were heavily bombed, urban warfare as bad as at Stalingrad.

"But as you see, I survived," he says.

We arranged to meet several days later at his home, and after we parted company, I fell in with several old *Ost Front kampfers* (Eastern Front veterans) from Valder's division, their conversation crackling with words like *verschleppt* (arrested), *erschossen* (shot), *verwundet* (wounded).

"I fought for both sides," one old veteran says. He shows me two oft-folded photographs that he fishes out of his billfold. In one he wears a Soviet uniform, in the other, an SS uniform. At one point, he draws his pitted face near my own to whisper, in my grandfather's dialect no less, "I was at Auschwitz. I was an interpreter. Only an interpreter."

I shrink back and quickly make my way to the lowest convention center level, where I find younger Volksdeutsche, born wherever the Soviet deportation trains dumped their parents or grandparents after the war in Central Asia, who know little or nothing of the Black Sea colonies of their parents and grandparents.

In the 1990s, after the fall of communism, these aussiedlers and their children, motivated by German laws offering citizenship and compensation for losses in WWII, arrived in Germany at the rate of two hundred thousand per year, two million Volksdeutsche overall, known pejoratively as *fluchtlinge*, or refugees, and seen as an economic drain on Germany's resources, and the source of social problems. Many no longer spoke German, and seem more Russian than German. But they took language training courses, and began to assimilate into German society, and the older Russian-educated professionals such as doctors and engineers, competed for menial jobs with *gastenarbeiter* (guest workers) from the Third World.

Back in the lower section, an oom-pah band of accordions and brass instruments is playing songs with a distinctive melancholy Russian lilt, and the Catholic Volksdeutsche are dancing, Pius Gross, the American, paired up with Mrs. Kraft, the sister of his Siberian relative, and Valder, my elderly SS acquaintance is out on the improvised dance floor too, with his much younger dance partner, a Californian Volksdeutscher, dancing, it seems, with the abandon of someone trying to forget?

***

After the Bundestreffen I prepare to meet Valder, the former SS man. I hole up in my favorite Munich hotel, drinking room-service coffee, and studying documents and plat maps concerning my step-grandfather's birthplace, and Valder's home village, once was a substantial village of several thousand, one in a string of sizable German Catholic colonies founded in the first decade of the nineteenth century in the Kutschurgan Valley.

I'm trying to learn whether long columns of Romanian Jews, the so-called *elend-zug* (processions of misery) came into the vicinity of the Kutschurgan colonies, and, if so, did local Volksdeutsche police destroy them?

Israeli war crimes investigators in the early 1960s had the same suspicion. They'd sent local authorities in the Federal Republic of Germany a list of questions to ask Volksdeutsche resettled there. Most questions focused on Obersturmfuehrer

Norbert Paschowell, the ruthless former police commandant of the Catholic district. There was scant evidence, just one claim, by a former inhabitant of Selz, the district capital, that Jews were murdered en masse in the Kutschurgan Valley during Paschowell's tenure. How many, or exactly where, he wouldn't, or couldn't, say. Just that murders took place.

That's what I'm explaining to my non-Volksdeutsche friend several days later, as we ride the city bus from our hotel in a Munich suburb to visit Valder.

"What are you going to ask him?" my friend says.

"I want to ask what he knows about the murder of Jews," I say.

"You mean you are going to ambush him?"

"You can't ambush these old SS men," I say as we got off the bus.

"He thinks we're coming for a quiet lunch. Not discuss the Holocaust. Anyway, there he is."

"Over here Fossler," Valder says, waving from in front of his nearby apartment building.

As we walk his direction, I'm thinking that if Germany had won the war, Valder would be ensconced on his veranda in his native Ukraine, surveying his vast acreage awarded for his soldiering on the Ost Front, waited on by his Slavic servant/ slaves, not retired to this modest, leafy Munich suburb.

Valder's lively gaze, which betrays the wariness of an old combat veteran, alights on my companion, and I introduce them. He slips his arm inside hers in a courtly manner. He has misunderstood her name as that of the heroine from his favorite movie. "Oh, like Scarlet in *Gone with the Wind*," he says, and he escorts us inside.

Wilhelmina, his wife of half a century but a decade younger than Valder, shows us around the immaculate apartment, walls covered by several gold and red carpets, Slavic in style, a lacquered balalaika hanging from a peg, and various family photos, including one his grandson had enlarged, showing a helmeted Valder in SS uniform, astride a white horse, rifle slung over his shoulder.

We seat ourselves at a heavy table, opposite the large picture window crowded with greenery, and share a meal, a mix of Germanic orderliness and Volksdeutsche warmth, eating spaetzle which Valder made himself, and sipping their favorite red wine, a Riesling, grown from grapes in the surrounding hills.

My friend, despite speaking no German, is enthralled by Valder, by his energetic stories, of famines and war and epidemics, of his courageous mother, brandishing a scythe in the women's revolt against the Selz collective, forcing the communists to allow families to keep a single cow so children could have milk.

One anecdote concerned his current adventures, driving his Mercedes convertible 240 km/hour in the fast lane of the autobahn, and his tour of the United States, where, stopped for speeding by an LA policeman, this veteran of the fiercest fighting in WWII—in the battle for Budapest, Valder's commanding officer ordered the decimated platoon to a doomed counterattack toward onrushing Soviet tanks— quickly flattens his palms on the car hood, a gesture of submission from American cop shows he watches on German television.

"Yah Valder, you weren't such a big SS man then," his wife teases.

When Wilhelmina and my friend go outside for a walk, Valder opens our second bottle of wine, and we do some serious drinking, and it's then I finally ask about his being a seventeen-year-old policeman in his village in Transnistria.

"My job was to patrol the streets," he says. "I carried an old Russian carbine."

"Patrolling for bandits and partisans and infiltrators," I say. "And communists?"

"There were none left," he says. "The Einsatzgruppen took care of them."

"And Jews?"

"Yes, a tailor and a shoemaker in the village. The Einsatz killed them too."

"I mean Jews forced out of Bessarabia," I say. "Many came along the main road from Tiraspol to Odessa. Did those columns get near your village?"

"*Keine Ahnung,*" Valder says quickly. (No idea.)

I mention the names of policemen, and the name of the local police chief head who helped train him.

"Common names in my village," Valder says with a shrug.

"Paschowell?" I say.

"Ach yah, everyone knew Obersturmfuehrer Paschowell was a swine-hund."

"And Sturmfuehrer R.?" I say, mentioning the baby-killing SS driver transferred from Rastadt to Selz in 1942 or 1943. It's then that Valder looks startled, shifting noticeably, an indication of stress, so says my psychotherapist friend Crenir; but the ladies, chatting happily in Pidgin English, return and sit down with us again at the table, so he never does answer the question.

"Time to sing," Valder announces.

He takes his lacquered balalaika off a peg on the wall, and strumming the instrument he'd learned to play in Central

Asia, where his family fled in 1933, to escape the Ukrainian famine, leads us in singing for an hour or more, melancholy Volksdeutsche songs, with a distinctive Russian lilt, and my American friend learns and sings the words to "*Schoen ist die Jugend*," a song about youth, so beautiful yes, which once gone, never returns.

"Ach yah," Wilhelmina oozes, as we finally say good-bye. "We haf hat such a nice time."

Valder accompanies us to the bus stop and boards with us, gripping the overhead straps for balance by our seat, and as the bus swerves on its way, the door making pneumatic swooshing sounds, he continues to flirt with my friend, describing the various exotic places he'd visited in Europe, with his wife and friends from their Catholic church. The bus, I note, is half full, Valder the only elderly man, still energetic and strong, while two million soldiers of his generation lay long buried on the Eastern Front.

Valder can't say enough about their beloved priest, about his kindness and decency, and I sense whatever the former policeman might have done in Transnistria, he'd long since confessed as much to his priest.

Several stops later, after hugging my friend good-bye, and vigorously pumping my hand, Valder steps out of the bus, into the scented evening.

Later, over a night cap in the hotel bar with my friend, I'm busy sulking, guilty about my dark thoughts about Valder. What my American friend says only makes me feel worse: "How could you ever think such a nice man killed Jews?"

***

I MAKE ENEMIES

Several months later, I'm standing at a podium in a large meeting room at the International Germans from Russia Conference in Caspar, Wyoming.

After reciting my presentation's title, "Volksdeutsche Police in Transnistria: Witnesses and Beneficiaries, Heroes and Perpetrators in the Mass Murder of Jews in Ukraine, 1941–1944," I sketch out the results of my Fulbright research.

As I recite numbers and dates and locations of massacres, the audience falls into a tense silence, and I can't say I'm surprised, since American Volksdeutsche have fond feelings toward their ancestral villages on the steppe. I avoid mention of any specific policemen, knowing that among the bobbing grey heads in my audience, are people with the same last names as the killers, and, to balance my presentation, I mention how Volksdeutsche, like the Lipperts of Neudorf, and the Duckarts of Landau, hid Jews, and I also repeat what Duissmann told me in Odessa, that without the help of the Volksdeutsche many Jews would not have survived.

Despite what I think is my balanced approach, chairs scrape, and there are irritated whispers, and briefcases slap shut. Part of the way through my presentation several people get up and leave, and at the end, an elderly expert on genealogical research pokes an accusatory finger at me, and before leaving shouts, "In those same ravines where, so you say, Jews were killed, the Soviet secret police shot and killed many of our people."

(He is wrong about Volksdeutsche being executed at the ravines. Most were shot in the prisons in Tiraspol, Odessa, and Nikolaev. But he's correct in making a connection between the murder of German colonists in the 1930s and the later murder of the Jews.)

Remaining audience members ask questions. Were the Volksdeutsche anti-Semitic? How large were the killing fields?

Did the Volksdeutsche villagers know of the murders? I answer as best as I can. Several stunned people come forward and my stack of handouts listing the murder sites quickly disappears.

Afterward I retreat with Volksdeutsche friends to a dimly lit hotel bar in the conference center, where a long haired cowboy band in scruffy attire sets up on a low stage. We drink beer, eat German fare served to convention goers, and share quirky jokes and stories from our Dakota German hometowns. I tell the story about how, as a seventeen year old, I stood at the free-throw line during the title game of the 1965 McIntosh County Basketball Tournament, while the opposing cheering section, to distract me, thundered out an infamous German dialect cheer, about liver sausage, headcheese, and fat.

We laughed about those simple times, and then, as the band began to play, and a blond woman of mixed American Volksdeutsche and Ukrainian ancestry and her husband, a sullen Saxon from Germany, seated themselves at our table, the jovial atmosphere curdled.

"So, Fossler, I heard your speech," the blond woman says, drumming her fingernails on the wooden table, and when I see her husband pulling in his neck, I know a personal attack is forthcoming.

"I tink you are a Jew lover," she says. "From all you says in your so-called speech."

She continues her diatribe. "What about all villages erased from the earth?" she fumes. "Like Sulz in 1937. What about everyone shot and deported to Siberia? What about the suffering von die Volksdeutsche?"

I remind myself, drawing on my experience dealing with the personal attacks and half veiled threats of Marxist university professors, to respond quietly.

When my antagonist is finished, I make roughly the same argument I'd made to my own mother that day in her condominium, that if the Volksdeutsche admitted their police units were involved in the Holocaust, even if forced, and that members of this group are beneficiaries of genocide, if unwittingly, then historians will more readily accept the ways the Volksdeutsche were brutalized not only by the Soviets, who murdered one million, but also by the Nazis.

"Und those bones you say you find by our villages from the Jews," she says, bristling. "Is garbage that the dogs haf buried and dug up."

Mimicking how dogs dig, pawing at the air, my antagonist manages to upend our drinks, sending a small flood of ice cubes and alcohol across the table. We dab at the mess with napkins, thankful for the distraction. Someone orders more drinks all around, and for a time we feign civility.

Truth is, I feel sympathetic toward my blond antagonist, and I try to explain to her how, a decade earlier, I'd felt similarly upset. It was just after reading a scholarly article that accused a Volksdeutsche, Karl Stumpp, a revered postwar patriarch of the Germans from Russia Society in America, of having murdered a Jew in Transnistria, where he, Stumpp, had been sent by Leibbrandt to survey the Volksdeutsche villages. Stumpp, with whom I felt a personal connection, because our research overlapped, and because, my senior year in high school, he'd given a presentation in the New Odessa Lutheran Church where I'd been baptized.

Crunching ice between her flashing white teeth, my antagonist will have none of it. So I finally leave the cowboy bar, going down a long hallway hung with a kaleidoscope of colorful banners of German from Russia chapters from the US and Canada, whose quaint names, like *Die Deutsche Kinder*, or Children of German Descent, and *Die Deutsche Stammbaum*, or Branches of the Germanic Tree, are stitched in Gothic script, against idyllic backgrounds of barns and plows and the prairie.

While crossing the hotel registration area, headed for my room, I hear my name. Turning, I see a grey-haired fellow, seated with what looked like six or seven of his elderly siblings and their mates, on the faux-leather lobby furniture. Europeans, Germans, I told myself, seeing that all or most were dressed in light silk and linen for the hot weather, unusual garb for Dakota Germans.

"Our family lived in Transnistria during the war," the older grey-haired fellow says. "Most of us were born there."

"Except our little brother here," one says, nudging a portly, younger man.

"Yass, yass, we heard your presentation," the younger, double-chinned brother says, stroking his straggly grey beard and sounding like a humanities professor giving a classroom lecture. "Since you mentioned our village, Helenental, then surely you must know of Ras-dal-nay-ja?"

"No, I don't," I say, wondering why he pronounced each syllable of that Ukrainian city so slowly, so dripping with sarcasm. "I entered Helenental from the east. Rasdalnaya must be somewhere to the west."

Turning to his siblings, the younger brother now speaks in clipped, haughty British English, with just a burr of German accent. (Later I learn he lived and taught in London.) "Why this poor fellow doesn't even know where Rasdalnayja is. What a farce."

With a geriatric creak of knees, the group rose en masse, shuffling away, a fragment of further sarcasm floating back to me, something about "that American's obvious geographical stupidity."

Angry and confused, I head for my room.

Part of the way there, an elderly, out-of-breath lady, and one of the family members, calls out to me. "Please, stop. We just had a conversation with you in the lobby."

"That wasn't a conversation," I say. "That was an ambush."

She pulls from her designer purse a map, unfolding it with a rigorous snap, and pointing, first, to the Helenental where her family once lived, and then, fifty miles to the north and east, to the Helenental where there'd been police murders.

"There are two different Helenentals," she says, fixing her fierce blue eyes on me.

"I thought that might be the case," I say.

"Please don't judge my brothers too harshly," she says. "They think they are right about everything."

"I'm used to that from American academics."

"Yes, they are college professors, like yourself, good progressives," she pleads, wrong about my politics. "Not like the scum, and that low-life rabble that killed Jews in Transnistria."

As she chattered away, I tried to gauge her age. Old enough to have belonged to the *Bund Deutsche Madel* in Transnistria, the female equivalent of the Hitler Youth. Old enough to remember trucks heaped with clothing. Old enough to have worn that clothing. And old enough, also, to remember the killings.

Later, I pace my hotel room. The elderly siblings, the woman says, are all progressives, politically. That makes sense. Being a conservative or republican entails a risk, at least in academic circles, of being labeled a Fascist or a reactionary or a Nazi: accusations that for her family members, with their Transnistrian roots, would have been particularly painful. So the family became the German equivalent of American liberals, positioned on the opposite end of the political spectrum, closer to the communism/Marxism that destroyed

Volksdeutsche culture on the steppe. Cloaked in progressivism, they stood for a better world, and thus repositioned, how could anyone identify them with the dark old world of the Nazis? But because they knew I knew about Transnistria, about the murder of the Jews by Volksdeutsche police, they felt vulnerable. Which was why they attacked me.

Before bed, I empty my pockets on my nightstand, a tangle of car keys, hotel key cards, and convention-goer cards, including the one belonging to my cowboy bar antagonist, which her husband had given me.

There on her card, spelled out in ornate gothic letters below her contact information, is her personal credo, ironic in light of her refusal to accept Jews were killed in her ancestral village: "If you don't understand your past, how can you have a future?"

***

After a long day of emotional landmines, not all of which I'd negotiated with dignity, or grace, I settle in to read Solzhenitsyn's *Two Hundred Years Together*, an examination of the shared history of Jews and Russia, printed in German because no US publisher would touch it. At the onset of the Russian Revolution, Solzhenitsyn claimed, the attitude of the Jews toward the Bolsheviks was hostile, but after gaining freedom due to the revolution in most spheres of life, social, political, and cultural, these Jews "did not stand in the way of other Jews who were Bolsheviks, and who then exercised their newly acquired power to cruel excess."

As questionable as that is—even if it echoes something said by Height, one of the foremost scholars of the Volksdeutsche—Solzhenitsyn did make a moral point that if Russian Jews try to justify this heavy involvement of Jews in the government apparatus, and their participation in atrocities, that would be like the German people finding excuses for the Hitler period (or the Volksdeutsche excusing their policemen in the Holocaust).

Instead of excuses, Solzhenitsyn says, it would serve both the Jews (and Volksdeutsche), to answer for the cut-throats in each of their groups, not distancing themselves from those so vigorously involved in torture and killings. This applied, I thought, to the elderly siblings with whom I'd sparred, all born in Ukraine, all distancing themselves from the perpetrators they labeled as "scum" and "low-life rabble."

Which told me the elderly siblings didn't want to answer morally for their past, including whatever might be shameful. By answering, I meant trying to comprehend, to look at their ethnic past and ascertain their own role, their own errors, if any, or the errors of their fellow Volksdeutsche. Each ethnic group, Solzhenitsyn says, should answer for the murderers in their midst, as if members of our own family, and "if we release ourselves from any responsibility for the actions of our national kin, the very concept of a people loses its meaning." Yet here they were, the elderly siblings, attending the convention, and claiming Volksdeutsche ethnicity that they didn't want to fully own.

***

The next morning, over an early breakfast in the convention center cafe, I'm brooding, the darkest angels of my nature accusing me of ambition and egotism for bringing, the day before, the mass murders into the public eye at the Germans from Russia convention. I'm smarting from the various criticisms, veiled and otherwise, and even a snarky comment, obviously aimed at me, by a retired high school librarian as I walk past her that very morning. "Now everybody will think our society is a bunch of Nazis."

By stressing that the Volksdeutsche had also saved many Jews in Transnistria, I've sought, naively, to insulate myself from criticism. What did I expect, I ask myself that morning, because hundreds, even thousands of American Volksdeutsche were deeply invested in the German from Russia Societies and club chapters, and the meetings, often enough, stood at the heart of their social lives. It was not only a genealogical club, but also a support group, cooking club, singing group, and therapy session. Being German from Russia was, someone joked, less a label than a diagnosis. Who but another Volksdeutsche could understand our contradictions, our religiosity, our archaic words and accents?

We are an exclusive club, carrying remnants of a rich, but dying folk culture, rooted within the eighteenth century. But the society's membership, as I'd noted from the grey heads at my presentation, was dwindling, and due to demographics alone, the society would disappear entirely in another decade or two.

***

A couple of hours later, in the long convention hallway, I meet a man of retirement age, his plastic convention name tag dangling around his neck like a noose. Across it—in large block letters—the family name of one of the Holocaust's bloodiest genocidaires: E.

He's nondescript looking enough, wearing Girbaux jeans and a black Hawaiian silk shirt with white sailing ships, and his only real sign of age are three horizontal lines etched deep into his forehead.

"Vere you born in Ukrainia?" he asks.

"No. I was born on the prairie. And you?"

"Klein Rastadt," he says.

"Yes, I have been there," I say.

His forehead lines rise in surprise, and he guides me by the elbow to a leather couch against the wall.

"We can talk more easily over here. So you know Klein Rastadt? And Rastadt?"

"Yes, I have stayed in Rastadt many times," I say. "Overnight in the L. house on August Eleventh Street."

"As a child, I visited relatives in Rastadt," he says. "My uncle…from Rastadt, he is flying from Germany, to stay with me in Chicago."

"Did he ever speak of events in Rastadt during the war?" I say.

"No, no. He does not talk," he says. "And there is another uncle of mine nobody ever mentions."

"I've seen your last name in documents," I say finally.

"Documents?"

"Yes, documents. But are you sure you want to know this?"

"Truth is truth," he says, spreading his arms wide in a gesture of acceptance. For an instant, he looks just like the picture I snapped of Sascha that day outside Rastadt when he was showing me the circumference of the oven on whose edge he stood.

"This is a Soviet secret police execution list," I say, pointing to several names. "Several men with your last name."

"My grandfather and father and a cousin," he says. "All Volksdeutsche have relatives on that execution list."

"Other documents are worse," I say, sounding like my mother, subtle, evasive.

"Worse? What can be worse than the execution list?"

"Documents that describe Rastadt during the German Occupation," I say, delving into my satchel for an eyewitness account, which I hand to him, and this is the testimony he reads:

Yes, I knew of the murder of Jews in my home area. I saw how in January and February of 1942, Jews were led to their slaughter. This was in Rastadt. I saw from a distance of several hundred meters how the Jews were brought here. The Jews were from Odessa. Where else would they find that many Jews? They were brought on foot and in wagons and in sleds. That was a cold winter, 1941–42, and many nearly dead Jews were brought here. There were men, women, and children of all ages. How many times were Jews brought here I can't exactly say, but at least ten times, maybe up to twenty times. And that doesn't include those times under cover of night when the Jews were brought here and killed.

His lips moving with the words, the lines on his forehead lifting in surprise, he finishes and then handing me back the document, says in a whisper: "That fits. Yah."

I should have stopped then. When I saw his fingers shaking. But I pursued the topic. Out of callousness? Or perhaps— what was Alice's word—*gruendlichkeit*, thoroughness? I don't know, but I continue.

"I found a confession in the archives in Ukraine," I say.

"Confession?" he says, eyeing me warily.

"Yes, I have it here," I say, head down, delving into my satchel. "Maybe it's your uncle? The one your family didn't talk about."

"I must go now," he says.

When I look up, he strolls away, his Hawaiian shirt disappearing in a crowd in the hallway, where all of the Volksdeutsche seem to part and accept him before closing their ranks around him.

***

I'm standing near the registration table on the last day of the convention, when an angry voice behind me, heavy with accent, says, "Stalin was a Chew."

When I glance around, I see a knot of elderly convention-goers, retired farmers and their wives, bandy legged men in German from Russia chapter vests, women in prairie grandmother bonnets and wide gingham dresses, and in their midst a short, stocky woman in a pants suit, holding forth about Stalin.

Mrs. F.—that's what her name tag says—is spewing a hate-filled diatribe, full of all the lies and crude simplifications she can muster, to attempt to justify the Holocaust, from the establishment of Soviet collectivization in 1929 to the extermination of ten million Ukrainian and Volksdeutsche peasants.

"All the work of Chews, like Kaganovitsch and Berman, and others," Mrs. F. says, glancing around at her small audience. "Chust like the famine."

The Jews, she huffs, controlled Germany's economy before WWII, and today the world diamond industry and 90 percent of the shoreline of Manhattan, but she reserves her most vitriolic rant for the current Israeli state, and I thought, how strange when a raging anti-Semite made many of the same anger-filled arguments I've heard from university humanities professors.

"The Chews can't face the fact that seven million others also died in the war. They weren't the only victims. Not by a long shot," Mrs. F. says, hunching over like Quasimodo, and sidling away a few steps to illustrate the manner in which, she says, Jewish liars recoil from the truth.

All these slanders, I'm sure, because Mrs. F. is too young to remember Transnistria, likely came from her father or other relatives, for there were at least three F. family members on the Hoffnungstal police roster, detailed to arrest Jews, if not murder them, and if she believed that the Jews were responsible for the earlier suffering of the Volksdeutsche, then nobody need face the moral consequences of killing Jews.

"My presentation is at three o'clock this afternoon," I finally say. "I'll give another view about what happened in Transnistria."

"What I say is absolute truth," Mrs. F. huffs, stalking away in the manner she earlier mimicked. "Und there is no other view."

***

At the Volksdeutsche sing-along that evening, Mrs. F. thumps into a folding chair beside me. She's the first person there to make a request—*"Fuhre Mich"* (Come Savior, Lead Me)—a well-known Volksdeutsche religious hymn, sung on deathbeds and at weddings and at funerals, and also my mother's favorite, one I've heard at evangelical revival services as a child.

"But before ve sing," Mrs. F. announces to the twenty gathered to sing together. "I tell you, this song vas sung at my own paptism in the Hoffnungstal church in 1941. So as we sing, let's remember our rich heritich."

As the powerful church voices of Dakota Volksdeutsche fill the convention meeting room, I suddenly realize who baptized Mrs. F. as a baby in 1941 on that special Sunday when sacraments, denied for a decade under the Soviets, were given en masse to Hoffnungstalers. The person who cradled her against his black SS uniform while he dipped the index finger of his right hand into the baptismal font and traced the sign of the Christian cross on her tiny forehead—that person was none other than Hauptsturmfuehrer Theophil Weingartner.

That finger with which the cross was traced on Mrs. F.'s forehead might have been, if Weingartner was guilty, the same finger with which at the klinge he'd pulled the trigger of his Luger, and I wonder if his restless, and perhaps cruel spirit, like the demons entering the swine in the Biblical parable, has passed into this lady, fidgeting beside me.

When we begin our final song—an old revival hymn, *Gott ist die Liebe*—those dark thoughts fall away from me. The haunting, repetitive strains make me grateful that my grandparents, heeding the Sibyl's prophecy, spared the American generations of our people the suffering and death under the Soviets, and all the victimization under the Nazis.

Along with that gratitude comes a sudden rush of sympathy for Mrs. F., but as I turn to speak to her, to be kind to her, and maybe nudge her away from her vicious anti-Semitism, I see, through the trembling blur of my tears, that she is gone, already departed from our songfest.

***

OUT OF THE FLAMES

After the conference, I take stock. It has been eight long years since I glimpsed the photo of Weingartner. Strange how something the size of a large postage stamp, could affect the course of my life. During those years, I filled in the largest blank spots in Volksdeutsche history. Now, when anyone googled Gradofka, or Podoleanca, or Bogdanovka or Lichtenfeld, they'd gain access to my website, to information and numerous photos about my journey along the Road of Death.

I've paid a price, I know. My memories of my grandfather seem tainted, and Lichtenfeld, whose shimmering aura I'd so fervently imagined, and once thought of as the primal hearth of my grandfather's family, now seemed a place of blood and death, and along with those soothing voices of my ethnic past, which sometimes floated back to me, came the stark

313

realization that the same dialect, used to give orders to the police by the Volksdeutsche local commanders was also the language of murder.

Sometimes there seemed no escape from reminders of my grim research.

Once, driving across the prairie to a family wedding, I turned into a primitive roadside park twelve miles from my hometown, going under a metallic archway to check a squealing fan belt, a false alarm.

It felt good to be back in my own heimat, my emotional home, so I sat at a picnic table of warped two by eights, and enjoyed the autumnal scent of dried leaves, the surrounding lobed hills littered with craggy glacial rocks, and the long circular row of rusting equipment, harrows and combines and rakes of an earlier farm era, which marked the perimeter of the park. Wondering what local *Volksdeutsche* farmer donated the acres for this homely rest stop, I circled around to the front of the metal archway, where across its top the park's name was spelled in hammered metal letters, gleaming in the late afternoon sun. I didn't like what I found.

The park—D. Park—had the same family name as the infamous squad leader at Lichtenfeld, awarded a gold watch for his assiduous Jew killing. Ambushed, car tires spinning, I quickly left the park, and continuing on to the wedding, I pondered the contradiction between the Dakota immigrant farmer, donating his land for a prairie park, and also the fire station in the nearby town, and the Volksdeutsche policeman detailed to the Holocaust murder pits. Thank God, I thought, for the prairie, our ethnic ark.

Later, milling around at the crowded wedding reception, an elderly lady, cradling a newborn against her bosom, makes her way past me, and when someone calls to her, "Where did you find the little one," the lady replies, "Oh I stole this baby away from Jill." So for an instant I'm back at the ovens of

Gradofka, listening to the brother telling me about his sister, the baby his mother stole from the flames.

Those are two remnants of my research that haunt me, and a third, and the most insistent, is the story of the naked Jewish beauty who pulled her Volksdeutsche executioner into the oven. It's a story that, my first year back from Ukraine, I repeat compulsively. To startled Christian friends as we sip coffee before church services. To my sister-in-law over the phone. To a table of academics in the university lunchroom. And one day to a filmmaker friend, who suggests that, using the incident as a focal point, we write a film script.

Over the next six months, we meet Saturday afternoons at a Barnes and Noble. Eventually we finish a full-length script, "Angel from the Flames," an unlikely love story between the naked Jewish beauty and the policeman ordered to kill her, who ends up hiding on a Dakota farm among his Volksdeutsche relatives.

Much of the script is cut whole cloth from my Nazi obsessed childhood, except for the part of the plot where the naked woman pulls her would-be executioner with her into the flames of an oven.

Later, when the former policeman leaves his farm for the first time in decades and visits his son in New York City, an elderly Jew there recognizes him: "I know you. You were at the ovens in Gradofka. You were one of the beasts."

Who would believe such a hackneyed plot, I ask my coauthor when we finished the script, never guessing that our work of fiction foreshadows what I'm about to uncover in real life.

***

DRECK

On the hottest day that next summer, I'm in a community center on the Western Canadian prairie, sweating like a butcher. The makeshift, wobbly podium I'm standing at is an upright cardboard box propped on a low table, and the out-of-date public address system shrieks like a banshee, but as the people there, seated at long tables laugh and smile at my Volksdeutsche jokes. I'm relaxed and happier than I've been in a while.

We eat a catered meal together, the Canadians and I. They trace their origins to the same cluster of Volksdeutsche villages as my own, arriving too late for Dakota homestead land, and instead settled in Canada, and who, as we chat, slot me into the genealogical puzzle of the prairie Volksdeutsche. "Oh, your grandmother was a Boschee? There are Boschees up here." It feels like I'm back in New Odessa again, at Sauerkraut Day, and as I meet and shake hands with hundreds of Canadians of Volksdeutsche ancestry, I feel a little like an ethnic rock star.

Several meetings seem foreordained, and point me, without my even knowing it then, back to my Dakota hometown in my search for police genocidaires, the first, when an aging Robert Redford look-alike, with startling blue eyes, introduces himself—"Mr. Fossler, my name is Adolf Brost." I know from his last name and the Germanized way he says mine, that he's from Josefstal, my stepfather's ancestral village in Eastern Transnistria.

"Yes, I lived in Josefstal," Adolf says. "And my family came to Canada, by way of Germany, after World War Two."

We fall into an easy intimacy, Adolf and I, born of our common origins, and the next day we travel to his upscale home in Edmonton, a prairie city of just under a million. In his high-ceilinged living room, we're joined off and on by his wife and by Johanna, his sister, a retired farm wife. We speak late and long.

Speaking of his family, there is the usual mantra of arrests and executions, of collective officials probing the earth with long, thin rods for hidden caches of grain and examining feces to uncover hidden grain, of emaciated villagers eating rotten horse flesh, pets, acacia blossoms, of survivors, too weak for sustained digging, and watching helplessly as heavy rains washed corpses from shallow graves, and mangy dogs loped village streets, human body parts clamped in their jaws. Our conversation finally shifts from their family's suffering in the Soviet 1930s to the German Occupation, when Josefstal was rescued by the Nazis who marched through their village streets and set up police units.

"Were they armed?" I ask. "The police?"

"Ach, no, no," Adolf says.

"They didn't carry weapons? Are you sure?"

"Just sticks to patrol," Adolf says.

Together, Adolf and his sister tell me of the murder of a Jewish family from Josefstal, parents first, and a week later, likely after the VoMi bureaucrats didn't find sufficient Aryan characteristics, the children, first the girl, and then the boy, cut down by an unnamed executioner's final bullet.

"Helga told that same story in Josefstal," I say.

"Everyone in Josefstal knew the story. They lived it," Johanna says, her voice disembodied and sad, coming from beyond the circle of light.

"Who fired the shots?" I say. "A German military officer? A member of the Einsatzgruppen?"

Silence.

"Local police?" I say.

"Like I told you," Adolf says with finality, getting up to drive his wife somewhere. "The local police just carried sticks."

After her brother left, Johanna moved from the long shadows to a long couch near where I sat.

"Did Helga mention Yakov Leidel?" she says.

"Yes, I think so," I say.

"Did she tell you he patrolled the streets of the village wearing a Nazi arm band and a pistol?"

"Yacov Leidel was armed?" I say. "But your brother said the police just carried small sticks. Why did he—?"

"He's younger and doesn't want to remember," she says. "Leidel is his cousin, our cousin."

"What did you talk about while I was gone?" Adolf says when he returns.

"About Yakov," Johanna says.

"Did you tell him how Yakov's family was chased from their home," Adolf says. "Five different times by the Soviet secret police."

"No, no," Johanna says. "We didn't talk about that. It's too late to get so upset."

"Well, okay," Adolf says. "Time we all went to bed."

***

After an early breakfast of kuchen-pie at a marble counter in his immaculate kitchen, Adolf whisks me in his new car around Edmonton, Alberta, a bustling city infused with money from nearby oilfields.

"It's a great place to live," he says. "Four hundred times bigger than Josefstal."

He pointed out the structures he helped build, first as a carpenter, then a supervisor, amassing a small fortune in real estate—a long way from his humble beginnings on the steppe.

His father, he says, arrested without cause by the Soviets, and slated for execution in 1937, was saved when a Jew heading the local collective vouched for his integrity, and somehow the entire family, during the evacuation of Transnistria and the rest of the war in Germany, managed to stay intact, making their way, after the war, to Canada.

"In Canada, we got lonesome for our people," Adolf says. "So we sometimes went down to North Dakota to visit relatives."

"You had relatives in North Dakota?" I say.

"In your hometown," he says. "We fit right in. We'd been writing them letters after the war."

Driving the wide avenues of his adopted city, we marveled at the tangle of marriage and blood at the heart of our common Volksdeutsche culture, Black Sea Germans scattered across Germany and Canada and the United States, descendants of the original founders of our ancestral villages between the Dniester and Bug Rivers.

"That's where I met Leidel, my cousin," he says.

"In my hometown?"

"At a Volksdeutsche reunion in the 1960s," Adolf says. "I didn't believe he'd survived."

They'd exchanged visits, Adolf and Johanna and their families motoring to Leidel's home in South Dakota, and the former policeman and his family coming up to Canada.

"When Yakov was dying, we drove down to see him."

It's an odd, transitory moment: Adolf, clutching his steering wheel, his ruddy features suffused with anger.

"Why did I need to know his dreck?" Adolf says. "Even if he was dying."

"What did Yakov Leidel tell you?"

"Nothing I wanted to hear," Adolf says. "Nothing I want to talk about."

The rest of the day, relaxing in Adolf's backyard and that night in his guest bedroom, I wonder what Leidel, the former policeman told Adolf on his death bed. Something terrible. About killing Jews? And what was Leidel doing in New Odessa, my hometown?

The next morning Johanna appears to say good-bye, and Adolf shakes my hand through the open window of my rental car, and says, "I'm happy we could meet and visit."

Ask him, I tell myself that day in the driveway. Even if he looks youthful, he is eighty years old. He has a bad heart. Ask him. This is your last chance. So ask him.

"Adolf, what did Leidel tell you?"

"Ach, lass gehe—Let it go," Adolf says, using the dialect phrase my grandmother always used, and I know that whatever Leidel told Adolf will sink away into the sea of time and be lost forever—or so I think.

In a long, scenic drive through scenic southern Alberta, I pass through several small towns that sport life-size dinosaur effigies and fossil shops. On the way back to the interstate, I drive fast, bugs and grasshoppers spattering my car's windshield, exploding there like bullets.

***

Several hours later, I'm driving up and down the streets of a little Canadian prairie town that has two weathered and no-longer-functional grain elevators along some rusted railroad tracks and a dozen rows of modest homes banked against a one block main street.

It's a courtesy call on Theresa, a ninety-year-old Volksdeutsche lady from the German Festival, who after my joke-telling session, handed me her address and said, enigmatically, "You should visit your relatives. So come see me."

Around the back of a modest home on a corner, under a canopy of Chinese elms, I find Theresa sitting under a sun umbrella with an old dial phone in her lap, its long cord snaking across the uneven boards of her deck and disappearing under her back door.

"Come and sit down," Theresa says. "When I saw your car I called my son. He'll be right over."

We are related, she says, in at least two different ways, and she exchanged letters with my grandparents in New Odessa, receiving much help, she says, money and food and clothing, that allowed many in her family to survive.

"I've translated some of those letters," I say. "In one letter your mother wrote that you were swelling up."

"You did?" she says, brushing her hand over her cheeks, over what seemed a million tiny, cuneiform hieroglyphics incised there, marks of swelling I'd seen on other survivors of the genocidal famine of 1933. "Everyone swelled. All of Josefstal. All your relatives."

Her son arrives, a tall, nervous local real estate agent with a tight, angular jaw; he sat beside me, and puffing vigorously on a cigarette, quickly usurped the conversation. Was he nervous his mother was telling me, a stranger, too much?

"He was born there," Theresa says, nodding at her son.

"In Transnistria?" I say.

"Yes, Transnistria."

"Just after the German invasion," the son says.

"He grew up here, in Canada," Theresa says. "We came after the war."

"He looks like a Delke to me," I say, mentioning my stepfather's last name.

"His grandfather was a Delke," she says.

"So I guess he should look like a Delke," I say, laughing.

"He looks like his father's side. A lot like Yakov Leidel."

"Yakov Leidel?" I say, surprised. "You knew Yakov Leidel?"

"Yakov Leidel was my husband's brother," Theresa says.

"And your husband was Rheinhold Leidel?" I say, having seen that name on a list of Josefstal policemen compiled by German war crimes officials. An asterisk and appended note said, "*Ausgewandert nach Kanada.*" (Immigrated to Canada.)

"Rheinhold was in the Selbstschutz," Theresa says. "With Yakov Leidel."

"Selbstschutz?" Again I'm surprised. I've only seen that term in documents.

"That means the Josefstal police," Theresa says, thinking I didn't understand.

"Did your husband talk about his time in the police?" I ask.

"It wasn't for him. So he quit."

"He didn't do anything wrong," the son blurts out. He stabs out his cigarette in the ashtray on the circular table between us, then lights another.

"Did your husband talk about Yakov Leidel?" I say.

"All the time," Theresa says.

"So you knew Yakov in Ukraine and in Canada? What was he like?

"Why ask me?" Theresa says. "I thought you knew him?"

"Why would you think I knew him?"

"Yakov's sponsor, his uncle, lived in your hometown," she say. "Yakov was always talking about that place in North Dakota."

"New Odessa?"

"Yes, New Odessa."

"So Yakov Leidel's uncle lived in New Odessa?" I say.

"Four of his uncles lived there."

"Who was Yakov's sponsor?"

"The Leidel, Christian," Theresa says, inverting the names in the old Volksdeutsche manner.

"What else do you know about Yakov Leidel?"

"I know Yakov went to New Odessa a lot to see his relatives there."

"Like Mom always says," the son says, grinding out the stub of another cigarette. "If you have relatives, you visit them."

***

IN HITLER'S BASEMENT

Back home the next day, I study my Transnistrian wall map. The one with the red pushpins indicating murder sites.

Josefstal was a single dot in empty space. No mass murders there. None I know of. Yet all around in each direction—at Worms, ten miles northwest; at Kolosofka station, twenty miles away; at Speyer, seven miles north; at Neu Kandel ten miles west; at Berezovka, twenty miles west—there were mass murders. Yet my jaunt to Canada has raised questions about Josefstal, about Yakov Leidel. I decide to follow the thread and learn more about the former policeman.

Leidel was a familiar name in New Odessa. They were a prominent family, having arrived in several waves of settlers from Josefstal in the first decade of the twentieth century. There were Leidels among the bustling farm kids ferried to school in town by large yellow school buses, and Leidels in town, taller and more studious than their rural counterparts. I knew most of them. But not the person Theresa in Canada mentioned—"the Leidel Christian." So I phone my mother, my best source about our hometown.

"Do you remember Leidels?"

"Of course I remember Leidels," she says. "Why wouldn't I?"

"Christian Leidel?" I say.

"Yes. Don't you remember? I lived in Hitler's basement?"

"Hitler's basement?" I say, wondering if dementia has clouded her judgement.

"That old guy you and your friends always called Hitler," she says.

"That was Christian Leidel?"

"The Leidel Christian," she says, reversing the name, the old way, like Theresa in Canada. "You remember after your stepfather died—"

"You sold our house and moved to the end of the block," I say.

"Yes, into Hitler's basement apartment," she says. "I lived there two years."

"I visited you there. Several times."

"But why are you so interested in Old Hitler?"

"I'm trying to find someone Hitler sponsored after the war."

"You mean Yakov Leidel?" my mother says.

"You knew him?"

"Of course."

"Why of course?"

"I talked with him a lot. We had coffee together," she says, fastidious about her words. "Whenever Yakov and his wife came to visit his uncle, they invited me up to visit."

"When you were living in Hitler's basement apartment?" I ask.

"Yes, Yakov came down and asked me to join them. He was always flirting with me."

"What was he like? Yakov Leidel I mean."

"Like anyone born in the old country."

"What did you talk about?" I say. "When you were invited for coffee?"

"Relatives. We talked about relatives. What else?"

I grew up listening to my aging aunts and uncles on Sunday afternoons in our living room, or in a semicircle of chairs on our front lawn, reciting the Biblical begats, the who married whom of our intricate genealogical puzzle.

"So Yakov was related to a lot of people in town?" I say.

"Of course. To the Netzingers and others."

"Wasn't your stepmother a Netzinger," I say, aghast.

"She was Yakov Leidel's grandmother."

"Yakov Leidel's grandmother?"

"Yakov's mother stayed in the old country."

"But his grandmother came to the prairie?" I say. "So we are related to Yakov Leidel?"

"Yakov's mother was my *stiefschwester.*"

"Your stepsister?" I say.

"Yes."

"So Yakov Leidel is my step cousin?"

"Yes. We're all related. By marriage or blood."

Hearing that word, *blood*, I cringe.

***

I entered my prairie hometown in the stark midmorning light, a shudder going up my spine. I was feeling anxious and guilty. How will the locals react if they learn Holocaust killers bore their last names? Or that a Transnistrian policeman, and maybe a killer of Jews, was related to local families? I don't know, and during my stay in town, I don't want to find out.

I check into the Prairie Oasis, a rundown motel on New Odessa's eastern edge. It had a quasi-Western motif, soiled carpets, low-ceilinged hallways, and the worst Internet evaluations of any motel in North Dakota—"a local embarrassment." It's an assessment that assures a quiet stay in my hometown.

My motel room, as requested, contains two king-size beds. It also features a blond desk and chairs from the 1960s. Across them I spread all the documents, everything from scrawled notes of telephone conversations to back issues of German from Russia society publications to old letters from New Odessa's bilingual newspaper—everything I've gathered about Leidel, and so I set to work, there, in New Odessa, where the various strands of my research, my childhood experiences, the Volksdeutsche villages in Transnistria, and Leidel, have come together in a Gordian knot, one I want to unravel.

Late into that first evening and into the next day, I focus on the first third of Leidel's life, which is contemporaneous with, and roughly congruent to, that first part of the lives of other Transnistrian genocidaires. He was a baby during WWI, a toddler during the Ukrainian Civil War, when anarchists and revolutionaries attacked the German colonies, and a teenager during Stalin's collectivization, when Leidel's mother was among those who starved, and then, four years later, in 1937, his father was among the twenty-five thousand Black Sea Germans executed.

Over several decades, Leidel's parents in Josefstal steadily communicated with their friends and relatives, especially with Leidel's grandparents, on the Dakota prairie. They often spoke warmly of New Odessa to their son, and over the years Leidel witnessed his parents' joy at the arrival of letters, of money, of packages of food and clothing that drew them back from the brink of starvation. One day, Leidel's father made Leidel memorize and repeat back to him a simple address, Leidel, New Odessa, North Dakota, USA. "If something happens to me and your mother," he told his son, "write my brothers in New Odessa. They will help you."

One evening, I take a break from the research, and going along the narrow buckled sidewalks of New Odessa, I retrace my childhood paper route. My former customers' homes are different, remodeled, larger than I remembered. In a number of those same homes—as I know from old letters I've translated—sad scenes played themselves out in the 1930s, as retired farmers, pacing on arthritic knees over bulging linoleum floors, read final messages from relatives in Soviet Ukraine: "Dear brother, if this continues, by spring, we will eat each other. They want to annihilate us, the Germans on the steppe. Our souls cry to the heavens. I'll love you until death."

The Dakota Germans never knew, or if they knew never say, anything about their relatives' suffering. The pioneers were remembered as always bent over their German-language newspapers, which acted as clearing houses for German colonist affairs across Europe and America, and in those newspapers, they at times found Nazi anti-Semitic propaganda, which echoed the slurs against the Israelites in their personal letters from the old country: "The Jews now have us in their hands." In 1939, a front page opinion piece, penned by a resident of a town thirty miles from New Odessa, was an anti-Semitic screed: "Jewish Imperialism."

Back in my motel room, moving like a chess player matching wits against multiple players, I continue to piece together Leidel's life. During the 1930s the collectivization era, when doubly damned as the son of a prosperous kulak, and of Germanic ancestry, he'd often dodged arrest, and as a new wave of Volksdeutsche executions ratcheted higher, his communist brother-in-law, unable to protect him any longer, warned him to join the local communist party.

He did, despite his lifelong hatred for the regime that destroyed his parents. Thus, he remained unscathed until just after the German invasion in 1941, when the Soviet secret police arrested the twenty five year old Leidel, and two dozen other villagers of military age in Josefstal, placing them under armed guard in several horse-pulled wagons, that set out on the road to Nikolaev, to put them in the prison there.

Leidel knew his decade of luck had ended. All he could expect at the secure redbrick prison on the bluffs of the Bug River at Nikolaev was imprisonment, torture, and death. But fate intervened. Overhead in the clear skies a dogfight took place between a Nazi fighter airplane and a Soviet aircraft. It set off a terrific clamor, and the Soviet commissar ordered an underling to take the prisoners into a nearby field and shoot them. Instead, the men somehow managed to get free. It was another of Leidel's many brushes with death.

During the first weeks of the German Occupation, Leidel's name was on the list of known communist party members, as Einsatzgruppen units swept the area, executing Jews, communists, and Volksdeutsche collaborators with the Soviets. The question was, how in two months, September/ October, 1941, did Leidel, known for chasing women, and playing an accordion at weddings, become a policeman? Especially one with enough power, including the power of life and death, to protect his communist brother-in-law from Nazi death squads. Unless he, Leidel, was a member of those death squads?

During the evacuation of Transnistria, Leidel was an armed scout, riding far ahead of the wagon train on a fast horse, securing provisions for livestock, sometimes at gunpoint. Back in the German Reich, Leidel was quickly drafted into the Wehrmacht, fighting at war's end in several battles on the collapsing Eastern Front, and escaping Stalin's forcible repatriation of Volksdeutsche, legally Soviet citizens, but none of whom wanted to return to the Soviet Union.

For Leidel, that was another close call, about which he later expressed great relief, and the pivotal event which convinced him to get as far from the Soviets as possible. Was that because he feared being put on trial in the Soviet Union, where witnesses might be arrayed against him? I don't know, and so I plunge back into the documents, seeking answers, seeking clues.

After the war, in the bombed out remnants of Berlin's Anhalter train station, he met the mouthy teenager he used to chase off the streets as a policeman in Josefstal, now a fetching young woman, and the two of them, moving in Josefstal refugee circles, quickly married, had their first child, after which Leidel began to focus on reaching America, the golden land.

In 1949, with Red Cross help, he scrawled the address his father made him memorize seventeen years earlier across the face of an envelope, and sent his first letter to Dakota relatives who departed Josefstal before he was born, a feather dropped into a canyon; they quickly responded, and during a year-long correspondence sent him clothing, canned goods, even a hundred pound sack of flour, and then in 1950, an invitation to come to America.

Leidel fulfilled the legal requirements under the Displaced Persons Act, affidavits were signed and witnessed in Germany and the United States, with the former policeman rightly stating he'd been married in a church in Germany, falsely claiming his birthplace there, not in Ukraine. Is that an indication he was running from something?

Boarding a military ship manned by a civilian crew, supported by the International Refugee Organization, and carrying several thousand European refugees, the Leidels crossed the Atlantic Ocean to New York in 1952, his family's passage funded by a Jewish organization, a fact not lost on the former policeman. He also realized, midway, that the bulk of the passengers were Jews, some survivors of death camps— "They had a place to go and we didn't," he says—and even if it was the Jews, during the worst part of the crossing, who were first to offer help, nursing his seasick wife and caring for his son, he felt surrounded by a people he'd formally vowed to destroy a decade earlier.

That was in the autumn of 1941, during his police training, which consisted of propaganda formulated by Leibbrandt at the Eastern Ministry about the dangers of Jewish Bolshevism, and culminated at a pyre of burning logs on the open steppe—meant to symbolize the burning of Jews—where the police recruits chanted, in unison, their vow of allegiance to Hitler.

From New York the Leidel's rode the train to the heart of the continent, disembarking at a prairie rail station in New Odessa, North Dakota, a block from where I then lived, a five-year-old in my parents' home.

Waiting for him in the wainscoted small town depot, were Leidel's Dakota relatives, his uncles and their families, and, also, it seemed at first glance to Leidel's young wife, who scooped up her son and drew back in horror, Adolf Hitler, the Nazi dictator, not in his military uniform, but a pair of grease-spotted coveralls with the circular impression of a snooze can worn into its breast pocket.

"This is my Uncle Christian," Leidel said, introducing to his wife the rough looking character who, with his square moustache so strongly resembled the German dictator. "He is the person who sponsored us."

For several weeks Leidel and his wife and child slept in Hitler Leidel's wood-heated summer kitchen, apart from the tiny farm home, which was miles from town. They were shocked by the frontier-like living conditions, by the moonscape view of the snow-hummocked prairie, the lack of indoor plumbing, and cold tramp to the smelly outhouse. With electricity available only a couple of hours a day, and then only if a battery system was hooked up, Leidel's wife, especially, pined for the conveniences she'd left behind in postwar Germany.

In the spring of 1952, the local newspaper ran a brief article, "Displaced Persons Seek New Happiness in Rural Community," along with a photo of the young family posed behind a small world globe from the grade school. Leidel told the reporter they were willing to work hard, to chase their American dream. He wanted to farm, like his Dakota uncles, and hoped his son would also become one. All he wanted, he said, was to forget the past.

"Ach yah, I remember Hitler," a bearded relative tells me over drinks in the redbrick bar on Main Street once owned by my great uncles. He describes how—on Saturday nights in the mid-1950s, when farm families parked their large-finned cars on main street to shop and socialize after a long week in their fields—local groups played live music in the adjoining dance hall, waltzes and polkas and Germanic-accented popular tunes, and sometimes the elderly farmer, Hitler, sloughing his greasy coveralls for a white shirt and dauber polished Sunday shoes, played a primitive Volksdeutsche percussion instrument—the bones or pig knuckles—clicked in such a lively performance that, despite his doleful appearance, drew much applause, especially from his handsome young nephew, drinking beer and speaking German dialect with the rest of the Leidel relatives.

Old Hitler and his nephew shared a love of music. Leidel liked to brag that he used to "dance like the dickens." And as I know from my own documents, the former policeman, both before and during the German Occupation of Josefstal, played both drums and concertina for local weddings, Nazi May Day festivities, and the April twentieth Fuehrer birthday fete at the far edge of the Nazi colonial empire in Transnistria.

"I met up with Hitler Leidel in the early 1960s," one of my former classmates tells me. "I was working for an outfit out of Fargo, Ulteig Engineers."

His crew was surveying a power line across McIntosh County, and an old farmer and Yakov Leidel, emerged from a rusted pickup and confronted them in his pasture. "This is my lant. Chust what do you tink you are doing out here?"

The engineers showed him their tripod and measuring rods, and pointed to their truck door logo, as evidence that, as representatives of the company, they had legal access to survey his land, which satisfied the grizzled old farmer.

"The old guy was just a little weird, with all his Nazi talk," my former classmate says. "And if I remember right, he buttonholed us for more than an hour."

That day in the pasture, Hitler Leidel, his nephew listening quietly, praised the advanced weaponry and technology of the Nazi war machine, and also the great leader who put the German people back to work in the 1930s.

My old classmate casts a wary glance around the mostly empty cafe, whispering that the old farmer seemed anti-Semitic. He said the Nazis couldn't have killed six million Jews because there weren't that many Jews to kill, and that if they wanted to know about the Jews, the engineers should ask his nephew, there at his elbow, just who it was that killed his parents in the old country.

"That's more than you want to know about Old Hitler Leidel," my friend says. "Just don't associate my name with any of this. I have to live here."

Several months later, Leidel and his young wife and child bade their sponsor good-bye, and moved to South Dakota, where he found work in a mine, and instead of cutting limestone blocks in the long dark tunnels of the Josefstal quarry, as he'd once done, working for a Jew, he now dug lead and gold and other minerals, unafraid, he said, of the deep descent into the earth. He'd survived worse, he'd said.

His Dakota relatives continued to visit Leidel and his family, and even an aging Hitler Leidel motored south in his old Studebaker, stocking Leidel's larder each summer with fresh garden vegetables, and after autumn butchering, with sides of beef and jars of canned chicken. Leidel and his family, in turn, spent holidays in New Odessa, and attended the funerals of his elderly relatives.

A photo from the mid-1950s, shows Leidel and his wife, and two children, in front of their modest, clapboard home. The former policeman wears an expensive plaid suit, though an uncertain smile wreathes his movie-star good looks. There is something else in his face, in his eyes, an uncertain cast, reminiscent of Weingartner in the Fresno photo.

Leidel joined clubs and local organizations, indicators of his assimilation into the American mainstream, attended church regularly, sitting on the church council, and even naming his youngest child after the offspring of an uncle in New Odessa. His old life in Europe was not entirely forgotten, for he often sent money and food items and his used clothing to his beleaguered relatives, those caught up in the Soviet dragnet at the end of WWII, and forced into Siberian exile.

Each Memorial Day, Leidel placed flowers on his grandparents' graves at the family church in Jackrabbit Valley, twenty miles south of New Odessa, and in the mid-1980s, he and his wife attended the church's hundredth anniversary, singing patriotic and religious songs, and listening as representatives of the various Netzinger siblings took turns at the microphone, briefly reciting the history of each family branch in America.

When it was Leidel's turn—his mother was the only Netzinger sibling to remain in Ukraine—he took to the podium, dressed in a long-sleeved white shirt, wearing a cowboy string tie, its clasp fashioned from the same Black Hills gold he mined.

Gazing nervously over the crowd of 150 relatives from across the United States, and apologizing for his thick German accent—"No ticker than ours," someone shouted in support—the former policeman related the sad fate of the Leidels and Netzingers in Josefstal, his mother starved, father was executed, and he and his siblings were chased by the Soviet secret police. He sketched out his wartime experiences in the Wehrmacht, and then added, in closing, "America is a great, good country, and I thank God, and my relatives, especially the Leidel, Christian, for bringing me here."

Taking their places at the long picnic tables, and sharing the Volksdeutsche meal, catered by a small town cafe, Leidel and his wife enjoyed themselves, sitting among the most relatives he'd seen since leaving Josefstal.

***

One afternoon I take a break. Using a borrowed key, I gain entry to the town library, located in the stuccoed city hall at the far end of Main Street. I'm curious to know if the books I read on Saturday afternoons of my childhood are still there. In the stacks—a series of metal shelves from the local mercantile store—I search for and quickly find, noting my lopsided schoolboy signature scrawled across the cards in their back-cover pockets, the books I'd been reading, about the time my grandfather was telling me about Lichtenfeld, and the old country, books about golden Mycenae, and Schliemann's Troy, and one book, Halliburton's *Complete Book of Marvels*, which I repeatedly checked out over several years, and which described his nighttime plunge, in the ancient city of Chichen Itza, into the cenote, the Mayan well of death. There was another book I checked out and read too, fifty years earlier, about cenotes, with descriptions of how these sacred wells were geological formations that ancient Mayans saw as openings into the dark spirit underworld, and as I examined the photos in the half-light, I had a strange realization

The cenotes seemed larger versions of those ovens, the same ominous brown color, the same circular, steep-sided shafts down which human sacrifices were hurled to blood-hungry Mayan Gods. Which explained why Gradofka's lime-ovens, the first time I saw them, seemed so familiar, and struck in me a chord of inexplicable recognition.

Another evening, in my old neighborhood, I found our former home, still shaded by several thick cottonwoods planted half a century earlier by my stepfather, its clapboards shedding paint, and, directly across the street, I searched for where our cardboard Hitler bunker once stood.

335

But the once-tilting lot, where the bunker lay hidden in a tangled greenery of fragrant wormwood and pigweed and thistles, had since been contoured out of existence, and in its place, huge-tired green combines, in echelon, and next to them, a ranch-style home with a backyard swing set. It's impossible to get my bearings. Hitler's real bunker in Berlin had been easier to locate.

On the opposite end of the block, I find the brown-shingled, ranch-style home, with double garage, into which Hitler Leidel and his wife retired, now vacated, and in whose basement—Hitler's basement as my brothers and I used to call it—my mother had once lived in the mid-1970s. My only memory of Old Hitler dates from that time—on my way through the garage door to my mother's apartment, I glimpsed the old farmer, his square moustache now grey, slumped in a ladder-back chair on the cement driveway. It was just after his first stroke, his cane lay across his lap, and his ever-faithful wife was hovering nearby.

Yakov Leidel and five male cousins were pallbearers. From the country church with its copper-sheathed steeple in Jackrabbit Valley, where the funeral was held, they carried Hitler Leidel's remains to the nearby, lonely, lilac-overgrown country cemetery, where he was laid to rest next to Leidel's grandmother, my step-grandmother, and surely, as the weight of the coffin pulled on his shoulder socket, Yakov Leidel felt gratitude for his sponsor, who brought him to America, and who, perhaps, in doing so, shielded him from the probing questions of German war crimes prosecutors.

***

That same evening, in my old neighborhood, and just catty-corner from the old farmer's house, I find the other Hitler house, the one in which Larry and I, as fifth graders, thought the dictator real lived, its dark asphalt siding upgraded to modern metal clapboards, its once straggly lawn, beneath which we fantasized the stacks of hidden Nazi gold, now resodded and green.

From the intersection—there is no traffic in the quiet evening—I snapped photos to capture this weird conjunction, the two Hitler houses so close, and so, on my way back to the motel, I couldn't help but think: how strange and prescient our childhood imaginings, taproots sinking deep into our collective history, prefiguring my current Holocaust research.

How even possible, these dark intimations and raptures of futurity, except from God's guiding hand? How even possible the coincidence that Yakov Leidel once wore what all of the Transnistrian genocidaires wore during their three years of killing, a Nazi armband, a black swastika against a red background? He not only wore it, but in exactly the same place, his upper left arm, which was where my grade school buddies and I, in our Hitler bunker, and into our biceps, engraved those bloody swastikas.

***

On my last full day in New Odessa, I decide to visit a Dakota German genealogist who knew Yakov Leidel.

If anyone was privy to the former policeman's secrets, it would be Otto. That's what I tell myself as I leave the Prairie Oasis, and take the winding asphalt road between smooth-shaped hills topped with large boulders, eleven miles to a neighboring prairie town.

Otto's house is easy to find. It reflects his passion for all things Volksdeutsche, remodeled with *fachwerk* (crisscrossed beams embedded in a stuccoed exterior) to resemble a seventeenth century farmhouse from Alsace, France, once the *ur-heimat* (the original home) of many Black Sea Germans.

Once I'd spoken on the phone about his startling claim that some Alsatian Volksdeutsche had Jewish ancestry. It's a connection, Otto claimed, stemming from sixteenth-century

Spain, when Jews fleeing Torquemada's bloody Inquisition, went to Alsace, intermarrying with German-speaking farmers. Which meant, Otto told me, that some Alsatian Germans claiming free acreage in the first decades of the nineteenth century in Czarist Ukraine, were, in fact, of Jewish ancestry. That all made sense to me, since the Nazis couldn't always tell the difference between Volksdeutsche and Jews. One family of German colonists in my grandmother's village narrowly escaped an Einsatzgruppen antitank ditch slaughter. "You look like Jews. How can you not be Jews," an SD officer told them, thrusting their identification papers back to them. "Now get out of here." German colonists in Odessa played on that ethnic confusion, giving their identity cards to Jews, saving many lives, as Duissmann affirmed. If Otto's theory was true—and I had my doubts, mostly because Otto as an amateur historian was prone to reading into documents what he wanted to find— then Volksdeutsche police murdered not only fellow Soviet citizens, but even some of their own relatives.

Otto, who met me at the front door, resembled one of those Shepardic Jews from whom he claimed Volksdeutsche were descended, greying hair combed back from a triangular face, blue eyes, ruined from deciphering Germanic script in archaic church registries, scrutinizing me myopically from behind thick-lensed glasses.

"Kumm herein," he says, inviting me into his living room, cluttered with back issues of Volksdeutsche journals, printed Internet documents, and genealogical charts, pinned to the walls, and hanging like loose strips of wallpaper. It's a scholar's home, notwithstanding my doubts about him, which reaffirm my sense that with academic training, Otto might have risen from his current position as an eccentric provincial living off a trust fund, to the ranks of noted historians.

"I heard you were back in New Odessa," Otto says, motioning me to sit down. "Asking questions."

"That's me," I say. "Always digging up dirt."

"Well, no, I didn't mean it that way," Otto says.

"On the way here I thought of your research about Jews being related to the Volksdeutsche."

"Funny you'd say that," he says, looking over his bifocals. "I have more in that regard."

"Which is?"

"Something that happened in the 1850s."

The Czarist government, he says, recognizing the German colonists as singularly equipped to teach agricultural methods to ghettoized Jews, relocated 450 Volksdeutsche to live and work in twenty different Jewish villages.

"The result of that relocation was interesting," Otto says.

Moving nimbly for a man of his girth, he goes from the couch opposite me to a small library table. After rummaging in a stack of papers, he returns with a long unfurling document, a genealogical chart, that he hands to me.

"Besides improved agriculture. There was also intermarriage between the two minorities."

"Is this accurate?" I say, not believing what the chart indicated. "Yakov Leidel had Jewish ancestry."

"I thought you knew," he says.

"So our people weren't such pure Germans after all?" I say, using a term that bothered me, that was, in effect, a Nazi term.

I'm still working on it," Otto says.

An old saying flitted through my mind: "*Alt wie a Kuh, und immer noch dazu.*" (Old as a cow and still learning.) Which was why Volksdeutsche humor seemed similar to Jewish humor. Because it often was Jewish humor. And those stories of secret Jewish ancestry I'd heard over the years, and dismissed as apocryphal nonsense, and wishful thinking for some exotic ancestry: those were, it seemed, in many cases true.

"There is a terrible irony in all this," I say. "Did Yakov tell you about his time in the Josefstal police?"

"Yes, of course," Otto says. "We spent a lot of time together before he passed away."

"What did he tell you?"

"That he was a courier. He carried messages."

"Messages?"

"Important ones," Otto says. "Between Josefstal and the district SS headquarters in Speyer. That's what he told me."

"Josefstal was in the Speyer district?"

"Yes. That's what Yakov told me."

I hate hearing that. Speyer is a substantial Catholic village in the Beresan, near Leidel's Josefstal. Speyer, on the way to Gradofka, where I'd often stopped, to kneel and pray near the refurbished church, and there, overseen by the tender pathos of Byzantine-like images of apostles in the recessed window niches, ask for God's guidance. Speyer, a balm and healing counterpoint to the SS baby killers with pig-like features that stumbled through my dreams.

"If Josefstal was in the Speyer district," I say, thinking aloud. "That means Yakov was on that district's police unit, answerable to its district SS commandant, Eckart."

"Yakov often talked about Eckart," Otto says. "The man who hired him, he says. He never said Eckart was SS."

I tell Otto everything I know about the psychopath Eckart, said to speak eight languages in his capacity as a liaison between the VoMi and the Romanian command in Transnistria, known for shooting anyone he wanted, poisoned early in his tenure by a jealous SS colleague so that his war crimes went unresearched.

"One thing that Yakov told me," Otto says. "Eckart always relied on volunteers. For what, I don't know."

"For the killings."

"Killings?" he says, his thin lips quivering.

"Killing of gypsies, partisans, enemies of the Reich," I say.

"And Jews?"

"Yes."

"You think our Yakov was involved?" Otto says, crestfallen. "But why?"

"Orders, perhaps. Or he volunteered. Or prove himself to Eckart. Or revenge."

"He never told me that," Otto says. "Not in the final interview I did with him."

"You interviewed him?"

Otto goes to his desk again. He hands me a forty-page interview he's paid a local high school student to type up from a cassette tape, an obviously shoddy job.

"It's full of errors," Otto says. "We're not all educated college professors like you."

"I don't mind the errors," I say. "I bet even the Rosetta Stone had errors."

Together, at Otto's Formica kitchen table, we divided the interview pages, like I did with Dmitri in Ukraine.

"What are we looking for?" Otto say.

"Whatever shows Leidel's propensity for violence. Anything."

Heads bowed, we search for clues.

"Here is a passage I remember," Otto says, a bit later, looking over his thick bifocals.

"Read it to me."

In a weary voice, Otto read a passage, buried deep in the verbatim transcript, about displaced Josefstalers socializing in postwar Germany. He mentions one of my stepfather's relatives, Rudolf Delke, a strapping SS man hardened on the Eastern Front, who once taunted Leidel's attractive, young wife, for marrying such a poor prospect.

The volatile Leidel hunted Delke. He found him on a dance floor at a club, dragged him off, and, here Otto's voice quavered, as he read Leidel's words: "I beat the shit out of him. And then I tore his new suit off of him."

"What does that say about Yakov?" Otto says.

"It may be what rough ex-soldiers did postwar," I say. "But it may also show Leidel's vengeful nature. Who knows?"

Not much later, Otto stabbed his stubby forefinger at the middle of a page, and looked up at me quizzically: "This is something I don't remember."

In the passage Leidel described local informers responsible for the exile and death of countless Josefstalers, a common fate during the 1930s in Transnistria. "I knew who the informers were, and when the German army came in," Leidel said. "They shot these German communists. But I won't tell you their names. I have stories you would never believe. Things so horrible I don't want to think or talk about them."

"That sounds like a veiled confession," I say.

"I don't remember Yakov saying that. So maybe you are right."

"About what?"

"That our people just want to do genealogy," Otto says. "Most of us don't really want to know our grim history. Me included, I'm afraid."

"I understand that. Genealogical charts don't show blood. If it's any solace, there are things I'd rather not know either."

"He's your relative too," Otto says, as if reading my thoughts. "This can't be easy for you either."

"I'm trying to follow the light of truth," I say, my words coming, it seemed, from somewhere both distant, and, also, inside myself.

"Then follow the light. Wherever it leads. *Verstehe?* (Understand?)

***

That evening, I stretch out on one of the king-size beds in my motel room, to read myself to sleep, and get an early start home the next morning. The book I'm reading at the time, not exactly a soporific, *The Things They Cannot Say*, about soldiers and killing, includes this passage:

> Watching people being killed, especially those you know, is a memory that can't be erased. But actually doing the killing, or being fully complicit in it, is a lifelong sentence to contemplate the nature of one's own character, endlessly asking, "Am I good or am I evil?" and slowly growing mad at the equivocation of this trick question, whose answer is definitely yes. When someone kills in war there's a psychological triage that occurs. The individual must find meaning in the act. Because killing is a refutation of our humanity,

there must be a justification, to prevent the mind from defaulting to the judgement of murderer.

Leidel surely justified the murders he'd committed. By telling himself it was wartime? That he was a policeman protecting Josefstal? That he was following orders? That he was avenging all the suffering and deaths of his loved ones under the supposedly Jewish-Bolshevik regime? In Holocaust literature, somewhere, I'd read that couriers given important documents to carry, or perform other important tasks, often identified strongly with their superiors, doing things they might not have otherwise done.

I know I'll never sleep, not with those thoughts and everything I'd learned from Otto of Eckart and Leidel and my own Jewish ancestry, racketing around in my head. So in several trips, I tote everything, all the documents and books, the files and folders to my car, dumping them out in the backseat, and then check out of my motel room and headed homeward. My car cresting the first rise outside of New Odessa, and with the setting sun spreading a molten glow along the horizon behind me, I realize that while I was in town I'd suppressed all thoughts of the fiery ovens, and Leidel's possible connection to them.

Later, a brief but fierce rain shower darkens the highway, and wafts the scent of lakes and wet hay into my car, scents of childhood, of work, reminding me of the elderly pioneers I knew, a decent, kind, religious people. Once, the Volksdeutsche of Transnistria, the people from whom they'd come, had also been prosperous, hardworking, religious. Until the tsunami-like waves of Soviet terror. What can you expect, I ask myself, using Dmitri's words and logic, from people who'd endured that? Not much. Still, it's important to realize that Leidel, and other policemen like him, were only a subset of the overall group, and did not represent all Volksdeutsche.

Leidel was not shy about publicity. There were photographs of him in a variety of Volksdeutsche newsletters and publications. Seen by thousands. Would a murderer act that way? Or did he perhaps know, through the intricate Volksdeutsche grapevine, that those who could testify against him were long dead? Or did he know he'd killed all possible witnesses?

Active members of the Germans from Russia Society throughout the 1970s, the Leidels hated the organization's name because it reminded them of a place they'd sooner forget, while faithfully attending the annual conventions, especially in later years, and donning their finery for the occasion.

"Oh how quaint!" convention-goers warbled, snapping photos of the Leidels, posing in clothing that no Dakota German ever wore, that some mistakenly thought was October Fest apparel, but really resembled the costumes, as shown in Nazi propaganda stills of Transnistria, that the Volksdeutsche wore for May Day and Hitler Birthday festivities—both seemingly unaware: Leidel, in a plumed hat cocked jauntily on his head, a pair of short lederhosen, and tube socks stretched over his boney shins, and his wife, in her dirndl, a close-fitting colored blouse, embroidered with tiny edelweiss flowers: the spitting image of Eva Braun, Hitler's mistress, as filmed during WWII on the Berchtesgarden balcony.

In the early 1990s, Leidel wrote a brief, lively account for a publication read by thousands of a tearful reunion with a brother he'd not seen for fifty years. As Leidel described it, he'd flown from South Dakota, and his brother from Siberia, and they'd met in Germany. Such reunions were commonplace in that period—I'd witnessed several myself— as Volksdeutsche, separated by war, and returning from the far reaches of the former Soviet Empire, were reunited with scarcely remembered family members. They wept together, getting reacquainted, with Leidel trying to convince his brother—his Christian belief seemed authentic—"to accept God and Christianity," but his broken-down sibling rejected the attempt.

In the mid-1990s, Leidel's wife decided to make a return trip to Josefstal, their former village in Ukraine, which they left half a century earlier, but despite the fact that he'd recently flown to Germany, so it wasn't fear of flying, he refused to accompany her. Why? Unless he feared post-communist Ukrainian authorities, who might have access to SS police rosters, so he'd actually be risking arrest and trial, even at this late a date. Why take the chance? In that way, if indeed that was his thinking, he resembled other genocidaires I knew, or those I thought were genocidaires, like Old Peter, who categorically refused to return to their home villages.

Those were my thoughts, driving the prairie at night, so that by the time I neared my home in Red River Valley, I felt I'd reached a dead end in my research. That night, after all my obsessing about him, Leidel appeared in my dreams, on a fine white horse, wearing his Nazi arm-band, and his field-grey cap, turned backward, so its death's head insignia faced me as he rode away.

***

Not much later, rising from the curse-ridden depths of our ethnic strata, another agony thrusts itself to the surface. It comes in the form of a phone call.

"Ron, I need to tell you one more thing about Hoffnungstal," says the caller, whose soft lisp, and lingering German accent, tell me it was Timotheus, the retired US Special Forces soldier, and Helmut's best friend, with whom I haven't spoken for several years.

"Maybe someday you will remember this and write about it," he says, not knowing that I was already writing about it, and just as with Regina, I knew he was going to tell me so that people he didn't know, and would never see, would know the truth of the collective blood curse of our inexplicable history.

"After Helmut's mother died in 1940," Timotheus says. "Helmut's grandfather moved into the house on Bueckele Street, just down from the mayor's office a couple of blocks."

"Yes," I know Bueckele Street," I say. "I visited that house when I was in Hoffnungstal."

"That was the happiest time of Helmut's life. Living there with his grandfather."

"With his father too," I say.

"His father was there, yes," he says. "But there was nothing happy about that. You'll understand in a bit."

"Helmut told me he grew very close to his grandfather in that time," I say.

"The old man really cared deeply for Helmut," he says. "He cut Helmut's hair and played old religious songs for him."

"On a squeezebox accordion that my great grandmother sent him from New Odessa, North Dakota."

"I see you know that story," Timotheus says, surprised. "I'll tell you one you don't know."

"About the Jews of Freiburg?" I say.

"Yes and no. First, let me tell you what happened once Helmut's father was named mayor by Hauptsturmfuehrer Weingartner."

"To replace the mayor who protected the Jews?"

"Yes. Helmut's father made sure the census edict was posted," he says. "And so the Freiberg Jews came into Hoffnungstal to register, and once they lined up to register at the mayor's Amt, they were arrested."

"Then killed by the Einsatzgruppe at the klinge," I say.

"Then, when the Hoffnungstalers learned of the murders," Timotheus says. "Everyone, most everyone, was very angry."

"Most everyone?"

"Not Helmut's father," he says.

"So the Hoffnungstalers spoke out against the murders? But not Helmut's father?"

"Helmut's grandfather went to the mayor's Amt, the office, to confront his son."

"His son, the mayor?"

"And Hauptsturmfuehrer Weingartner," Timotheus says.

"What did the old man say to them?"

"The old man didn't say, he shouted."

"What did he shout?"

"You know," Timotheus says, gathering himself. "Things like 'I was their *shabbat goy*. I helped them on their holy days. I helped them and they helped me. We were friends. They were innocent. You killed your own son's friends.'"

"What happened?"

Timotheus made a whistling sound between his teeth.

"Helmut's grandfather disappeared?" I say.

"Yes."

"So Weingartner gave the order to arrest the old man, and—"

"No," he says.

"Who then?"

"The mayor."

"The mayor had his own father arrested?"

"Yes, and the grandfather ended up at the klinge."

"Shot by Weingartner?"

"Nein," Timotheus says, the only time in our conversation he uses a German word.

"Who did the killing?" I say. "Not Weingartner? Or Sturmfuehrer H.?"

"Nein," Timotheus says, again. "The mayor. Using his own pistol."

"The mayor killed his own father?"

"Yes, yes."

"Did Helmut witness the killing?"

"Possible," Timotheus says. "Very possible."

"More than very possible?"

"Yes. You could say that."

"Who buried the body of the grandfather?"

"Not the mayor," Timotheus says.

"Helmut?"

"The mayor tossed Helmut a shovel. He told him, 'You loved him so much, you bury him.'"

"So that was Helmut's trauma."

"That I can say for certain," Timotheus says.

***

"So you once worked for Hauptsturmfuehrer Weingartner?" I say. "In Hoffnungstal."

I can't believe my luck. Several phone calls based on a single obscure clue buried deep in a document have led me to phone ninety-three-year-old Esther L., who has been living in California for half a century.

"Yes, I was the Hauptsturmfuehrer's secretary in Hoffnungstal," she snaps. "But I don't talk about him or the Jews."

"Why not?" I say, a little too quickly.

"Because people might tape-record what you say."

349

"I am not recording this."

"They will use it against you later. Even if they say they won't. Perhaps you will do this, Herr Vossler?"

"Well, take a chance," I say, with a forced laughed, and when she laughed too, I felt another door opening into the bloody and complex saga of Hoffnungstal.

Despite her earlier protestations about not talking about the Jews, Esther tells me of several of her friends, Jewish girls from Freiburg, with whom she often went to dances in Hoffnungstal, and she always had so much fun.

"Do you know who Leibbrandt was?" she says, abruptly.

"My relatives in Fresno knew him. And I have read about him."

"He was one of *unsera Leute*," she says, using the German term for our people. "And a high official in Hitler's Eastern Ministry."

"You knew him?" I say.

"Knew him? I danced with him," she says, proudly, her voice young and buoyant, like Regina's when she spoke of Weingartner.

Esther met Leibbrandt, she says, in the fall of 1942 or 1943. She was a secretary and receptionist in Weingartner's headquarters, copying out church records (which certified the Hoffnungstalers as members of Hitler's master race), when Leibbrandt, touring the East, and wearing his Eastern Ministries uniform, with its tight-fitting tunic, approached her desk.

"Oh it was important business," she says. "The Ost Minister brought Weingartner the names of those who murdered his family in the 1930s."

"What happened to those people?" I say.

"What always happens to spies. Spitze, we called them."

"Executed at *D' klinge?*" I say.

"That's all I want to say. No more talk of Jews."

"So tell me about Leibbrandt."

"Everyone in Hoffnungstal knew him," she says. "The entire room lit up when he entered it. Yes, he was a lively man, and he always had a joke for you."

"So you danced with Leibbrandt?"

"Ach, yes, did we ever dance. It was at the harvest celebration. I even flirted with him."

Leibbrandt whirled her around the dance floor, she says, and half breathless between waltzes, asked her how a village girl could dance so well, and she told him that before the war she'd studied dance in Odessa.

"What else did you do? Besides dance and flirt with Leibbrandt?" I say, more teasing than anything, and by not probing, I inadvertently nudged her into an admission.

"I burned documents," Esther says. "At the end, before the evacuation."

"Documents?"

"Police rosters," she says. "Weingartner's orders."

"What kind of orders?" I say.

"All I'm telling you is that I burned them."

"What about Weingartner's order to search the wine cellars? And find those trying to hide and stay behind?"

"I see you know about that. But you are wrong. That order came from the evacuation authorities. Not from my Hauptsturmfuehrer."

"If anyone was found, trying to remain behind. Then what?"

"They were shot," she says. "It was the same across Transnistria."

"What about the dozen prisoners in the jail?"

"That was the Hauptsturmfuerher's last order in Hoffnungstal."

"How do you know?"

"I typed it."

"What was the order?"

"To empty the jail," Esther says. "More than that, I won't tell you."

***

Whether the police murdered those dozen prisoners from the Hoffnungstal jail is not clear. Perhaps one of "Weingartner's people" remained behind to oversee, or do, the killing. It couldn't have been L., because he was chauffeuring the Hauptsturmfuerher in his staff car at the head of the long wagon train heading west. It couldn't have been Sturmfuehrer HJ either, because he was seen that final day getting into a VoMi lorry with his new wife, and the Hoffnungstal church ledgers in his possession. That left only Obersturmfuehrer H., Weingartner's main executioner. So it was anyone's guess.

Perhaps, there were no final murders. That's what I want to believe about the final day, about the final hours of the existence of the German colony of Hoffnungstal, that the fifteen man police unit, despite their orders to eliminate the prisoners, opened the jail, and set everyone free. If so, it was a small act of rebellion. Long overdue. An act of human dignity and freedom. A shaking loose of Nazi shackles. And the first tiny step—of which this book is another—to atone for all those innocents murdered at twilight and buried in the sandy soil of the place called the Blade.

***

Crenir, my psychologist friend and I, angle our way across campus. We take our time. It's been awhile since we'd talked. We breathe in the air scented with flowering crab blossom and lilacs. The sidewalks are crowded with backpack-toting summer school students. We'd been talking about Helmut, about the trauma he'd overcome to become a decent person, a good father, a good husband. We'd been talking about the elderly lady who had once been the secretary for Weingartner, about the final orders.

"So that is the end of your book?" Crenir says.

"Not really," I say, and despite the beautiful day, I bemoan the fact that I've spent more than a decade of my life, plus my retirement savings, "on all of this business."

"Business?" Crenir says. "Isn't that what Regina called the murder of the Jews?"

"Well, yes," I say, chastened. "But I'm wondering why I ever began this project."

"Because of the dream of white uniformed soldiers," he says.

"I don't remember telling you that."

"Well, you did."

We clomp up the cupped stairs of the oldest building on campus, and in his cramped, book-lined office, he snaps on the air conditioner, and as the ancient machine stirs the sluggish air, he says, "Tell me again. Why can't you finish your book?"

"I don't know enough," I say.

353

I launch into a rambling account, about Wasserthal, about the Volksdeutsche there, combing the ashes for gold the victims carried to their deaths in the ovens there.

"Or is it because you don't want to be another Volksdeutscher benefitting from genocide?"

"Something like that."

"Then give voice to all the victims," Crenir says. "And to those police forced to murder."

"Not all were forced."

I hand Crenir a publicity pamphlet of an annual tour, offered by a prairie university to the former German colonies in Ukraine, and I see his brow furrow as he reads the inflated phraseology, of the "indescribable, awe-inspiring joy of exploring your vibrant cultural heritage."

"I can see you don't think American Volksdeutsche will appreciate the fact their ancestral villages were involved in the Holocaust?" he says.

"You can say that again."

"Aren't the Volksdeutsche in general, as a group, decent and concerned with justice?"

"Yes, I think that's true. Good, decent people, despite a troubled history."

"So finish your book. Seek the truth. Seek justice."

"Well…" I mumble.

"Is there another reason you don't finish your book?"

"You tell me," I say, defensively.

"You don't like judging your relative Leidel."

"I couldn't forgive myself if I was wrong."

"About Leidel being a murderer?"

"Yes."

"But you don't think you are wrong?"

"No, I don't," I say, adding, in homage to Dimitri, "Just my opinion."

***

One day, I drive to a recycling center. I toss out the accumulated notes and discarded pages and drafts of this yet uncompleted book and other reminders of what I consider a failed project. I also stop at the local Goodwill store, where I stand by the receptacle bin, struggling to decide whether I should jettison my battered leather satchel.

It's gone everywhere with me, a symbol of my Transnistrian adventure, of a dozen years of my life. It's been slung over my shoulder, propped always in sight, and tucked under the front seat of Anatolis's Nissan and Mikhail's Volga. It has held several handheld tape recorders, two cameras, a well-thumbed, pocket-sized Gideon's *New Testament*, thistle-impaled sweaters and burr-infested socks, yellowing secret police interrogations, verbatim court confessions, a thick folder of names of executed Volksdeutsche, a sheaf of local and district maps, and dozens of village plat maps, and food given as gifts—everything from homemade cheeses, to blocks of honey-comb, to grapes, to bottles of *champanski* and red wine, one of which, judging by the stained, abraded leather, had broken, likely on the final, rugged path from Krasna-Vladimorovka to Lichtenfeld. There are also, I notice, splotches of dried blood.

I press my memory. Where was that from? From Bondarevka when a guard dog bit Laryssa's ankle? Or from Kolosovo, when, clearing dirt from the fragments of a child's skull shattered by an Einsatzgruppen bullet, my Swiss army knife slipped, and I'd cut my thumb, and red droplets boiled from the wound? Or from the Bakshala River, where I'd tripped at a Vorwerker killing site, and torn open my knee?

The satchel's zippers still work, even the repaired long one, whose metal teeth mesh perfectly, and from the deep front pocket, I retrieve two empty cartridges and a pristine bullet point. How did that metal pass through the customs and TSA screeners on my way home? A bigger question: where did I find the cartridges? Likely at one of the string of multisyllabic sites that include Jastrabino, Novo Kantakouska, and Novogregorievka, sites which now seem a dizzying blur of pits and ravines. Strange, for someone like me, who a friend once called "a memory artist," not to remember. Part of me fears forgetting, but maybe forgetting is a good thing. It means my strung-tight nerves are healing. It means I'm disentangling myself from the crushing coils of the Transnistrian Holocaust.

In a side pocket, I find a fragment of baked clay. I turn it over in my fingers. Embedded in the brown matrix, glistening and brilliant white specks. Laryssa gave it to me one day at Gradofka, when she'd done something out of character, breaking loose from the oven wall that fragment, which she'd placed in my palm, and closing my fingers over it, and telling me in soft, tour-guide tones: "If you look closely, you will see bits of dentine and bone. Do you understand? That is from the victims burnt in the ovens." Standing by the receptacle bin, as I wrap the shard carefully in my handkerchief—it's human remains after all—and slip it into my pocket and make a mental note to consult a rabbi for the proper method of internment, the memory of my last visit to Gradofka stirs in me.

It's a bitter afternoon, early winter, and from my rental car I stride over a series of iron-like wheel ruts, and go up the slope to where the oven shafts open. A piercing wind, sweeping off the steppe, takes my breath away. I return to my rental car, and retrieve a long scarf that Sonia knitted for me, and swath it in layers around my face. Near the lip of an oven, I sit down on the sere grass and rock, clasping my knees, my eyes squeezed shut, shimmering arcs dancing on the inside of my lids.

Dogs bark in the distance. A drunk bellows. I stretch out on the sere grass, and using my satchel as a pillow, peer through the gap in my scarf—which is what the killers saw on those cold winter days—as twilight falls over the steppe, and light drains away, and clouds collapse into darkness.

I'm chilled, shaking like an anchorite. Not that I mind. Visiting Gradofka, or any such sites, should be uncomfortable. All visitors should score as deep an impression in their memories, in their hearts, as possible. That last time at Gradofka, my thoughts grow vague and troubled, snagged on odd questions. Such as, is that wheeling overhead kaleidoscope of stars the same stars the Jews saw before they were fed into the oven flames? My teeth clatter, and my muscles spasm from the cold. I think: if there was a plaque, or marker, what should it say? Perhaps: "At this place, God turned away His face."

My thoughts congeal around the fact that it would take more than a plaque, it would take a book, and that, with my glacial pace of composition, would take years. A hopeless task. So let future historians, armed with documents and statistics enter the Kingdom of Death—perhaps through the door I've tried to carve into the cliffs of our ethnic memory: let them write the definitive book about this slaughterhouse. All I offer is a gratuitous act of self-imposed penance for all the Volksdeutsche police had done, been forced to do.

Leaving for Nikolaev that night, the headlights of my rental car probing the dark, I don't yet know that I'm already in flight, and not much later, after my final visit to Lichtenfeld, I'd be borne along on a river of blood, swept from the Kingdom of Death, and back to the American prairie, back to my own ethnic ark, where I write this now.

***

COERCION AND HATRED

After a decade of chasing the ghosts of Transnistria, of leaning on intuition and prayer, I feel like an orphan, adrift on a sea of ironies, contradictions, and thorny facts.

Such as the fact that in the latter 1930s, Soviet mass violence against the Volksdeutsche shifted away from class-based hatred, away from dispossessing the colonists as wealthy kulaks, to the perception of them as outsiders to be eradicated.

Such as the fact that during Stalin's Great Terror, in 1937, many Volksdeutsche were accused of supposed links and cultural ties to Nazi Germany, which the Soviets viewed as an ideological and military threat. Which was, or seemed, the mirror image of the Nazi view of Jews, because of the perceived prominence of Jews within the communist party, a perceived prominence that led the Nazis to associate Jews—not unfairly according to Solzhenitsyn—as especially supportive, at least initially, of the murderous Soviet regime and communism in general.

Such as the fact that the Nazi regime, like the Soviet regime, thought in terms of whole ethnic groups, not individuals, and, as a result, the Nazis interpreted the Soviet crimes against the Volksdeutsche—some in that minority agreed, from fear of their lives, or after being propagandized— as crimes committed by Jews against Germans, rather than what they were: crimes of the Soviet repressive apparatus. In that respect, it seemed to me, the Holocaust might better be understood, at least in part, as a European tribal conflict, like the ongoing struggle between the Shia and Sunni factions of Islam.

Such as the fact that the Volksdeutsche, drafted and otherwise coerced by their Nazi masters, ended up in a proportionally higher rate than other minorities in SS units, local police units, as well as death camp guards and other personnel; not necessarily because of a greater propensity to be killers, or Jew haters, but due to the proximity of their German colonies to where the Holocaust took place across Eastern Europe, Ukraine, and Transnistria, so that as the murder campaign spread continent-wide, the Nazis increasingly relied on local, indigenous authorities and commands, and that drew the Volksdeutsche, who knew the language of the Nazis, in disproportionate numbers into the ranks of the perpetrators.

Regardless, the Volksdeutsche paid a steep price for their perceived collaboration with the Nazis, and suffered from the mere fact of being Volksdeutsche, witness the ten million souls collectively blamed, and in many cases, violently expelled, during the postwar *Vertriebung,* or forced relocation, from their Eastern European homelands, where they had lived for generations.

What would happen, I wonder, if the crimes against the Jews went unconfessed, unadmitted? Would the children and grandchildren of the former policemen, like the sons of Atreus in the Greek tragedy of Aeschylus, blindly act out all that was hidden, all that lay buried, creating a pathological, guilt-ridden culture? The literature professor in me thought so, which was why I'd long sought—from a Transnistrian Volksdeutsche, from someone there at the time—a confession, or an admission, that yes, the Volksdeutsche police murdered seventy thousand Jews in Transnistria, bringing the atrocities out of the realm of shame and guilt, and into the light of truth.

Such an admission was unlikely in the extreme, and could only come from someone with a long view of Volksdeutsche history, someone on stilts, who could see beyond the fear and paranoia, beyond his or her own personal and familial suffering under the Soviets, beyond the dead bodies of nearly a million fellow Volksdeutsche starved and executed and worked to death, whose bones were scattered across eleven time zones of the former Soviet Empire.

What had been needed, in addition to the Nuremberg trials and other postwar tribunals, was a forum, a Transnistrian truth-and-reconciliation committee, like that of post-apartheid South Africa. A safe place where the policemen—a special cohort who murdered, in the main, from fear of losing their own lives—could confess. Earlier, setting loose those howling ghosts of the Holocaust might have brought some closure, some finality. Now, however, it was too late; even if granted amnesty, how many of the rapidly aging and dying Transnistrians, especially the former Volksdeutsche policemen, so defensive, so full of shame, so fearful of prosecution even this late, would ever agree to sing in such a dark choir?

***

The drunken phone call—another call set into motion by those forces I didn't understand, and in part by my own earlier efforts—reached me in the middle of the night.

"*Hasht g'sehna?*" a voice says in perfect German dialect.

"Who is this?" I say, groggy with sleep. It can't be Dmitri, who only speaks High German, or Don, my hometown friend, because he never called late.

"Haf you seen it?" the voice says in English this time.

So I know it's Valder, calling from Munich, Germany, the former policeman, over ninety now, with whom several years ago now, I'd shared that meal, the fine wine, and the uncomfortable questions about his past.

"Yes, I saw it," I say.

It was a recent *New York Times* article, with a lurid, if accurate, title: "Michael Seifert, 86; Infamous Nazi guard in Italy was 'Beast of Bolzano.'" Valder stumbled upon it in his daily perusal of international newspapers at his favorite cafe in Munich.

Seifert was a Volksdeutsche, as the article explained, who settled postwar in Canada, and after being convicted and imprisoned in Italy of war crimes, he'd passed away two years

360

later in 2010. A single case that demonstrated clearly that courts in Germany and elsewhere meant to deter future war crimes by showing there was no statute of limitations, even on old Nazi war criminals like Seifert.

"You knew Seifert from the SS?" I say. "Was he in the Maria Theresa Division with you?"

"No," he says. "I knew the Seifert, Michael, from my home area."

"What was he like?"

"Ach, what was anyone like?" Valder says, angrily, so I know he's drunk, or drinking, a bottle of the wine he so favors. "Here, listen," he says.

In an outraged, old man's voice, he reads a snippet from the article. "'Michael Seifert grew up between the looming shadows of Nazi Germany and Stalinist Russia. His father was a postal worker until 1933, when he lost his job on suspicion of supporting Hitler.' Does anyone even know what that meant then?" Valder says.

"I doubt it."

"It means arrest und torture und d' rat cage."

"It's journalism," I say. "The focus is on Seifert's conviction, not—"

"A dozen of your relatives were shot by the Soviets. You told me yourself. Engelhardts and Usselmanns and Schmidts. All people I knew."

"More like twenty," I say.

"And you defend this article? While your relatives twist in their graves?"

"Are you saying Seifert didn't torture and murder prisoners at the Nazi transit camp in Italy?"

"He was making *Rache*. How do you say that in English?"

"Revenge," I say. "But revenge implies guilt. These were innocents."

"Hitler's Commissar Order treated them all the same way. Partisans, informers, communists, gypsies, Jews. Und not all were innocent."

"Treated the same way? You mean murdered."

Our conversation bumps to a halt. I never hear from him again, and two years later, an e-mail arrives, along with his brief obituary, assembled by his wife, which omits that he was in the Waffen SS, an outlawed organization. But it does mention his police training, a benign reference it seems, but one that places Valder in Transnistria in 1942, a time and place where a quarter of a million Jews and gypsies were being slaughtered.

***

The day after Easter Sunday. I'm pedaling my mountain bike on the edge of East Grand Forks, along a gravel road stretching between a series of long potato warehouses so like Soviet collective barns, and cultivated black fields, whose greening shoots look like those I'd seen at Suha Balka. As my younger sister told me, "Ron, Ukraine is still renting a place in your head."

When my cell phone vibrates, I park my bike behind the final potato warehouse, out of the buffeting wind. It's Johanna, my Edmonton relative, in whose accented voice I recognize a quiet urgency, which reminds me that there has always been something unsaid between us about Transnistria. After my Canadian visit, I've had only sporadic contact with her. Now, after the usual inquiries of the health of our family members, she tells me why she is calling.

"Most of my friends haf died. Und many of those born in Ukrainia haf not died mit a clear heart."

In the open field a jackrabbit stands alert, ears stiff. It turns slightly, as if listening to whispers from a forgotten world, its fur still winter white, like the white uniformed soldiers from my dream so long ago.

"Today I tell you things I have not yet told you," she says. "Because you had the courage to ask about Yakov Leidel."

There is a long pause. She takes a deep breath.

"You remember, I told you Josefstal police were armed," Johanna says.

"Even if your brother told me they weren't?"

"Yes. Yakov Leidel carried a pistol and rifle, and everyone…"

A crackling silence. Broken fragments of speech. A dropped call? The ghosts of Transnistria eluding me again?

"Johanna, are you still there?" I say.

"Everyone in Josefstal was proud of the Yakov. Even if he was a show off."

Another long pause.

"Why were they proud?" I say.

"Because he was a member of the SS police," she says. "One of our village's very own young men."

"Given such responsibility?"

"Yes. Protecting us. And taking back what was stolen from us in Soviet times."

Another pause.

"What was done was done partly because of *Zwang*," she says.

"*Zwang?*" I say.

"Yes, *Zwang,*" she says. "I don't know the English word?"

Deep in the fallowed cropland behind the long potato barns, there are, I feel certain, long buried rocks, wedging upward, toward the sunlight.

"Coercion?" I say. "Force?"

"Yes, force. Orders made it easier."

"But you said 'partly.' If part was Zwang, what was the other part?"

"The other was *Hass,*" she says, hissing the ugly German word for hate. "For all we suffered under the Soviets."

"So Zwang and Hass? Coercion and hate?"

"You must understand," Johanna says, her voice cracking with emotion. "Our young people, their parents and grandparents shot and starved…the misery…Ach mein Gott."

"What about Yakov Leidel?"

"Ron, it is not easy to kill a person."

"So Yakov Leidel did kill?"

"When Yakov was sick and dying, we drove down from Canada to South Dakota, to see him. In Sioux Falls."

"Your brother told me the same. Was that when Yakov told you?" I say, being purposely vague.

"We talked late into the night. Yakov kept using one word—*reward.*"

"Reward?"

"He liked that word," she says. "He used it whenever he spoke of those who died."

"You mean those he killed?"

"He told us the police went to surrounding villages. To make *sauberungs-aktion*. A Nazi word."

"Cleansed?" I say.

"Yes, cleansed."

"Johanna, was there a kalk-oven in Josefstal? Where killings were done?"

The realization coursing through me like an electric current answers my own question. Of course. The sloping place to which Helga pointed while I snapped a photograph. Half buried. Yes. That was the kalk-oven. Why hadn't I realized it before? With my eye, with my well-trained archaeological eye? Because I didn't want to see it, like I didn't want to see the ovens around Lichtenfeld, because I didn't want another oven in another ancestral village.

"It's true. We lost our feeling for others," Johanna says softly, not answering my question, yet echoing Regina's comment of a good, decent people, some grown hard and indifferent. "We could see the pain in our young men's eyes."

"For what they'd done under the Nazis?"

"Yes."

"What did they do?"

Silence. Then she says, "That's why they needed men like Yakov."

"To point to the informers and Volksdeutsche communists," I say, giving her slow sips of the old poison, like Dmitri had done with me.

"Yes."

"And after that? To shoot them?"

Silence.

She can't say Yakov Leidel murdered Jews. Can't say her cousin was a part of the Holocaust. Yet no answer is also an answer.

"There were Jews hiding across Transnistria," I say. "Jews escaped from ghettos and labor camps and from those long columns."

Silence.

"Hunted down by Yakov and the police," I say. "And taken to the kalk-oven."

"We thought of the Jews as the chosen people. We would never have harmed them. Yakov never could have killed anyone innocent."

"You don't want to believe he killed innocents? Yet there was killing of Jews."

"You are right. I don't want to believe that," she says, sighing. "Ach yah, a tragedy, what our boys did."

"What young men like Yakob chose to do?" I say. "For their own advantage?"

"Yes," she says. "Our Yakov had *Hochmut*. Ach yah."

"Pride?" I say.

"Yes, about his appearance. He was poor. He never had good clothing. Then he became a policeman."

"And had good clothing? From those he murdered?"

"Yakov had first pick," Johanna says. "He even sold some clothes."

She mentions names of several policemen who helped Leidel, men related to us both, men whose names, as a final sacrifice to the gods of forgetting I have erased. They are blotted out by what she tells me next.

"Ron, yes, Yakov und the others. They were part of this terrible act, this terrible crime."

Then another silence.

"Maybe this was not true elsewhere, but in Josefstal," she says, "it was done at least in part by their own choice."

It's the admission I've thought I would never hear, and on the heels of my hearing it, I am struck a stunning blow, like a forearm shiver in football. So I recall little after that, except that as I bid her good-bye—it's the last time we will ever speak—she sounds at peace, and for the first time in over a decade, so do I.

I pedal the final stretch homeward, gravel crunching beneath my tires, jostling ruts giving way to smooth asphalt. For the first time in several years I enter my study quickly, without trepidation, and clattering away on the keyboard, steadily, I write this, the final part of this book, these very words that, like the other clues and coincidences given me over the years, come from beyond myself, as if dictation from an eternal scribe.

My quest did not begin, I realize, with the dream of white uniformed soldiers, nor the photo of SS Hauptsturmfuehrer Weingartner, but earlier, with the forgotten empire of childhood, with what my grandfather told me, with the time that the shimmering aura of Lichtenfeld first opened in my own mind's eye.

That aura was not, as I'd come to believe, the awful glow of the kalk-ovens, but the light of this world, given in trust, a guide on my own soul's journey, foreordained, like my Eichmann nickname, and the cenotes, and the bloody swastika I'd carved into my arm, to never let me forget, to lead me forward, to discover the ovens and ravines, and all those lost, broken places in the Kingdom of Death and hasten the day when all the estranged and separated ashes of victim and perpetrator, of Jew and Volksdeutsche alike, along with my guilt for writing this book, could be swept in a torrent of blood into the primordial sea, and all things long secret and hidden finally laid upon the altar of God's judgment.

***

ACKNOWLEDGMENTS

Many people contributed to this book. Joshua Vossler, my son, designed the cover, the map, and gave general support. Eric Steinhart guided me to the Ludwigsburg archives. Others who helped include Ken and Kristina Gray, Robin Andersen, Russ Chelak, Debbie Beick, Gerda Fadden, Pauline Lippert Litvin, Robert Schneider, and Alma Woehl Engelhardt, my mother. Thanks to Canadian friends and relatives, Merv Weiss, Adolf Roth, Anna Fischer Roth, Tim and Carmen Geiger, and Rose Marie Sackela. Thanks to Ukrainians, Inna Strucknova, Dr. Serge Yelisarov; Feodor Sheremet, Nick and Nina Chapernoy, Leonid Duissmann, Rosa Weinstein, Dr. Vladimir Chernitsky, Dr. Juri Kotlar, and Dr. Serge Makarchuk. Sources who passed on during the fifteen years I worked on this book include my stepfather Basch Engelhardt, Johan Hieb, Johan and Theodor Krein, Auguste Koenig Ackermann, Rheinhold Kramer, and my good friends Walter and Anette Bamesberger.

SOURCES

Primary source materials, plus my personal notes and drafts, are housed at the Germans from Russia Heritage Collection at North Dakota State University Library in Fargo, North Dakota. Interested readers may also consult the source page, my web-site at www.ronvossler.com, or my e-mail at ron.vossler@gmail.com.

Sources used and consulted are too numerous to list individually. The general categories include oral history accounts, family anecdotes, genealogical charts, letters and articles and editorials in various Dakota German-language newspapers, small town centennial books, memoirs, travelogues, phone and film interviews, material from Volksdeutsche magazines in Germany and the United States, numerous personal conversations recorded in my diaries, Jewish survivor accounts from *Yad Vashem*, my field journals, hundreds of hours from my library of filmed and tape-recorded interviews, Nazi-era newspapers from Germany and Transnistria, and archival materials from Ukraine, Moldova, and Germany. The most valuable material concerning Nazi-Occupied Transnistria came from the Bundesarchiv, Ludwigsburg, Germany. Sources I've most depended on include the following:

Aly, Goetz. *Hitler's Beneficiaries*. (New York: Metropolitan Books/Henry Holt and Company, 2006).

Ancel, Jean. *Transnitria, 1941–1942: The Romanian Mass Murder Campaigns*. Trans. by Rachel Garfinkel and Karen Gold. 3 Vols. (Tel Aviv: The Goldstein-Goren Diaspora Research Center, Tel Aviv University, 2003.)

Dean, Martin. *Collaboration in the Holocaust: Crimes of the Local Police in Belorussia and Ukraine, 1941–1944*. (New York: St. Martin's Press, 2000).

Ehrenburg, Illya and Grossman, Vasily. *The Complete Black Book of Russian Jewry.* (New Brunswick and London: Transaction Publishers, 2002).

Friedlander, Saul. *The Years of Extermination: Nazi Germany and the Jews, 1939–1945.* (Harper Perennial, New York, 2008).

Goldhagen, Daniel Jonah. *Hitler's Willing Executioners: Ordinary Germans and the Holocaust.* (Vintage Books, New York, 1997).

Gross, David. *Lost Time: On Remembering and Forgetting in Late Modern Culture.* (University of Massachusetts Press, Amherst: 2000).

Gross, Jan T. *Neighbors: The Destruction of the Jewish Community in Jedwabne, Poland.* (Princeton University Press, Princeton and Oxford, 2001).

Haar, Ingo, and Michael Fahlbusch. *German Scholars and Ethnic Cleansing, 1919–1945.* (Berghahn Books, New York-Oxford, 2005).

Height, Joseph. *Paradise on the Steppe.* (Bismarck, North Dakota: North Dakota Society of Germans from Russia, 1973).

Hilberg, Raul. *The Destruction of the European Jews.* (Chicago: Quadrangle Books, 1967).

Ioanid, Radu. *The Holocaust in Romania.* Translated by Marc Masurovsky (Chicago: 2000).

Lewy, Guenter. *The Nazi Persecution of the Jews.* (Oxford University Press, New York, 2000).

Lincoln, W. Bruce. *Armageddon: The Russians in War and Revolution.* (New York and Oxford, Oxford University Press, 1986).

Lower, Wendy. *Hitler's Furies: German Women in the Nazi Killing Fields*. (Boston and New York, Mariner Books, 2014).

Philipps, John. *The Germans by the Black Sea between the Bug and the Dniester Rivers*. (Fargo, North Dakota: Germans from Russia Heritage Collection, North Dakota State University Libraries, 2000).

Reitlinger, Gerald. *The House Built on Sand: The Conflicts of German Policy in Russia, 1939–1945*. (New York, The Viking Press, 1960).

Rhodes, Richard. *Masters of Death: The SS Einsatzgruppen and the Invention of the Holocaust*. (New York, Vintage Books, 2003).

Sites, Kevin. *The Things They Cannot Say*. (Harper Perennial: New York, 2013.)

Snyder, Timothy. *Bloodlands: Europe between Hitler and Stalin*. (Basic Books: New York, 2012).

Solschenitzyn, Alexander. *ZweiHundert Jahre zusammen: Die Juden in der Sowjetunion*. (Muenchen, Deutschland, Herbig Verlag, 2004).

Steinhart, Eric C. *The Transnitria's Ethnic Germans and the Holocaust, 1941–1942*. (Chapel Hill: Unpublished Master's Thesis. University of North Carolina, Chapel Hill, 2006).

Vossler, Ronald and Joshua Vossler. *The Old God Still Lives: Ethnic Germans in Czarist and Soviet Ukraine Write Their American Relatives, 1915–1924*. (Fargo, North Dakota: The Germans from Russia Heritage Collection, North Dakota State University Libraries, 2005)